The Victorian Woman Question in Contemporary
Feminist Fiction

Also by Jeannette King

TRAGEDY IN THE VICTORIAN NOVEL: Theory and Practice in the Novels of George Eliot, Thomas Hardy and Henry James

AN OPEN GUIDE TO 'JANE EYRE'

DORIS LESSING

WOMEN AND THE WORD: Contemporary Women Novelists and the Bible

The Victorian Woman Question in Contemporary Feminist Fiction

Jeannette King
*Senior Lecturer in Women's Studies in the Department of English
University of Aberdeen*

palgrave
macmillan

First published 2005 by
PALGRAVE MACMILLAN
Houndmills, Basingstoke, Hampshire RG21 6XS and
175 Fifth Avenue, New York, N.Y. 10010
Companies and representatives throughout the world

PALGRAVE MACMILLAN is the global academic imprint of the Palgrave Macmillan division of St. Martin's Press, LLC and of Palgrave Macmillan Ltd. Macmillan® is a registered trademark in the United States, United Kingdom and other countries. Palgrave is a registered trademark in the European Union and other countries.

ISBN-13: 978–1–4039–1727–0 hardback
ISBN-10: 1–4039–1727–2 hardback

This book is printed on paper suitable for recycling and made from fully managed and sustained forest sources.

A catalogue record for this book is available from the British Library.

Library of Congress Cataloging-in-Publication Data
King, Jeannette.
    The Victorian woman question in contemporary feminist fiction / Jeannette King.
        p. cm.
Includes bibliographical references and index.
ISBN 1–4039–1727–2 (cloth)
    1. Feminist fiction, English—History and criticism.   2. Historical fiction, English—History and criticism.   3. English fiction—20th century—History and criticism.   4. English fiction—Women authors—History and criticism.   5. Feminism and literature—English-speaking countries—History—20th century.   6. Women and literature—English-speaking countries—History—20th century.   7. Women—Great Britain—History—19th century—Historiography.   8. Feminism in literature.   9. Sex role in literature.   10. Women in literature.   I. Title.

PR888.F45K56 2005
823'.8093522—dc22

2004061222

Transferred to digital print 2007
Printed and bound in Great Britain by
CPI Antony Rowe, Chippenham and Eastbourne

To Pam

Contents

Acknowledgements

I owe the inspiration for this book partly to my late colleague and friend, Robin Gilmour, who had his own plans for a book on contemporary fiction 'using the Victorians', which he was sadly unable to complete. His essay on the subject, however, to which I refer in the Introduction, gives some indication of the project's scope and potential. The focus of my study is more specific, but would, I hope, have had his approval.

The ideas central to my research were generated over some time, and revised in response to discussions with colleagues at Aberdeen and elsewhere. I was grateful for the opportunity to give papers at the 'Hystorical Fictions' conference held by the University of Wales in Swansea (2003), and at my own department's Research Seminar, and would like to thank all those whose comments helped me to refine my thoughts. I owe particular thanks to Nancy Wachowich for her guidance with regard to research on gender and polar exploration.

During the writing process, many more people gave me the benefit of their time and thoughts. I owe a particular debt to Mary Joannou, whose sympathetic reading of my earliest chapters showed that she understood exactly what I was trying to do, and whose suggestions helped me to do it better. More personal thanks are due to Liz Allen, Jo Watson and Isobel Murray, who read and commented on chapters at various crucial stages in the writing process. Special thanks are due – yet again – to Pam Morris and Flora Alexander for the wisdom and critical rigour they brought to bear on my arguments, as well as for large measures of loving encouragement. Their unfailing support this year as always has meant more than I can say.

But, however much they enrich life, books – read or written – are not all of life. The rest of it belongs to my very dear friends, and above all to my family – Jon, Dan and Jane. Without their love and support, completing this book this year would probably have been impossible. It would certainly have meant very little.

Aberdeen
September 2004

Introduction

Why, in the last decades of the twentieth century, should so many women novelists have looked back a hundred years for the subjects of their fiction? Why should the Victorians hold so much interest for the age of superwomen and ladettes? What, in particular, is the interest of Victorian constructions of gender and sexuality for modern feminists? These were the questions that drove the research for this monograph. Clearly no single set of explanations will do as an answer, but my concern is less with the motivation of individual novelists than with the significance of this body of writing as a literary and cultural phenomenon.

Contemporary women novelists have not confined themselves to the Victorian period, of course. Many have looked back further. In both Britain and the United States, the lives of individuals prominent in the late eighteenth and early nineteenth century have provided the occasion for feminist explorations. Michèle Roberts's *Fair Exchange* (1999) is based on episodes in the lives of Mary Wollstonecraft and William Wordsworth, imaginatively reconstructing their secret affairs, while the American Susan Sontag revisits the romance of Emma Hamilton and Admiral Lord Nelson in *The Volcano Lover: A Romance* (1992). Other writers construct lives for those of whom very little is known, such as the young woman who became a surgeon general in the British army early in the nineteenth century, whose life is so vividly imagined in Patricia Duncker's *James Miranda Barry* (1999). In other cases historical events provide a context for totally fictional characters, such as Valerie Martin's Manon Gaudet, whose experience of a slave rebellion on her husband's plantation is the focus of Martin's 2003 Orange prizewinner, *Property*. Jeanette Winterson's *The Passion* (1987) similarly tells a fantastical tale about a cook in Napoleon's army and a gondolier's daughter. Novels which take the reader even further back in time include Winterson's

1

Sexing the Cherry (1989), a story of Rabelaisian characters caught up in the English Civil War, and Rose Tremain's *Restoration* (1989), which deals with the period immediately following the Protectorate. The same range of approaches characterises novels set in more recent times. While Pat Barker's *Regeneration* trilogy (1991–5) is based on the well-documented lives of the poets of the First World War and the doctors who treated them, Anna McGrail's *Mrs Einstein* (1998) constructs a fictional biography for the famous scientist's daughter Lieserl, and the American novelist Amy Tan reconstructs the more anonymous lives of women in early twentieth-century China in *The Kitchen God's Wife* (1991). This is clearly not a comprehensive list, but it indicates the depth of interest which the past held for women writing in the final decades of the twentieth century.

I would argue, nevertheless, that interest in the Victorian period is particularly strong, and that novels set in that period tend to be characterised by their engagement with gender issues. Jean Rhys's *Wide Sargasso Sea*, published in 1966, is arguably the literary progenitor of this trend. In telling the story of the first Mrs Rochester, the madwoman in the attic of Charlotte Brontë's *Jane Eyre*, Rhys carried out a post-colonial and feminist reading of Brontë's canonical original, which has itself become almost canonical. Bertha's 'madness' is shown to be largely Rochester's own construction. It is the product of a patriarchal and imperialist ideology which identifies his wife's sexuality as a sign of degeneracy always liable to slide into insanity, and furthermore associates it with the colonised 'Other' she represents. But despite its popularity in recent years, this novel was a relatively isolated phenomenon at the time, although in 1969 John Fowles published *The French Lieutenant's Woman*, which has become probably the most famous pastiche of the Victorian novel. In contrast, most women novelists of the time were concerned with the difficulties and opportunities presented to women in the 1960s, rather than the 1860s.

In the 1980s and 1990s, however, the situation changed dramatically with the revival in popularity of historical fiction in general, although it may be a mistake to consider historical fiction as a distinct genre, given the range of writing it encompasses. This range is evident in the long tradition of historical fiction by women. Some of the most popular writers in that tradition, like Dorothy L. Sayers and Georgette Heyer, have written within such specific genres as detective fiction and historical romance. Others, like Rosemary Sutcliffe and Mary Renault, have virtually created a genre of their own with their novels of Roman Britain and Bronze Age Greece respectively. This has made it easy to dismiss their work as romantic or escapist. It certainly has not had the same impact on the academic curriculum as *Wide Sargasso Sea*, or met with the same critical acclaim, but as women's writing in general continues to be re-examined and revalued, here too there are signs of change. Sarah Waters, one of the most successful of current practitioners, argues that women have not only dominated the genre since the 1920s, but have used it to 'map out an alternative, female historical landscape', which often 'constitutes a radical rewriting of traditional, male-centred historical narrative'.[1] By making female experience central to their narratives, such novels gave women back their place in history, not just as victims but as agents. The novel Waters cites as an example, Maude Meagher's *The Green Scamander* (1933), reconstructs the culture of the Amazons, retelling the events leading up to the meeting of their queen, Penthesilia, with the more famous Achilles outside the walls of Troy. But what these novels by women had in common with each other and with all historical fiction was that they satisfied the appetite for knowledge of the past, still apparently insatiable today, judging by the prominence and prestige of historical television series, and the popularity of history and biography with the reading public.

What perhaps characterises more recent historical fiction, however, is its more direct engagement with the historical process itself, often blending historical documentation and events with its imagined narratives and characters. This characteristic relates the new historical fiction to postmodern trends in historiography itself. Since historians cannot use the actual past as a standard for historical accounts, but have to rely on someone's narrative – oral or documentary – postmodernists argue that history can only ever be contested versions of the past. If any piece of historical writing is, in effect, one tale among many, then an imaginative construction of a life of which little is known, but which has a basis in documented fact, may have its own claim to a kind of 'truth'. A.S. Byatt, one of the most eminent of the historical novelists discussed in this monograph, puts it with typical clarity: 'The idea that "all history is fiction" led to a new interest in fiction as history.'[2] Byatt herself, like Victoria Glendinning, whose novel *Electricity* is discussed in Chapter 4, is a scholar with experience of critical biography, well qualified to embark on writing 'fiction as history'. Postmodernists have a particular interest in adopting new, marginal perspectives on events, and in decentring recorded history, which directly intersects with the concerns of feminist historians and novelists alike. Historical fiction by women is part of the wider project, pioneered by second wave feminism, of rewriting history from a female perspective, and recovering the lives of women who have been excluded or marginalised. Byatt speaks for many when she explains that the original impulse behind her novella *The Conjugial Angel* was 'revisionist and feminist. It would tell the untold story of Emily [Tennyson], as compared to the often-told story of Arthur and Alfred in which Emily is a minor actress' (*On Histories and Stories*, p. 104). Novelists like Michèle Roberts cite historical sources in their novels, acknowledging their debts to the feminist academic research of the 1970s and 1980s, while both Toni Morrison's *Beloved* and Margaret Atwood's *Alias Grace* are based on historical cases of women accused of murder. Such fiction has sometimes been called 'hysterical history', using fiction to question the claims to objectivity of more traditional accounts.[3] *Beloved* gives a voice and life to the silenced slaves of the American South which radically challenge not only white accounts of slavery, but the white male-dominated tradition of nineteenth-century fiction. If, according to Fredric Jameson, using history responsibly means bringing to the surface of the text the 'repressed and buried reality' of class struggle,[4] it surely also means bringing to the surface the reality of women's struggle for a voice, particularly the struggle of those oppressed by both gender and race.

Modern novelists are also able to speak about issues which were unspeakable for women of the past, notably areas surrounding sexuality and the body. Their ability to celebrate female sexuality will be most evident in my discussion of Angela Carter's *Nights at the Circus* and Sarah Waters' *Tipping the Velvet*. This greater freedom is particularly evident in the lesbian historical fiction which Waters has made such a popular and a critical success. Waters suggests that lesbians have a special affinity with historical fiction, demonstrating how a novel like Meagher's *The Green Scamander* 'seduces its readers into complicity with a lesbian textual economy in which both the spaces between female bodies, and the gaps and ellipses between sentences and words, are resonant and highly charged' (p. 17). As Terry Castle points out, lesbianism has been manifest in the Western literary imagination primarily as an absence. In Victorian fiction, for instance, lesbians appear only as ghostly, spectral presences.[5] Novels like *Tipping the Velvet* bring that shadowy figure into the light, and make it possible to explore what lesbian lives may have been like, in the absence of historical evidence.

The specific appeal of the Victorian period for late twentieth-century women writers can be accounted for partly by the general resurgence of interest in the Victorians, an interest which reached a climax with the centenary of Victoria's death in 2001, but which has not gone away. In his exemplary essay on the use of the Victorian age in fiction written between 1970 and 2000, Robin Gilmour points to the concomitant growth in paperback publication of Victorian fiction, which includes little-known titles alongside the popular classics.[6] It has been argued that such novels simply participate in what Jameson calls postmodernism's 'nostalgia mode', creating the past through the recreation of its surfaces, without ever allowing the original to assert itself. But Dana Shiller counters that argument by asserting that what she calls 'neo-Victorian fiction' reinvents the Victorians, rather than effacing them, through 'its careful reconstruction of the Victorian past' (p. 545). Byatt again is a strong voice for the defence, setting out as she does in her own work to rescue 'the complicated Victorian thinkers from modern diminishing parodies' and from 'disparaging mockery' (*On Histories and Stories*, p. 79). Less well known than Byatt, but working in similar territory, Andrea Barrett, in *The Voyage of the Narwhal*, suggests the complex intellectual background to nineteenth-century natural history and exploration in a narrative about the gulf between male and female aspiration. All the novels discussed in this monograph engage fully with the discourses of nineteenth-century scientific and cultural life in such a way as to convey to the reader something of the period's complex mindset, rather than simply its changing fashions. This kind of historical fiction emphasises, in Shiller's words, the 'textualization of the past' (p. 546). This is a crucial emphasis, since, as Linda Anderson has argued, the 'reclaiming of history' by women may simply reconstitute 'reality' as it is, if it ignores 'how that existence is textually mediated'.[7]

For writers interested in gender issues, the simultaneous consolidation and subversion of patriarchal gender discourse during the Victorian period make it an important one, which women novelists have revisited in a number of ways. Some have followed in Rhys's path, but have directed their revisionary approach to canonical fiction by men. Emma Tennant's *Two Women of London* (1989) offers a modern and female reworking of R.L. Stevenson's *Dr Jekyll and Mr Hyde*. Her next novel *Tess* (1993) is a postmodern response to Hardy's *Tess of the d'Urbervilles*. *Tess* juxtaposes a contemporary narrative, shadowed by Hardy's novel, with material from Hardy's biography in a way that asks the reader to question the distinction between fact and fiction, and to enjoy the intertextual play of narratives. Valerie Martin's *Mary Reilly* (1990) tells Jekyll's story through the eyes of a new female character, while in the United States, Sena Jeter Naslund's *Ahab's Wife* (1999) fleshes out an eventful biography for the woman referred to so fleetingly in Melville's *Moby Dick*. These novels are part of a widespread revisioning of canonical male-authored texts, including the Ancient Classics and the Bible, about which I have written elsewhere.[8] While some may display the playful intertextuality of postmodernist fiction, each of them also challenges the images of women constructed by the literature of the past, the values inscribed in those images, and their enduring power.

It is possible, then, to see a confluence of influences at work: to argue that a renewed interest in historical fiction intersected with a renewed interest in the Victorian period to create a very productive field for the feminist revisioning which has been such an important critical and imaginative impulse in the late twentieth century. Revisiting Victorian women's lives provides an opportunity to challenge the answers which nineteenth-century society produced in response to 'the Woman Question'. But the novelists dealt with in this book are not merely carrying out a historical exercise. Their interest is, I believe, in what the Victorian period can add to the modern reader's understanding of gender. As David Glover and Cora Kaplan put it, 'Modern feminist critics use the Victorian period to revisit the unresolved issues of what kind of opposition gender is, and what kind of ethics and politics can be assigned to "traditional" femininity.'[9] The crucial term here is 'unresolved'. Gender is as politically charged an issue now as it was at the end of the nineteenth century, and continues to be debated in both the popular and academic press. If we are in the middle of another shift in what we know and think about gender, in the 'post-feminist' mood that prevails at the beginning of the twenty-first century, we need to know how our beliefs came about, and how much has been excluded or forgotten in what we know.

One significant growth area within gender studies is, therefore, research into the development and codification of ideas about gender, which has fed from and into disciplines such as history, anthropology, science, theology and literature. This book grows out of and contributes to that inter-disciplinary exploration, as well as to the revisiting of Victorian womanhood – and to a lesser extent manhood – in contemporary writing. It analyses the ways in which late twentieth-century feminist fiction engages with the discourses of science, literature and religion that shaped Victorian ideas about gender. In outlining this discursive background, I have tried to avoid presenting too monolithic a view of Victorian culture and belief, although it is sometimes hard to do so, given the weight carried by the more dominant views of women. Wherever possible I have indicated degrees of dissension, and the underlying tensions inherent in any ideology.

The chapters that follow discuss a selection of highly individual novels, all set in the second half of the nineteenth century. They include the work of some, but by no means all, of the novelists mentioned in this Introduction. The novels are presented chronologically according to the different decades in which they are set. That sequence tells a story – or rather, two stories. In contextualising the novels in relation to Victorian gender discourse, it identifies the issues which contributed to the growing debate about 'the Woman Question'. But it also tells the story, seen through the eyes of twentieth-century feminists, of how women increasingly subverted the control exercised by that discourse. To conclude, and since gender cannot be understood in isolation from class and race, the final chapter on Morrison's *Beloved* provides a response – if not an answer – to the question raised by the first chapter. The variety of forms which these novels take illustrates what Gilmour calls 'the truly experimental aspect' (p. 199) of this fictional preoccupation with the Victorians.

1
What is a Woman? Victorian Constructions of Femininity

> In general (for I neither can nor will state any thing but what is most known,) how much more pure, tender, delicate, irritable, affectionate, flexible, and patient, is woman than man.
>
> – John Caspar Lavater, *Essays on Physiognomy*[1]

> For men at most differ as Heaven and earth,
> But women, worst and best, as Heaven and Hell.
>
> – Alfred Lord Tennyson, 'Merlin and Vivien'[2]

While both these quotations emphasise the difference between women and men, they appear to offer contrasting views of women, the first conveying a far more flattering view of women in general than the second. And yet the first, from the Swiss pastor John Lavater's *Essays on Physiognomy*, is much closer in attitude to the second, taken from Tennyson's Arthurian epic, *Idylls of the King*, than at first appears. Lavater's essays on the science of physiognomy, of judging character by appearance, first appeared in 1789, but remained, according to Jenny Bourne Taylor and Sally Shuttleworth, the most influential text in its field throughout the nineteenth century. The ninth edition was published in 1855, only a year before Tennyson wrote 'Merlin and Vivien'. The essay 'Male and Female' includes 'A Word on the Physiognomical Relation of the Sexes', which describes male and female appearance in a series of binary oppositions of the kind which Hélène Cixous sees as characteristic of Western thought about the sexes.[3] Many of these opposed physiological attributes lend themselves to interpretation in moral terms, generally implying female weakness, as in the opening lines, 'Man is the most firm – woman the most flexible. Man is the straightest – woman the most

8

bending.'[4] While Lavater presents woman as man's saviour, without whom he is 'but half a man [...] but half human' (p. 17), he simultaneously suggests the ever-present possibility of her fall from grace by quoting Paul's Epistle to Timothy: 'She shall be saved in childbearing, *if* they continue in faith, and charity, and holiness, with sobriety' (p. 16, my italics). That qualification is crucial, since it explains the contradiction evident throughout the nineteenth century between the desire to define woman as a single category, and an equally powerful desire to distinguish between what Tennyson's Merlin calls 'worst and best' women.

Together, these two quotations illustrate the interconnectedness of different spheres of knowledge in the Victorian period. As Robin Gilmour points out in his influential study of its intellectual climate, there was little attempt to keep science, literature and theology in different intellectual compartments: they shared a common discourse.[5] Moreover, in spite of Lavater's claim to only state 'what is known', he presents as 'knowledge' a view of male and female attributes as subjective as that of Merlin's response to the sorceress Vivien, anticipating the extent to which received wisdom permeates thinking about gender in every discipline of the time.

Even such powerful discourses as those of theology and science did not go uncontested, however, or proceed at a regular pace. The 'woman question', in particular as it bore on women's demand for emancipation from the duties of motherhood and family life, was hotly debated throughout the Victorian period, as my discussion of the gender debate later in this chapter will show. Nor is it possible to ascribe the position of Victorian women to a male conspiracy. There were many women, including feminists, who argued that woman's highest fulfilment came from motherhood. Even Elizabeth Blackwell (1821–1910), the world's first trained, registered woman doctor, gave a series of lectures in 1852 with the message that girls must take care of their bodies to make them perfect vessels for motherhood.[6] Male views on the subject ranged from John Stuart Mill's *The Subjection of Women* (1869), which presented powerful arguments for improvements to women's legal situation and for giving women the vote, to the critic John Ruskin's classic lecture 'Of Queen's Gardens' (1865), which presents a Romantic idealisation of woman's role as guardian of the 'sacred place', home. The general weight of opinion was, however, in Ruskin's favour, as is indicated by the denunciations which followed Mill's publication.[7] This chapter cannot hope to deal in detail with the full complexity of this debate, but it attempts to indicate the dominant themes and trends, while pointing the reader in the direction of fuller, more authoritative studies.[8] Moreover, since its purpose is to provide a context for twentieth-century fiction which engages with late nineteenth-century discourses of femininity, the chapter concentrates on the intersection of scientific, religious and literary discourses relating to Victorian women, rather than on the reality of their lives. For, as Carroll Smith-Rosenberg and Charles Rosenberg argue,

> Role definitions exist on a level of prescription beyond their embodiment in the individuality and behaviour of particular historical persons. They exist rather as a formally agreed upon set of characteristics understood by and acceptable to a significant proportion of the population [...]. They exist as parameters with which and against which individuals must either conform or define their deviance.[9]

Religious prescriptions and cultural reflections

At the beginning of the Victorian period the most important influence on such definitions of women's role was religion, reflected not only in legislation and social practice, but also in the wider culture, in art and literature, women's magazines and conduct books. The two most powerful images of woman that emerge from the Bible, or at least from the interpretation of it that has dominated Western thought for two thousand years, underpinned the division of Victorian womanhood into the polarised extremes of 'madonnas' and 'magdalenes', a distinction which – however simplistic – played an important part in the popular imagination. Eve, leading man away from God through the temptations of the flesh, is associated with evil and disobedience, justifying the subsequent subordination of woman to man. The contrasting image of the Virgin Mary embodies the obedience to God's wishes of which Eve was incapable, and is completely free from the taint of sexuality which surrounds representations of Eve. In addition, as the mother of Christ, Mary provides the ultimate model of maternal devotion and silent submissiveness. These two representations of women, and the narratives in which they are embedded, provide a rationale for the division of women into 'angels' and 'abortions', to use Lavater's terms. Only by being obedient, denying their bodies and seeking fulfilment in maternity can women be sure of a place within the first category.

Images of the Madonna and of angels therefore contribute to the formation of the Victorian feminine ideal, in both visual and literary representations. What emerges out of this iconography is a highly idealised picture of woman as disembodied, spiritual and, above all, chaste. Chastity, moreover, meant for many not only a lack of sexual experience, but a lack of sexual feeling, or 'passionlessness'. Associated with the rise of evangelical religion between the 1790s and 1830s, the ideology of passionlessness made it possible for women to attain the apparently impossible goal of emulating the virgin mother: mothers were able to remain sexless, 'virgin' in a sense, because they remained sexually unaroused. This ideology also enhanced women's moral power. As Nancy Cott argues, 'By replacing sexual with moral motives and determinants, the ideology of passionlessness favored women's power and self-respect.'[10]

In Coventry Patmore's narrative poem, 'The Angel in the House' (1854–63), the figure of the sexless angel crosses into domestic ideology, embodying all the Christian virtues of love, purity and self-sacrifice so as to act as moral centre of the family. Paradoxically, the religious doubt and anxiety generated by the materialism of the new sciences gave rise to an impulse to deny the materiality of women in order to maintain an element of spirituality in a godless universe. Gilmour points out that for the positivist Auguste Comte, for instance, 'Woman, as Madonna, was to occupy a central place in worship' (p. 105). Women were expected to fill the vacuum left by the death of religious certainty, revered not only as the embodiment of virtue themselves, but as the guardians of male virtue. The idea of virtue itself became in the mid-Victorian period, in Mary Poovey's words, 'depoliticized, moralized, and associated with the domestic sphere, which was being abstracted at the same time [. . .] from the so-called public sphere of competition, self-interest, and economic aggression'.[11] The categorical division of life into public and private spheres during the Victorian period has been challenged in recent years, both by historians who contest the distinction between the public and the private,[12] and by those who question the extent to which women were confined to their 'proper sphere'. Amanda Vickery, in particular, sees the vocabulary of separate spheres as 'a conservative response to an unprecedented *expansion* in the opportunities, ambitions and experience of late Georgian and Victorian women', and argues that while 'the public/private dichotomy may, therefore, serve as a loose description of a very long-standing difference between the lives of women and men', there is no evidence that it led to the transformation of relations between the sexes in the Victorian period.[13] Eileen Yeo similarly argues that 'powerful voices from religion, science and the state produced stronger prescriptions about the gendering of public and private spheres for a variety of reasons including their fear of women's activity as part of wider social "disorder"' in her introduction to a collection of essays which go on to show how Victorian women negotiated these barriers to their entry into the public sphere.[14] The novelists with whom this study is concerned, while reconstructing those 'powerful voices' and their repressive effects, also illustrate, through their fictions, Vickery's view that 'Victorian women emerge as no less spirited, capable, and, most importantly, diverse a crew as in any other century' (p. 390).

As new sciences developed during the century, however, they increasingly jettisoned the kind of religious sanctions Lavater invoked to validate his theories. Poovey argues that as early as the 1830s 'naturalistic explanations of difference were posing a serious challenge to scriptural explanations of the same thing' (p. 7). But while the explanations may have changed, the belief in sexual difference, and the nature of that difference, remained remarkably similar. Ironically, therefore, the same sciences that most threatened religious authority in some areas came to its aid to shore up traditional ideas about gender. And where religion could only state, albeit with divine authority, what women should be, and condemn those that failed to achieve this ideal, science aspired to say what women objectively were – a verdict from which there was no appeal, for scientific claims to objectivity tend to carry greater weight than the more overtly ideological claims of religion or literature. As Foucault has shown, scientific discourse has a pre-eminently normative function, since apparently disinterested systems of knowledge create norms and laws which make possible judgement and exclusion on the basis of perceived 'deviance' from those laws.[15] This became increasingly the case as science became more emotionally and intellectually central to Victorian culture. As Gilmour puts it, after the 1860s, with the growing acceptance of evolutionary accounts of human origins,

> science became an increasingly confident and imperial ideology, laying claims to fields of human behaviour previously thought closed to it. From the structure of society to the workings of the subconscious mind and the nature of religious experience itself, 'science' was widely seen as the magic key that opened every door. (pp. 111–12)

The role of science as the 'magic key' to the understanding of gender is the main focus of the rest of this chapter, since this is the area with which the novelists discussed in this study are – directly or indirectly – most engaged in their own representations of Victorian womanhood.

The biological sciences

The biological sciences aspired to the pursuit of universal laws, to identifying the underlying principles that governed life. Basing their authority on 'nature', they were able to present apparently neutral accounts of sex difference which established a definition of 'woman' as a homogeneous group differentiated far more from men than from each other, with different educational needs and different social functions. As Alison Winter has suggested, gender, therefore, became a particularly significant variable for defining intellectual identities and social roles, in contrast to earlier periods when gender was less important than gentility in determining credibility.[16] Being 'universal', these ideas of difference were generally transatlantic in currency, which perhaps explains numerous references to 'Victorian America' in current scholarship.[17] I shall, therefore, use examples from both British and North American scientific and medical writing throughout this chapter, in order to establish its relevance to the North American fiction to be discussed in later chapters.

Some of the most assertive statements about sexual difference stem from simple anatomical observations being used as the basis for judgements about mental operations. Numerous discussions centred on the question of brain size. Thomas Laycock (1812–76), a lecturer in clinical medicine, writes in 1860, 'Experience shows that woman has less capability than man for dealing with the abstract in philosophy, science, and art, and this fact is in accordance with the less development of the frontal convolutions',[18] showing how scientific 'facts' might be extrapolated from observations based on the cultural status quo. Even in 1887, George Romanes (1848–94), a physiologist and psychologist influential on both sides of the Atlantic, argues that, since there is a five-ounce weight difference between the female and male brains, 'on merely anatomical grounds we should be prepared to expect a marked inferiority of intellectual power in the former'. He further claims that women's relative physical weakness makes them 'less able to sustain the fatigue of serious or prolonged brain action' so that they can never hope to equal men mentally.[19] Susan Sleeth Mosedale, in an essay exploring the influence of gender ideology on scientists' findings, accuses Romanes of letting popular beliefs about women interfere with his reasoning. She quotes his tendency to refer to women's inferior mental traits as 'proverbial', 'a matter of ordinary comment' and 'a matter of universal recognition'.[20] When more sophisticated measuring led to the realisation that a female's brain, although absolutely lighter than a male's, was relatively heavier when compared with body weight, attempts were made to devise new indices to support male intellectual superiority. The response of Paul Broca, one of the leaders in the field of differential intelligence, is typically circular in its reasoning:

We might ask if the small size of the female brain depends exclusively upon the small size of her body [...]. But we must not forget that women are, on the average, a little less intelligent than men, a difference which we should not exaggerate but which is, none the less, real. We are therefore permitted to suppose that the relatively small size of the female brain depends in part on her physical inferiority and in part upon her intellectual inferiority.[21]

Brain function was also thought to differ in men and women. Phrenologists argued that specific mental faculties, located in specific parts of the brain, could be investigated by feeling bumps on the outside of the head, and tabulated areas of difference in the brain indicating emotional differences in the sexes. George Coombe, the Scottish populariser of phrenology, claimed that its founder, the Austrian Franz Gall, could tell whether a brain had belonged to a man or a woman, if it were presented to him in water, since the cerebellum, the seat of sexual love, was larger in the male, as compared to the part of the brain indicating the love of the young, more pronounced in women (Russett, p. 19). Even Victorian neurophysiologists, as Ornella Moscucci points out, drew gendered distinctions between different parts of the brain: the 'higher brain levels which were the locus of mind, and lower levels which functioned automatically by reflex action', governing bodily functions. The higher intellectual faculties played the dominant role in men, while the 'automatic' sectors of brain were more dominant in women because of the imbalance of physical over mental events in women.[22] This again rather circular argument can be traced back to the much earlier association of woman with body, and man with mind. Women's powers of reason were inevitably lower than those of men, since reasoning was not their primary function. From such premises it was easy to draw even more tendentious conclusions, based on the usual appeal to 'nature', such as that 'there seems to be a natural incompatibility between science and the female brain'.[23]

What woman was suited for was apparently indicated by her larger pelvis, at least in European women. The sexologist Henry Havelock Ellis (1859–1939) writes in his influential study, *Man and Woman: A Study of Human Secondary Sexual Characteristics* (1894), that the pelvis of some of the 'dark races is ape-like in its narrowness and small capacity', in contrast to the wider European pelvis which was 'the proof of high evolution and the promise of capable maternity' (quoted in Russett, p. 29). Long before this, however, advances in physiology which led to a new understanding of the female reproductive system confirmed woman's primary role. In 1845, Dr Adam Raciborski discovered that ovulation was involuntary,[24] so that by the mid-nineteenth century the ovaries were seen as the essence of femininity, and reproduction as woman's essential function.[25] The first definition of gynaecology – 'the doctrine of the nature and diseases of women' – was published in 1849,[26] and the formal recognition of this area of medicine fostered the view that the physiology and pathology of the female reproductive system provided the key to understanding her mental, psychological and moral 'nature'. As one doctor explained in 1880, 'Ovulation fixes woman's place in the animal economy [...]. With the act of menstruation is wound up the whole essential character of her system.'[27] A Professor Hubbard from New Haven, an American physician, explained in 1870 that it was 'as if the Almighty, in creating the female sex, *had taken the uterus and built up a woman around it*',[28] suggesting that the medical profession still sought scriptural authority for their findings.

However commonplace this emphasis on the difference between the male and female body may seem to the modern reader, it is worth noting that it represents a distinct change from earlier anatomical schemes. In his essay on the relationship between reproduction and sexuality, Thomas Laqueur points out that, until the eighteenth century, the female body was seen as an inferior and inverted version of the male – female reproductive organs being merely undeveloped homologues of the male. In the nineteenth century, this homological view came increasingly under attack from scientists like Walter Heape, a militant anti-suffragist and Reader in Zoology at Cambridge: 'the reproductive system is not only structurally but functionally fundamentally different in the Male and the Female; and since all other organs and systems of organs are affected by this system, it is certain that the Male and Female are essentially different throughout'. Scientists like Heape were ready to use such knowledge, moreover, to argue that 'the accurate adjustment of society depends on proper observation of this fact' (quoted in Laqueur, p. 31).

This view of the female reproductive system as homologous to the male meant, moreover, that female orgasm was considered necessary for conception. Laqueur quotes Jane Sharp's 1671 midwifery guide, last reprinted in 1728, which argues that the clitoris is the female penis: 'It will stand and fall as the yard [vernacular for penis] doth and makes women lustful and take delight in copulation' (p. 14). In contrast, nineteenth-century anatomy saw menstruation as the trigger for conception. The 'ovular' theory of menstruation suggested that the release of the egg caused menstruation, at which time women were at their most fertile and experienced most sexual desire, the equivalent of an animal on heat: Charles Locock's entry in *The Cyclopaedia of Practical Medicine* (revised edition, 1854) compared a woman menstruating to a rabbit 'during the state of genital excitement called the time of heat'.[29] Since sexual intercourse during menstruation was discouraged, the possible link between female sexuality and reproduction was not widely promulgated. By such means physicians could keep maternity and sexuality distinctly separate.[30] Involuntary ovulation and conception made female pleasure irrelevant to reproduction.

The idea of female sexual pleasure was itself a subject of considerable debate. On the one hand, there was a body of scientific and medical writing supporting the concept of 'passionlessness' which was so important ideologically to definitions of the female. W.R. Greg, a liberal manufacturer, even when writing on prostitution in the *Westminster Review* in 1850, articulates the view that women are rarely subject to desire, because 'there is a radical and essential difference between the sexes.... In men, in general, the sexual desire is inherent and spontaneous, and belongs to the condition of puberty. In the other sex, the desire is dormant, if not non-existent, till excited' (quoted in *Uneven Developments*, p. 5). One of the most well-known authorities on the subject, Dr William Acton (1813–75), has been widely quoted as stating that most women are not 'troubled' by sexual feelings:

> The best mothers, wives, and managers of households, know little or nothing of sexual indulgences...As a general rule, a modest woman seldom desires any sexual gratification for herself. She submits to her husband, but only to please him; and, but for the desire for matrimony would far rather be relieved from his attentions.[31]

But, as Taylor and Shuttleworth point out, it is important to be aware of the context of this statement, which Acton is making to reassure prospective husbands that their wives will not make frightening demands on them. He is, however, extremely critical of otherwise model wives who 'not only evince no sexual feeling, but, on the contrary, scruple not to declare their aversion to the least manifestation of it' (p. 181).

Others make the implications of Acton's criticism more explicit, arguing that sex was a vital element in the bonding process, essential to a happy marriage for both parties. The American John Humphrey Noyes, for instance, argued that sex was an essential and irreplaceable form of human affection, with an important social function.[32] There is clearly a tension here between preserving the ideal of the 'pure-hearted' woman, and recognising the importance of sexuality within marriage.

Some doctors were even ready to acknowledge the force of female sexual desire. Henry Maudsley (1835–1918), one of the most influential psychiatrists of the later nineteenth century, went so far as to argue that women 'suffer more than men do from the entire deprivation of sexual intercourse' (quoted in *Embodied Selves*, p. 206). Medical men, dealing with the reality of their patients' lives, were perhaps more inclined to accede to the possibility of female sexuality than those writing from a purely ideological standpoint.

Discussions of the female reproductive system also tended to take a pathologised view of the female body as a whole, seeing women as semi-permanent invalids. A standard American work on female diseases, published in 1843, stated that women were liable to twice as much sickness as men, most of it stemming from the womb.[33] One of the most popular models of disease in the second half of the nineteenth century was that of the 'reflex irritation', which held that any disorder of the reproductive organs could cause pathological reactions in other parts of the body. As one physician explained, 'These diseases will be found, on due investigation, to be in reality, no disease at all, but merely the sympathetic reaction or the symptoms of one disease, namely, a disease of the womb.'[34] For some physicians this provided an all-purpose diagnosis, turning every health problem presenting in a woman into a 'woman's problem'. Even as sympathetic an analyst of sexual difference as Havelock Ellis writes of the female reproductive system using almost biblical imagery to suggest a threat which is not merely physiological but moral: 'even in the healthiest woman a worm, however harmless and unperceived, gnaws periodically at the roots of life' (quoted in Russett, p. 31).

Unsurprisingly, women's 'natural functions' themselves were similarly medicalised. From menarche to menopause, women were supposedly at risk because of the menstrual discharge, which was not only thought liable to 'derangement' in itself, but to affect the nature of disease in other parts of the body: as Locock's *Cyclopaedia* entry puts it, 'very few diseases can exist, and very few plans of treatment be recommended, without the presence of the menses in some way influencing the nature of the symptoms or the remedies to be applied' (quoted in *Embodied Selves*, p. 202). Young women who had reached puberty were prescribed a regimen for menstruation that remained relatively consistent throughout the nineteenth century: fresh air, moderate exercise, rest, domestic tasks and a simple diet; and the avoidance of liquor, corsets and strong emotions. Again, however, as Showalter points out, there was some debate in a number of journals about the supposedly debilitating nature of menstruation, several writers arguing that there need be no disruption of normal life. Shuttleworth and Taylor quote part of Clifford Allbutt's 1884 lecture, 'On Visceral Neuroses', as a similar corrective to the view that the uterus was the source of all disorder (quoted in *Embodied Selves*, p. 206).

The perceived infirmity of the female body inevitably had an impact on ideas about female education, the conflict between the demands of the reproductive body and those of the intellect being starkly depicted. An argument from physics[35] was used to explain the nature of women's physiological economy, since the laws of conservation of energy meant that too much energy was expended by the reproductive organs to be available for any other interests a woman might have. As Poovey explains, 'The model of the human body implicit in this physiology is that of a closed system containing a fixed quantity of energy; if stimulation or expenditure occurs in one part of the system, corresponding depletion or excitation must occur in another.'[36] It was dangerous for any woman to expend energy on anything other than her primary reproductive purpose, as the consequences could be grave not only for herself, but for her children: 'She would become weak and nervous, perhaps sterile, or more commonly, and in a sense more dangerously for society, capable of bearing only sickly and neurotic children – children able to produce only feebler and more degenerate versions of themselves' (quoted in Smith-Rosenberg and Rosenberg, p. 340).

But it was not simply that the female system could not cope with both the demands of education and the demands of the reproductive cycle. Education in itself was generally thought deleterious to female health. As Edward H. Clarke puts it in his oddly named attack on female education, *Sex in Education, or, A Fair Chance for Girls* (1873), 'The results are monstrous brains and puny bodies; abnormally active cerebration, and abnormally weak digestion; flowing thought and constipated bowels; lofty aspirations and neuralgic sensations' (quoted in Smith-Rosenberg and Rosenberg, p. 340). Charles Meigs (1792–1869), a leader in nineteenth-century obstetrics in America, agreed with this view, stating that, after five or six weeks of education, a previously healthy woman would 'lose the habit of menstruation', depriving her body for the sake of her mind.[37] G. Stanley Hall, one of the founding fathers of American psychology, offered one of the most reactionary plans for educational reform: 'broaden by retarding, ... keep the purely mental back and by every method ... bring the intuitions to the front', for girls must be educated 'primarily and chiefly for motherhood' (quoted in Russett, p. 61).

A number of important and distinguished women and men, however, provided alternative explanations for the poor state of women's health. These included tight corsets and sedentary lives, devoid of fresh air and physical exercise. Such explanations were particularly to be heard in America in the second half of the nineteenth century.[38] Those campaigning for women's education argued that boredom and idleness were more likely than education to be the cause of illness. This was the response of Elizabeth Garrett Anderson, the first woman to train as a doctor in Britain, to Henry Maudsley's article on the dangers of 'brain-forcing' in women.[39] It was a long time, however, before such voices were listened to and their recommendations acted on.

In the meantime female physiology, it appeared, meant women were unsuited to anything other than their 'natural' role as mothers. And to reinforce this sense of motherhood as woman's normal destiny, many physicians pointed to the even greater incidence of physical and emotional difficulties experienced by women who failed to give birth.[40] As has already been implied, such medical and scientific views of the female body were not so much the product of advances in those areas of knowledge, as ideological interpretations of that knowledge. Some scientific advances could have led to an emphasis on the similarities between the sexes, rather than the differences between them. Laqueur points, for example, to advances in developmental anatomy, which 'pointed to the common origins of both sexes in a morphologically androgenous embryo and thus not to their intrinsic difference' (p. 3). Instead, he goes on, as 'science was increasingly viewed as providing insight into the fundamental truths of creation', with nature as 'the only foundation of the moral order' (p. 35), biology could be used to provide authoritative evidence for radical differences between the sexes, and for patriarchal social structures.

An unhealthy mind in an unhealthy body?

Differences between the sexes were not limited to their physical differences, since these had their impact on the mental processes too. Some of the links made were very simplistic. As late as 1882, *The Popular Science Monthly* published an article by Miss M.A. Hardaker on 'Science and the Woman Question' which included the assertion that 'the sum total of food converted into thought by women can never equal the sum total of food converted into thought by men. It follows, therefore, that *men will always think more than women*.'[41] The gynaecologist James Oliver presented a more complex view of the case in 1889:

> The difference between the man and the woman is not stamped on any one organ of the body, neither is it revealed in the function or group of functions manifested by the organs of generation, it is rather an association of such, and is the outcome of a peculiar molecular and molar state belonging to every organ and structure of the body. The difference is universal or constitutional; it pervades the whole mind and body of the individual.[42]

In many cases subjective judgements were presented as fact with little or no reference to empirical evidence. Romanes, for instance, argued that woman's relative physical weakness led inevitably to such failings as her 'resort to petty arts and pretty ways for the securing of [her] aims', as well as her more commendable 'deeply-rooted desire to please the opposite sex which, beginning in the terror of a slave, has ended in the devotion of a wife' (quoted in Mosedale, p. 18).

And just as the female body was seen to be subject to the demands and vagaries of the reproductive system, so was the female nervous system. In one sense the centrality of woman's reproductive function was thought to have positive consequences on her emotional life. Involuntary ovulation provided a 'scientific' basis for maternal instinct, described by Peter Gaskell in 1833 as 'truly an instinct in the strictest acceptation of the word' (quoted in Poovey, p. 7). More often, however, woman's reproductive function was seen as the cause of intellectual and emotional problems. Because of the cyclical nature of those functions – the short, but recurrent cycles of menstruation and childbearing, and the longer cycle marked out by menarche and menopause, all women were subject to 'periodicity', which made her nervous system inherently unstable. Worse may follow, since, according to Dr Isaac Ray (1808–81), 'with women, it is but a step from extreme nervous susceptibility to downright hysteria, and from that to overt insanity. In the sexual evolution, in pregnancy, in the parturient period, in lactation, strange thoughts, extraordinary feelings, unseasonable appetites, criminal impulses, may haunt a mind at other times innocent and pure.'[43] During menstruation itself women are described as susceptible to a 'temporary insanity' and 'undoubtedly more prone than men to commit any unusual or outrageous act'.[44] Such arguments were sometimes used to defend women convicted of crimes like abortion, otherwise incomprehensible in women.

The links made between female physiology and insanity, and in turn between insanity and impure thoughts, are particularly significant, since they echo the anxieties articulated in other discourses about every woman's potential for sin, trapped as she is in her body. The greatest danger to a woman's mental health, as to her moral worth, came from her sexuality, which scientists, like moralists, tried to keep distinct from maternity. The representation of cause and effect here is at times circular, drawing on the traditional associations between insanity and sexuality. The insane had long been considered to be prone to sexual depravity, with women excelling men in this respect. T. Claye Shaw's report on 'The Sexes in Lunacy' observes that 'women in acute states of insanity are abusive, indiscriminately violent, impulsive, obscene and wayward out of all proportion to what men are'.[45] Now female sexuality could itself be seen as evidence of insanity, particularly of that variety known as 'moral insanity', which Elaine Showalter suggests redefined madness 'not as a loss of reason, but as deviance from socially accepted behavior'. She quotes James Cowles Prichard's original definition of the concept, in 1835, as 'a morbid perversion of the natural feelings, affections, inclinations, temper, habits, moral dispositions, and natural impulses, without any remarkable disorder or defect of the intellect, or knowing and reasoning faculties'.[46] Depending so heavily on current ideas of what was 'natural', such a concept of insanity made its diagnosis and treatment highly ideological, as Showalter's study of 'the female malady' shows. For those who conceived of passionlessness as a physiological norm, rather than merely an ideal, any evidence of sexuality in a woman could be deemed deviant. The sexual woman was represented as not only bad, but sick and unnatural, because unwomanly. And aberrant sexuality was often linked with other kinds of gender transgression. In America, Wood points to 'an underlying logic running through popular books by physicians on women's diseases to the effect that ladies get sick *because* they are unfeminine – in other words, sexually aggressive, intellectually ambitious, and defective in proper womanly submission and selflessness' (p. 8).

Hysteria was a less dramatic, but much more common, form of female mental infirmity. Earlier perceptions of the disorder had linked it to the womb, from which it derived its name,[47] and these were reinforced by the view that all physical female diseases had their origin in the uterus. But during the course of the century this perception tended to be reversed, shifting the point of origin away from the womb to the nervous system itself, the emotions then registering themselves as bodily symptoms. John Connolly, a pioneer of moral management of the insane, took a half-way position between these two perspectives, arguing that women were particularly vulnerable to hysteria because of the stress placed on the uterine economy, but that these stresses were emotional as well as physiological. In spite of shifting attention away from the womb, however, this view did not break the link between hysteria and femininity. While men might also succumb to hysteria, they were far less vulnerable than women, since they were thought to have far greater control of their emotions. Romanes cautioned that 'in women, as contrasted with men, [the emotions] are almost always less under control of the will – more apt to break away [...] from restraint of reason' (quoted in Russett, p. 42). Feelings were thus gendered, just as much as physiology, and naturalised by reference to physiology.

Moreover, the feelings most likely to give rise to hysteria were sexual feelings, and it is here that the complexity of Victorian attitudes towards female sexuality becomes most apparent. While female insanity was associated with the illicit expression of sexual feelings, hysteria was associated with their repression. Robert Brudenell Carter (1828–1918), in *On the Pathology and Treatment of Hysteria* (1853), removed the illness still further from organic origins, observing that the predominance of female, as opposed to male, hysterics was due to the socially enforced repression of woman's sexual passions – the most 'violent' female emotion. Unmarried women in particular, unable to satisfy their sexual desires in any other way, were liable to either an addiction to masturbation or hysteria.[48] Rather, however, than recommending that such sexual restraints should be lifted, Carter and others used his observation as evidence of the unnaturalness of the unmarried state for women. For such disorders, therefore, popular domestic manuals based on Connolly's advice recommended marriage – by implication sexual relations – and pregnancy.[49]

At the end of the century Sigmund Freud's *Studies on Hysteria* (1895) provided a more systematic theory of hysteria based on his understanding of the consciousness as split. In his view hysteria was the result of psychological conflict which the sufferer was unable to express except through bodily symptoms. Typically that conflict was the result of sexual desires which young women in particular were unable to articulate, or even acknowledge, since they lay repressed in the unconscious. Since Freud's theories relate female hysteria to sexuality in this way, hysteria became read as evidence of a guilty sexual secret. As his later account of the 'Dora' case states, 'where there is no knowledge of sexual processes even in the unconscious, no hysterical symptom will arise; and where hysteria is found, there can no longer be any question of "innocence of mind"' (quoted in Ender, p. 12).

In looking behind the visible symptoms of women's diseases to try to ascertain what the symptom was 'saying', Freud acknowledged the reality of female desire, as well as showing that hysteria cannot be cured by social control, since its roots lie in the unconscious and therefore are only amenable to treatment by psychoanalytic means. And in acknowledging the role of repression, he also acknowledged the element of social control responsible for hysteria. He did not, however, see these controls as unnecessary constraints on the needs and aspirations of young women, even if, in the process of being forbidden any sexual curiosity, girls were scared away from any form of knowledge, so that their intellect was suppressed along with their sexuality. Like others, he believed women's greater vulnerability to feelings in general made them incapable of overcoming sexual feeling through self-control, so they must be brought up to suppress it. Freud concluded, with most of his male contemporaries, that all forms of knowledge, whether sexual or not, were too dangerous to female mental health to be encouraged, even while acknowledging the legitimacy of the desire. Writing with Breuer, he regrets:

> Adolescents who are later to become hysterical are for the most part lively, gifted and full of intellectual interests before they fall ill. [...] They include girls who get out of bed at night so as secretly to carry on some study that their parents have forbidden for fear of their overworking. [...] The overflowing productivity of their minds has led one of my friends to assert that hysterics are the flower of mankind, as sterile, no doubt, but as beautiful as double flowers.[50]

Advances in the understanding of the relationship between body and mind did not, therefore, lead to any 'advanced' thinking about female roles. To see the body and mind as inseparable might have put an end to the dualism that placed woman/body and man/mind in opposition, but instead simply reinforced the opposition between men and women by insisting on the differences between male and female physiology. As Taylor and Shuttleworth point out, physiological explanations of the influence of the reproductive system on thought and feeling were used as a rationale for Victorian attitudes towards woman, which oscillated wildly between the poles of difference, the body and spirituality. They quote in evidence the physician John Gideon Millingen (1782–1862) who made the paradoxical assertion in 1848: 'Woman, with her exalted spiritualism, is more under the control of matter' (p. 169). The idea of female sexuality being latent but repressed shifted the crude angel/whore distinction into a sense that any apparent 'angel' could be harbouring a potential 'whore' if sufficient supervision were not exercised. Cott argues that what began as ideology became medical 'knowledge' in mid-century, so that later in the century doctors could take over the role of ministers, advising on sexual and 'moral' problems among women. What Moscucci calls the development of 'obstetric jurisprudence' meant that so-called knowledge about women's physiology and pathology was applied to the regulation of social life, suggesting 'that the maintenance of the public order depended on the medical surveillance of women's sexual functions' (p. 107).

Evolutionary theory and the social sciences

> Woman's excellence over man is not, in truth, in the manifestation of force of intellect and energy of will, but in the sphere of wisdom, and love, and moral power.
>
> The natural history of man is in accordance with these scientific data. The less intellectual and physical energy of woman has deter-mined her social position in all ages and all races. (Laycock, 1860, *Embodied Selves*, p. 177)

Laycock's comments, in addition to illustrating the confusion of 'scientific data' with received wisdom, show how biological and medical views of sexual difference were, in the second half of the nineteenth century, given added authority by the findings of newer sciences wider in scope. The work of Charles Darwin, in particular, reinforced the view that the differences between men and women extended beyond the reproductive system to secondary sexual characteristics. All such differences, according to Darwin, could be explained by the process of evolution. *The Origin of Species* (1859), primarily a biological work, argued that evolution occurred because those individuals of a species whose characteristics best fitted them for survival were the ones who contributed most offspring to the next generation, to whom the parents passed on those character-istics. In this way, the adaptation of the species to its environment gradually improved. *The Descent of Man and Selection in Relation to Sex* (1871), primarily a work of anthropology, added the principle of sexual selection, according to which males contend for and are selected by females on the basis of their superiority. The chosen male then transmits his superiority to his male offspring, so that only males evolve as a result of sexual selection. Men and women are, therefore, as they are because of a mixture of natural and sexual selection.

Because woman is not involved in the competitive process of sexual selection, she inevitably lags behind man in evolutionary terms. Darwin's view of evolution places her closer to the child than to the adult male, a view echoed in literature of the period.[51] She 'retains a closer resemblance to the young of her own species'. In moral and intellectual development women, like the 'primitive' races, are like children compared to the evolved male adults of civilised races. Even her superior qualities confirm her place on a lower rung of the evolutionary ladder, since Darwin accepts the generally held view that 'with women the powers of intuition, of rapid perception, and perhaps of imitation, are more strongly marked than in man', only to argue that some of these faculties are 'characteristic of the lower races, and therefore of a past and lower state of civilization' (*Descent*, quoted in Tuana, pp. 37, 38). The 'science' of craniology was sometimes used to support such arguments, relating female skulls to those of non-European races and infants (see Tuana, p. 46). In 1887, Edward Drinker Cope (1840–97), leader of the American school of neo-Lamarckians, presented a similar argument by reference to recapitulation theory – the idea that the development of the individual recapitulates the development of the species. In his view, because woman reaches maturity before man, her development is arrested at a less advanced stage, resulting in the retention of infantile or primitive qualities which males grow out of: 'Probably, most men can recollect some early period of their lives when the emotional nature predominated...this is the "woman stage" of character.'[52]

Woman's development was also arrested by the primacy of the maternal function. The principle of the conservation of energy, according to Darwin, determines that females expend so much energy on foetal development that they have less energy than males for developmental variations. For Laycock, that function is part of a natural law which unites woman with the lowest creatures in creation: 'So low down in the scale of creation as we can go, wherever there is a discoverable distinction of sex, we find that maternity is the first and most fundamental duty of the female' (*Embodied Selves*, p. 177). And once it became popular belief that characteristics acquired as a result of damage from disease and improper lifestyles were transmitted through heredity, inappropriate female behaviour had to be condemned for its deleterious effect on the health of society at large, which could only be safeguarded by the production of healthy children. Education, therefore, already thought to be a danger to the reproductive system, was also seen as a potential danger to the future health of the species: 'better that the future mothers of the state should be robust, hearty, healthy women, than that, by over study, they entail upon their descendants the germs of disease'.[53] Men also have a distinct role to play in the survival of the species since, Darwin argues, biology dictates that men 'maintain themselves and their families'. But this role can be fulfilled in a variety of ways, and will increase male superiority over women since 'this will tend to keep up or increase their mental powers, and, as a consequence, the present inequality between the sexes' (*Descent*, quoted in Tuana, p. 66). As the species evolves, man becomes more varied, woman less so, because of her specialised reproductive function. And since increased differentiation is a key factor in the evolutionary process, man's more rapid development continues to be inevitable. What Darwin therefore adds to the debate about sexual difference is a sexual hierarchy determined by the evolutionary process and therefore beyond question.

Within this perspective the Victorian woman's domestic role and submission to man is not necessary simply for the preservation of the family, or even society, but of the race. Woman's reproductive organs defined her role in terms of irresistible racial needs. Poovey points out that, even before Darwin, the uterus was seen as the most important organ not only in the female body, but of the 'Race'. She quotes from W. Tyler Smith's lecture series on obstetrics (1847–8): 'the uterus is to the Race what the heart is to the Individual: it is the organ of circulation to the species' (p. 35). The idea of an evolutionary imperative reinforced existing ideas that women had a moral responsibility to fulfil their role as mothers, and to accept their subordination to men. Although Darwin does not express approval for the 'present inequality' of the sexes, his work provided telling arguments as to its inevitability.[54] Since evolution increases sexual role differentiation, woman becoming increasingly specialised for motherhood, man becoming increasingly varied in function, any attempt to minimise sexual difference would result in the degeneration of the human race. At the same time, Darwin's readiness to fall back on what is 'generally admitted' about gender indicates why Gillian Beer calls *The Descent* 'the most culturally dependent of Darwin's works, drawing for its evidence and affirmations on the works of ethnographers, race-theorists, and primatologists of the 1860s, themselves often affected by Darwin', making the 'circle of evidence [...] disturbingly untroubled since materials are passed round and back from one field to another'.[55]

That 'circle of evidence' can be observed in the work of the social sciences, also attempting, like science, to identify 'laws', in their case the laws underlying society. The influence of Darwinism can be seen first in the development of anthropology, which was essentially a creation of the nineteenth century. When considering the role of anthropology in the gender debate, Moscucci notes that it developed at the same time as gynaecology developed as a fully established medical specialism, and she argues that it had a similar agenda. The task of the gynaecologist 'involved an evaluation of the balance between instinct and reason, of the senses and the moral faculties, of the relationship between organisation and environment – the very themes round which the natural history of man, one of the chief components of the science of anthropology, was organised' (p. 31). Anthropological findings could be used to endorse the sexual differences – both physical and mental – identified by biologists and used to justify role differentiation. Gilmour notes that differences in cranial shape, for instance, proved that 'women's strengths were emotional rather than logical, sympathetic and domestic rather than rational and worldly; and that for them to enter the public domain of political debate was to risk losing their countervailing power, which could best be exercised in the home' (p. 191). As a category for anthropological enquiry, woman is defined by her specialisation for reproduction, any differences between races and cultures being largely overridden by their shared sex.[56]

Anthropologists also accepted the Darwinian view that such sexual differentiation was an essential component of evolution, as can be seen from James McGrigor Allan's statement in a lecture to London anthropologists in 1869: 'inequality of the sexes increases with the progress of civilization'.[57] The work of social anthropologists between 1860 and 1890 proved that family life as experienced by middle-class Victorians was not a natural institution, but only one of many possible social arrangements. The research of men like Bachofen and Briffault confirmed the existence of matriarchal societies prior to patriarchal societies.[58] However, since the matriarchal period was dominated by the female fertility principle, it was argued that patriarchy represented the emancipation of man from dependence on Nature and therefore the highest stage of human evolution. Moreover, according to the 'law' of the division of labour, the exemption of woman from productive labour, so that she might devote herself to the bearing and rearing of children, was a characteristic of the most advanced societies. However much the lives of working-class women contravened this 'law', the Victorian middle-class family, centred around a permanent maternal presence but governed by the more highly developed male, could be seen as the final product of a long evolutionary process.[59] The evolutionary anthropologists thus added their voices to those protesting against female emancipation of any kind. As Allan asks:

> Is it possible to conceive a more contemptible and deplorable spectacle than that of the female [...] who, having undertaken, and having appointed to her, by nature, those functions, in the proper fulfillment

of which consist the charm and glory of the sex, deliberately neglects and abdicates the sacred duties and privileges of wife and mother, to make herself ridiculous by meddling in and muddling men's work? (quoted in Tuana, p. 164)

Allan's references to the 'charm and glory' of the female sex and to the 'sacred duties and privileges' of her role, may echo the idealisation of women found in other discourses of the period, but adds to it the weight of natural law.

Herbert Spencer (1820–1903), one of the foremost sociological and psychological theorists of the period, was equally insistent that the biological sciences provided the model for social development. His essay 'Progress: Its Law and Cause', arguing that all forms of evolution involved a move from simpler to more complex forms, that 'organic process consists in a change from the homogeneous to the heterogeneous',[60] preceded the publication of Darwin's theories, but his later work was influenced by them. Like Darwin, Spencer drew on the theory of the conservation of energy to argue that woman's development was arrested because each organism had a limited amount of energy, with separate organs competing for limited resources, and the demands of the reproductive system meant woman had less available energy than man for intellectual and psychic growth. However, where Darwin's theory of evolution was not a theory of progress, but an account of the machinery by which simple forms develop into complex forms, Spencer was confident that biological development was inevitably a matter of 'Progress', as the title of his essay suggests. He therefore brought a moral dimension to the neutral concept of natural selection, as his coinage of the phrase, 'the survival of the fittest' – so often ascribed to Darwin – indicates.

Woman's moral sense was seen as central to the survival of the species, her capacity for feeling and sympathy being as important as male intellect and justice. Nevertheless her relative lack of these 'masculine' qualities debarred her from public life: 'there is a perceptible falling short in those two faculties, intellectual and emotional, which are the latest products of human evolution – the power of abstract reasoning and that most abstract of the emotions, the sentiment of justice'.[61] Women, Spencer argues, respond to appeals to pity rather than equity, and seek immediate public good without thought of distant public evils. There is also in his writing an anxiety about female sexuality which has significant repercussions for his view of the family. Sexuality was, in Spencer's view, a characteristic of natural, 'primitive' man that had to be controlled in the interests of civilisation. In the safety of her own home, the Victorian lady was protected from the sexual and material dangers of primitive life, so had been able to evolve to her highest form. Not only her own interests, but those of her children demanded that she remain in such seclusion. As the weaker partner, moreover, woman had developed secondary sexual characteristics which increased the chance of survival, and which were passed on to her daughters. Among these were 'powers of disguising their feelings' (quoted in Mosedale, pp. 11–12). This potential duplicity meant that, while revered, woman also needed to be carefully supervised and controlled. The Victorian family, which ensured control of the passions, refinement and decency and the domestication of women, was thus in Spencer's view sanctioned not by Nature, but by civilisation. That is, woman's essential character was determined by Nature, but the ideal of womanhood could be achieved only by conforming to the patriarchal structures evolved over centuries.

Social scientists like Spencer were endeavouring to situate the idea of difference within a framework where biologically determined attributes enabled each sex to play contrasted but equally important roles, increasingly differentiated by the forces of civilisation. A crucial concept here is 'complementarity', which enabled feminine identity to be seen as the necessary counterpart to masculinity. Londa Schiebinger has traced this concept back to the eighteenth century and Rousseau, arguing that even then it developed new foundations for old arguments, identifying a natural basis for sexual difference conducive to social stability, since it ascribed a value to the private sphere and woman's place in it.[62] According to this theory, woman's 'equality' was guaranteed by her difference from man, which gave her an essential and esteemed role in society. Whatever the scientific basis of this concept, in the Victorian period it had much wider currency. Ruskin sums up this principle in 'Of Queen's Gardens' (1865): 'Each has what the other has not: each completes the other, and is completed by the other: they are in nothing alike, and the happiness and perfection of both depends on each asking and receiving from the other what the other only can give' (quoted in Gilmour, p. 190). John Stuart Mill, however, was quick to point out how easily such notions could lead to ideas of female inferiority and provide a rationale for male domination: 'All women are brought up from the very earliest years in the belief that their ideal of character is the very opposite to that of men: not self will, and government by self control, but submission, and yielding to the control of others.' He describes as 'tiresome cant' the saying that 'women are better than men' by those 'who are totally opposed to treating them as if they were as good' (quoted in Russett, pp. 130, 137). But towards the end of the century, particularly in America, many feminists also supported the idea of complementarity, although drawing different conclusions, asserting 'temperamental and intellectual differences between the sexes as the very reason for greater feminine participation in public life' (Russett, p. 98).

So what of man – the 'complement' to the female?[63] Were his nature and role equally determined by biology? His superior strength and brain size were certainly seen as the source of his superior intellectual skills, but neither his intellect nor his nervous system was seen to be in thrall to the influence of the bodily functions, as they were in woman. Although fatherhood was seen as evidence of true masculinity, male physicians assured the public that the male reproductive system exerted no parallel degree of control over man's body. Male sexual impulses, moreover, were subject to a man's will, the emotional and instinctual functions being more firmly controlled by the brain. Male continence, virtuous and willed repression of carnal desire, figured as an ideal almost as much for the respectable Victorian male as for his female counterpart, but it was to be achieved by self-control rather than by supervision, as it was in women. Apart from venereal disease, excessive masturbation, particularly in youth, was thought to pose the greatest danger to the male body and mind, and was pre-eminently represented as resulting from a lack of proper self-control, and as evidence of 'an unmanliness despised by men' (James Paget, quoted in *Embodied Selves*, p. 223).[64] Man's relationship to his body was, therefore, seen to be completely different from woman's, underlining the extent to which Victorian manhood, as the product of civilisation, was separated from woman, still more tied to Nature. Such 'facts' about man were held as self-evident, even though the development of gynaecology was not paralleled by any equivalent study of male reproductive biology. Only woman required a separately defined area of medical knowledge, since only she deviated from the 'human' norm represented by man. 'The Sex Question' usually meant 'the Woman Question', since only women were perceived as being defined by their sex. Man, in contrast, literally signified mankind as the focus of analysis in areas such as history, philosophy and anthropology. His role was only defined and limited by the limits of humanity itself – at least if he were a white middle-class Anglo-Saxon.

Entering the gender debate

The ideas of the evolutionists were readily absorbed into the popular debate about 'the Woman Question'. But this debate was not, in reality, so much about determining the nature of femininity as about what Glover and Kaplan call 'femininity's function as the mainstay of nation and state through the affective relations of the family'.[65] The theory of complementarity provided a 'scientific' rationale for the doctrine of separate spheres, while equal education, it was argued, was bound to lead to the moral degeneration of the race by creating unfit mothers. Whatever anxieties men may have felt on the domestic or professional front about the demand for emancipation could, therefore, be masked by the apparent urgency of the need to avoid wholesale degeneration of the species. Such arguments are typically expressed by an anonymous reviewer in the conservative *Saturday Review* in 1871:

> if our better halves alter the conditions which have raised us from the condition of orang-outangs, a relapse into savagery is quite possible... the advance of our race has been marked by an increasing diversity between men and women, which makes one, not the contradiction, but the complement of the other [...] so that it appears to be a direct retrogression to assimilate the work of the highly-developed woman to that of her mate [...]. The agitation for women's so-called emancipation should be strenuously resisted.[66]

Victorian ideologies of gender, moreover, overlapped with ideologies of class. As Patricia Ingham puts it,

> These apparently functional descriptions made available a positive image of the middle classes, differentiating them from and justifying control over the lower. For by uniting himself in marriage to a satisfactory exponent of femininity, a typical exponent of middle-class masculinity could subsume her identity into his and become possessed of her high-mindedness and purity, along with a domestic haven of comfort.[67]

When gender differences were questioned, therefore, much more was at stake than the relationship between a man and his wife. As Marxist thinking and the drive for social reform challenged hierarchies based on class, it became even more urgent to reinforce the idea of a hierarchy between men and women. To quote Ingham again, 'The old certainties of gender needed constant shoring up to prevent social disintegration of the kind that was widely feared' (p. 161).

Threats to those certainties took various forms. Educational opportunities expanded with the founding of Queen's College in 1848 and Bedford College the following year, and the subsequent opening of more schools and colleges for the daughters of the middle classes. And the success of the campaign against the Contagious Diseases Acts, repealed in 1886, showed women could organise themselves on gender issues. But Gilmour suggests that there was in fact a double politics of gender at work. The outer struggle for rights was embodied in the organised suffragist campaigns which formally began with Barbara Bodichon's setting up of the Women's Suffrage Committee in 1866, and in liberalising legislation which gave women greater control of their own destinies.[68] But there was also an 'inner struggle of both men and women to cope with the demands of powerful but failing cultural stereotypes' (p. 189). Those struggles were closely related, with women's changing roles often being held responsible for deviations from their 'nature'. These 'deviations' were in turn taken as evidence of the 'unnaturalness' of those roles. The 'New Woman' of the late nineteenth century provoked particular horror in some quarters, since her perceived 'masculinity' transgressed the boundaries of both sexual roles and sexual difference. Even a sexual radical like Havelock Ellis argued, in his 1895 study of homosexuality in women, that emancipation had given rise to an increase in feminine criminality, feminine insanity and female homosexuality.[69] Gilmour sums up the different levels at which the threat of the New Woman's activity might be felt: he argues that the active woman posed a threat to virtue, since domestic and sexual virtue required female passivity. She also threatened the mystique of masculine professional prestige. Finally she challenged the 'existential pact between the sexes', based on the Romantic concept of woman as 'guarantor of the selfhood of the man' (p. 193). Although the white male might represent the very pinnacle of the human species, for any woman to aspire to any of the characteristics which constituted that masculinity was to break that pact.

Even women whose 'transgressions' against their natural role might not be voluntary were a source of anxiety. In 1862 W.R. Greg described the 'redundant' woman as one of the pressing issues of the age, expressing his concern about those who were forced to lead independent lives, rather than 'completing, sweetening, and embellishing the existence of others'.[70] Complementarity here seems to mean marginality rather than the equality which its exponents usually claimed for it. Nor was the perpetual virginity of the old maid admired, as the reverence elsewhere accorded to chastity might lead one to expect. Instead it was pathologised, and represented as an object of pity or disgust. An article by an anonymous writer on 'Woman in her Psychological Relations' in the *Journal of Psychological Medicine and Mental Pathology* (1851) argues that 'the non-fulfilment of their duties as *women* involves its punishment'. He describes the post-menopausal single woman as typically masculine in both body and mind:

> Sometimes, indeed, the male characteristics are in part developed [...] and a hoarser voice accompanies a slight development of the beard [...]. The woman approximates in fact to a man, or in one word, she is a *virago*. She becomes strong-minded; is masculine in her pursuits, severe in her temper, bold and unfeminine in her manners. This unwomanly condition undoubtedly renders her repulsive to man, while her envious, overbearing temper, renders her offensive to her own sex. (quoted in *Embodied Selves*, p. 175)

Although life-cycle changes may be largely responsible for the qualities found to be so repellently masculine, there is an underlying suggestion here that the failure to fulfil a woman's duties in the first place may have been a contributory factor, the consequent 'punishment' therefore being deserved. As W. Balls-Headley in his influential book *The Evolution of the Diseases of Women* (1894) puts it, the 'sexual instinct' is 'the essence and the *raison d'être* of woman's form, the expression of the cause of her existence as a woman; it is the evidence of her ancestral debt; of the instinctive necessity that the female reproductive cell must meet the male fecundating cell; the object is the propagation of the race' (quoted in Moscucci, p. 28).

Similar physiological changes could, of course, be expected in women who had fulfilled their duty. As Moscucci points out, doctors argued that female beauty was due to the activity of the ovaries, creating the softness and roundness associated with procreative activity. After the menopause, women were likely to become angular, and by definition 'unfeminine'. Instead of being congratulated for finally being free from the pernicious influence of her reproductive processes, for no longer being a prisoner of her body, the post-menopausal woman is seen as an unsatisfactory unsexed being, in what the gynaecologist Braxton Hicks calls 'the neutral man–woman state' (quoted in Moscucci, p. 103). In one of the many contradictions in Victorian gender ideology, the female condition is seen as a bar to achieving that full humanity represented by the male, but to lose that femaleness is to lose a woman's *raison d'être*, to become almost less than human.[71] Further light may be thrown on this hostility to the 'unsexed' woman by Cott's analysis of the function of 'passionlessness'. Cott makes a very persuasive case for seeing the concept of the passionless woman from a feminist perspective, as a means of combating the sexual/carnal characterisation which caused women to be excluded from important 'human' (that is, male) pursuits. She argues that by denying any carnal motivation, women could redefine themselves as spiritual/moral beings, allowing them to develop self-esteem and to develop their 'human' faculties (p. 233). The idea of woman's moral superiority generally, however, seems to have been absorbed into the concept of complementarity, and any threats which women presented to received ideas of gender difference could be contained by calling into question that 'female' identity on which her place in society depended.

The emphasis on gender difference, then as now, depended on the suppression of similarities between the sexes. As the feminist theorist Gayle Rubin writes:

> Far from being an expression of natural differences, exclusive gender identity is the suppression of natural similarities. It requires repression: in men, of whatever is the local version of 'feminine' traits; in women, of the local definition of 'masculine' traits. The division of the sexes has the effect of repressing some of the personality characteristics of virtually everyone, men and women.[72]

Even in the nineteenth century, however, there was some interest in 'natural similarities'. Moscucci refers to a number of attempts to reconcile the concept of sexual difference with the idea of a human nature common to both, citing the fascination with the idea of the latent hermaphroditism or bisexuality of humans. Evidence for such a possibility was sought in embryology, and the discovery that the sex organs shared a common origin in foetal life. Sir James Young Simpson (1811–70), an eminent Edinburgh obstetrician, went further, arguing that the young of both sexes were in an androgynous state before puberty, when the male became more highly developed as an individual (p. 21).

The big argument continued to be, however, whether woman could ever become as 'highly developed' as man. As Moscucci points out, central to Darwinism is the belief that organisms interact with their environment, and that with time the resultant changes are incorporated into the organism's biological make-up. This implicitly acknowledges that distinctions between men and women are also bound up with the history of the human species, rather than being immutably given and fixed in nature. A study of Eskimo women by the physician John Robertson (1797–1876) seemed to confirm this when he reported that moral changes induced by religious teaching had altered the physiological processes of puberty and menopause. Similarly, in 1894, when Havelock Ellis published *Man and Woman*, which summarised data on anatomical, physiological and cranial sex differences accumulated since 1860, so that it represents the consensus of medical and scientific opinion at the time, he appeared to acknowledge the impact of social forces on perceived sexual differences. He writes, 'We have to recognise that our present knowledge of men and women cannot tell us what they might be or what they ought to be, but what they actually are, under the conditions of civilisation' (Moscucci, pp. 23, 27).

What women 'might be', however, in the eyes of most writers on the subject is best indicated by the contrast Romanes draws between their 'theoretical equality' and their 'natural inequality'. Although he acknowledges the role education had played in 'the mental differences between men and women', and claims that women's 'theoretical equality' was increasingly recognised as civilisation advanced, he concludes that it was unlikely that women would ever recover the ground lost to them in the past, since 'it must take many centuries for heredity to produce the missing five ounces of the female brain', so that their 'natural inequality' was likely to persist (quoted in *Embodied Selves*, pp. 385–6).[73] Darwin agreed that this inequality was likely to be continued by the evolutionary process. Characteristics acquired early in life are generally passed on to both sexes, so that any advantages accruing to boys through education should be inherited equally by male and female children. Darwin therefore refuted the idea that education could be to blame for inequality in mental power. Any hope of the mental powers of women in general improving would depend on daughters inheriting superior qualities acquired by their mothers in early adulthood, and on only those mothers breeding. Even then, the likelihood was that men would continue to develop faster, because of the continuing struggle to compete in the process of sexual selection. Romanes welcomed improvements in women's education and the impact of the women's movement in all areas of life, but with the proviso that neither should diminish in any way the distinctively 'feminine' qualities. Any idea of equality seems to remain firmly embedded within the theory of complementarity, providing justification for the doctrine of separate spheres, just as similar arguments about racial difference were used to justify doctrines of separate development.

It therefore becomes clear why, as Flavia Alaya has pointed out, John Stuart Mill devoted almost the entire opening section of *The Subjection of Women* (1869) to 'the pernicious effects of "arguments from nature", even among those who considered themselves enlightened, upon any discussion of the freedom or potential of women'. Darwin himself, in spite of his thesis that species evolve through interaction with their environment, rejects the argument that women's inferior achievements in the past were the result of their subjugation, and ignores Mill's caution, quoted by Alaya, that 'a negative fact at most leaves the question uncertain and open to psychological discussion'.[74] The 'arguments from nature', moreover, identify woman with Nature, which, since the Enlightenment, had been opposed to reason, the sciences and law, all that constitutes civilised society. As 'Other' to culture, Nature – and consequently woman – was an object of both curiosity and fear, something to be explored, investigated and ultimately tamed and mastered. For it is the very 'otherness' of Nature – and woman – that makes scientific study possible. The biological and medical evidence of the time provided further justification for woman being the object of both surveillance and intervention. As Gallagher and Laqueur comment, 'the nature of Woman becomes Nature itself, but a Nature peculiarly demanding of interpretive medical authority and intervention' (p. xi). They are referring here specifically to Poovey's essay on medical interventions, but their comments apply equally to other attempts to 'know' and therefore control. In 1883, Alfred Wiltshire looked forward to the day when the physiology of reproduction would be brought 'within the dominion of science, and cease to be a wonderment and mystery'.[75]

Wiltshire's statement about the role of science also echoes the Romantic attitude to woman, and Nature itself, as a mystery for the male author(ity) to explore. Where ideas about gender are concerned, there is a striking overlap between the discourses of science and Romanticism which, together with religious discourse, were implicated in maintaining Victorian definitions of femininity. As Gillian Beer's pioneering work on science and literature has established, scientists used literary quotation and allusion in their work, as literary writers used scientific quotation and allusion in theirs.[76] Romanes, for instance, ends his discussion of the differences between men and women by quoting a literary text which played a key role in the gender debate. To conclude his attempt to reconcile the idea of female emancipation with the idea of sexual difference, he quotes from Tennyson's 'The Princess' (1847), a long narrative poem devoted to the question of women's education:

> The woman's cause is man's: they rise or sink
> Together, dwarfed or god-like, bond or free:
> [.   .   .   .   .]
> For woman is not undevelopt man,
> But diverse: could we make her as the man,
> Sweet Love were slain: his dearest bond is this,

Not like to like, but like in difference.
Yet in the long years liker must they grow;
The man be more of woman, she of man;
He gain in sweetness and in moral height,
Nor lose the wrestling thews that throw the world;
She mental breadth, nor fail in childward care,
Nor lose the child-like in the larger mind;

(lines 243–4, 259–68, *The Poems of Tennyson*, pp. 837–9)

The fiction with which this book is concerned constructs scenarios which demonstrate the effects of the definitions and discourses outlined in this chapter, conveying the anxiety felt about the concept of womanhood during this period. But its female protagonists also attempt to achieve autonomy from the male control inscribed in the language of religion, science and Romanticism. Often drawing on feminist academic research in the 1970s and 1980s, some of which I have referred to here, the novels suggest the points of resistance available in any discourse, and particularly in those so riven with contradictions as the gender ideologies of the late Victorian period.

2
The Darwinian Moment: The Woman that Never Evolved

Darwin did not explicitly address the question of gender until *The Descent of Man and Selection in Relation to Sex* (1871). Fiona Erskine, however, has presented persuasive arguments to suggest that from 1859, *The Origin of Species*[1] 'provided a mechanism for converting culturally entrenched ideas of female inferiority into permanent, biologically determined, sexual hierarchy'.[2] Even in the 1850s, anthropologists used evolutionary theory to provide a scientific basis for the idea of separate spheres, and from the 1860s on, an abundance of essays, pamphlets and lectures was written to demonstrate how natural and sexual selection had operated to make women physically and mentally inferior to men. Because males had to compete for females, they became progressively stronger and 'fitter', in every sense, so inevitably evolved faster than females. In addition, women had evolved for the single specialised function of motherhood. Finally there was an implied parallel between the evolution of the sexes and the evolution of separate races, or even species, since the *Origin* states that the two sexes might be regarded in the light of two separate species, and links the arrested development of women with that of savages.

Erskine also points out, however, that *The Origin of Species* was initially received as a radical publication, not only by those conscious of its implications for religious orthodoxy but by supporters of women's rights, who saw the idea of environmental adaptation as an argument to suggest women's roles were not fixed and immutable but could respond to the growing pressures for greater equality. She cites American feminists writing in the 1880s, like Olive Schreiner, who saw women's current restlessness as evidence that sex roles had become maladaptive in evolutionary terms, and the Women's Movement as a movement of the sexes towards common occupations and interests. Charlotte Perkins Gilman, too, believed that if women participated more in the struggle for survival, it would reduce the degree of sexual divergence caused by sexual selection.

The novels discussed in this chapter are set in the periods following Darwin's two most significant publications, *The Voyage of the Beagle* (1839)[3] and *The Origin of Species* (1859). The title of Andrea Barrett's prizewinning novel *The Voyage of the Narwhal 1855–1856*, first published in the United States in 1998, directly evokes not only Darwin's work, but that of other travel writers of the period, while the title of A.S. Byatt's novella, *Morpho Eugenia*, published in Britain in 1992 and set in the 1860s, evokes the process of collection and species classification that was one of the functions of such journeys.[4] Gilian Beer's work on 'Darwin's plots' has shown that the influence of evolutionary discourse was apparent in a far wider range of writing than was once thought,[5] and this is reflected in the use of the discourse of natural history and exploration in both novels. In these modern contexts, however, these discourses co-exist with others which attempt to resist their dominance. A crucial term in both novels is 'observation', which is, to quote Beer, 'the crowning outcome of development' (*Open Fields*, p. 205). The role of the observer puts the subject into a position of authority over the observed object, whether that object be inanimate or animate, animal or human. Throughout *The Voyage of the Beagle* Darwin repeatedly uses the phrase 'I observed', as if off-setting the subjectivity of the first person with an assertion of objectivity. But he himself is well aware of how easily language can turn observation into judgement by introducing cultural norms: describing the recapturing of an elderly female slave in Rio de Janeiro, he recounts that 'sooner than again be led into slavery, [she] dashed herself to pieces from the summit of the mountain. In a Roman matron this would have been called the noble love of freedom: in a poor negress it is mere brutal obstinacy.'[6] Emily Martin, quoting from Johannes Fabian, agrees that the emphasis on observation means 'the ability to "visualise" a culture or society almost becomes synonymous with understanding it'.[7] She goes on, moreover, to suggest the particular relevance of this idea to gender issues, since vision is the 'key culprit in the scrutiny, surveillance, domination, control, and exertion of authority over the body, particularly over the bodies of women'. Barrett and Byatt suggest both the ideological implications of observation as a scientific tool, in relation to gender and race, and its limitations.

The Voyage of the Narwhal and *Morpho Eugenia* suggest, therefore, that despite the hopes of feminists, the evolution of women's rights was frustrated rather than furthered by Darwinian ideas about the evolution of species. Although written and set on different sides of the Atlantic, the two stories show striking similarities in plot. In each case, the 'hero', a natural historian in the Darwinian mould, experiences professional failure but is ultimately 'rescued' by one of the many so-called surplus women who posed such a problem for Victorian commentators.[8] The surface plot of masculine discovery has underlying it, therefore, a narrative of female emancipation. These narratives embody precisely that threat to separate-sphere ideology which Darwinian anti-feminists feared, since that ideology not only defined women's role as protectors of future generations, but helped to distance Victorian civilisation from the 'lower' races.

Separate species and separate spheres: Andrea Barrett, *The Voyage of the Narwhal 1855–1856*

> You like tales of adventure, in which the hero truly explores that wide world. But the novel [*The Wide, Wide World*, popular with women readers] is about tyranny, really; the tyranny of family and circumstances, and how one survives when running away isn't an option. Which it never is for women like us. (p. 271)

Andrea Barrett's novel *The Voyage of the Narwhal 1855–1856*[9] appears to belong to the first type of book described above, evoking nineteenth-century accounts of scientific exploration even in its appearance, each chapter being prefaced by a nineteenth-century engraving and quotation. But its subtext places it in the second category. Barrett's double narrative compares men's and women's lives within a society preoccupied by debates about the evolution of species and species difference, interpreted by some as racial difference. These explicit considerations of difference reverberate to the modern reader with regard to the gender differences embodied in that double narrative structure, and to the concept of separate spheres represented as given in the world of the novel.

For the reader with even a general knowledge of Darwin, both the novel's title and the central character's name will evoke the history of evolutionary theory. Erasmus Darwin Wells, named after Charles Darwin's grandfather, an early exponent of such ideas, joins the *Narwhal* on its voyage to the Arctic as its naturalist. Such voyages contributed to the development of evolutionary theory, because their narratives concern human encounters with both the natural world and the humans who inhabited it.[10] Through the crew's encounters with the 'Esquimaux',[11] the novel enters the debate about species development, a subject contentious enough for Erasmus to argue about it even with Jan Boerhaave, his closest friend on board. Boerhaave, the ship's surgeon, believes, like many naturalists of the time, that the native people they observe are uniquely adapted, like the animal population, to their environment, and therefore that different races like the Esquimaux must have been created separately in successive creations, constituting separate species.[12] Within the American context a second issue drives this debate – slavery. Even Erasmus's liberal brothers lean towards the idea of separate species when discussing African Americans, 'so essentially *different* from us' (p. 271). And although their friend Browning responds with the theological argument that all are descended from Adam and Eve and therefore one creation, it is left to a minor female character to relate the question of difference to social and economic equality, rejecting Agassiz's polygenism because of the ammunition it provides to the supporters of slavery. As Erasmus retorts to Boerhaave's assertion that separate does not mean inferior, 'differentiation always implies ranking' (p. 121). The observations of natural historians could be used to reinforce colonial ideology, even if they were not its product. One of the anti-slavery papers describes the pro-slavery father of the explorer Kane[13] as 'the Columbus of the new world of slave-whips and shackles which he has just annexed' (p. 147), making an ironical reflection on the link between slavery and exploration.

Exploration is also, however, associated with images of masculinity that were integral to Victorian gender ideology. It has been pointed out that the Royal Geographical Society, for instance, continued to present exploration as a battle with Nature, testing the manliness of the explorer to the limits, even after the decline of opportunities for spectacular feats of exploration had led to a new emphasis on the mapping and measuring of known territories, because tales of adventure were more likely to attract new subscribers. And no woman, unsurprisingly, received the Society's gold medal for exploration before the First World War.[14] The presumption that exploration required uniquely masculine qualities was particularly strong with regard to Arctic exploration. Lisa Bloom argues that nineteenth- and early twentieth-century narratives of polar exploration played a prominent part in the social construction of masculinity and legitimised the exclusion of women from the discourse of exploration:

As all-male activities, the explorations symbolically enacted the men's own battle to become men. The difficulty of life in desolate and freezing regions provided the ideal mythic site where men could show themselves as heroes capable of superhuman feats. They could demonstrate, in a clichéd phrase of polar exploration narratives, 'the boundlessness of the individual spirit.' Such claims were hardly likely to accrue to women living within the bounded spaces of everyday life, marriage, and the workplace. The polar explorer represented the epitome of manliness.[15]

In addition to the fortitude and courage such journeys required, male rivalry was fostered by the race to find the mythical polar sea, and the Arctic also allowed for the realisation of manhood through the apparent sexual compliance of Esquimaux women. The degree to which Erasmus and the *Narwhal*'s commander, his childhood friend Zechariah (Zeke) Voorhees, conform to this ideal of masculinity largely determines their public reputation and their fortunes.

Zeke's ulterior motive is, indeed, to search for an open polar sea, and take home more detailed maps of the coastline, but the ostensible purpose of the voyage is to look for signs of Sir John Franklin's expedition in search of a northwest passage. Historically the search for Franklin, the driving force for the novel's plot, precipitated another controversial debate relating to evolution in both Britain and the United States, this time from an anthropological perspective. As Erasmus explains, Dr John Rae of the Hudson's Bay Company, while carrying out a geographical survey in the region, had purchased relics of Franklin from a group of Esquimaux, who claimed not only that the explorers were all dead, but that they had found evidence of cannibalism. Rae's findings were not, however, accepted back home, since they were incompatible with what was 'known': according to Erasmus, the Admiralty stated, 'Englishmen don't eat Englishmen' (p. 49). The novel lends credence to Rae's story when Joe, the ship's interpreter, is told by a Netsilik woman that the tribe had found human remains that had been interfered with, and a sailor's boot containing pieces of boiled flesh. This episode added a sensational element to the comparative study of different cultures and their development. It triggered a debate between Rae and Charles Dickens, which set Rae's faith in the credibility of the natives, who understood better than anyone what people could be driven to in those conditions, against Dickens's faith in the English gentleman as the ultimate product of the evolutionary process. Dickens's view was reinforced by the Victorian division of cultures into the 'nomadic' and the 'settled', only the settled giving rise to 'civilisation'. The fundamental question here is whether the difference between the 'gentleman' and the 'savage' fades in the struggle to adapt to a hostile environment. Were the two races indeed different enough to be regarded as different species?[16]

The Franklin expedition also added the element of heroic altruism to the ideology of masculinity associated with polar exploration. According to Bloom, the view of polar exploration as a humanistic enterprise involving great self-sacrifice dates from this expedition, or rather to the search parties sent after it, because 'these men and ships were sent out to the Arctic not for material gain, but rather to save their fellow countrymen from death or to bring back their bodies' (p. 118). She points out that Tennyson's poem *Ulysses*, which celebrates heroic self-sacrifice in the Romantic tradition, was originally dedicated to Franklin. Sir Clements Markham, president of the Royal Geographical Society, in 1893 looked back on the 1840s/1850s, the period in which the novel is set, as the most memorable period in polar exploration because of those 'examples of heroism and devotion which must entrance mankind for all times' (quoted in Bloom, p. 120). These are the images with which Zeke conceals his more worldly aspirations.

This heroic sense of mission, reinforced by the idea of 'difference', made it easy to see the indigenous population not only as part of the region's natural history, and therefore objects of study, but as inferior and exploitable. Although the *Narwhal*'s crew acknowledge that they have much to learn from the Esquimaux about how to survive in their world, there is no respect for differences of custom and belief that cannot be appropriated or turned to practical advantage. Finding a meteorite, Zeke and even Erasmus want to take this important discovery home, even though Joe argues that the natives need them: 'They call them *saviksue*, they believe they have a soul' (p. 79). While the Esquimaux have reverence for people and environment alike, the explorers have reverence for neither. To Zeke, a skull from an Esquimaux grave is no less collectible than a meteorite, in spite of Joe's objection that the spirits of the Esquimaux dead cannot rest if their graves are disturbed. In contrast, when the crew find the graves of Franklin's men, and Dr Boerhaave suggests exhuming them to find the cause of death, Zeke refuses on the grounds that they are Englishmen, and are entitled to rest in peace.

Ultimately the indigenous people become collectible objects themselves: Zeke's prize specimens are live. Although Zeke persuades Nessark's tribe that the *angekok* or spirit of the tribe wishes Nessark's English-speaking wife Annie and her son to return to Philadelphia with him, Zeke's true motive, Ned suggests, is to secure his reputation, to authenticate his story and make him a hero.[17] Erasmus imagines him saying, 'You collected bones and twigs, and then lost them. [...] I've brought back people. Not skulls, not brains in a jar: living, breathing people.' On his return Zeke immediately embarks on a lecture tour to show off his 'Esquimaux specimens' (p. 307). Although his published journal describes Annie and Tom as 'excellent representatives of their race, intelligent and agreeable', his emphasis now shifts to what differentiates their world from his, since that is their commercial selling point. In line with popular practice in Europe and North America at the time, they act out their daily routines in tableaux from Esquimaux life, displaying their cultural 'otherness'. Erasmus's charge that Zeke is exhibiting Annie like a Hottentot Venus implies her total objectification.[18] When Annie and Tom are not being exhibited, Zeke keeps them in the repository in Erasmus's home, among all the other specimens.

But if the journey of exploration is part of the colonial enterprise, so is the writing of that journey. Whatever the ostensible purpose of the exploration, Beer argues that once it is 'condensed within a pattern of expectation that assumes a range of development in human societies moving from primitive to civilized a particularly ample authority can be claimed, since the civilized is assumed to be the place from which the writer starts and to which he returns. The writing is itself civilization at work on the unruly' (*Open Fields*, p. 58). Language can serve the colonising impulse, since even mapping involves more than objective observation and measurement. And as Bloom notes, the absence of settlements made it particularly easy to perceive the polar regions as blank spaces which lent themselves to ideas of 'discovery' and naming. Naming land or sea is not merely a form of appropriation, by which a country asserts claims over territory, but a form of displacement since it so often involves imposing a name on what has already been named by its inhabitants. The ideological mystification involved in the discourse of exploration can therefore render the indigenous population invisible. The Captain of the *Harmony*, whose ship finally rescues the crew of the *Narwhal*, makes an impassioned indictment of the 'discovery men':

> men who go off on exploring expeditions, with funding and fanfare and special clothes, thinking you'll discover something. When every place you go some whaling ship has already been. [...] I've met Russian discovery ships, and English, and French, and never known them to discover much of anything. (p. 244)

Yet while drawing legitimate attention to the neglected role of men driven by the more practical concerns of whaling, the Captain himself is sufficiently the product of colonial ideology to ignore the presence of the Esquimaux before the whalers.

The Voyage of the Narwhal is therefore both about a journey and about the processes of representation which turn journey into narrative and narrative into history. The novel's title points to this dual activity, referring both to the voyage and to the book which Zeke writes about it, 'aping the famous works of exploration' (p. 331), in Alexandra's words. Anyone creating a record of their journey can shape the narrative of events according to socially validated goals and ideals which will lend the narrative authority and credibility. Zeke's account presents a story of successful European endeavour in inhospitable and exotic regions which reinforces colonial ideology and the assumptions of its readers. He knows, moreover, that whoever controls the written narrative of the journey determines its 'history', which is why he takes charge of all the journals and notes written by the crew, repeating the action of Erasmus's first commander, Charles Wilkes. He is then free to present events in such a way as to validate his view that the expedition's problems resulted from failure to respect his authority. His presentation of the expedition's story constitutes yet another act of appropriation.

This narrative also constructs Zeke as a hero, since, like his lecture, it presents a tale of solitary heroic endeavour which relegates the rest of the crew to the periphery of his story, there merely to throw into greater relief his own strength of character in surviving alone. As Erasmus notes, it is all '"I" and "me" and "mine"' (p. 338). And Zeke is sustained by the ideology inscribed in the discourse of exploration, which cloaks his ruthless self-interest in a veneer of honourable endeavour and ambition. He asks Erasmus, 'Wouldn't you like to have your name on something here? [...] Wouldn't it be wonderful to discover something altogether new?' (p. 75). In addition to finding endorsement for his behaviour in colonial ideology, Zeke also seeks it in nineteenth-century patriarchy, constantly referring to the memory of Erasmus's father to validate his behaviour. He claims that he, rather than Erasmus, is Mr Wells's heir, accusing Erasmus of failing to live up to his father's expectations whenever he hesitates to support Zeke's plans because of the risk they pose to the crew. Even Zeke's relationship with Annie in Anatoak reflects this need for filial recognition: 'The life he'd lived with her and her family was the life Erasmus's father had taught him to seek; his dream shifted and he was part of that family, the true son, the son Mr Wells had always wanted' (p. 390). Erasmus himself is all too conscious of failing to take on his father's authority, particularly with regard to his sister, knowing he should have asked Zeke 'fatherly questions' about their engagement. In contrast Zeke is eager to act 'in the name of the father' and become the head of the household, ultimately usurping Erasmus's position. As Erasmus recognises, his own house 'was the home Zeke had always craved; he'd slipped into it the minute Erasmus lost his place' (p. 317).

However, while Zeke conforms to the idea of the hero constructed by the discourse of exploration, the novel also deconstructs that idea. It reveals the egotism which is the dark side of the 'heroic' explorer as he becomes increasingly authoritarian, manipulating the men into going north at the risk of their lives. That egotism is starkly evident in his treatment of his greatest 'discovery', Annie and Tom. Even when she is dying, his main concern is that he will lose her help with his book, with the record of his encounters and vision. He has no interest in natural history or in acquiring new knowledge, keeping no record of what he sees on the journey. In presenting himself as 'a regular Robinson Crusoe' (p. 309), Zeke is, as Ned suggests, rather 'making up an adventure tale than reporting what he saw' (p. 329). But although this becomes the public version of the *Narwhal's* voyage, it is challenged by the different narratives that constitute the novel, including the diaries of Alexandra and Ned and the letters of Dr Boerhaave. Above all Erasmus, through whom much of the narrative is focalised, provides a version of events which embodies alternative ideals to those of the heroic adventurer. Zeke's dream of individual glory is opposed by Erasmus's dream of coming home as 'a sort of hero: that steady, older naturalist who has been of inestimable aid to the commander, and made all the important observations' (p. 114). His ideal is one of community, of being part of a small group sharing scientific interests and achievements. But Zeke refuses to allow Erasmus the time he needs to study the wildlife to achieve his goals, just as Wilkes had done in the 1838 expedition. A similar emphasis on community, rather than individualism, characterises Erasmus's leadership when he is forced to accept responsibility for abandoning the *Narwhal* and bringing the crew home. Zeke's individualism threatens the welfare of any group, as the Esquimaux recognise. Annie remembers:

> Her tribe was one great person, each of them a limb, an organ, a bone. Onto the hand her family formed, Zeke had come like an extra finger. They'd welcomed him, but he'd had no understanding of the way they were joined together. He saw himself as a singular

being, a delusion they'd found laughable and terrifying all at once. (p. 319)

The contrast between Zeke and Erasmus, therefore, is a contrast between different cultural values. The ideal of mutual support and nurturance essential to the survival of a community is opposed to the ideal of autonomous individualism which motivates the quest for heroic status.

Erasmus's ideals, therefore, distance him from the colonial ideology inscribed in the discourse of exploration. Dr Boerhaave comments, quoting Thoreau: 'it is easier to sail many thousand miles through cold and storm and cannibals, in a government ship, with five hundred men and boys to assist one, than it is to explore the private sea, the Atlantic and Pacific Ocean of one's being alone' (p. 198). While Zeke journeys alone across the ice, Erasmus journeys into himself, learning to question the assumptions with which he started out. The evidence of Franklin's possible cannibalism breaks down the distinctions he once drew between the white and non-white races, causing him to look back and see Wilkes's brutal punishment of man-eating natives in a new light. Back in Philadelphia, he finds the skull of a 'Feejee' chief in a museum, and his new awareness prompts him to wonder how that person had become a skull, and to recall with shame how he himself had 'gawked' at the islanders as if they were apes, a separate species. Erasmus's desire to write is equally free from the colonising impulse to appropriate and control the narrative of events, since he rejects the idea of monologic truth so often associated with patriarchal thought. As a painter he wishes he could show a scene 'as if through a fan of eyes. Widening out from [his] single perspective to several viewpoints, then many, so the whole picture might appear and not just [his] version of it' (p. 27).

Erasmus therefore fails to ensure that his version of events prevails. In contrast to Dr Kane, who also lost a ship and three men, but returned to find himself a great hero,[19] he offers a story without a hero, which therefore fails to win popular acceptance. The denial of Erasmus's heroic status by the popular press, and Zeke's questioning of his right to be considered his father's son, implicitly cast doubt on his masculinity, within the meaning of that term in the Victorian period. That doubt is reinforced by what can be seen as a process of 'feminisation' resulting from the voyage. The crippling loss of his toes due to frostbite is a form of castration, like the blinding of Charlotte Brontë's Rochester in *Jane Eyre*, one of the archetypal Victorian novels about gender. It constitutes a symbolic endorsement of Zeke's attacks on his manliness for failing to accompany Zeke on his final journey north. Like Rochester's, this disability makes him newly dependent on the women in the household. Indeed it places him in a similar position to them: his movement becomes as restricted as that of a Chinese woman with bound feet, since his new shoes are the same size as his mother's, which he has treasured since her death. Erasmus is reduced to passivity, to remaining within the private sphere of the home, waiting – to heal, to learn to walk again, to find out what the future will hold – just as Lavinia and Alexandra have waited in his and Zeke's absence. Before the voyage, Erasmus knew none of the servants' names: they were Lavinia's territory. Now he knows them all. As if to further emasculate him, Zeke tells Erasmus he has always belonged at home. In the repository, which in his father's lifetime was full of living things, but is now a fossilised version of that past, he recognises that his own life will not, as he had once imagined, be like that of his father.

Paradoxically, however, Erasmus now proves himself, rather than Zeke, to be his father's true intellectual heir. He had learned from his father the value of the mythical as a means of understanding humanity and the inexplicable workings of the universe. The myths were 'stories, not science – but useful as a way of thinking about the great variety and mutability of human nature'. But the classical stories also provided warnings of 'the perils of not observing the world directly' (pp. 23–4), a warning which Erasmus's father repeats to his son in dreams. Erasmus believes his strength is for just such observation and recording, in contrast to Zeke, whose 'vision' often stands in the way of accurate observation. The book about the Arctic which Alexandra encourages him to write will incorporate his father's principles:

> the narrative would pull his readers along on a journey, as an imaginary ship moved from place to place and through the seasons. [. . .] He described a sequence of verbal portraits, a natural history that caught each place at a particular time of the year. He wouldn't be in the story, Erasmus said. He'd be erased, he'd be invisible. It would be as if readers gazed at a series of detailed landscape paintings. As if they were making the journey themselves, but without discomfort or discord. (pp. 292–3)

Truthfulness of observation is here combined with the use of the imagination to enable the reader to share the experience of the journey. And in wishing to eliminate both the heroics associated with 'adventure tales', and the ego of the observer, Erasmus also minimises the masculine associations of exploration and observation. The process of revaluation is completed when he accepts his brother Copernicus's suggestion that he should bring the lives of the Esquimaux into his book. Erasmus is forced to recognise that the Arctic is not simply the object of his male, colonial gaze, but the home of people whose knowledge of it far exceeds any that can be derived from observation alone. His feeling that observing people was not his business had been motivated by a kind of egotism, since 'by not passing judgment on the people he saw, he'd hoped to avoid having anyone pass judgment on him' (p. 386). He has to learn that he too is subject to observation and evaluation.

The 'feminisation' of Erasmus is, therefore, ultimately positive rather than negative in its effects, enabling him to develop the powers of empathy that make his earlier visions of a sharing community a reality. When he first tries to help Annie, his male ego causes him to misinterpret her request to 'go home', because he believes she is repeating what Zeke has just said to him – 'Go home' (p. 362). His own sense of rejection and jealousy precludes real empathy. But after her death he ensures that at least her son Tom goes home. Erasmus's final journey is therefore carried out in an entirely different spirit from that of the earlier voyage. His purpose is not appropriation, but restitution. Tom is restored to his family, and his original name restored to him. And before leaving for the Arctic, Erasmus takes the child to the West, together with Alexandra and Copernicus, where he finally experiences community, not the community of scholars he once dreamed of, but what Alexandra calls a new kind of community or family – three adults sharing responsibility for a child. There are no separate spheres here.

But the most significant difference between the two journeys is the presence of Alexandra, for the structure of the narrative deconstructs the nature of Victorian femininity as well as masculinity. Her emergence from the shadows of the male adventure story until she herself becomes part of the adventure dramatises the increasing demand of Victorian women for participation in the public sphere. But the first two books of the novel testify to the doctrine of separate spheres, the lives of Lavinia and Alexandra featuring almost as footnotes to the historic exploits of the male characters. Alexandra imagines how Lavinia must have 'watched her world shrink and shrink, while her brothers' worlds expanded' (p. 261). And she knows how expectation can determine aspiration. Even when invited to join her brothers while their father reads to them, Lavinia tells Alexandra that she only half listened, since there was no point in sharing their learning, when she knew she would always remain at home. Instead, like most young women of the time, Lavinia learns to invest everything in personal relationships. Lavinia exemplifies the traditional role of the woman for whom love is, in Byron's words, her 'whole existence'. Fearing for Zeke's life, she acknowledges that her life has meaning only through him: 'without Zeke, what am I?' (p. 265). The vulnerability of such women was identified at the time by George Eliot, who describes their predicament in her letters:

> We women are always in danger of living too exclusively in the affections; and though our affections are perhaps the best gift we have, we ought also to have our share of the more independent life – some joy in things for their own sake. It is piteous to see the helplessness of sweet women when their affections are disappointed – because all their teaching has been, that they can only delight in study of any kind for the sake of a personal love. They have never contemplated an independent delight in ideas as an experience which they could confess without being laughed at. Yet surely women need this sort of defence against passionate affliction even more than men.[20]

In contrast, Alexandra illustrates the position of the 'surplus woman'.[21] Although unmarried, she is no less dependent than Lavinia, since she is doubly marginalised by lack of husband and lack of money. In spite of her thirst for knowledge, she must choose either to become Lavinia's companion, and feel like an unpaid servant, or remain the typical maiden aunt in her brother's household, where she feels 'a dense net of obligations' (p. 295), and must obey his orders. Even when she travels West, she feels the restrictions which her sex and lack of financial independence impose on her. When Copernicus laments that he has travelled too much, her response is, 'Imagine being able to say that [...]. *Too much*; when all she'd ever felt was *Not enough*' (p. 385).

But if Alexandra's dissatisfactions are explicitly feminist in nature, so is her readiness to challenge the restrictions of her world. Employed to work on plates for Dr Kane's book about his Arctic journey, Alexandra recognises that illustration is one of the naturalist's most important tools, affecting the reader's understanding as much as the text. Some illustrations, like Agassiz's drawings of the 'Hyperborean', are more the product of preconception and prejudice than of observation. As Erasmus notes, they distort reality to make 'an attack on the unity of races, an attempt to prove their separate creation' (p. 274). In contrast, Alexandra's abilities prove equal to Erasmus's. Initially unacknowledged as the author of her engravings, her achievement, like that of so many women, remains invisible, subsumed to male interests. But the work enables her to escape the private and enter the public sphere, opening up new worlds for her, both literally and metaphorically. She comments, 'When I'm working everything else drops away and I enter the scene I'm engraving. As if I've entered a larger life' (p. 146). Engraving is, moreover, another form of authorship, a means of shaping reality, through which Alexandra adopts the position of the observer, rather than remaining the potential object of the male gaze.

Alexandra's dreams of Arctic adventure take her far beyond the domestic sphere, and ultimately become reality in a journey which constitutes another form of transgression, since it also involves the flouting of sexual conventions. Not only does she want to see everything, she wants Erasmus to see her. While her words 'Look at me' (p. 387), echoed in a very similar context in *Morpho Eugenia*, appear to make her the passive recipient of the male gaze, her assertiveness gives her control of his gaze, just as she takes control of their relationship by entering his room at night. She insists on her right to be considered as a sexual being, rather than one of those 'surplus' women who were expected to sublimate all their desires in subservient domesticity within another family. Alexandra, like A.S. Byatt's Matty Crompton, articulates two equally powerful desires, both flouting the norms of femininity – sexual desire and the desire to experience the wider world. She claims both sexual and intellectual satisfaction. In doing so, she rejects the binary oppositions not only between male and female, but between intellect and feeling, mind and body.

The novel's ending, therefore, replicates that of the traditional three-volume Victorian novel ending in marriage, but brings to it a twentieth-century perspective in not only allowing for the satisfaction of Alexandra's ambitions, but also blurring the gender boundaries between her and Erasmus. As Erasmus becomes part of the private sphere, he becomes as dependent on her as she is on him, the novel here echoing the ending of *Jane Eyre*, where Rochester is reduced to dependence on his former servant. But where Rochester, on being 'tamed' in this way, remains confined with Jane in the domestic world, Erasmus's 'feminisation' opens up new possibilities for both himself and Alexandra, making real the dream of shared endeavour which the exclusively male world of exploration appeared to preclude.

For the heroic iconography of Arctic exploration as an all-male endeavour should not blind the modern reader, as it did so many contemporaries, to the fact that some women did endure the hardships of the Arctic – or to the even more obvious fact that 'Esquimaux' women endured these hardships for life.[22] To a woman like Annie, the 'heroic' white explorer Kane and his men therefore seem childlike, incompetent and foolish: 'They'd been like children, dependent on her tribe for clothes, food, sledges, dogs; surrounded by things which were of no use to them and bereft of women. Like children they gave their names to the landscape, pretending to discover places her people had known for generations' (pp. 343–4). Her own journey to Philadelphia is equally a journey of exploration, in which she travels long distances to an alien world, exposed to an unfamiliar culture, unfamiliar food and unfamiliar diseases.[23] In this context, she is the observer, the Americans the observed: 'She'd been sent here like a shard of splintered mirror [...], to capture an image of the world beyond her home' (p. 358). But where Zeke and Erasmus feel they are acting in the name of the father, Annie's mission comes from her mother. She is not there to appropriate, but to learn all she can about the alien world which threatens her own, in order to protect her family and her people. Where Victorian scientists like the American zoologist W.K. Brooks saw women as the conservators of the culture, while men were the explorers (Russett, p. 95), Annie breaks down the boundaries between the two roles. Similarly, her sexual relationship with Zeke, although totally acceptable to her tribe, places her, like Alexandra, beyond the pale of respectable Victorian woman-hood. Annie therefore presents a challenge to that ideology every bit as powerful as Alexandra's.

Moreover, while Annie finds her alien new environment as deadly as many Arctic explorers found theirs, her system of beliefs enables her to escape from it after her death. When Zeke arranges for the flesh to be stripped from her bones so that her skeleton may be exhibited in the museum, to secure his reputation and his fortune, she in a sense evades this horrific violation because, as Tom puts it, the men had 'only made visible the process she'd begun' (p. 372). Knowing her body will never return home to be prepared for the life beyond, she determines to return in spirit:

> By the strength of her thought alone, she must strip her body of flesh and blood and be able to see herself as a skeleton. Each bone, each tiny bone, clear before her eyes. Then the sacred language would descend, allowing her to name the parts of her body that would endure. When she named the last bone she'd be free; her spirit could travel and she could watch over her son. (p. 363)[24]

Naming her bones is an act of re-possession, freeing her from the alien name and role that have been imposed on her. To Zeke and the other white explorers she is primarily a sexual body, like all the Esquimaux women known only as wives, never named themselves. But in death she transcends her own body and becomes again part of the 'body that was her tribe' (p. 358). Like Alexandra, she challenges the binaries that would objectify her, and identify her entirely with her body.

Above all, by showing the impact of racial and gender ideologies on this single figure, the novel dramatises the links between them. Whatever her status in the life of the tribe, in the white world Annie is doubly exploited, belonging both to a separate sphere and a separate 'species'. When she succumbs to fever, Annie recalls Zeke's arrival in her homeland in images which convey the different levels of threat concealed by apparently benevolent motives: he was 'a walking finger who pointed at her and then turned into the barrel of a rifle. The rifle had brought her tribe meat and fed the children.' But Zeke had not understood his connection to 'the body that was her tribe. [...] When she coughed a bullet seemed to enter her lungs' (p. 358). As racially other, Annie is sexually available to Zeke, but in spite of the obviously phallic imagery of the rifle, the violation she undergoes at his hands is more than simply sexual, since it represents the degradation and dehumanisation of her people at the hands of the white coloniser. She becomes a spectacle – racially, an object of scientific observation, and sexually, an object of the male gaze. On stage during Zeke's lecture tour she is reduced to the level of a performing animal. When he whistles, she and Tom appear on a sled pulled by beagles, not Zeke's own dogs, since, as Erasmus observes, 'Zeke would not subject his own pets to this' (p. 338). And when Annie's remains are displayed in a glass case in a public space, her 'difference' is in one sense writ large, since it would be inconceivable for a white man or woman to be displayed in this way. Yet reduced to skeletal form in this way, the obvious signifiers of her race and gender – her difference – are simultaneously erased.[25] Issues of visibility and invisibility here meet in ways that reveal the contradictions inherent in ideologies of gender and race.

If Annie's story echoes Alexandra's in its challenge to gender ideology, the gulf between them nevertheless remains enormous, demonstrating the parallels between nineteenth-century perceptions of gender difference and racial difference. Both women and the non-white races were seen to be less evolved than the European white male, and if the differences between men's and women's lives appeared less distinct in the Arctic than in Philadelphia, then this was only proof of the less evolved nature of Esquimaux society. As discussed in Chapter 1, the most evolved societies were those in which gender differentiation was greatest.

Writing late in the nineteenth century, the German neurologist Richard von Krafft-Ebing (1840–1902) equates advances in civilisation with the development of the patriarchal family in terms which make explicit the link between colonial and gender ideologies: in a 'spirit of colonisation [...] man establishes a household', and the 'community of women ceases' (*Psychopathia Sexualis* (1886), quoted in Gilman, p. 249). Such arguments were used as weapons against women's greater political and sexual freedom in the United States and Britain. The non-white woman therefore provides the most dramatic embodiment of 'difference', of two kinds of colonised 'Other', a subject to which I shall return in Chapter 6.

Darwin and Romantic love: A.S. Byatt, *Morpho Eugenia*

> Darwinian ideas affected two kinds of narrative that were venerable parts of the forms of Western art. They affected not only the idea of religion – creation, salvation, immortality – but the quite different idea of romantic love. (A.S. Byatt)[26]

Set in the early 1860s, A.S. Byatt's novella, *Morpho Eugenia*,[27] demonstrates her thorough familiarity with Darwinism, dealing with the impact of *The Origin of the Species* after its publication in 1859, and also anticipating his theories of sexual selection. Her own account of the novella shows her familiarity also with the inter-relationship between scientific and other writing in the Victorian period, so that the story in a sense fictionalises the ideas Beer analyses. Its title refers to the shapely beauty of both the butterfly it designates and the story's heroine, Eugenia. But the word *morpho* is the root of the word *metamorphosis*, a change of shape, suggesting the idea of transformation which is central both to the novella and to 'Darwin's plots' – the story of how simple organisms gradually evolve into complex ones. The novella is essentially about ways of responding, consciously or not, to those plots, and about the different discourses through which those responses are articulated. But Beer also emphasises that scientists work 'with the thought-sets historically active in their communities', 'the shared stories of their time', and these include the gender myths of the period as well as more enduring stories of love and romance. The responses articulated in the novella, therefore, also suggest 'the *intimacy* between intellectual issues and emotional desires and fears' (*Open Fields*, p. 8).

From the outset of the story, its central character, a naturalist called William Adamson, employed to classify and catalogue Harald Alabaster's extensive but rather random collection, finds himself drawn into the central intellectual debate of the period. Originally a clergyman, Lord Alabaster's declared aim is to write a book which will defend the 'natural theological' explanations of life which Darwin's work repudiated, 'a book which shall demonstrate – with some kind of intellectual respectability – that it is not impossible that the world is the work of a Creator, a Designer' (p. 33).[28] He relies on analogy to impose moral meaning on the actions of bees and ants, using anthropomorphic terms like 'altruism' and 'self-sacrifice' to describe behaviour patterns which ensure the survival of the nest. From such interpretations he moves readily to the 'argument from love' (p. 89), to the idea that a loving Father in Heaven must direct such providential behaviour. Byatt herself describes Harald's use of analogy to reconcile Darwinian discourse with religious discourse as dangerous, so that when William, a confirmed Darwinist, rejects Harald's arguments as 'a specious analogy' (p. 89), he appears to be her spokesman. Insisting we must resist the temptation to approach the natural world anthropomorphically, he also appears to represent Byatt's view that anthropomorphism is 'a form of self-deception', in which 'we turn other creatures into images of ourselves' (*Histories*, p. 80). In the course of the novella, however, the author reveals the limitations of William's perspective – his faith in his own objectivity, and in science as an objective master-discourse. William fails to take account of Darwin's warning that there are 'no facts without theory' (quoted in *Open Fields*, p. 157).

Privileged by his position as a white male at the top of the evolutionary ladder, William is confident of his superior status as observer over what he observes, and of the authority which his scientific knowledge lends him. Margaret Pearce suggests that he 'views the world as if he were subject, and all others are objects, gazed upon by him, observed by him. He represents the characters through a masculine, unitary gaze, centring himself in the story.'[29] William is son of Adam, so named, according to Byatt, because 'like Linnaeus, he named the unknown insects in the tropics' (*Histories*, p. 81). But as son of Adam he is still at the beginning of the story of his own 'descent', a term which, as Beer points out, tells a double, contrary story – man's 'fall from his Adamic myth or his genetic descent (ascent) from his primate forebears' (*Darwin's Plots*, p. 108). He remembers the Amazon rain forest of his last expedition as a kind of Eden, 'in so many ways the innocent, the unfallen world, the virgin forest, the wild people in the interior who are as unaware of modern ways – modern evils – as our first parents'. He observes, more-over, that 'the connection of the woman and the snake in the garden is made even out there, as though it is indeed part of some universal pattern of symbols' (p. 30). William's readiness to interpret this world in this way suggests that he is not himself immune from the influence of traditional religious discourse, even though he adopts an anthropological perspective.

That anthropological perspective is evident even in his first response to Eugenia, the Alabasters' daughter. Understanding the meaning of the ritual of a country house ball, he observes: 'Her shoulders and bust rose white and flawless from the froth of tulle and tarlatan like Aphrodite from the foam. [...] She was both proudly naked and wholly untouchable. [...] These dances were designed to arouse his desire in exactly this way' (p. 6). And he registers that her behaviour is similar in function to the very different behaviour of women in the Amazon, where he was 'grabbed and nuzzled and rubbed and cuddled with great vigour by women with brown breasts glistening with sweat and oil, and with shameless fingers' (p. 7). While recognising that he is 'at once detached anthropologist and fairytale prince trapped by invisible gates and silken bonds in an enchanted castle' (p. 21), he believes the two roles can remain separate, detached observation remaining undisturbed even by Eugenia's 'cloud of magic dust' (p. 20). But while outside he remains 'his hunting, scanning self' (p. 37), he fails to register the processes of natural and sexual selection at work within the house. Like George Eliot's Dr Lydgate, progressive scientist hero of *Middlemarch*, William suffers from 'spots of commonness', blind spots deriving from the Victorian gender myths which contribute to his ideological entrapment. He is a victim of the idealisation of women as asexual beings. Preoccupied with Eugenia's physicality, in particular with her mouth and breasts, so that even during their wedding ceremony he is not conscious, as he feels he should be, of 'two souls speaking their vows together' (p. 64), he nevertheless cannot conceive of similar feelings on her part. She is 'marble and untouchable', so that he is 'afraid of smutching her, as the soil smutched the snow in the poem. [...] How the innocent female must fear the power of the male, he thought, and with reason, so soft, so white, so untouched, so untouchable' (p. 66). His references to her evoke the virginal purity of the Victorian Madonna, in contrast to his own 'dirty and dangerous' male desires (p. 8). Seeing their wedding night as an ordeal required of innocent young girls to propagate the species, William attributes Eugenia's unexpected responsiveness to instinct, comparing her to a bird in a nest, because his idealisation of her cannot accommodate the possibility of any prior sexual experience. And yet there are cultural limits to this idealisation. Although he attacks Eugenia's brother Edgar for his sexual abuse and impregnation of Amy, one of the household servants, William is forced to consider that there might be in Brazil 'pale-eyed dark-skinned infants with his blood in their veins' (p. 147). William is a victim not only of the gender ideology underlying the myth of Romantic love, designed to conceal the reality of sexual desire, but of the ideology of Victorian anthropology, which placed the non-white races, and the non-white woman in particular, on a much lower scale on the evolutionary ladder where sexual desire was uncontrolled by higher impulses.

If William's scientific objectivity is compromised by his role as a lover, his faith in the unique value of scientific discourse also proves to be misplaced. The temptation to use metaphor and anthropomorphic language when describing the natural world is inherent in language itself, which is anthropocentric, even if the material world is not. William's own observations make use of metaphor, particularly those dead metaphors which embody received wisdom, and those metaphors are implicit acts of interpretation, which indicate the overlapping of his two worlds. He himself is not, however, always alert to their significance. When he observes the young ladies 'cocooned in silk' (p. 60) before his wedding, and calls his bride *Morpho Eugenia*, he is merely making comparisons based on perceived similarities of form, rather than considering any deeper similarities in function. He is ready to compare the beauty of the ladies to the beauty of the butterflies he observed in the jungle, but fails to consider the function of that beauty. He has yet to learn that metaphor can be a form of discovery just as much as scientific analysis. As Byatt says of her own use of metaphor in her story, through metaphor 'you discover *precisely* and intellectually something that you always knew instinctively' (*Histories*, p. 118).

Maintaining the separation between the human world of romance in which he participates and the natural world he studies, therefore, William fails initially to make the connections to which his own metaphors point him. He attempts to pass on to Matty Compton, the Alabaster family's poor relation, some of his knowledge of insect life, but when she tries to draw a parallel between ant slaves and the *'machine-slaves'* of the cotton mills, he insists, 'Men are not ants' (p. 100). He observes that among butterflies the brightest flaunt their colours 'as a kind of warning. They are the males, of course, making themselves brilliant for their brown mates. [...] Whereas here we men wear carapaces like black beetles' (p. 7). But although observing that the roles of male and female in the insect world are reversed in the human world, he fails to register the 'warning' that such a reversal entails. His resistance to these connections is most apparent when his two worlds meet in the conservatory, where he collects a host of butterflies to delight Eugenia. Here a cloud of Emperor moths is drawn irresistibly to a caged female. When one gets trapped in Eugenia's lace, her resulting distress is the trigger for William's declaration of love, and this entrapment of the male insect becomes a repeated motif through which Eugenia is able to summon William to her bed whenever she desires. Scientific objectivity is again compromised by the ideology of Romantic love, which cannot acknowledge that it is the female who has set the trap.

When William creates a formicary to teach the Alabaster children some natural history, his study of ant society leads, however, to a growing recognition that ants and men are not as different as he at first thought. His first sight of Lady Alabaster leads him to feel that 'this immobile, vacantly amiable presence was a source of power in the household' (p. 27), but it is only later that he recognises her role is the same as that of the Queen in the ant colony, her only purpose being to breed. And like the Queen she is supported in this function by workers, the same sex as herself, but so different in function as to be almost unrecognisable as the same:

> They had come like a cloud of young wasps from under the roof of the house, pale-faced and blear-eyed, bobbing silently to him as he passed. Some were no more than children, hardly different from the little girls in the nursery, except that the latter were delicately swathed in petticoats, and frills, and soft festoons of muslin, and these were for the most part skinny, with close-fitting, unornamental bodices and whisking dark skirts, wearing formidably starched white caps over their hair. (p. 49)

After marriage he becomes aware that Eugenia's role is the same as her mother's. As she grows fatter with pregnancy, he notes her 'creamy second chin', and the 'white nest' (p. 70) of the bed in which she now sleeps alone, leaving William to hover in the doorway just like Lord Alabaster in the doorway of his wife's 'little nest'. Her dependency on the workers is emphasised by her admission that without her maid Bella she cannot even dress herself. William increasingly recognises himself as the male drone.

The country house, furthermore, appears to function as a single unit, as William believes the ant nest does. When he is recalled to the house one day to find his wife in bed with her brother, and learns that this incestuous relationship has existed since Eugenia's youth, Matty suggests that the mysterious message asking William to return came in a sense through the house itself, through 'the invisible people' who know everything that goes on: 'now and then *the house* simply decides that something must happen' (p. 155). Like worker ants intervening on behalf of the Spirit of the Nest when male ants fight for the Queen, the workers acted collectively for the good of the household to try to stop the mating of two siblings, which is clearly not beneficial in breeding terms. When he allows the connections between the two worlds to emerge, William is able to bring his scientific understanding to bear on his understanding of gender roles, rather than allowing that understanding to fall victim to gender ideology.

In contrast, although Matty is like William socially situated between the family and the 'invisible people', unlike him she never becomes one of the family, nor does she wear the ideological blinkers of Romantic love. She is therefore able to exploit her marginal position to observe and analyse the Alabaster household far more accurately than William. She belongs to the class of workers and women that Beer characterises as 'peripheral, powerless' in the scientific world in the nineteenth century, yet whose 'scrutiny of scientific practice or scientific discourse is felt as disturbing' (*Open Fields*, p. 206). When William explains the role of the individual in ant society, her caustic response is, 'Maybe they are all perfectly content in their stations' (p. 38). Without the benefit of his scientific training in objectivity or his scientific terms of reference, she is nevertheless quicker than him to make sense of the world around her by making connections between the human world and the natural world.

As a woman, lacking the authority to make 'scientific' truth claims, Matty instead uses metaphoric discourse to write a fable about the insect world, and implicitly to suggest the limitations of William's point of view. Its title, *Things are Not What they Seem*, alerts the reader to the need to go beyond surface observation. The hero Seth and his companions, for instance, find that their apparent benefactor, the fairy Mrs Cottitoe Pan Demos, is a Circe-like creature who turns them all into animals. Seth alone has eaten too little of her feast to be transformed, so is simply made a swineherd, 'for the good of the household' (p. 123). Beer's comment on the way that literary language operates explains the effectiveness of the fable as a discreet way of commenting on William's situation – his enchantment by Eugenia and subsequent absorption into the Alabaster household. She argues that such language

> moves, often openly, and with great flexibility from level to level, achieving much of its intensity by means of allusion and connotation

across levels. Such language opens out connections which technical discourses exclude from notice [...]. The free and multiple movement across levels in literary language is its characteristic resource for discovery. (*Open Fields*, p. 164)

This literary use of language is nevertheless not wholly antithetical to the way language is used in the scientific world. Darwin himself was concerned, Beer suggests, 'to demonstrate as far as possible the accord between scientific usage and common speech. His interest in etymology established language-history as a more than metaphorical instance of kinships hidden through descent and dissemination' (*Darwin's Plots*, p. 49). Darwin hoped that advances in scientific knowledge would reveal that what first appeared to be purely metaphorical was 'plain signification', that connections indicated in figurative language had their basis in scientific fact. Richard Todd points out that the names acquired by insects in the course of history signify their meaning for a given culture, but that the Linnaean system of classification, 'though admittedly one of unprecedented signification, is actually no different from the old haphazard namings in the sense that it, too, must rely on metaphor'.[30] Matty's representation of the insects who rescue Seth from the enchanted garden makes her natural history suitable for her intended child-reader. But it also shows her awareness that their common names reflect relationships that are not just metaphorical. She sees the Elephant Hawk Moth, for instance, as 'a kind of *walking figure of speech*' (p. 141), and once she begins to explore the etymologies of the creatures in her story, the language of this system itself drives the story, creating its own relationships and plots. As her alter ego Mistress Mouffet tells Seth, names are 'a way of weaving the world together, by relating the creatures to other creatures and a kind of *metamorphosis* [...] out of a *metaphor* which is a figure of speech for carrying one idea into another' (p. 132).

Both literary and scientific language can therefore be used to convey the concept of metamorphosis, or transformation, which, as the underlying principle of evolution, is central to natural history. This is evident as much in the nineteenth-century interest in fairy tale and myth as in its interest in the equally marvellous metamorphoses in the life cycle of frogs and butterflies. Matty's fable describes many such moments of metamorphosis, reflecting the transformations of the human world with which she is involved. The transformations of identity undergone by Seth, for example, represent the changes in William's personality, brought out by his dramatically changing circumstances. In Matty's case, however, such transformations embody not so much new phases in her personality as different dimensions of it, previously concealed by what Byatt calls Matilda's masquerade as Matty. The multiple representations of her own self in the fable resist any one-to-one identification with her character, but are highly suggestive. Seth's various rescuers are obvious manifestations of the woman who ultimately rescues William from Bredely Hall. The 'minute creature' who shrinks Seth to enable him to escape from a cavern evokes the almost invisible member of the household who helps William to escape the frustrating tedium of his married life by encouraging him to write *The Swarming City: A Natural History of a Woodland Society*, a scientific, but popular study of the local ant colonies. When he discovers Eugenia's incestuous relationship, and Matty announces that she has made all the arrangements necessary for him to leave England with her to take up his old life as a collector, William makes the connection to the fable explicit: he calls Matty 'a good Fairy' (p. 156), recalling the great Fairy who ensures Seth's final escape from the garden. This Fairy is also known as the Sphinx, who both sets and answers riddles, just as Matty does in the card game which reveals to William her knowledge of Eugenia's incest. The game too is a form of transformation, in which Matty changes letters around to turn 'Insect' to 'Incest', while William's reshuffling of the cards returns to her the word 'Sphinx', acknowledging her skill and perspicacity. And it is a Sphinx moth which literally rescues Seth from the garden by carrying him over its walls.

But whatever light the fable throws on the Alabaster household, it is also about natural history. The great Fairy is more than a fabulous representation of Matty. She is also Dame Kind, Nature, in part a personification of natural selection. Byatt relates her to Darwin's and Edmund Spenser's Dame Nature, 'who hath both kinds in one', male and female, and to Tennyson's Nature in *In Memoriam* (*Histories*, pp. 120–1). Seth dreams of the destruction and waste which is an inevitable part of the process of natural selection, hearing a voice quoting Tennyson's 'I care for nothing, all must go', but he also hears a voice saying 'Fear no more' (p. 138); and his trust in Dame Kind saves and restores him. William too is saved by his trust in Matty and Nature, in so far as it embodies the possibility – in the individual, as in the species – of transformation and growth. This seems to be the significance of the ending of the novella. On board ship in mid-Atlantic, Matty and William are brought a butterfly by Captain Papagay.[31] The butterfly is wildly off course but – as Matty observes – 'still alive, and bright'. Papagay responds, 'That is the main thing. [...] To be alive. As long as you are alive, everything is surprising, rightly seen' (p. 160).

In writing this fable of natural history, Matty is carrying out an activity regarded as perfectly acceptable for Victorian ladies. As Carolyn Merchant observes, in Britain as in America, 'middle-class women, whose direct impact on nature through production had decreased, found opportunities to influence consciousness about nature by educating themselves in the natural sciences, by writing children's books, and later by preserving nature through women's clubs'.[32] *Morpho Eugenia*, however, suggests that an intelligent woman of the period might subvert that activity for more radical ends. Matty writes to acquire an independent income, and in writing her way out of the Alabaster household, she also precipitates William's departure. She is therefore guilty of transgressing the moral standards expected of her by committing both fornication and adultery. Her determination to accompany William to the Amazon is a further refusal to observe the limits of her sex, since it is in defiance of William's assertion that the Amazon 'is no place for a woman' (p. 156). His comments on the Amazon ants could aptly be applied to her, since these ants appear to act contrary to their sexual function: they 'never excavate nests nor care for their young. Their name is probably bestowed because like the classical Amazon warriors, who were all women, led by a fierce queen, they have substituted belligerence for the delicate domestic virtues associated with the female sex' (p. 99). Matty's acts of transgression mean she has in effect ceased to be a woman, according to Victorian gender ideology. As Byatt comments, she is 'not confined to her biological identity' (*Histories*, p. 117).

But it is perhaps more accurate to say that Matty has never been represented as a woman within the terms of the discourse which dominates William's view of women. If Matty can tell him, 'You do not know that I am a woman' (p. 156), this is because she lacks the characteristics that for him define femininity and are epitomised in Eugenia. Byatt sets up the two women in distinct opposition: '*Morpho Eugenia*, the aphrodisiac butterfly of sexual selection against Matty, the Sphinx, the night-flyer, who "hath both kinds in one", lion and woman' (*Histories*, p. 121). In contrast to Eugenia, Matty's mouth is 'hard, not soft, but full of life' (p. 157). Her dark anonymous clothes make her more like the men in their 'black carapaces' than the ladies in their butterfly-like finery. William makes similar assumptions about the differences in women's mental activity, assuming that women are 'expert in emotional matters' (p. 69), and that Eugenia will be uninterested in his ambitions, but Matty shares his intellectual engagement with the natural world and the questions it raises about humanity's place within it. Because she transgresses gender boundaries in this way, William thinks of her as 'sexless' (p. 105), but this representation simply sums up all that resists categorisation and confinement by gender. Once Matty has achieved her independence, she too undergoes transformation, releasing her hair to make William see her as a woman, a transformation expressed in her insistence that he uses the name Matilda instead of Matty. Like Barrett's Alexandra, she says, '*Look at me*' (p. 157). Insisting that, although 'surplus', she remains sexual, and taking command of their relationship, she too contravenes female stereotypes.

The idealisation of women of which William is a victim is largely the product, I have suggested, of the myth of Romantic love. As Byatt's description of Eugenia as 'the aphrodisiac butterfly of sexual selection' suggests, however, such a view is not entirely out of keeping with his position as a scientist, since it was reinforced by Darwinian ideas about sexual selection. Sarah Blaffer Hrdy points out that

> to Darwin, elusiveness was as integral to female sexual identity as ardor was to that of their male pursuers. As he put it, the female is 'less eager to mate than the male'. She 'requires to be courted; she is coy, and may often be seen endeavoring for a long time to escape' until, impressed by his superiority, she chooses the 'best' male, endowing her offspring with such superior traits as he offers.[33]

All this can be observed in Eugenia's behaviour. She expresses herself unworthy of love, having unwittingly – she claims – caused the death of a previous fiancé, until deciding William will make a suitable husband. In making a clear distinction between human and animal sexuality, Darwinism sanctions the kind of idealisation which conceals a reality less acceptable to Victorian eyes.

For the reality is that it is not Matty who is – like the Amazon ants – 'irrevocably dependent and parasitic' (p. 99), but the Alabaster women. Their needs dominate a household 'run for and by women' (p. 76), and for them Matty plays the role of one of the 'barren females, or nuns, who attend to the feeding, building, and nurturing of the whole society and its city' in support of the 'only *one* true female, the Queen' (p. 85). The analogies set up in the novella between the human world and the insect world deconstruct the gender myths of Romantic love by setting them in the context of the processes of sexual selection in the animal kingdom. In the process, Byatt not only suggests the human and animal world are closer than Darwin's theory of sexual selection would indicate, she also draws attention to the contradictions inherent in Victorian gender ideology, to which evolutionary theory contributes. The 'coy' female of courtship becomes the devouring 'Queen', who represents the 'unevolved' woman of Darwinian theory, the woman specialised only for motherhood. The lives of Eugenia and Lady Alabaster parody William's description of the Queen ant:

> as the workers take over the running of the nursery and the provision of food, they will forget that they ever saw the sun. [...] They become egg-laying machines, gross and glistening, endlessly licked, caressed, soothed and smoothed – veritable Prisoners of Love. *This* is the true nature of the Venus under the Mountain, in this miniature world a creature immobilised by her function of breeding. (p. 102)

William's passionate post-nuptial relationship with Eugenia ends abruptly once she becomes pregnant, and only revives when she is again ready to breed. His life becomes seasonal, revolving around Eugenia's pregnancies, and the apparently irresistible force of her desire, since the role of men within this household is simply to impregnate their mates and pass on their genetic inheritance, like the male ants whose 'whole existence is directed *only* to the nuptial dance and the fertilisation of the queens' (p. 103). The woman worshipped as the Goddess of Love becomes a primitive mother goddess.

The evolutionary imperative to continue the species is, moreover, reinforced by the imperative to improve the species through breeding practices that will improve the offspring's biological inheritance. Such practices are even more important where there is a major social and financial inheritance to secure. The novella's treatment of Eugenia's marriage to William demonstrates how human selection can aid natural selection, both individual and social values playing their part in the search for a mate, since, as Beer puts it, 'Succession and inheritance form the "hidden bond" which knits all nature past and present together, just as succession and inheritance organise society and sustain hegemony' (*Darwin's Plots*, p. 196). This is why Lord Alabaster accepts William as a valuable, though impoverished and low-blooded, addition to the family: 'You have courage, and intelligence, and kindness [...]. All families stand in need of these qualities if they are to survive' (p. 56). Eugenia's children will ensure the continuance of the family face as well as the family fortune, but William discovers that those he calls the 'white' children, so true to their maternal Alabaster 'stock', may be the product of her incestuous relationship with her brother Edgar. In evolutionary terms, her greatest transgression as a woman is not, therefore, her adultery. Against her plea that her behaviour was natural,

William opposes the irrefutable argument that 'breeders know [...] even first-cousin marriages produce inherited defects'. She is damned for being solely interested in 'self-nurture and self-communion' (p. 159), rather than in her responsibility for the evolution of the race.

But Eugenia's behaviour can also be interpreted in the light of late twentieth-century ideas about evolution. Her ability to draw William to her bed whenever she desires a child is typical of the behaviour of most primates, according to Hrdy, whose research suggests that females 'are, and always have been, the chief custodians of the breeding potential of the species' (p. 18). Hrdy's challenge to Darwin's theory of sexual selection was first articulated within Darwin's own lifetime, although largely ignored. Antoinette Brown Blackwell, an American, published a critique of *The Descent of Man* in 1875 which argues that women compete in the process of sexual selection just as much as men. Darwin's thesis that among humans the male dominates choice, unlike all the other species, where the female holds the power of selection, ignores the probability that, as Hrdy puts it, 'selection favored females who were assertive, sexually active, or highly competitive, who adroitly manipulated male consorts' (p. 14). Such a view acknowledges the link between maternity and sexuality over which Victorian ideology drew a veil. Eugenia has precisely those sexual characteristics which will reinforce her breeding potential: her soft roundness is not only a sign of female beauty, but a signifier of reproductive potential, according to nineteenth-century scientific studies of the female body. William responds particularly to her breasts, which have both an erotic and maternal function. When she weeps, her slightly pink and swollen eyes mimic aroused sexual organs; in William they elicit both sexual desire and the protective role of the potential father. *Morpho Eugenia* demonstrates that in a society troubled by the problem of 'surplus women' – as Lady Alabaster puts it, 'there are always more ladies' (p. 4) – competition among women is inevitable. William, it should be remembered, is seduced by not one, but two women – Eugenia and Matty – although each uses very different means.

Blackwell also complains that Darwin's account of the evolution of the male fails to be matched by any sense of the evolution of the female: 'he seems never to have thought of looking to see whether or not the females had developed equivalent feminine characters'.[34] For Hrdy, this includes his failure to explain the evolution of the sexual appetite of the human female, who may engage in intercourse even when it cannot lead to conception. Hrdy rejects the hypothesis that perpetual female receptivity evolved as a bonding mechanism, to ensure male interest in their offspring, on the grounds that it does not take account of similar patterns in other primates, where males take very little part in the care of offspring. Instead she argues that female primates mate with a number of partners in order to create confusion about paternity, thus increasing the number of potential fathers with an interest in the welfare of her offspring. 'To the extent that her subsequent offspring benefit, the female has benefited from her seeming nymphomania' (p. 174). Eugenia quite openly acknowledges such a motive, telling William that she made sure she did not know the paternity of her children. Even her adultery can be explained in evolutionary, as well as in individualistic terms.

Morpho Eugenia therefore suggests the hold that Darwinian ideas of gender difference have had on succeeding generations, including our own. Those ideas have at their base an insistence on difference – not only the difference between men and women, but the difference between humans and other species as regards sexual roles. The novella shows too how this scientific discourse overlapped with the discourse of Romantic love. But it also mounts a challenge to such discourse, and suggests how a highly evolved woman, as opposed to the unevolved woman of Darwinian theory, might replace it with a more flexible discourse of her own, and so release herself from its control.

3
'Criminals, Idiots, Women and Minors': Deviant Minds in Deviant Bodies

In 1845 an American called Marion Sims described himself as 'a colonizing and conquering hero'. He continues, 'I saw everything as no man had ever seen before.'[1] Sims was not, however, an explorer or naturalist, like the fictional heroes previously discussed, but a gynaecologist, describing his adventures into the unknown with the aid of a speculum. For, as already indicated, Victorian discovery was not restricted to geographical exploration or scientific study of the physical universe, but included the exploration and 'mapping' of the female body.[2] And increasingly, the female mind, so vulnerable to infection from the diseases of the body, became the subject of detailed 'scientific' investigation too. The results suggested that the female body is always the potential source of deviance, particularly of sexual deviance, and consequently requires constant observation, in the form of surveillance, and treatment or even punishment. For this pathologised view of femininity was given the force of law. Legal discourse was, Carol Smart suggests, interwoven with the discourses of medicine and science 'to bring into being the problematic female subject who is constantly in need of surveillance and regulation'.[3] She points out that medical professionals were frequently called in to give evidence to Parliamentary Select Committees on topics like prostitution and infanticide, and that the second half of the nineteenth century was marked by a surge of legislative activity designed to regulate female sexual and reproductive behaviour, focusing particularly on practices such as birth control and baby farming which enabled women to escape the burden of motherhood which was, according to Victorian ideology, their destiny.[4]

The phrase quoted in this chapter's title is a contemporary response to this idea of the female as essentially deviant which highlights the association drawn between women and those others who 'deviate' sufficiently from the norm of the rational white male to be deemed incapable of exercising the right to vote. It forms the title of an article published in 1868 by Frances Power Cobbe (1822–1904), who wrote extensively on the condition of women for the periodical press, and refers to 'the four categories under which persons are now excluded from many civil, and all political rights in England'. Cobbe goes on: 'They were complacently quoted this year by the *Times* as every way fit and proper exceptions; but yet it has appeared to not a few, that the place assigned to Women among them is hardly any longer suitable.' Cobbe points out that married women were in effect denied a legal existence, since 'the husband and wife are assumed to be one person, and that person is the husband'. She furthermore exposes the contradiction inherent in arguing that women are inferior to and weaker than their husbands, but denying them 'all the support and protection which it is possible to interpose between so poor a creature and the strong being always standing over her'.[5] While Cobbe argues that women no longer deserve to be listed among the excluded, one could argue that it was hardly necessary to have included them as a separate category in the first place, since they were by implication subsumed in the others: woman's reproductive system rendered her always potentially deviant and unstable, if not legally criminal or insane, while in evolutionary terms she stood closer to a child than an adult male.

The link between deviance and female sexuality is particularly evident in medical discourse on hysteria.[6] Robert Brudenell Carter's influential study of hysteria, published in 1853, linked the condition specifically to sexual feelings, which he describes as the most violent feelings in women. Hysteria was both the result of the indulgence of sexual desires, and the cause of a preoccupation with the reproductive organs which led to talk and behaviour considered to be indecent. As he explains:

> The occasional occurrence of nymphomania may be taken as a case in point, and may be explained on the ground that attention to the emotions concerned in producing hysteria has weakened the sense of decency for a time, by engrossing the whole nervous force for the contemplation of an object of desire.

The path from hysteria to degeneracy and even criminality was all too smooth, particularly for the lower classes. Carter describes hysteria as being 'much concerned in the first errors of many prostitutes', and more likely to result from the sexual emotions of lower-class women, since 'the advance of civilisation and the ever-increasing complications of social intercourse' gave rise to other equally powerful emotions among the educated.[7] Sander Gilman goes so far as to argue that a basic assumption underpinning William Acton's study *Prostitution, Considered in its Moral, Social, and Sanitary Aspects* (1857) is that the potential for prostitution is inherent in lower-class women. And he cites Cesare Lombroso's influential criminological study, *The Delinquent Female: The Prostitute and the Normal Woman* (1893), which makes the same connections from a different perspective, seeing prostitutes as congenital degenerates: 'Their abnormal predisposition can be seen in the gradations from occasional prostitution to moral insanity.'[8] The perceived absence of moral qualities in lower-class women, moreover, enabled the dominant middle classes to locate their anxiety about female sexuality well away from their own homes, specifically amongst the class to which most prostitutes belonged. In Ingham's words, 'In the dominant discourse of the period [the fallen woman] signifies the inescapable corruption of the working classes, which must be contained at any cost' (p. 25).

The eminent French physician Pierre Briquet suggests, however, that hysteria is an almost inevitable risk associated with femininity: 'woman's destiny is to feel, but to feel is almost hysteria'. He goes on:

> In order to fulfil the great and noble mission devolved upon her, it was indispensable that [woman] be endowed with a great susceptibility to affective impressions, that she be able somehow to feel everything in herself, and unfortunately, here as in everything else, the good can also produce evil, hysteria thus comes from this great susceptibility to affections. Let us imagine a man endowed with the faculty of being affected in the same way as woman, he would become hysterical and consequently unfit for his predestined role, namely, that of protection and strength. Hysteria in a man means the overthrow of the laws constitutive of our society.[9]

The sanction here is social rather than criminal law, but the consequence is the same: to be fit for her proper sphere a woman is inherently vulnerable to hysterical illness, which renders her unfit for anything outside her proper sphere.

If women were victims of their own bodies, and their propensity for deviance, those same bodies were usually the focus of treatment. At the most brutal end of the spectrum, clitoridectomy was designed then, as in more recent times, to encourage chastity by removing the source of sexual pleasure.[10] Less drastic was the rest cure, which focused on immobilising and fattening up the female body, and was famously described by Charlotte Perkins Gilman in her short story, *The Yellow Wallpaper*.[11] Even at the more liberal end, forms of surveillance were intended to control a woman's movements rather than to remove those restrictions identified by the more enlightened as the cause of frustration and illness. Carter's suggested treatment, for instance, is based on a view of the female hysteric as a delinquent child who needed to be handled by an unassailable authority:

> The patient should be placed exactly in the position of a child at school, where the command of the master is enforced by the parent, even if the latter does not perfectly agree with him. [...] The relatives will often think themselves quite competent to exercise a general surveillance over the treatment, and to question the propriety of this or that procedure. But no privilege of this kind must on any account be allowed; because, even if their judgments were always correct, such an exercise of them would tend to lower the professional man in the opinion of the patient by establishing a court of appeal from his decision. (p. 146)

Surveillance is in fact implicit in all these medical and semi-juridical discourses, which attempt to police the boundaries between what is perceived as normal and what is perceived as pathological. And their ultimate goal is, as Foucault has pointed out, to exercise power through disciplinary means rather than through the imposition of external force. Briquet, for instance, suggests calming the hysteric through the power of the gaze ('*par la force du regard*', quoted in Ender, p. 44), anticipating Foucault's analysis of the power that lies in an 'inspecting gaze, a gaze which each individual under its weight will end by interiorising to the point that he is his own overseer, each individual thus exercising this surveillance over, and against, himself'.[12] Feminist critics such as Laura Mulvey have written on the particular force of this view of power for women, historically the subject of the male gaze. Antony Easthope agrees that 'visual dominance, seeing and knowing everything, comes from a particularly masculine perspective [...]. To keep in sight means to keep under control.'[13] Those women whose non-conformity or even criminality made evident their failure to self-regulate through self-surveillance and self-discipline required more overt external forms of surveillance and control at the hands of the medical and legal profession.

These regimes are at the centre of Margaret Atwood's *Alias Grace* and Sarah Waters' *Affinity*, which extend the critique of scientific knowledge and authority discussed in the previous chapter into a similar critique of the judicial system, showing how in both cases the claim to objectivity is tainted by the male-centred view dominant in Victorian gender discourse. But that critique is also implicit in the forms of the novels, which are as resistant to the formal conventions of the mid-Victorian realist tradition as they are to the assumptions inscribed in them. Literary history suggests, moreover, that those assumptions are in turn closely related to the principles of scientific study. Just as the Victorian scientist believed that disciplined, impersonal observation of the material world and its inhabitants would result in objective knowledge which would further human progress, so the tradition of realist fiction assumes the existence of objective truths which, through careful observation, can be accurately represented and shared with the reader. Like those doctors and scientists who hoped, through observation of the body, to penetrate to the human interior, so the writer of realist fiction adopts the position of the privileged observer who, from a basis of detailed external description, penetrates the inner lives of his or her characters. In contrast, as inheritors of post-structuralist views of life and of fiction, Atwood and Waters continually refuse to grant the reader any such certainty.

More specifically, as novels about crime, concerned with the guilt or innocence of the convicted criminal, *Alias Grace* and *Affinity* are reminiscent of a category of fiction which has been associated more than most other genres with both realism and science. Dedicated, like both, to the pursuit of knowledge, the detective novel, as Jeremy Tambling argues, 'grows out of the realist text – is, indeed, in the germ of its idea the condition on which the realist text is based'.[14] Catherine Belsey similarly suggests that detective fiction evolved in part as a consequence of the prestige of science: 'The stories begin in enigma, mystery, the impossible, and conclude with an explanation which makes it clear that logical deduction and scientific method render all mysteries accountable to reason.'[15] Such novels focus on the unravelling of secrets and mysteries not dissimilar to those associated with the question, 'What is a woman?'.

However, while Belsey argues that 'shadowy, mysterious and often silent women' haunt nineteenth-century crime fiction, in *Alias Grace* and *Affinity* they take centre stage. While the silence of their Victorian predecessors often conceals female sexuality, 'investing it with a dark and magical quality' (p. 114), in these recent examples sexuality is both the magnet that attracts others to them and the crime that requires such intensive scrutiny and punishment, even if often unacknowledged as such. And since Atwood and Waters construct fictions in which the truth claims of any of the narratives they contain are constantly being called into question, and in which 'reality' can be no more than one person's interpretation of existence, their female criminals remain undetectable and unknowable. Grace Marks and Selina Dawes implicitly reject the terms by which Victorian gender discourse attempts to categorise them, and undermine the certainties of the processes of detection and judgement central to nineteenth-century fiction. Their remaining mystery throws into sharp relief the inadequacy of so-called scientific knowledge to define or contain them.

Madwoman or bad woman? Margaret Atwood, *Alias Grace*

Although Margaret Atwood's *Alias Grace*[16] takes place in Canada, the Victorian values and character of this part of the empire are repeatedly vaunted as distinguishing it from its more 'democratic' and 'progressive' American neighbour, so that the discourses deployed in the narrative relate closely to the British examples examined so far. The eponymous heroine, based on the historical case of Grace Marks, has already been convicted of murder when the novel opens in 1851, but so deeply does her crime transgress the female ideal that the authorities are still driven either to find her innocent, or to classify her as 'criminal', 'idiot' or 'minor' in order to explain that transgression. The alternative is to believe that Grace embodies the feared dark side of female identity, the deviance always potentially present in the sexualised female body – that she is, simply, 'woman'. Jamie Walsh, Grace's erstwhile admirer, articulates the dualistic options available when she turns in his eyes from being 'an angel [...] fit to be idolized and worshipped [...] to a demon' (p. 418).[17]

The anxiety which a woman like Grace causes is evident not only in the loss of freedom and perpetual surveillance which her thirty years of imprisonment entail, but in the scientific scrutiny to which she is also subjected. The central question posed by this rich case-study is whether she can best be classified in criminological or psychiatric terms: is she bad or mad? And this uncertainty is reflected in her movement between the prison and the asylum. Marks's earliest biographer, Susanna Moodie, visited her in both locations, and was moved to hope that her guilt could be attributed to 'the incipient workings of this frightful malady'. In either case, questions of gender keep coming to the fore. In the early years of her incarceration, Grace is diagnosed as a hysteric, that most female of conditions, but in the asylum she quickly recognises the gender inequalities which have brought so many of her fellow inmates there.

Most she believes to be sane, except when drunk, some taking refuge in the asylum to escape domestic violence because 'he was the mad one but nobody would lock him up' (p. 34), or to find shelter in winter. Grace nevertheless understands the protection that her uncertain mental status accords her; and to some of the asylum doctors, Grace's 'madness' is indeed a deliberate sham, releasing her from the stricter regime of the penitentiary, and further evidence of her wickedness. To provide 'scientific' evidence, a visiting doctor measures Grace's head, using the popular science of phrenology to establish a typology which will enable criminals to be identified even before they commit any crimes. Even Moodie's account draws on the pseudo-scientific language of physiognomy to validate her judgement, describing Grace's 'long curved chin, which gives, as it always does to most persons who have this facial defect, a cunning, cruel expression'.[18]

What all these judges of Grace's character really want, however, is for Grace to judge herself, to confess. Unlike the classic detective novel which ends in confession, Atwood's novel is dominated by confession, since Grace's first-person narrative is structured around the efforts of the representatives of state power – legal, religious and medical – to extract a confession from her. Grace hides behind the amnesia which, she claims, overcame her at the time of the murder to avoid such statements. But confession is presented to her as the only route to freedom. In legal terms, she cannot be pardoned until she admits her guilt, and Reverend Verringer, the prison chaplain, urges confession because 'the truth shall make you free' (p. 91). Believing her to be innocent of murder, he nevertheless demands that she recognise the spiritual authority which enables him to forgive her sins, just as the courts have the legal authority to grant her pardon. Throughout her incarceration, chaplains urge, 'Confess, confess. Let me forgive and pity. Let me get up a Petition for you. Tell me all.' But Grace knows that 'once you start feeling sorry for yourself, they've got you where they want you' (p. 39). For the price of physical freedom is the subjugation implicit in becoming a confessing subject, as Tambling explains: 'Those addressed by a confessional discourse are "interpellated", [...] and are subjected, i.e. made to define themselves in a discourse given to them, and in which they must name and misname themselves' (p. 2). Confession, he goes on, thus produces 'the subject it wants' (p. 54).

External forms of scrutiny, therefore, ultimately give way – as they do historically, according to Foucault – to more intrusive techniques designed to secure confession. And in a society where science is taking the place once occupied by religion, the role of the priest is reinforced, if not replaced, by that of the doctor. As Tambling points out, physicians and lawyers are described in Mary Braddon's novel, *Lady Audley's Secret* (1862), as 'the confessors of this prosaic nineteenth century' (p. 134). Verringer accordingly cedes his role as confessor to the high-minded young scientist, Dr Simon Jordan, who sees the pursuit of truth as his life's goal, although his interest is not in morality, but in the workings of the mind; he uses the principle of association and the analysis of dreams to explore Grace's unconscious, techniques which can be seen as precursors of psychoanalysis.[19] Their conversations are a diagnostic tool which will give him not only knowledge of her inner secrets, but power over her fate. That power is, however, only a more tangible form of the power represented by all such knowledge, which gives Jordan, as a doctor in a 'position of all-knowing authority' (p. 335), power to define what Grace is – mad or bad.

This is evidently also a gendered process. Dr Jordan represents the power of the male medical profession over women in an acute form, since he can explore both their physical interior, with his 'forbidden knowledge' (p. 94), and their minds. His language is characterised by images of penetration: he acknowledges that he approaches Grace's mind 'as if it is a locked box, to which [he] must find the right key'.[20] He tries in vain 'to open her up like an oyster' (p. 153). Grace herself experiences a sense of personal violation, in which she is to some extent complicit. She qualifies her initial claim that she feels torn open like a peach with the words, 'not even torn open, but too ripe and splitting open of its own accord', but she proves impenetrable, since 'inside the peach there's a stone' (p. 79). The more sinister implications of this desire are figured in Jordan's dream of being examined, and watched himself as he is about to dissect a poor woman. The presence in the dream of a candlestick, the last item he took for Grace to 'associate' with, links this examination with his psychological dissection of Grace. On removing the sheets, he finds not a corpse but a warm absence, a reminder that Grace is a living being constantly evading his grasp.

On waking, Jordan finds himself penetrating Rachel, his landlady, so that the sexual dimensions of his supposedly scientific investigation are fully exposed. For his desire to penetrate Grace is not purely metaphorical: he wants to 'know' Grace in the biblical sense. When the moment comes for him to approach the subject of the murder with Grace, disturbed as he is by his own increasingly violent sexual fantasies of Rachel, his language is suggestive of other mysteries – that of the female interior, of unnameable female sexuality: 'They are nearing the blank mystery, the area of erasure; they are entering the forest of amnesia, where things have lost their names' (p. 342). Above all he also wants to know her sexual status. Like the newspapers interested in 'true confessions', and the chaplain who tries to extract from her the salacious details, Jordan's interest is increasingly not so much the state of her mind as the state of her body. When she is supposedly under hypnosis, he cannot resist asking the thing he wants to know most, whether Grace was McDermott's paramour.

While Jordan's terminology may differ from Verringer's, his ideology is remarkably similar where gender is concerned, both religion and science inducing what Foucault calls the 'hysterization of women's bodies', seen to be 'thoroughly saturated with sexuality'.[21] He represents himself as a Yankee democrat reformer, advancing knowledge by remaining free and disinterested, and his experiences in Paris and London have freed him from any illusions as to 'the innate refinement of women' that were so much a part of Victorian gender ideology:

> He has seen madwomen tearing off their clothes and displaying their naked bodies; he has seen prostitutes of the lowest sort do the same. He's seen women drunk and swearing, struggling together like wrestlers, pulling the hair from each other's heads. [...] He's known them to make away with their own infants, and to sell their young daughters to wealthy men who hope that by raping children they will avoid disease. (p. 100)

Such knowledge does not, however, protect him from those blind spots regarding gender difference which he, like Byatt's William Adamson, shares with George Eliot's pioneering doctor, Dr Lydgate. Instead he uses this knowledge as a rationale for a false idealisation which will secure the distinction between 'angels' and 'whores', arguing there is 'all the more reason to safeguard the purity of those still pure. In such a cause, hypocrisy is surely justified: one must present what ought to be true as if it really is.' This is his motivation for accepting at face value Rachel's pretence of sleepwalking into his bed: in contrast to the prostitute who feigns pleasure, she must feign resistance to maintain the fiction of her respectability. Such double-thinking clearly accounts for his anticipation of a marriage in which procreation would take place 'unseen, prudently veiled in white cotton' (p. 102), and drives his desire to find Grace innocent, in spite of his knowledge that without her extraordinary experiences she would be 'tepid, bland, and tasteless' (p. 453).

Jordan's belief in Grace's innocence enables him, moreover, to maintain an image of himself as what Grace's lawyer calls a Saint George figure.

Before meeting her, he imagines her as 'a nun in a cloister, a maiden in a towered dungeon, awaiting the next day's burning at the stake, or else the last-minute champion come to rescue her. The cornered woman; the penitential dress falling straight down, concealing feet that were surely bare.' In reality Grace is very different: 'straighter, taller, more self-possessed, wearing the conventional dress of the Penitentiary, with a striped blue and white skirt beneath which were two feet, not naked at all but enclosed in ordinary shoes' (p. 68). And his own self-image as a protector of women proves to be equally fictitious. Grace's lawyer accuses Jordan of being like him, rescuing the maiden in order to have her himself, so that Jordan stands accused of exploiting her vulnerability just as much as any man exploiting a prostitute. For all his professed feelings for Grace, he abandons her and her 'case' as soon as they threaten his professional status, his money giving him a power of escape which is denied to women like Rachel and Grace. His memory of his first sexual experience with a servant as an image of a more innocent time suggests he is in denial about the exploitation of women by men, and particularly of poor women by rich men. His lovemaking with Rachel becomes increasingly violent as he is subject to violent images that arrive out of nowhere, and are totally out of character in this 'mild-tempered man' who nevertheless thinks of Rachel's 'naked feet, shell-thin, exposed and vulnerable, tied together with – where has this come from? – an ordinary piece of twine' (p. 337). This link between sexuality, violence and power is the dark side of the Saint George figure. The novel suggests, moreover, that Jordan's repression of this link is characteristic of Victorian ideology, since it is also evident in the man who does finally 'rescue' Grace by marrying her. The pleasure Jamie Walsh derives from this rescue is increased by the knowledge of her suffering, and he is sexually aroused by her account of the murderer McDermott's brutal attempts to seduce her, suggesting an element of sadism in the sexual desires of even the gentlest of men.

But how is it that Dr Jordan's idealisation of himself is thus exposed, given that, as the confessor, he is not himself exposed to public examination? He stands at the centre of the naming process by which, to quote Tambling again, 'The hysterical, the mad, the sexually perverted and women are produced as the other of the [...] bourgeois subject, assumed to be male, normal, heterosexual and white' (p. 6). Nevertheless, Atwood uses a focalised narrative to ensure that Jordan becomes a confessing subject to the reader, if not to those around him. She uses dreams and associations to reveal the workings of his unconscious, just as he does with Grace. At the end of the novel, recovering from his Civil

War experiences, he too claims to suffer amnesia, in his case regarding what took place in Kingston. To restore his memory, his mother shows him everyday objects that were once important to him, just as he once showed Grace homely articles to trigger memories of her hidden past. The novel draws attention to further similarities between Jordan's situation and Grace's. When Rachel wants him to kill her husband, he appears to accept, just as Grace claims she did when McDermott asked her to help him murder Kinnear and Nancy. Jordan imagines carrying it out and then killing Rachel to be rid of her, achieving a curious displacement of his feelings by asking himself whether she is 'insane or a moral degenerate' (p. 477), once again naming the Other. The effect is to suggest how little divides the respectable from the criminal or even insane. As Jordan acknowledges, 'The difference between a civilized man and a barbarous fiend – a madman, say – lies, perhaps, merely in a thin veneer of willed self-restraint' (p. 163). He does not, however, apply this observation to women.

Ironically Grace ultimately confesses less than her confessor, adopting strategies which suggest that the power relations of the confessional can be overturned. She resists the power of the gaze through her own powers of observation, which make Jordan feel like 'the subject of some unexplained experiment' (p. 68), as if he, rather than she, was being examined. For she is able to exploit his vulnerability to Victorian gender ideology by mimicking that femininity which in his scheme of things vouchsafes her innocence. Her contacts with the Governor's household have given her voice a 'ladylike' sensibility and improved her manners. There she has learned a form of concealment, adopting the totally smooth exterior of the lady that reveals nothing, her hands folded in her lap 'in the proper way' (p. 23). Having also learned the discourse of feminine innocence which denies the body, she gives Jordan literal-minded answers, naïve or prim enough for an innocent sixteen-year old whose life stopped short when she was imprisoned, making him feel at fault for raising sexual matters. Jordan's professional training tells him that the body may indeed conceal secrets, or only reveal them in hysterical form, and that 'what he wants is what she refuses to tell; what she chooses perhaps not even to know' (p. 374). But his ideological inheritance regarding women means he desires above all to believe in what he thinks he sees.

Grace is aware that he wants confirmation of what he already believes. She therefore offers Jordan an extended 'confession' that will give him the answer he wants. At her trial, on her lawyer's advice, she confessed to helping to commit the second murder under duress, fearing for her own life, and this admission of legal culpability, coupled with her youth, created an image of the murderess as victim which enabled her to avoid hanging. Although she later repudiated the confession, she maintains this image of victimhood in the narrative of her early life that she gives Jordan. Young, female and an Irish immigrant,[22] Grace's story typifies the experience of the multiply oppressed. On arrival in Toronto, the twelve-year old Grace leaves her abusive father only to become vulnerable to sexual harassment and abuse by those who employ her as a maid. Her narrative therefore constitutes an indictment of the laws that condemned her, but failed to protect her, vividly illustrating Cobbe's argument. Like the painting of Susannah and the Elders on the wall of the murder victim, Thomas Kinnear, it suggests that women are always held responsible for male desire, and are liable to be falsely accused, even when they are the innocent victims. The inequalities of class reinforce those of gender. Grace's comment that gentlemen 'do not have to clear up the messes they make' is applicable metaphorically as well as literally. She compares them to children, because 'they do not have to think ahead, or worry about the consequences of what they do' (p. 249), reversing the usual Victorian view of women as childlike. Grace's narrative accords sufficiently with Jordan's medical experience to be convincing. He has enough knowledge of the bodies of working-class women to challenge, like Cobbe, the concept of the 'weaker sex': 'their spines and musculature were on the average no feebler than those of men' (p. 84). And he has enough knowledge of their lives to challenge the view, quoted at the beginning of this chapter, that the lower classes had a natural propensity for prostitution, which he instead recognises as a sane alternative to starvation. Deconstructing the associations between sexuality and madness, he points out that 'if women are seduced and abandoned they're supposed to go mad, but if they survive, and seduce in their turn, then they were mad to begin with' (p. 349). Moreover, to read Grace's story as an example of victimisation accords with Verringer's desire to prove her innocence, for which he is paying Dr Jordan well.

But without denying the historical validity of stories like Grace's, within the context of the novel the reader also needs to be aware that this view of Grace invites complicity with the Victorian view of the woman as a child or minor, unable to take responsibility for her own actions. And while this view may be appropriate in relation to the twelve-year-old Grace, a different reading may be needed for the older Grace. Her friend Mary Whitney clearly is such a victim, dying as a result of a botched abortion, after being made pregnant by her employer's son; she knows that giving birth would mean her dismissal, and probably a future of prostitution to support herself and her child. Grace's story, however, can be read as an account of how she avoids the fate which befalls Mary and so many like her – as an account of her resistance to victimhood. Seen in this light, Grace's actions throughout are a sane response to her situation, indicating a strong survival instinct worthy of the most Darwinian view of human life. But if Grace's narrative is at one level about how Grace avoids becoming another Mary Whitney, at another level it is about how she becomes Mary – or rather how Mary becomes part of her, the self she needs in order to survive. Mary acts as surrogate mother to Grace, explaining all the facts of life pertinent to a solitary pubescent working-class female. After Mary's death, Grace hears her friend calling *'Let me in'* (p. 207), and faints; when she comes round, she does not know who she is, since Grace is 'lost, and gone into the lake' (p. 208), suggesting she has been taken over by Mary's personality. This episode marks the death of the earlier innocent Grace and the birth of a more knowledgeable Grace who bears the fruits of Mary's experience, and uses her name as an alias. In prison she calls on her memories of her friend to bring into play a cruder and stronger persona able to deal with her keepers' jokes and innuendo. But in order to preserve the 'alias' of female grace and innocence, which is her only chance of release, Grace must conceal this more knowing, sexualised self.

What is less clear is how far she is also engaged in unconscious repression of a sexually experienced, even murderous self, since the splitting of the self is, according to Lacanians, a universal survival strategy. Even in prison her conforming self is under threat, since Grace remembers or dreams (her narrative consistently leaves such questions open) being outside a room containing Kinnear and Nancy, and demanding to be let in, just as Mary's voice did, the repressed sexual self demanding admission. But notions of admission and escape shift in significance throughout the narrative, at times suggesting a split subject, at others conveying Grace's perception of her life history as something constructed by others, inside which she is trapped, and from which she begs God to release her. The relationship between 'Grace' and 'Mary', and the two selves they represent, is brought to a dramatic climax when Grace is hypnotised by Dr Jerome DuPont, alias her old friend Jerome the peddler.[23] Apparently in a hypnotic trance, in a voice 'remarkable for its violence' (p. 471), Grace makes the ambiguous statement, 'It was my kerchief that strangled her.' She goes on, 'And this time the gentleman died as well, for once' (p. 466), as if to suggest that Kinnear's murder was a form of revenge for Mary's death. The same voice, however, immediately exonerates Grace: 'Grace knew nothing about it!' (p. 467). It explains that Mary, on her death, had to borrow Grace's body, because Grace forgot to open the window, referring to the folk belief that if a window were not left open, the dead soul would be unable to escape. The recurrence of the window image suggests that the threshold between Grace's personality and Mary's has been crossed under hypnosis, bringing the repressed self to the fore. Both Verringer and 'DuPont' are happy to accept an interpretation which frees Grace of responsibility for 'Mary's' actions, although the clergyman describes her condition as a form of possession, while DuPont calls it 'double consciousness' – two personalities with different sets of memories, if one accepts 'that we are what we remember' (p. 471).[24] For Jordan, the choice of terminology is more problematic, since he knows that the concept of *dédoublement* will not be acceptable either to the Minister of Justice, ending all chance of releasing Grace, or to the medical profession, making him a laughing stock. And, as always, this vindication comes at a price: Grace is diagnosed as psychologically deviant, reinforcing the stereotypical view of woman as inherently unstable, prone to hysteria and insanity, her innocence always under threat from darker forces.

There remains, however, the possibility that Grace is more in control than she seems, using the situation to construct another alias that will serve her fight for freedom. She may be consciously using the persona of Mary to articulate the sexuality which she is usually forced to repress, enjoying the opportunity to turn the tables on Jordan by observing his behaviour with the Governor's nubile daughter Lydia, and penetrating his sexual secrets, as he has tried – unsuccessfully – to penetrate hers. The fake nature of DuPont's 'scientific' credentials also leads the reader to anticipate a fake performance, but his shaken response afterwards creates a high level of ambiguity. His comment that usually 'the subject remains under the control of the operator' (p. 470) suggests that the planned performance has evaded him. Grace's supreme piece of acting might be her success in persuading even him that the planned fakery turned into genuine hypnosis.[25] This most intrusive form of public surveillance is thus foiled like every other: the demonstration which was intended to elicit Grace's confession, establishing her innocence and guilt beyond doubt, merely constructs another version of her story.[26]

Grace's resistance therefore constitutes a refusal to interiorise any of the identities she is offered by her confessors, or the ideology inscribed in them. In Tambling's words, 'The history of confession is that of the power at the centre inducing people at the margins to internalise what is said about them – to accept that discourse and live it, and thereby to live their oppression' (p. 6). But Grace resists the exercise of power through these medical and judicial discourses. Her insistence on retaining control of her own narrative and her own secrets is a statement about identity in a narrative which from the outset questions the very concept of a stable identity. She asks herself whether identity is simply what is written about someone, one's reputation:

> I think of all the things that have been written about me – that I am an inhuman female demon, that I am an innocent victim of a black-guard forced against my will and in danger of my own life, that I was too ignorant to know how to act and that to hang me would be judicial murder, [...] that I am of a sullen disposition with a quarrelsome temper, that I have the appearance of a person rather above my humble station, that I am a good girl with a pliable nature and no harm is told of me, that I am cunning and devious, that I am soft in the head and little better than an idiot. And I wonder, how can I be all of these different things at once? (p. 25)

But she is able to turn this idea to her own advantage. If we are what we remember, as 'DuPont' suggests after the hypnotism, then Grace's 'amnesia' frees her from her past and enables her to construct a new identity, even while acknowledging that all identity is at best a patchwork, constructed in part by other people. When she arrives in the United States after the murder, she feels she has never existed because she has left no trace of herself behind. She continues, with an obvious reference to her own name, that she has left 'no marks. [...] It is almost the same as being innocent' (p. 398). Apart from another teasing suggestion that she may in fact be guilty – but guilty of what? – this statement suggests the possibility of wiping out the past and constructing a new identity. When, after her release from prison, she marries Jamie Walsh, she can be said to marry her mirror-image – 'a self-made man' (p. 523) – as she is a self-made woman.

But how can Grace be said to construct her own identity when the language of her story, even when not directed to Jordan, only admits to different degrees of certainty, to things that 'might' have happened or 'surely' could not have, so that the status of the whole narrative remains uncertain? When she comments on the charges laid against her that 'there are other things they said I did, which I said I could not remember' (pp. 342–3), the reader is uncertain whether to interpret 'I said' as an admission of misinformation. And we have no other 'truth' to measure her account against. But if words are unreliable, there may be more enlightenment in the non-verbal. The novel ends with Grace making a Tree of Paradise quilt – the first quilt she has made for herself. She changes the traditional pattern because she believes that the Tree of Life and the Tree of Knowledge were one, since you would die whether you ate of it or not, but if you ate of it, you would at least die less ignorant. Rejecting the patriarchal view that ignorance is a prerequisite for innocence, particularly in women, she decides moreover to add a border of snakes entwined, accepting the necessary presence of temptation and sin even in Paradise. Finally, she decides to add triangles of cloth taken from Mary's petticoat, her own prison nightdress, and Nancy's dress, concluding that they will all be 'a part of the pattern. And so [they] will all be together' (p. 534). As women, victims of patriarchy, they have more in common than separates them. And as women, they have both human frailty and their place in Paradise. Grace shapes the pieces of her life into a new pattern, superimposing it on patriarchal narratives like the biblical one which have shaped hers.

To endorse the symbolic significance of this final act of narrative, each of the novel's chapters is headed by the name of a quilt pattern which relates, sometimes obliquely, to the chapter's content. Grace herself refers to quilts as flags, to alert the reader to their role as signifiers. She explains to Jordan why women draw attention to the bed by placing such 'flags' on them:

> It's for a warning. Because you may think a bed is a peaceful thing, Sir, and to you it may mean rest and comfort and a good night's sleep. But it isn't so for everyone; and there are many dangerous things that may take place in a bed. It is where we are born, and that is our first peril in life; and it is where the women give birth, which is often their last. And it is where the act takes place between men and women that I will not mention to you, Sir, but I suppose you know what it is; and some call it love, and others despair, or else merely an indignity which they must suffer through. And finally beds are what we sleep in, and where we dream, and often where we die. (p. 186)

The bed is the place where all the most important – and dangerous – events in a woman's life take place, in so far as a woman's life centres on her body and its reproductive functions.

By identifying herself so closely with the body, Grace seems in danger of aligning herself with that discourse which sees woman's nature as entirely the product of her physical organism. Nor is it clear that she has succeeded in shaping a life free from either gender ideology or biology.

Her eventual release is due not to any confession or narrative she weaves but to institutional observations of her 'exemplary conduct' (p. 483). And at the end of the novel, neither Grace nor the reader knows what the future holds: whether her story ends with birth or death depends on whether she has a foetus inside her or the same kind of tumour that killed her mother. Even if it is a foetus, her comments on the bed remind the reader how closely linked birth and death were at that time. In spite of finding herself subject to those biological imperatives so central to discourses of femininity, Grace nevertheless refuses to be interpellated as a guilty subject within those discourses. Remaining an enigma, 'alias Grace', to both her confessors and the reader, and thwarting the search for any 'real' Grace by inquisitors like Dr Jordan, Grace's story therefore bears testimony both to the power of gender discourse and the determining force of biology for women of the Victorian period, and to the possibility of the individual subject challenging, if not entirely transcending, that power.

Criminal influence: Sarah Waters, *Affinity*

Like *Alias Grace*, Sarah Waters' novel *Affinity*[27] explores the perceived relationship between female criminality, class and sexuality in the Victorian period. Set in Britain in the 1870s, this novel – like Atwood's – deals with a young woman prisoner visited by a representative of the middle classes who is expected to exert an improving influence. As Ingham puts it, 'the gravity of female criminality [...] was usually seen to involve what were called "crimes of morality" and was measured by the failure of working-class women to live up to the middle-class model' (p. 26). Both visitors, however, increasingly find themselves under the influence of the prisoner. The purpose of their visits is therefore subverted by forces which threaten Victorian gender ideology.[28] Female sexuality is the force that undermines Dr Jordan's authority, but in *Affinity* the increasing popularity of spiritualism, and the power of female friendship provide the threat. For Margaret Prior, the lady visitor, is bound to the prisoner Selina Dawes by an 'affinity' which threatens the heterosexual norms of Victorian society. When Margaret imagines introducing Selina to her family, she wonders what would frighten them most: 'her being a spirit-medium, or a convict, or a girl' (p. 315).

Both novels suggest that most of the female prison population are victims of poverty and sexual exploitation. And *Affinity*, like *Alias Grace*, depicts a prison system which not only punishes those women by depriving them of their freedom, but imposes forms of surveillance which will lead the prisoners to interiorise that sense of guilt which will turn them into 'proper' women. Waters describes the prison building in terms similar to Jeremy Bentham's panopticon, designed to ensure every prisoner could always be seen without knowing when:[29] 'The tower is set at the centre of the pentagon yards, so that the view from it is all of the walls and barred windows that make up the interior face of the women's building' (p. 10). Furthermore, the inspection flap, which the prisoners call 'the eye', in their cell doors makes it possible for them to be observed more closely at any time. This degree of surveillance is not simply intended to deter anti-social behaviour but is itself a form of punishment. Selina understands that the fact that all the world may look at her is a declaration that she has lost all right to privacy. Visitors may even watch the new intake taking their baths. Such observation is intended to encourage introspection, leading to repentance.

The prison regime and its high levels of surveillance are equally, however, intended to prevent the development of close emotional ties within its female population. All communication between the women, spoken or written, is forbidden, ostensibly to prevent any conspiratorial activities, and to deprive the prisoners of any comfort that might alleviate the harshness of their punishment. But there is also a continuous if unspoken hint that something even more dangerous, something illicitly sexual, might develop. Outside the prison, intimate female friendship was generally held in high esteem, as a valuable source of support, particularly for women involved in the responsibilities of marriage and children. Lillian Faderman relates this view to Cott's theory of 'passionlessness' discussed earlier in this study:

> Since middle and upper-class women were separated from men not only in their daily occupations, but in their spiritual and leisure interests as well, outside of the practical necessities of raising a family there was little that tied the sexes together. But with other females a woman inhabited the same sphere, and she could be entirely trusting and unrestrained. She could share sentiment, her heart – all emotions that manly males had to repress in favour of 'rationality' – with another female. And regardless of the intensity of the feeling that might develop between them, they need not attribute it to the demon, sexuality, since women supposedly had none. (Faderman, p. 159)[30]

Since sexual relationships between women were not at this time publicly acknowledged to be possible, they were not criminalised. Nevertheless, the *Oxford English Dictionary* dates the first recorded use of the word 'lesbianism' as 1870, when A.J. Munby described it in his diary as 'equally loathsome' as sodomy. Miss Ridley's invitation to Margaret to watch the women bathing certainly has salacious undertones, as she reacts to Margaret's refusal with 'a sour kind of satisfaction, or amusement' (p. 80) at Margaret's possible discomfort over the sexual implications of such an act. Clearly a distinction is being suggested between the asexual 'lady' of Victorian ideology and the women of lower classes.

Among single women of all classes, however, such intense same-sex relationships, however chaste, represented a threat to patriarchy, particularly given the growing numbers of 'surplus women' as the century progressed. Faced with such competition, a young woman could not afford to be distracted from her proper goals of marriage and motherhood. Margaret, having lost her dearly loved friend Helen through marriage to her brother Stephen, later realises how carefully her own mother had been watching this relationship for signs that it was too close. And as she becomes more involved in the world of the prison, the distinctions assumed to exist between the lady visitor and the criminal are increasingly broken down, based as they are on these false ideologies of class and gender.

Ironically, some erosion of those distinctions was the function of lady visitors, because it was thought that even the thoughts and feelings of the prisoners, which surveillance could not penetrate, could be brought to conform to proper moral standards through example. As Mr Shillitoe, the prison governor, comments:

> Those poor unguarded hearts, they were like children's hearts, or savages' – they were impressible. [. . .] Let them see the miserable contrast between her speech, her manners, and their own poor ways, and they will grow meek, they will grow softened and subdued. (p. 11)

This view of the female criminal's susceptibility to influence is closely related to the Darwinian view of woman as the less evolved of the sexes, closer to the child or more 'primitive' races than the adult male. As a corollary, she is also thought likely to have become a criminal because of bad influences, the defence which saves Grace from the gallows. Margaret nevertheless resists such a view of Selina, on the grounds that her lack of correspondence with the outside world makes it unlikely that she is serving her sentence to protect a lover.

It is instead Selina who is the active influence. Margaret's belief in Selina's innocence, together with her own vulnerability, makes it inevitable that it should be the lady who comes under the prisoner's influence, rather than vice versa. Already 'under the influence' of chloral, an addictive sedative, her prison visiting is intended as a form of therapy after her suicide attempt following her father's death – and the loss of Helen, which she cannot so easily acknowledge. Selina therefore quickly fills the emotional and spiritual vacuum left in the life of this typical surplus woman. Initially encountered simply as a sigh, a hardly material presence, on first sight she reminds Margaret of 'a saint or an angel in a painting of Crivelli's', with 'something rather devotional about her pose, the stillness' (p. 27), a first impression which ultimately proves as misleading as Dr Jordan's image of Grace as a penitential martyr. Selina moreover offers herself as a confidante, a safe repository for those secret thoughts and desires which are otherwise confined to Margaret's diary: she suggests that Margaret 'might as well say [her] closest thoughts there, in her cell. Who did she have, to pass them on to?' (p. 111). And the notebook in turn provides the earliest evidence of Selina's growing influence: '*Selina* – she is making me write the name here, she is growing more real, more solid and quick, with every stroking of the nib across the page – *Selina*' (p. 117).

That influence has two sources, both potentially subversive of class distinctions. Selina's 'private sittings' as a spiritualist medium, according to the prosecutor at her trial, placed her in a position 'to exercise considerable influence over [her] lady sitters' (p. 145), although Selina defends this influence as a kind of spiritual healing. Margaret readily believes that her father communicates with her through Selina, dissuading her from thinking again of joining him through suicide. She interprets the mysterious 'tokens' that appear in her room at night as evidence of 'a quivering cord of dark matter', through which Selina herself will eventually escape the confines of her prison cell and come to her. Although she observes that the 'cord' is thickest at night when she takes laudanum, she does not perceive the possible cause and effect that becomes increasingly apparent to the reader. The possibility that Margaret is indeed suffering from hysteria is suggested when she has delusions about her brother wanting her medicine so that Selina will come to him too.

Selina's role as a spirit-medium also demonstrates that spiritualism can be a transgressive outlet for repressed female desire, as the following chapter will show in more detail. Her séances cater particularly for the emotional and physical yearnings of female clients, allowing ladies to enjoy 'spirit' kisses and physical 'comfort' in a manner which would otherwise be unthinkable. The wealthy Mrs Brink takes her into her own home so that Selina can unite her with the spirit of her dead mother, but her deepest desire is for physical contact: going to her employer's bedroom every night, Selina records in her diary that 'each night, she grows fiercer, she draws [Selina] nearer to her, saying "Will you come, O! Won't you come a little nearer? Do you know me? Will you kiss me?"' (p. 173). And Selina's spiritualist activities often involve 'immodest' acts. One of the most damaging allegations made at her trial is that Selina asked Madeleine Silvester, the alleged victim of her assault, to strip down to her petticoats, and did the same herself.

If spiritualism is an outlet for female desire, in this novel it serves more specifically as an outlet for same-sex desire, the second source of Selina's influence over Margaret, and arguably the central, though unspoken, form of 'deviance' in *Affinity*.[31] The representation of same-sex relationships is, however, highly ambiguous, as a result of the narrative's coded treatment of them. When Mrs Brink dies of a heart attack, the prosecution argues that this was caused by the shock of seeing Selina attack Madeleine. But Mrs Brink's final words, 'Not her, too?' (p. 2), possess considerable ambiguity. Are they an instinctive response of disappointment and jealousy that Selina also has an intimate relationship with Madeleine? Or has the bright light falling on the white legs and half-hidden face of 'Peter Quick', Selina's spirit-guide, revealed the truth – that the spirit-guide is in fact Ruth, Mrs Brink's own maid? In this case, Mrs Brink's reaction could express her realisation that Selina, too, is a fake, and in intimate collusion with Ruth. There is no way of determining her meaning from the text, but the overt sensuality of Mrs Brink's desires is given sexual overtones by some of the language used.[32] Selina describes Mrs Brink's voice as 'high & changed'; it seemed to 'have a hook upon it. I felt it begin to draw at me, finally it seemed to draw the very dress from off my back' (p. 173).

Margaret's representation of her own feelings in her diary appear to be less a case of deliberate obfuscation than a case of innocence or repression. Her early diary entries speak readily of her love for Helen, suggesting nothing shameful about her feelings, which belong to the tradition of passionate friendship evident in so many letters between Victorian women. As Faderman puts it, women saw the intensity of their feelings as 'an effusion of the spirit' (p. 159), and Margaret concurs that it is 'only love'. She is clearly not, however, innocent – in the sense of ignorant – of less legitimate feelings, the 'something gross and wrong' (p. 316) from which she insists on distancing herself. When the matron, Miss Manning, describes a pair of prisoners as 'pals [...] worse than any sweethearts', Margaret is disturbed to find the word 'pals' has '*that* particular meaning', and that she came close to acting as a go-between for the couple's 'dark passion' (p. 67).[33] She resists seeing either herself or Selina in such terms, convinced that 'no prisoner ever sought to make a *pal*' (p. 82) of Selina. Nevertheless the erotic potential of her relationship with both Selina and Helen is evident. Selina revives in Margaret the 'naked *Aurora* self' (p. 242)[34] she used to be with Helen, and which she invokes when she cries to her old friend, 'Don't go too near the bed! Don't you know it's haunted, by our old kisses? They'll come and frighten you' (p. 204).

Selina, moreover, helps Margaret to encode her desire in unworldly terms through the discourse of spiritualism, central to which is the concept of affinity. The *Oxford English Dictionary* entry for the term includes a quotation of 1868: 'All these Spiritualists accept the doctrine of special affinities between man and woman; affinities which imply a spiritual relation of the sexes higher and holier than that of marriage.' Margaret is persuaded by Selina's rhetoric that she is her 'affinity', because Selina uses that terminology to sanction same-sex love. In the afterlife, she explains, sexual identity will be discarded, so that each spirit will be free to return to its true partner, its 'affinity': 'we will all return to that piece of shining matter from which [our] souls were torn with another, two halves of the same'.[35] Since spirits transcend gender, they may find their 'affinity' in someone they would not expect to couple with while alive, someone kept from them 'by some false boundary' (p. 210). Selina is implicitly referring to the boundary of sexual difference enforced by what Adrienne Rich calls 'compulsory heterosexuality'.[36] Her arguments offer, moreover, a new reading of evolution which enables women to breach the gap between themselves and men by, in effect, ceasing to be women, by leaving their bodies behind. When Margaret laments the fact that she herself has not 'evolved' to the mature female condition of matrimony, Selina argues that for women to do what they have always done is for them to remain unevolved: 'it was doing the same thing always that kept us "bound to the earth;" [...] we were made to rise from it, but would never do that until we *changed*' (p. 209). Only when spirits realise, after death, that they have no gender can they be 'taken higher' (p. 210). As Margaret grows increasingly disturbed in her imaginings and emotionally dependent on Selina, she takes her feeling that she is 'growing subtle, insubstantial' as evidence that she is thus '*evolving*', becoming her own ghost (p. 289).

But if Margaret's diary entries are full of ambiguity and possible evasion, so too are Selina's. Some of her entries admit to learning the tricks of the spiritualist trade, such as how to make an object luminous, or prevent flowers from fading, although she tells Margaret that such deceptions were sometimes necessary to convince the sceptics. But her diary usually represents her experiences as genuine. Some cases could be put down to intelligent insight, such as when she 'sees' that a woman mourning the loss of her babies is going to lose two more, and some could be attributed to emotional and psychological pressures: her accounts of her attempts to raise the spirit of Mrs Brink's mother show the pressure on Selina to please a patroness who has rescued her from a miserable and economically uncertain future. Given the intensity of Mrs Brink's desire to believe, and the more knowing collusion of Ruth, testifying to the 'queer perfume' in the room (p. 173), this pressure may have enabled her to believe in her own powers.

Most problematic is her consistent attributing of any 'rough' or indecent behaviour to the spirit, Peter Quick. The lady that Margaret meets at the spiritualist library testifies both to Peter's roughness, and to his tendency to focus on the ladies. Since Selina has 'the face of an angel' (p. 153), any alleged impropriety is easily displaced onto this spirit which also abuses her, and her description of his first appearance suggests she is herself the victim of deception:

> Then it was not at all as I had thought it would be, there was a *man* there, I must write *his great arms, his black whiskers, his red lips.* I looked at him & I trembled, & I said in a whisper 'O God, are you real?' He heard my shaking voice & then his brow went smooth as water, & he smiled & nodded. Mrs Brink called 'What is it Miss Dawes, who is there?' I said 'I don't know what I should say' and he bent and put his mouth very close to my ear, saying 'Say it is your master.' (p. 193)

With hindsight, the reader can piece together a possible scenario in which Selina, expecting Ruth to appear as a spirit manifestation, is unprepared for her to appear as a man, as her emphasis suggests, so that she wonders – if only momentarily – whether the 'spirit' is real. The rest of the passage shows her seeking direction from 'Peter', a request which makes more sense once interpreted as a plea directed to Ruth, who is controlling the whole event. On first reading, however, the situation is, I would argue, far less clear, and the reader is faced with the choice of believing that Selina persuaded herself of his existence, or that she was aware of being involved in a hoax: either Selina is unable to acknowledge to herself that the 'powers' which make her unique and sought after are non-existent, or her diaries are a deliberate fabrication.

These difficulties of interpretation are arguably due, again, to the element of coding surrounding the representation of same-sex relationships, and particularly the figure of Peter Quick. While the behaviour of this male spirit-guide may be shockingly intimate, such behaviour in a female spirit-guide might be even more disturbing in a period beginning to acknowledge the possibility of sexual relationships between women. Once the reader becomes aware that 'Peter' is in fact Ruth, it becomes clear that 'his' behaviour breaches not only the bounds of permissible behaviour, but also the boundaries of heterosexuality. Later in her diary Selina continues to write as if Peter were real, but merely records what was said and done, rather than recording her feelings, as if half-conscious that her relations with Mrs Brink and her other clients may be illicit, and that she may one day need to defend her increasingly erotic activities by attributing them to Peter, who may be an unruly spirit, but has at least the merit of being male. The passionate nature of her attachment to Ruth is only revealed much later in the novel, although there are hints easily registered on second reading. Selina notes Ruth's ability to move like a ghost, which she puts to good use to move around unnoticed in the darkness of a séance. And after Peter's first manifestation, Ruth's brief 'Good girl' (p. 195), directed to Selina, suggests a not entirely detached approval. This suspicion is confirmed by a later dialogue with a new client, Miss d'Esterre, in which Ruth clearly takes the lead. Selina's defence of her behaviour to Margaret is a coded version of the truth, once we understand 'Peter' to be Ruth: Peter is 'her guardian, her familiar-spirit. He was her *control*. "He came for me, [...] and – what could I do then? I was his"' (p. 166). In spite of her humble origins, it is ironically Ruth who turns out to be the most powerful influence in the novel.

If Selina's diaries are a deliberate fabrication, then the novel completely subverts the convention that diaries provide insight into a character's truest and most secret thoughts and feelings, those that cannot be articulated elsewhere. Like Grace's interior monologue, they undermine the basic assumption of realist fiction that language is a medium which can convey fact, the truth, one of the assumptions also of Victorian science. Waters plays with those conventions and the expectations the reader brings to the diary form. Margaret's entries apparently conform to them, explicitly describing her current diary as a repository for those things she cannot or does not want to discuss with her family, and her previous diary as a record of the 'twisting thoughts' (p. 30) arising from her feelings for Helen, repeated later in similar 'twistings' about Selina. Since women's voices are, in Margaret's words, 'so easily stifled' (p. 229), diaries might seem to be guaranteed a kind of authenticity as the expression of a woman's subjectivity. I have argued, however, that Margaret's diary is characterised by evasion and ambiguity, and Selina's diary of her career in spiritualism provides no more of a confession than Grace's monologue. But, as in Grace's case, there is a rationale for such evasion. Conscious of what the exposure of her involvement in spiritualist fakery would mean, Selina has every reason for concealment in her diary in case of discovery. As Grace tells Jordan, servants know far more about their employers than their employers know about them, having access to the household's most intimate places and acts. Ruth exploits her knowledge of the contents of Margaret's diary while employed as a maid in Margaret's home. And Selina is far less ignorant of the activities of the lower classes than Margaret.

If Selina increasingly withholds her thoughts and feelings even from her diary, this suggests she is aware that they are transgressive, and that she needs to censor her self-representation. And there is evidence towards the end of her narrative that she is more consciously involved in deceit, since she is sufficiently in control herself to recruit unhappy young women as new spirit-mediums. Both her diary and Margaret's are narratives of intense personal change, and of revelation. The element of mystery and ambiguity preceding those revelations is, however, sustained by the novel's construction, which enables Waters to simultaneously hint and mystify to the very end. The novel is structured around parallel narratives – Selina's, describing her experiences as a medium between 1872 and 1873, before her imprisonment, and Margaret's, recounting her meetings with Selina in prison from 1874 to 1875. The reader therefore only learns the whole story as Margaret does, becoming to some extent caught up in the process of seduction to which Margaret is subjected, although the late twentieth-century reader, standing outside the narrative and reading Selina's diary in parallel, is likely to feel more scepticism about Selina.

These parallel narratives have, however, another important effect, which is to suggest that Selina is as much a victim of influence as Margaret. Selina is enthralled and arguably manipulated by Ruth, before she in turn enthrals and manipulates Margaret, using Margaret's desire for freedom from an emotional and intellectual prison to escape from her own very real imprisonment. Margaret realises 'with a kind of horror' (p. 309) how totally dependent she has become on Selina: putting on the velvet collar which attached Selina to her chair during séances, she feels herself pulled by Selina through the thread attached to it. But Selina is herself subjected to a similar kind of possession: the very last words of the novel, directed to Selina as she goes to satisfy Mrs Brink's needs, come from Ruth herself: 'Remember [...] whose girl you are' (p. 351).

The passion Margaret imagines Selina and Ruth sharing is the passion she herself feels. The fear and uncertainty that we detect in Selina's early diary entries are echoed in Margaret's. If there is a gap between the Selina of these entries and the Selina of Margaret's diaries, this is the product of bitter experience. Becoming the object of 'influence' – that is perhaps the true basis of the 'affinity' between them.

For by the end of the novel, Margaret realises there were no spirits, only her own longing, so that she is left facing a future so bleak that she refuses it. Her final suicidal thoughts are directed at Selina: 'Your twisting is done – you have the last thread of my heart. I wonder: when the thread grows slack, will you feel it?' (p. 351). But while the 'affinities' of spiritualism prove illusory, the concept of affinity emphasised in the novel's title is shown to be very real. Margaret's feelings for Selina are originally based on a sense of identification powerful enough to transcend the usual rigid distinctions of class, of guilt and innocence, because Selina continually forces Margaret to admit, 'You are like me' (p. 82). When Margaret asks her what she thinks of the prison, Selina replies, 'What would *you* make of it?', challenging Margaret to put herself in Selina's shoes and abandon the idea that the prisoners are essentially different from ladies like her. And Margaret does feel a strong sense of identity with those women who have attempted self-harm or even suicide, shocking a family dinner party by commenting on the arbitrary separation of the two groups of women: 'Don't you think that queer? That a common coarse-featured woman might drink morphia and be sent to gaol for it, while I am saved and sent to visit her – and all because I am a *lady*' (p. 254). The full extent of her identification with Selina becomes evident when Margaret sits in her closet in darkness. Trying to free herself from her clothes, she instead feels as if a screw is being tightened, an allusion to the straightjacket that Selina was forced to wear in the punishment cell; she feels she is with Selina, in the cell, but she is also re-enacting those moments Selina spent in a cupboard during her séances, feeling Selina's velvet collar around her neck, so that she in effect becomes Selina at this point. Although the novel's plot demonstrates Margaret's destruction through the abuse of this 'affinity', its parallel narratives and its exploration of same-sex relationships suggest an identity between vulnerable women that could ultimately become a source of strength. The possibility that women might bond with each other in the fight against patriarchy and its constraints was indeed the cause of growing anxiety as the nineteenth century advanced, an anxiety that is exuberantly defied in the novels discussed in Chapter 5.

4
Subversive Spirits: Spiritualism and Female Desire

The relationship between the female body and the spirit or 'word', divinely inspired, has always been problematic in patriarchal thinking, and the first chapter of this book indicated some of the religious and scientific arguments used in the nineteenth century to explain the perceived conflict between them. The world of spiritualism, however, as practised in late Victorian society, was one area of 'religious' experience in which women were able to participate actively, since it was commonly held that women were particularly gifted at communicating with the dead. Spiritualism, after all, began in 1848 in the home of two young American girls, Kate and Maggie Fox, who became famous as spirit-mediums. From there it spread to Europe, with the help of the popular press, largely through female mediumship, which became an often profitable career for middle-class and, occasionally, working-class women. Yet the nature and meaning of their participation are highly ambivalent. On the one hand, it appears to indicate that women can possess spiritual powers; on the other, it can be argued that the female medium is, as the term suggests, merely a passive vehicle, her body being used by the spirit messenger, just as the Virgin Mary was the vehicle for the Word of God made flesh. For Sir Arthur Conan Doyle, the novelist, the ideal medium was the stereotypical ideal Victorian woman – of relatively low intelligence, passive, innocent, intuitive and naïve. He writes, 'The clean slate is certainly most apt for the writing of a message.'[1] The novelists discussed in this chapter – Victoria Glendinning, A.S. Byatt and Michèle Roberts – clearly recognise that the ambivalence surrounding female mediumship is symptomatic of the contradictions arising out of both religious and scientific discourse about gender in this period. Their work contributes a fictional exploration of Victorian spiritualism to the analysis that has been carried out by feminist historians, and provides a less negative view of the phenomenon than that conveyed by *Affinity*. In their novels the female medium is a potentially subversive figure who, under the guise of acting as a medium for the words of others, breaches the constraints conventionally imposed on where, how and of what women may speak.

On the surface the medium appears to be a far from subversive figure, since spiritualism feeds on and reinforces very conventional images of femininity. A medium is, in the first place, a passive figure, whose role is to be receptive, and to transmit without distortion the voices of others. Furthermore she is frequently characterised as highly emotional, and even given to hysteria, particularly by critics of spiritualism, using terms all too familiar in nineteenth-century accounts of female psychology. Alex Owen, in her authoritative study of women's involvement in spiritualism, makes the point clearly:

> mediumship interacted with, and to some extent dramatised, pre-scriptive notions of femininity and female sexuality. A medium gave herself, sacrificed her 'self' to another. The possessed woman was inert, inactive, never responsible. [...] An activity which emphasised the centrality of the medium and the importance of the utterance rested on the assumption that it was not she who was the speaking and acting subject.[2]

And yet, the medium's surrender to possession by a spirit paradoxically grants her immense power – not only the power to cross the barriers between the living and the dead, but also the power to influence the beliefs and feelings of the living. As mediums, women were able to participate in the public sphere far more than was usually acceptable for respectable women. And although the voice with which the medium speaks is not her own – or rather, because the voice is not her own – she is able to transgress the prescribed female ideal without ever herself being culpable. To quote Owen again, 'Within the séance, and in the name of spirit possession, women openly and flagrantly transgressed gender norms. Female mediums, with the approval of those present, often assumed a male role and sometimes also a trance persona which was at total odds with the Victorian ideal of respectable womanhood' (p. 11).

The relationship between spiritualism and science is equally ambivalent. While conventional Christianity was felt by many to be under threat from nineteenth-century science, many spiritualists believed their practices

were a form of science, providing evidence for the afterlife. The paradoxical concept of 'spirit matter', which enabled spirits to materialise
and take on human form, was seen as the kind of proof which could
ultimately be verified by science, and the Society for Psychical Research
was consequently established in 1882 specifically to establish whether
such scientific proof of the spirit world could be found.[3] The female
medium could then be seen both as a highly spiritual being, and as an
object of scientific enquiry who could readily be restored to her 'natural'
place in the order of things by means of 'scientific' gender theory.

Through looking back at Victorian spiritualism from the perspectives
of twentieth-century feminist thought, Glendinning, Byatt and Roberts
highlight this ambivalence. In addition they use spiritualism as both an
expression of and a metaphor for female desire. Along with those Victorian
scientists who sought a psychological explanation for spiritualism,[4]
these novelists recognise that the experiences of the medium and her
audience might have their origins in the unconscious and its repressed
desires. For in addition to an acknowledged desire for contact with the
dead beloved, a desire so strong that several people at a séance might
claim a single manifestation as their own, these desires might relate more
covertly to female sexuality, since, in Owen's words, 'the very vocabulary
of trance mediumship oozed sexuality. Mediums surrendered and then
were entered, seized, possessed by another' (p. 218). The desire for some
manifestation of the body or voice of the beloved was apparently
achievable only through the mediation of another human body, rather
than through prayers to the divine, so that the practice of spiritualism
legitimated the body, female as well as male, in a way that runs contrary to
most religious thinking of the period. Séances themselves, moreover,
made sexual intrigue and the breaching of the usual norms of decorum
possible through the physical intimacy of linked hands and healing
touches, usually in darkness or candlelight. In Victoria Glendinning's
Electricity spiritualism does not occupy as central a role as it does in
Byatt's novella, but it nevertheless articulates the discursive relationships
between science and desire which feed into spiritualism. In *The Conjugial
Angel* the context for spiritualism is primarily literary. The novella
explores the means by which women become trapped in a Romantic
discourse of femininity which can impose a kind of living death upon
them, in which the world of the dead can seem equally real and powerful.
Finally, *In the Red Kitchen* highlights Victorian views of woman, and
particularly the female medium, as always the potential hysteric, but by
using spiritualism to link past and present, suggests the continuing
power of such gender constructions. Through analysing each author's

use of spiritualism to explore late nineteenth-century ideas of femininity in these different contexts, I hope to show how powerfully scientific, religious and literary discourses reinforced each other in matters of gender.

'Power words': Victoria Glendinning, *Electricity*

'Electricity' is in the literal sense one of the most obvious of 'power words'. But in Victoria Glendinning's novel of that name the heroine and narrator, Charlotte Mortimer, is not referring to electricity when she uses that phrase. She uses the phrase 'power words' to describe the language used by her doctor-relative Sir Bullingdon Huff. The doctor–patient relationship has often been used in women's writing – notably in Gilman's *The Yellow Wallpaper* – as a paradigm of male–female relationships in patriarchal society. In such texts the power that men possess over women is seen as not being limited to their right to prescribe what women may or may not do; they assert the more fundamental prerogative of diagnosing what women are, or should be. The medical profession thus exemplifies the mechanisms by which language sustains male authority. But in *Electricity*,[5] published one hundred years later, medical discourse is only one of the discourses competing to interpret experience and exercise power.[6] But while there appears to be an opposition between scientific discourse, including medicine, and the discourse of spiritualism – an opposition based on the conflict between scientific materialism and spirituality – it becomes evident that the worlds of science and spiritualism share a language, although they deploy it in different ways that are also gendered.

The novel is set in the 1880s, a time when the practical application of electricity in the home, in the form of electric lighting, was gaining momentum, following the invention of the incandescent lamp by Thomas Edison in 1879, and his construction of the first power station and distribution system in New York City in 1881.[7] The electric telegraph and the telephone had already transformed communications, and electric lighting threatened to transform people's perceptions similarly, as Charlotte observes: 'it conceals as much as it reveals. Everything is made significant, so nothing is' (p. 164). The novel also conveys the political and social unrest characteristic of the period, referring to the fear generated by Fenian bombings, and the debates over female suffrage, education and emancipation. Evidence that some of the professions were opening up to women is provided by Miss Marks, research assistant to Professor Ayrton, whose classes in electrical engineering Charlotte's fiancé, Peter Fisher, attends.[8] But such evidence of social transformation is merely used to reinforce prevailing gender ideologies: according to the family physician, women are constitutionally unfit for the fast-moving pace of modern life, so have greater need than ever to keep to their proper sphere. Even Charlotte herself, although restless and free-thinking, takes a conventional route through these contesting ideologies, choosing marriage rather than further education and the possibility of a profession. Although hoping to 'invent' herself (p. 43), she fears she has already been 're-invented' by her Aunt Susannah, who encourages her marriage, and by Peter himself.

Peter is particularly well placed to re-invent, since he is an electrical engineer, one of the new breed of professionals working with the technologies to which recent scientific discoveries gave rise, without themselves being scientists. But electricity means more to Peter than a livelihood; it provides a materialist explanation of all existence, since it is 'something that is present all of the time, an ingredient of all matter, of absolutely everything that is in the universe' (p. 10). The views he expresses here and elsewhere in the novel reflect two discoveries of the period. James Clerk Maxwell's equations published in 1864, which have been described as 'the major achievement of the period in physics' (Bernal, p. 567), united electrical, magnetic and optical phenomenon in a single universal force, electromagnetism, showing that all forces of Nature were related. Similarly the Law of the Conservation of Energy, which Bernal describes as the greatest physical discovery of the mid-nineteenth century (p. 588), established that energy cannot be created or destroyed, only changed in form, providing a principle of unification for all forms of energy.

To represent accurately this unseen force, observable only in its effects, post-Cartesian science has used mathematical symbols and equations, diagrams and chemical formulae. To represent it verbally, metaphor has to be employed, but those metaphors enable materialist interpretations to blur into an almost mystical view of life. Peter's own language incorporates both scientific and religious discourse which is itself metaphoric:

> God is power, is creation and destruction, is energy, is the divine spark, is the prime mover, is the Light of the World. [. . .] Lighten our darkness, we beseech Thee, O Lord. God is electricity. Electricity is God. [. . .] What if he isn't a He but the Thing itself? The unseen force. (pp. 24–5)

As Charlotte observes, 'He might have given up his religion, but he had found a new one' (p. 26). Peter envisions science as the religion of the future, filling the void created by scientific challenges to the Genesis account of creation and the new biblical criticism in what is often called the age of doubt. He describes power stations as 'the cathedrals of the future' (p. 159). Charlotte sardonically likens the day on which Peter will switch on the lights at Morrow Hall to 'the first day of creation: "Let there be light"' (p. 135), with Peter in the role of God. And Peter Fisher, whose name makes him sound like a New Testament evangelist, appropriately becomes the new religion's martyr when he is killed by electric shock while mending a faulty arc light.

This new 'religion', like the old, is administered almost exclusively by male 'priests'. And like the traditional priesthood, Peter desires converts who will share his belief in the monolithic truth of his vision of matter as everything. Charlotte appears to be just such a convert, admitting she has parroted what she has learned from him to Lord Godwin, Peter's first employer.[9] Even after Peter's death, she asserts that 'all matter is mere matter [...]. The lunacy of humanity is in believing that matter matters' (p. 244). But her punning use of language suggests her instinctive resistance to his 'monotheism'. When Peter tries to teach her technical terminology, she exploits the pluralistic significance of what he admits to be metaphors to create meanings other than those which he intends. Meaning therefore continually evades his control. While he believes he is preaching the gospel of science, Charlotte is hearing the language of love. When he talks of the sparks that fly from bodies that have been excited by touch, or, as the *Oxford English Dictionary* puts it, 'the state of excitation produced in such bodies by friction', she interprets his words in terms of human attraction.[10] She appropriates his terminology to describe 'his obsession with his science [as] in itself magnetic' (p. 25). He is, in fact, her 'metaphor' (p. 27) – a means to something beyond himself, which a woman cannot reach by direct means. Peter dismisses her interpretations as nonsense, typical of half-educated women, because they subvert his desire to impose his scientific vision upon her in clearly defined, closed terms.

There is, however, one discourse in the novel which assumes the characteristics of both scientific and religious thought – the discourse of spiritualism. The first séance Charlotte attends is organised by the Reverend Moss, whose wife informs her that spiritualism is a 'supplement to our holy religion. It enlarges the place in which the mind and spirit may range. It opens a special door into Heaven. [...] Christianity has its origins in psychic phenomena' (p. 145). The rituals of the séance have a church-like solemnity to them, requiring the same suspension of disbelief as those of the Mass which transforms wine into the blood of Christ.

At the same time, spiritualism shows parallels with Peter's 'religion' of science. Although Charlotte describes it as a 'search for effects', and therefore the opposite of science, which Peter describes as a 'search for causes' (p. 155), both spiritualism and electricity involve the operation of unseen forces, so are in a sense known by their 'effects'. Both are, moreover, described as forms of energy, relying on a conductor for the energy to flow. The medium, the conductor of the energy flow in the séance, herself needs 'psychic energy' (p. 146) in order for spiritual manifestations to occur. When Godwin, who becomes Charlotte's lover, describes the medium as 'the magnetic link between the sitters and the spirit world [...] a medium of communication' (p. 137), Charlotte points out that this is also how Peter describes electricity. The reference to magnetism is a reminder of how close were the links in many minds between the new 'sciences' of electricity, magnetism, mesmerism and spiritualism. And the principles which are so central to Peter's vision were seized on by spiritualists as providing support for their interpretation of the world: if energy is never destroyed, then it must continue to exist after death, they argued. And if everything can be reduced to matter, then surely the immortal soul, whose existence was guaranteed by the established church, can manifest itself in material form. The discursive link is made most forcefully in the novel by the seating arrangements for the séance, indicated in a diagram resembling an electrical circuit: people designated as negative-passives are seated alternating with those designated as positive-active, the former being the 'best conductors for spirit messages' (p. 154).

According to Godwin, however, it is not appropriate to try to prove the existence of the spirit world by scientific means, since spiritualism and science relate to different orders of experience: 'Occult phenomenon operate according to a different logic.' And he accurately identifies the source of conflict between science and spiritualism as a discursive one: 'People long to identify one final explanation of life. It would be so nice and tidy' (p. 138). The central issue here is the role of language in structuring our understanding and evaluation of experience. Peter wants to apply a single discourse to existence – that of scientific materialism – insisting that 'all events, whether physical or mental, are phenomena of matter' (p. 138), a view which many neurosurgeons today would support. He is impatient with the language of the paranormal, since terms like 'telepathy', 'clairvoyance' and 'resurrection' are inexact and unscientific, failing to explain the material bases of the processes they signify. But he admits that words like 'current' and 'flow' when applied to electricity are metaphors, the language of the familiar being used by scientists to designate the totally unfamiliar. Lay people are thus able to talk about science, although in the process they may blur distinctions crucial to scientists as they shift in and out of legitimate scientific discourse and the discourse of pseudo-science. Speaking of his wife's fear that animals would be killed if they grazed below electric wires, Charlotte's father comments, 'It's the magnetic fluid, isn't it? [...] People with the power cure diseases that way. Animal magnetism. [...] Mesmerism and all that' (p. 9). In spite of such confusions, Peter acknowledges that 'metaphors are ways of getting nearer truths' (p. 24), although he remains single-minded in his belief in metaphors being reducible to single meanings, and in a single truth: science will provide the key to unite all experience.

These questions of nomenclature and interpretation are, moreover, related to the question of who is empowered to name, revealing ideological conflicts at work. The differences between Peter's and Godwin's view of life and their discourse are partly determined by class. In Peter's world of technology, electricity means work and a means of achieving success. Godwin is also interested in scientific matters, but distinguishes his interest from his employee's: 'Electricity is Fisher's passion, as I myself am drawn to geology and botany. The inexhaustible lovely face of the earth' (p. 81). His interest in the natural sciences, a common aristocratic leisure pursuit, is partly aesthetic. The difference between Peter and Godwin can best be summed up by the traditional Science/Nature opposition, where science is seen as the analytical process by which man understands and structures the natural world. Where Peter talks of the invisible forces of electricity, a power in Nature only evident in its effects, Godwin is drawn to the 'wordless power of Nature made visible' (p. 172). Godwin loves amethyst because of the 'astonishing interior' (p. 132) revealed when the dull-looking geodes are split open. But his discourse is Romantic in both senses, the language he applies to the natural world paralleling the language of love and seduction, just as that of electricity does: he enjoys 'lovely faces' of all kinds. Godwin insists moreover that 'power is neutral. It knows no values. When we dread the power which transcends us, we call it evil. When we desire union with it, we call it divine' (p. 172). While this may be true in the natural world, the novel makes it clear that, when applied to the human world, power is anything but neutral, which is why the conflict between the discourses in which different kinds of power are inscribed is so intense. When Charlotte expresses her sympathy for Godwin's poor Irish tenants, she challenges a dominant discourse and its ideology, translating Godwin's impersonal language of economic exchange – 'the Irish rents [. . .] paid for the electrical installation, and the re-decorations' – into individual, human and moral terms: 'It did not seem quite right to me that a landlord should buy luxuries with money paid by poor people whom he did not know for the use of land in another country which he never visited' (p. 173). She is aware that his habitual discourse is marked by class, and that her place within that discourse, both as a woman and as the wife of an employee, is a subjected one. When she is introduced to his friends, he suggests she might like to be less impertinent, 'more like other ladies' (p. 145).

Godwin's claim that there are other kinds of power beside electricity – meaning sexual power – is therefore rather ingenuous. Although his seductive language attributes a woman like Charlotte with power, that power is highly circumscribed and unstable, not least because it depends on her ability to arouse male desire. Spiritualism, however, was an area in which, historically speaking, women were able to acquire a certain degree of power. Excluded from professional participation in the church, and denied access to the world of science by their relatively poor educational opportunities, as mediums they could have a public and potentially profitable role. When Charlotte takes up spiritualism as a means of earning a living after Peter's death, she is torn between a scepticism induced by Peter's teaching, and Godwin's faith in an alternative reality. Using the amethyst which was Godwin's gift as a kind of talisman, through which to connect herself to 'unseen forces' that will impart strength, she simultaneously aligns herself with Peter's sense of purpose: 'He had manipulated an invisible force for profit, and I intended to harness a rival force for the same purposes' (p. 191). If Charlotte's career in spiritualism is ultimately a failure, it is because she is herself too susceptible to influence, too much the passive medium, rather than in control of such unseen forces. After her Aunt Susannah's suicide, Susannah speaks through her niece, short-circuiting her, as Charlotte puts it. The presence of this formidable woman, even in spirit form, clearly inhibits Charlotte's response to the needs of her clients. Godwin's amethyst loses its power at this point too, suggesting that the force of Romantic love is also broken by this sceptical presence. And there is an equally decisive live influence – Thaddeus Thompson, one of Charlotte's clients, who embodies the voice of common sense in his refusal to be mystified by either electricity or spiritualism. Giving Charlotte an apple, he remarks, 'Apples keep the spirits away' (p. 223), a light-hearted enough statement which nevertheless predicts – or perhaps even procures – her failure.

Susannah and Thaddeus are intruding on a genuine power, nevertheless, which Charlotte discovers in herself through her career in spiritualism.

Even when that career reaches a disastrous climax in a séance relying entirely on fakery, she believes 'there was a power in that hushed, crowded room' (p. 227). But this is not the power to communicate with the dead, but the power to communicate with the unspoken desires and emotions of the living. The discourse of spiritualism, dealing with the receptivity of the medium, can therefore be replaced by the more modern, 'scientific' language of psychology, or the two can be merged: in Charlotte's words, 'the unconscious mind can make contact with the mind of another if the sensitive completely starves her conscious mind of stimulation, rendering her consciousness as transparent as glass, through which one can see to the deeper levels' (p. 199). But she also sums up her work more simply: 'Concentration, candlelight, sympathy and silence: they have a power of their own' (p. 209). The women who come to her for a dialogue with the dead are really seeking human understanding from the living, and the relief of emptying themselves of secrets to a stranger.

Peter's argument that most of the phenomena associated with spiritualism, such as table-tapping, are the result of the unconscious desires of séance members, does not therefore invalidate the medium's function. That function is moreover subversive, in so far as she is able to offer release to desires previously repressed. For this access to the 'dark' conflicts with the aims and language of both religion and science, in which the metaphors of light and enlightenment are central. Peter's response to talk of the unconscious is itself symptomatic: 'The unconscious mind is a cesspit. It is chaos. It is filth. It is darkness and disorder. It is to be controlled. That is the task of civilisation' (p. 139). Charlotte envisages one of the consequences of the electric age being fear of both silence and darkness: 'Where will the darkness go, driven out of the night sky by the glitter of the city?' (p. 246). She argues that light needs darkness, for while the Gospel of St Luke envisions the body being full of light, 'if there were no surrounding darkness, the incandescence would be invisible' (p. 247). What is driven out and unacknowledged can only give rise to fear.

The result of such repression is particularly evident in the Victorian period in the lives of women. In traditional patriarchal discourse, they have been associated with a darkness which has to be controlled or cured. This is most obvious in the tendency of medical discourse of the period to associate female insanity with sexuality. The point is made forcefully in the novel's most distressing scene by Bullingdon Huff, called in by Godwin to treat Charlotte's depression after Peter's death. His account of sexually abusing little girls in his care on the grounds that, in their madness, they desired it, and that it was a useful medical experiment, may not be typical, but similar views can be found in a number of medical textbooks of the period.[11] He concurs with the family physician consulted by Charlotte before her marriage, who relates the current 'epidemic of female insanity' (p. 118) to too much mental activity and/ or poor morality. Huff cites the scientific view that women are designed primarily for reproduction, so that if reproduction is prevented, they 'run out of control', allowing the 'lower nature' to predominate (p. 180). In Charlotte's case he diagnoses 'a systemic exhaustion of the sexual parts' (p. 179), which could be treated by the application of electric current to the sexual organs.[12] The use of electricity in medicine in this and other ways is only one of the normative and repressive forms of treatment of the mentally ill that Foucault traces in *Madness and Civilisation*,[13] and it suggests the power generated by the collusion of more than one profession sharing the same ideology. The dangers presented by unrestrained female sexuality, like those represented by the growing demand for female suffrage and education, call for strong controls, for which science offers both justification and means.

For ultimately, as Charlotte recognises, control is what her story has been about – the controlling power not only of institutions but of discourse, and the attempts of women to resist it. Aunt Susannah achieves what she wants within the constraints of marriage and family life by exploiting male sexual desire, and extends her limited control over her own body to her own death. 'In control to the end', she kills herself, plugging every orifice in her body so that there will be 'no loss of control' after death (pp. 237–8). But Charlotte also sees the futility of such attempts: 'Control cannot be sustained. How much vital energy is lost in the attempt!' (p. 248). And she has seen Peter die because he is not fully in control of the lethal power of electricity. Ironically, Charlotte feels most thoroughly in control as a medium, a feeling which she likens to a power surge. She clearly differentiates between power experienced as control over others and the power of human emotion, which she is able to tap into when she is most responsive to the feelings of others.

The major problem Charlotte and women like her face is their inability to control any of the discourses which dominate their lives and in which femininity is inscribed. After she meets Thompson, the apple grower, who speaks to her in the 'language of apples', she wishes she had her own language, 'an outside language. Mostly, women do not. Women have the languages of the bed, the kitchen and the nursery. These are indoor, inside languages. [...] Women are grounded birds. We have wings, but do not learn any of the languages necessary for flight' (p. 218). Above all, she has no language for the kind of semi-mystical experiences which constitute some of the most important moments in her life. When, for instance, she finds herself handling the amethyst talisman in a ritualistic way, she has 'no language for telling' why (p. 191). And when Mrs Bagshut tells Charlotte about the 'Borderland' of the spirit world, she uses the same term that Huff uses to describe female insanity, forced to borrow from the discourse of a masculine medical profession which has discredited the term. When Charlotte thinks about the 'Word' in a religious sense, she decides there are now too many words – too many conflicting discourses joggling for power – for it to be heard. And since there was no one around to hear that Word the first time, 'in the beginning' of creation, it would not in any case be recognised now because we can only recognise what we know. That original truth therefore remains unknown, knowable perhaps only in the silence which is also under threat. In so far as women's voices are silenced in this world, they may also represent an as-yet unknown truth.

But the novel ends more optimistically than this statement might imply, ultimately suggesting that women can begin to transcend the difficulties of their situation through language. Unlike Aunt Susannah, Charlotte is saved from thoughts of suicide when she finds the three peacock-patterned notebooks that Godwin has given her so that she can write about herself. The narrative contained in the novel is the product of the experiences it recounts, as represented by Charlotte herself, and the act of writing is a kind of exorcism or liberation, an 'emptying-out' of her memory which enables her to believe she can start afresh, that her 'real life begins now'. She may be 'an unsupported female with no useful connections, no qualifications, and [...] lame' (p. 249), but she is also intelligent and free, able to envision alternative futures. This open-endedness suggests that Charlotte rejects the kind of 'closed systems' embodied in the discourses with which she has wrestled, since these can result in a kind of entropy. The powerful appeal of 'sweet alluring entropy' is evident at the funeral of Charlotte's mother, when a reading from John Donne unites everything for Charlotte: 'Peter's vision of electrical power, Godwin's trust in the cycle of nature, my own belief in the doors that would be opened to me.' Donne's words evoke an image of heaven as the place where there shall be 'no darkness nor dazzling, but one equal light; no noise nor silence, but one equal music; no fears nor hopes, but one equal possession; no ends nor beginnings, but one equal eternity' (p. 115). But while this state has a kind of beauty and harmony which Peter characterises as a 'perfect distribution of all energy' (p. 28), it also threatens an end to the availability of energy, of the creative, driving force of desire, which is ultimately death.[14]

In writing her story, moreover, Charlotte is no longer dictated to by others, written into their discourses, but able to absorb their discourses into her narrative, thus achieving a kind of self-determination. And by showing the overlap between discourses, her eclecticism breaks down these closed systems. As Nicola Humble puts it: 'Charlotte's final triumph over the rationalist discourse of technology is in her use of its images to describe the profound irrationalism of spiritualism. [. . .] In such ways, a masculine discourse of power is transformed to describe a spectacle controlled by women.'[15] In this process Charlotte forges a kind of unity different from that which the more systematised discourses attempt to assert, a unity which includes the emotional and spiritual in a less reductionist way than Peter's scientific materialism demands. In her vision, the material can be a route to the spiritual, instead of subsuming it, or representing its opposite. She uses electricity as a metaphor for human communication, implicitly evoking what Angela Carter terms the electricity of desire[16] to suggest the power of that unseen force to attract the lover to the beloved. When Godwin nicknames Charlotte 'Wirewoman', he therefore unconsciously pays tribute to her ability to connect, and thus carry a new kind of female power and energy.

Gender and poetry: A.S. Byatt, *The Conjugial Angel*

The title of A.S. Byatt's novella, *The Conjugial Angel*,[17] evokes both the image of the angel in the house and the much earlier and very different concept of Emanuel Swedenborg, the eighteenth-century Swedish scientist and theologian, for whom an angel is a 'conjugial' being because it contains both sexes, signifying the marriage of goodness and wisdom. Swedenborgians also envisage an intimate relationship between body and soul, in contrast to the traditional patriarchal view of body and soul as being perpetually in conflict. Swedenborgianism therefore seems to sanction the needs of the body which Victorian women, in particular, were otherwise forced to deny. In her novella, Byatt explores the possibility of spiritualism, under Swedenborgian principles, allowing female desire to speak and to be answered. Like Glendinning, she sets the discourse of spiritualism in the context of more dominant Victorian discourses to explore just how far it does in fact challenge Victorian gender ideologies.

The woman at the centre of the novella, which takes place in 1875, is a historical figure, Emily Jesse. Now the wife of a successful sea captain, Emily was formerly the fiancée of Arthur Hallam, the beloved friend of her brother, Alfred Lord Tennyson, whose most famous poem, *In Memoriam*, was an act of mourning for Hallam. As described by Byatt's medium, Mrs Lilias Papagay, 'Mrs Jesse was the heroine of a tragic story' (p. 173), a story which has trapped her within its discourse since Hallam's death when Emily was only twenty-two. Hallam initially appears to offer her a way out of the 'beloved prison' of her family home, but being released from that 'unpoetic world' (pp. 230–1) into his world of Romance imposes its own constraints. Whereas she has previously imagined herself as 'a wild Byronic heroine' (p. 223), he envisions her as a 'faery' or dryad, meeting her in a Fairy Wood which belongs to the English tradition of Malory or Spenser, or the Greek tradition of sacred groves. Even the sofa on which he first kisses her is, in his letters, 'mixed with Chaucerian sighs out of some ideal Romance' (p. 179). This image of feminine beauty is notably unreal and ethereal, disembodied, as it must be to conform to the stereotype of feminine goodness, devoid of physical desires. For Emily's role in Hallam's Romantic fantasy depends on her conforming not simply to an ideal of feminine beauty, but to an ideal of female morality. Even his love letters are implicit with conditions: 'your faults [...] have in some degree the complexion of virtues, especially when accompanied with humility to confess, and endeavour to amend them' (pp. 230–1).

But, as has already been suggested, the gulf between good and bad women was no greater for the Victorians than the gulf between women and men. As Hallam tells Emily, reproducing neoplatonic beliefs widely held in the period, 'The Mind, the higher Mind, Nous, immerses itself in inert Matter, Hyle, and creates life and beauty. The Nous is male and the Hyle female.' Imbued with the contradictions which characterise Victorian gender ideology, the Romantic heroine is to be on the one hand disembodied, without physical desires, and yet on the other to be nothing but body – matter. Because she is not male, she cannot by definition be possessed of a mind. When Emily challenges such a view, she is told by Hallam that 'women shouldn't busy their pretty heads with all this theorising'. Other sexual differences follow from this basic opposition. As inert, mindless matter, women are essentially passive objects of beauty and goodness, whose purpose is to inspire men to true morality, because, as Hallam puts it: 'women are beautiful [...], and men are mere *lovers* of the beautiful, because women are naturally good and *feel* goodness in the chambers of their sweet hearts as their pure blood goes in and out, and we poor male things only apprehend truth because we are able to *feel* your virtues' (pp. 227–8).

Such a view of women was particularly powerful and fruitful for the poet, since Romantic idealisations of the feminine similarly ground women in the material by linking the maternal to Nature, following the much older precedent embodied in the term 'Mother Nature'. Where the poet is identified with language, and his subjectivity is the subject of the poem, woman/Nature is the object of the poem, providing stimulus for the poet's imagination and emotions, while remaining passive by herself. By projecting his moods or feelings onto woman/Nature, the poet appropriates and possesses woman/Nature. While ostensibly venerated as a spiritual being, woman in this context is inseparable from matter, but since matter here is identified as Nature, attention is displaced from the body and any sexual threat is eliminated. The inheritance of Romanticism continued to be felt in representations of women long after its official 'end' in the 1840s, and is evident in Byatt's representation of Arthur Hallam. Emily figures for him as an essentially static image: he tells her, 'What a picture you make, against the roses. [...] Don't move, I love to see you' (p. 227). She is to be looked at, and provide a muse, stimulating the imagination of the male poet, rather than being productive in any way herself.

But arguably the most damaging consequence of such thinking is not that women are unlike men. The further inference is that they are not fully human. They are denied a soul, as Hallam's comparison of Emily with Undine suggests. Undine is a spirit of the waters, created without a soul, until she marries and bears a human child, which exposes her to all the pains of mortality.[18] To be so unearthly is not to be fully human, and to become human by taking on a sexual and reproductive role is fraught with danger. It is, then, hardly surprising that Emily and the other young women in her secret poetry society should call themselves the Husks, a 'dry, lifeless name' (p. 233) suggesting the lifeless forms to which literary and cultural idealisation of the period reduce such women. Emily recalls that Hallam treated her like 'a mixture of a goddess, a house-angel, a small child and a pet lamb' (p. 218). While petted, protected and even in a sense worshipped, she is not regarded as an adult human being.

Emily's part in this Romance becomes tragic not so much because of the death of Hallam but because she is in effect expected to give up her life too. At the heart of the discourse of Romantic love lies an ideal of undying love which denies her any opportunity of happiness after Hallam's death. And this is reinforced by the ideal of female self-sacrifice, most fully embodied in motherhood, the Madonna being the paradigm, but also part of the wifely ideal. Lizbeth Goodman's comments on Letitia Landon's 'A Suttee', a popular poem of the period, are apposite. She argues that, although the practice of suttee, widow burning, was deplored by church and state in Britain, the poem (and custom) can be aligned with two conventional views: 'the romantic lover could and should have no existence apart from her beloved', and 'the wife must sacrifice herself for her husband'.[19] Although Emily is incapacitated by grief for a year,[20] and mourns for another eight, nothing less than perpetual mourning is required to prove her love for Hallam and her status as a woman. From 1861, after the death of Prince Albert, Queen Victoria provided a very public and influential model of such fidelity, her effigy on her tomb preserving her for ever as she was around the time of his death. But it has been argued that the story of Sleeping Beauty, the image of a woman frozen in time and a myth which conceals the pain of waiting, also appealed strongly to both masculine aesthetics and domestic politics throughout the Victorian period.[21] Although Emily is sustained by the Hallam family after Hallam's death, when she marries Captain Jesse nine years later, she feels trapped and suffocated by their unyielding, if quiet, disapproval. And Byatt includes in her novella Elizabeth Barrett Browning's denunciation of the marriage as a 'disgrace to womanhood' (p. 174). Even though Emily names her son Arthur Hallam Jesse, as a tribute to her former love, the child's very existence is living proof of her failure to maintain that 'perpetual maidenhood' (*In Memoriam*, VI, quoted on p. 234) which her brother envisages as the only proper response.

For only in her brother's poem does Emily adequately fulfil the role of self-sacrificing heroine. In this memorial she is fixed forever in the role of the grieving bereaved. Young Emily exists in the poem as a kind of shadow of her real self, while the reality of her later marriage is denied by omission, in contrast to the wedding of Alfred's other sister, which is celebrated in the poem's Epilogue. Emily's life becomes absorbed into and transformed by the poetry. The garden of Somersby, the Tennyson home and the scene of youthful happiness, is recreated in the poem so vividly that it now seems to exist only in the poem, and can only be remembered in the poet's words. Byatt suggests that it is by being inscribed in the poem in this way that Emily's life is sacrificed. Rather than feeling immortalised, the fictional Emily feels that the poem stands as a testament to her failure.[22] The poem 'strove to annihilate her' (p. 233) because Alfred has in effect displaced her as chief mourner, his mourning having 'undone and denied' hers (p. 229). Unlike his sister, he has lived up to the ideal of undying love and eternal devotion. This displacement is emphasised by the poem's gendering of that devotion. Editors have pointed out that Tennyson used as his model for the poem Greek and Roman elegies usually addressed to the beloved, lamenting loss while celebrating constancy in love (Shatto and Shaw, pp. 26–7);

the poet repeatedly takes on not only the role of a lover, but that of a specifically female lover, comparing his wait for Arthur's return to that of the young girl, the 'meek unconscious dove' (*In Memoriam*, VI, quoted on p. 233) that was his sister. He thinks of his own 'spirit as of a wife' (*In Memoriam*, quoted on p. 234). Throughout the poem, images of widows and widowers are repeatedly used to evoke the poet's sense of loss and desolation.[23] The poem immortalises the poet's fidelity as much as Hallam.

This displacement of Emily's role by Byatt's Tennyson raises important questions about the nature of Romantic love, and of sexual relations in general. The novella's account of Tennyson's relationship with his wife suggests he himself is not altogether comfortable in the role of Romantic lover. His admission that he is not a passionate man where she is concerned might simply reflect that idealisation of women which requires the suppression of their physicality. And his insistence that Hallam loved in 'a romantic glow' (p. 260), and was not therefore a sensual man could conform to the same structure of feeling. It is, however, challenged by Emily's own memories of her fiancé's excitement when they kiss. But Emily's memory of one day seeing the men with the 'two fingers of their trailing, relaxed arms, touching earth, pointing quietly at each other' (p. 228), with its reference to Michelangelo's painting of God and Adam in the Sistine Chapel, inevitably suggests a possible homo-eroticism in the relationship. This is reinforced by Tennyson's acknowledgment of the 'unaccustomed happiness [...] in his skin and flesh and bones' (p. 257) he felt with Hallam, and that there was 'more excitement in the space between his finger and Arthur's' than in his relationship with his wife. Tennyson compares their relationship with that of David and Jonathan, 'passing the love of women', but reassures himself with the thought that David was the 'greatest lover of women in the Bible' (p. 260).

The question of Tennyson's sexuality is, however, of less significance than what the representation of this relationship suggests about gender discourses of the period. The adoption of a feminine persona to embody his bereavement enables the poet to give vent to physical needs which run counter to more dominant constructions of the masculine ideal. The poem thus acknowledges the physical dimension to bereavement which is so deeply felt by the women who seek to renew contact with the dead through spiritualism. While the elderly poet represented in the novella has learned sufficient Victorian reticence to conceal his feelings in 'an impenetrable mist of vagueness', compounded of both 'the distracted vagueness of genius' and 'the thick cloak of the respectability of his Age' (p. 258), the man who wrote the poem a quarter of a century earlier was able to articulate what he still feels – the loss of the physical presence.

In both the poem and the novella this focuses on Hallam's hands: 'This was where Arthur met and temporarily mixed with him, in the English gentleman's grip. Manly, alive, a renewal of touch' (p. 255).[24] Cloaked in language calculated to avoid any suggestion of eroticism, the recurrent reference to hands is nevertheless an evocation of tenderness and desire. Whatever spiritual reunion might be possible after death, the poet's hands will always be empty, a void impossible to fill.

The idealisation at work here, therefore, goes beyond that of Romantic love. The young Hallam's *Theodicaea Novissima*, written for the Cambridge Apostles, speaks of the need for the passion of love which caused God to create Christ as 'an object of desire', making Divine love one with human love. If Emily sees Somersby as a world made by and for men, this is because her brother and her fiancé are drawn together by their identification with each other, which they see as the basis of the highest kind of love: the *Theodicaea Novissima* goes on to describe human love as 'the tendency towards a union so intimate, as virtually to amount to identification' (quoted on p. 217). The fact that Tennyson describes his own fiancée, Emily Sellwood, with the very words that Hallam used to describe his Emily on their first meeting is symptomatic of this total identification. Tennyson's desire to credit the excitement generated by his nearness to Hallam to 'the flashing-out of one soul to another' (p. 260) is not simply a denial of the possibility of homosexual desire, but an indication of the perceived difference between what is possible between men, who possess souls and creative minds, and what is possible between men and women separated by Victorian gender constructions.

The novella credits Tennyson with believing that, in some sense, 'all great human beings encompassed both sexes', modelled on Christ, who included in himself 'Wisdom and Justice, which were male, and Mercy and Pity, which were female'. The 'womanly aspects' he and Hallam possessed 'only increased their poetic sensibility, their manly energy' (p. 259). But rather than such arguments leading to sexual equality, they in effect make women redundant, except for reproductive purposes. Even the role of Muse, usually occupied by women in the discourse of Romantic love, is occupied in the novella by Hallam, who gives Tennyson the sense that the air was 'full of singing words that were the unformed atoms of his own creation to come' (p. 257). Many strands of Victorian scientific thought tended, as Chapter 1 suggested, to envisage the male as representing a 'human' ideal, which women's biological functions prevented them from achieving. It is, then, little wonder that Emily, on seeing the two men go off together, feels 'excluded from Paradise' (p. 227). Eve will not be needed until it is time to procreate.

If Tennyson's poetry does succeed in achieving the union of 'feminine' and 'masculine', then it also raises the possibility of uniting the body and the spirit which dualistic modes of thought keep apart. The novella quotes Hallam's saying of Keats, 'I restored a word to life, for him. Sensuous. My word. [...] Poems are the ghosts of sensations' (p. 251). The historical Hallam described Tennyson similarly as one of the 'Poets of Sensation'.[25] In the novella Tennyson justifies this view by referring to 'the inescapably sensuous nature of language', the 'matter-moulded forms of speech' (pp. 266–7); he claims that the form of his poetry can '*feel* its way through an argument', moving from abstract personifications of Love to 'pure animal sensuality' (p. 263). Writing can be a path to understanding that goes beyond the cerebral and theoretical to incorporate the lived reality of the body, because it has its roots in the physical, words themselves being in Tennyson's eyes sensuous things. Again the emphasis on the sensual rather than the theoretical evokes the feminine, rather than the masculine, according to traditional gender binaries, which Byatt's Tennyson here appears to deconstruct.

The fictional poet is most preoccupied, however, by his inability to move beyond the sensual to the spiritual. He is dissatisfied with the transcendental aspects of his poems, because they are unconnected with the sensuous pleasure of language, and he feels unable to make solid 'the world of spirit, of light' (p. 265). *In Memoriam* tapped deep into the psyche of an age haunted by a sense of doubt, because it articulates Tennyson's nightmare vision of a world reduced to matter, where the existence of another, spiritual dimension is in doubt. The poet's imagination is 'stirred by matter', which is more mysterious to him than mind, but the idea that his own thoughts were 'mere electric sparks emitted by a pale, clay-slimy mass of worm-like flesh' (p. 264) is horrifying. Whereas in Glendinning's *Electricity* Peter's imagination is stirred by a vision of the underlying structures and energy which matter represents, Tennyson's mind is, according to Byatt, moved by the horror of dissolution and death to which all are reduced, if there is nothing beyond matter. He remembers nearly fainting as a young man in London, overwhelmed by his vision of a future in which all the city's current inhabitants would be dead and in the ground. In place of *Genesis*'s vision of man being moulded out of clay by God, and intended for the highest of purposes, the poet sees man decaying into clay, for no purpose other than to provide food for worms:

the earth heaped and stacked with dead things, broken bright feathers and shrivelled moths, worms stretched and chewed and sliced and swallowed, stinking shoals of once bright fish, dried parrots and tigerskins limply and glassily snarling on hearths, mountains of human skulls mixed with monkey skulls and snake skulls and asses' jawbones and butterfly wings, mashed into humus and dust, fed on, regurgitated, blown in the wind, soaked in the rain, absorbed. (p. 262)

Darwin's evolutionary ladder here collapses into an undifferentiated mass, where death reduces all to compost and dust.

For Byatt's Tennyson the fear of death can only be transcended if there is something beyond it.[26] By repeatedly chanting his own name, and concentrating on his own self, he is paradoxically able to escape from himself into a kind of waking trance, in which 'he was everything, was God' (p. 265). Through the mind of Sophy Sheekhy, a medium possessed by the spirit of Arthur Hallam and also telepathically linked with Tennyson, this process is represented as a kind of rebirth, in which he fashions himself a cocoon, spinning threads from his mouth, as if the words he produces in his poetry can fashion that 'matter-moulded kind of *half-life*' (p. 268) for himself and Hallam which may be all the immortality now possible. In that same vision, however, Sophy sees Hallam being 'unmade' by the poet's actions, perhaps signifying that the immortality of the word metaphorically dissolves the living presence of the poem's subject, emphasising by comparison the 'airless, stinking mass' of the dead flesh (p. 274).

Sophy herself functions as a kind of parallel to Tennyson. She, too, is able to leave her body by hypnotising herself in the mirror, suggesting the possibility that the spirit can live on outside the husk of the body. And her shaking and jerking during the séance suggest she may, like the poet, be prone to epileptic seizures. Above all she shares his delight in poetry, and in particular its rhythms, which provide a route to the state of mind necessary for the medium to open herself up to the dead souls. When the dead Hallam appears to her, he calls her 'Pistis Sophia', whom he describes as 'the Angel in the Garden, before Man. The energetic principle of love for the beautiful' (p. 252), associating Sophy both with a being who exists before the creation of male and female as separate entities, and with the poetic mission Hallam shares with Tennyson. The name Sophia also suggests the only biblical representation of the divine which is associated with the female: according to the Gnostic Gospels, Pistis Sophia is the Holy Spirit of Wisdom, erased from the Holy Trinity by the orthodox Christian tradition so that the Trinity becomes entirely masculine.[27] Although Hallam refers to the belief that Sophia sent the first snake into Paradise, making the patriarchal association between woman and evil, in Gnostic tradition the snake was associated with the Mother Goddess and wisdom. And Hallam's reference to the frozen snake being warmed into life, apparently able to be born again as it sloughs off its old skin, indicates why the snake has also been a potent symbol of resurrection. All these associations, together with the parallelism between Sophy and Tennyson, suggest that it is possible for woman, too, to embody both the spiritual and the physical lives, to incorporate the best of both masculine and feminine.

But the relationship between body and spirit was for many Romantics and Victorians expressed most reassuringly in the philosophy of Swedenborg. For at the heart of his theology is a vision of the universe based on correspondence. In Byatt's novella that vision is explicitly articulated by Mr Hawke, one of the members of the séance: 'everything corresponds, from the most purely material to the most purely divine in the Divine Human' (p. 180). There is, therefore, no need to despise the material, in which the non-material is rooted: 'an affection is *an organic structure having life*' (p. 203), which it is sometimes possible to register in our senses. This perhaps prefigures the discovery by neurosurgeons that emotions can be demonstrated to have an effect on the organic matter of the brain. This sense of correspondence is also, of course, the basic principle on which the figurative language fundamental to poetry depends, and reflects the Romantic view of human love as an image of the divine: as Hallam puts it, both Keats and Dante suggest that 'pulsions of earthly Love' are the 'faint figuring' (p. 257) of divine love. It is, therefore, hardly surprising that the real Tennyson, like his fictional counterpart, should have found in Swedenborgian thought beliefs to reinforce his own spiritual longings.

Although not all Swedenborgians approved of spiritualism, spiritualism also assumes a relationship between the living and the dead, between body and spirit, that accords the body more respect than more orthodox Christian traditions have done.[28] This also makes it possible for spiritualists to believe that the living can communicate with the dead, since like Lilias Papagay they know that the world of the dead interpenetrates that of the living. What those at the séance require, moreover, is to achieve sensory contact with the dead. More specifically, in *The Conjugial Angel* the séance is represented as a means of enabling women to see, hear and touch their dead loved ones again. Whatever occurs during the séance is – however it is interpreted – fuelled by female desire. When Mrs Papagay acts as a medium for Mrs Hearnshaw's lost child, the language, working by metaphor and metonymy rather than analytical logic, conveys the physicality of the mother's longing for the touch of her dead child as well as her horror at repeatedly giving birth to death. But although this language has qualities appropriate to a child, it betrays its origins in Mrs Papagay through the inclusion of one of Captain Papagay's pet words, 'pudy', and its apparent familiarity with the erotic poetry of John Donne:[29]

> Hands hands across hands hand over under above between below hands little   pudy hands pudy plumpy hands Ring a Roses hands tossed with tangle on a   bald on a bald street skull not skull soft head heaven gates opened in small head cold hands so cold such cold hands no more cold ring a roses AMY AMY AMY AMY AMY love me I love you we love you in the rosy garden we love you your tears hurt us they burn our soft skins like ice burns here cold hands are rosy we love you. (p. 197)

What speaks through the voice of the medium is the voice of the female unconscious, of desires normally repressed. As mediums, therefore, women are able to articulate the forbidden in ways which under normal circumstances would not be tolerated in a public forum in respectable society. Their role is blatantly transgressive. When Mrs Papagay goes into the trances that make her communications possible, she ceases to be the proper lady, falling instead into a state which is 'distressing in its lack of control', her boots 'thrashing the carpet' and 'harsh voices [speaking] through her' (p. 169). She expresses a healthy scepticism towards the first 'message' she receives from her lost husband in the séance, since it is expressed in platitudes and generalities quite out of character with Arturo. But when she herself acts as a medium for him, the resultant outpouring includes oblique references to sexual slang a woman of her class would never have used in public or even have admitted to consciousness. These are words heard, remembered and deeply imbedded in her unconscious:

> Her respectable fingers wrote out imprecations in various languages she knew nothing of, and never sought to have translated, for she knew well enough *approximately* what they were, with their fs and cons and cuns, Arturo's little words of fury, Arturo's little words, also, of intense pleasure.

'Arturo' continues in language which in its repetition, its word-play, its emphasis on rhythm, its lack of syntactical order and logic, and its metaphorical richness has the characteristics of Kristeva's semiotic, associated with the female body:[30] 'Naughty-lus tangle-shells sand sand break break breaker c.f.f.c. naughty Lilias, infin che'l mar fu sopra noi richiuso' (p. 169). The automatic writing which only the women in the circle produce apparently legitimises the repressed desires of that body.

The séance also provides a forum for women's imaginative powers, an opportunity for them to take on the role of poet, rather than muse, as they construct narratives to articulate, if not satisfy, desire. There is a strong suggestion that a medium's power is the power of the imagination: Lilias Papagay, for instance, is like Shakespeare's poet and lover, 'of imagination all compact' (p. 163), a 'weaver of narratives' (p. 168) from the hints provided by the bereaved. This is not to belittle her ability, since while her imagination is capable of weaving a host of different stories for any individual, she senses when one is truer than others, although she has the humility to ask herself whether this can be called knowledge. As in *Electricity*, this power of understanding and perception derives from the ability to enter deeply into people's 'secret selves, their deepest desires and fears' (p. 171), and experience them as lived reality. In contrast, it is suggested that Tennyson's power lies in articulating his own grief in a form which will strike chords with the reading public, rather than in entering into the griefs of others, even those of his sister, who comments, 'No ghost would appear to *you*, Alfred, [...] you are not receptive' (p. 185).

Since the medium's role does, therefore, involve women conforming to the Victorian feminine ideal of passive and intuitive openness to the feelings and needs of others, the discourse of spiritualism does not ultimately subvert the gender constructions responsible for the subjection of Victorian women, even if it challenges the dualism of orthodox Christianity. This is even more true of Swedenborgianism, which maintains so many of the oppositions associated with male and female in patriarchal thought. Explaining the idea of 'conjugial love', Mr Hawke proclaims, 'in a heavenly Marriage, [...] truth is conjoined with good, understanding with will, thought with affection. For truth and understanding and thought are male, but good, will and affection are female' (p. 210).[31] Intellectual powers are male; affective powers are female, as they are for the fictional Tennyson and Hallam. There is nothing new here, nor in the privileging of the abstract, the word or spirit, over the fleshly body, gendered as female, in Hawke's description of the crucifixion as 'a necessary shedding of the corrupt humanity He had from the mother, in order to experience glorification and union with the Father'. The women in the séance feel suitably chastised for being 'too abundantly fleshly' (p. 278). Mr Hawke is still inclined to regard female flesh, in the form of Mrs Papagay, as a dangerous temptation. The séances in the novella, which tend to suffer from male domination, are in danger of simply reproducing Victorian gender hierarchies. Although Mr Hawke has no mediumistic powers himself, he is a central figure in their proceedings, ordained to speak as a wandering minister of the Church of Swedenborg. Even the articulation of female desire within the séance is ultimately subject to male censorship. Mrs Papagay's final piece of automatic writing is a poem which includes reference to the Angel's 'golden cock', and articulates her vision of one flesh in terms which are judged by Mr Hawke to be 'filthy imaginings' (p. 286), obscene enough to bring the séance to a stop. When the novella refers to the suspicion felt by some Swedenborgians towards spiritualism, because of its 'loose and dangerous power-play' (p. 188), it is the potential power acquired by women through spiritualism that seems the likely cause of this objection.

Nor do the spirit voices themselves always act as the authentic voice of female desire, particularly when they speak through Sophy Sheekhy. Often they seem complicit in the same ideology of Romantic love which has imprisoned Emily Jesse, and sent her to the séance seeking forgiveness for having betrayed her first love. The séance functions for her as a public confessional, just as it does for Mrs Hearnshaw, seeking forgiveness for having failed to keep her babies alive. Both feel they have failed in women's primary purposes: to be faithful and to nurture their young. The messages Emily receives from Sophy are an amalgam of quotations from the Book of Revelations, from *In Memoriam*, and from Hallam's *Theodicaea* and translation of Dante, all of which reproach her for her faithlessness. Taking a cynical view of Sophy's role, one could argue that she has done enough research to provide appropriate messages to fuel Emily's sense of guilt. When Hallam's ghost invades her room, he gives her a different message – that 'the mourning was painful to him' (p. 250) – but in the séance Sophy translates this as 'Tell her I wait' (p. 283). Sophy may have simply misread Emily's endless attempts to communicate with Hallam as a desire for just such a message. And yet she sees him as existing in an almost vampiric relationship with women, both with Emily and herself, as his cold, dead form lies down beside her, 'invading the very fibre of her nerves with his death' (p. 274). In her vision the dead cannot be separated from the living; they will claim their own as inevitably as death will. Women represent the living flesh to which the fear of death makes men cling. But at another level they function as signifiers of that otherworldly spirit which lives in Romantic poetry and offers transcendence over mortality and corruption. The Victorian ideology of womanhood draws its power from precisely such a contradiction.

The novella's ending, however, rejects such ideologies. Emily speaks in her own voice, rather than as medium, to refuse the 'extremely unfair arrangement' (p. 283) whereby she will share eternal bliss with Hallam, in denial of the life she has shared, for better or worse, with Richard Jesse. Richard's love for her is represented as more concrete and robust than Hallam's. He describes her as alive and vital, a 'real woman', and he knows in his 'bones – and [his] heart and liver and all [his] nerve-endings' (p. 241) – that they are right for each other. A 'man of action, not of words', he represents an obvious contrast to Hallam, and Emily in turn responds to him 'in a *bodily* way' (p. 239), as 'his hands and skin [speak] to her' (p. 242). Their relationship is grounded in the real world, rather than in literary discourse. It is similarly possible to read the dramatic re-appearance of Arturo Papagay as the product, psychologically of Lilias Papagay's desire, and her fidelity to the memory of a flesh and blood reality, rather than an imaginary creation. Arturo's return is a triumph of the material world every bit as much a 'miracle' as the re-appearance of the dead in the living world, and the journey that brings the tea from its origin to English drawing-rooms. It suggests that in order to survive, human love must acknowledge its base in the body. This idea is as relevant to Tennyson's intense sense of loss as to the female desires presented in the text. The novella can therefore be seen as a celebration of human love, in so far as that love acknowledges the female as subject, and not simply as the object of desire.

Spiritualism, psychology and history: Michèle Roberts, *In the Red Kitchen*

Victorian and twentieth-century women meet in Michèle Roberts's *In the Red Kitchen*.[32] The central protagonist in each century communes, moreover, with the spirit of an Ancient Egyptian princess, introducing yet another historical period into the novel. The movement between these three time zones adds to the exploration of Victorian gender discourses a sense of what unites these women and in particular of the forces that threaten to silence them. All three periods come together symbolically when the twentieth-century Hattie King visits the Victorian necropolis in London, which she sees as an 'Ancient Egyptian city', a 'stone swamp', with 'columns in the shape of palm trunks', inhabited by a sphinx-like figure (p. 116). Here she finds the gravestones of Flora and Rosina Milk, the Victorian women who once inhabited her house, and whose story arguably dominates the novel, providing an exploration of the role of the new science of psychology in defining and controlling femininity, an exploration which again centres around the phenomenon of spiritualism.

The story of Flora Milk, a young working-class girl, is based on the true life story of Florence Cook, one of the most famous Victorian mediums, who came into prominence in the 1870s.[33] As a woman, Flora is subjected to the same religious discourses at work in *Electricity* and *The Conjugial Angel*. Her role as a medium in the household of Sir William Prentiss, a wealthy scientist, is to provide spiritual and emotional comfort to his wife Minny, as she recovers from the death of her baby. Minny's narrative, taking the form of letters to her mother, initially represents Flora in terms of the purity and spirituality expected of a young girl: she is as 'pure as an angel', demonstrating 'a religious vocation' (p. 34), her physical beauty confirming 'her indisputable beauty of soul' (p. 49). That purity is, however, challenged by Flora's sister Rosina in the letter which opens the novel. Rosina uses the language of the Church fathers to denounce her sister as a 'monster in silk skirts. She looks like a woman, but she's a devil underneath, the part you can't see.'[34] According to her, Flora 'sucks the life out of people' and bewitches them, 'stealing their lifeblood', and would in earlier times have been burnt as a witch (p. 1). Her language suggests how women like Flora provoked such fear, for female sexuality is literally as well as metaphorically bewitching enough to tempt men away from their higher duties, and all the more pernicious when it is concealed.

The presence of another discourse, however – that of class – adds further complexities to that sexual ideology. When Sir William takes Flora to Paris to see the famous Dr Charcot, her account claims they are lovers and that her lower-class status is part of her attraction: 'he expected a certain coarseness. It excited him. Also it allowed him to stay cold, in control' (p. 108). In contrast to Minny's gentlewomanly denial of any sexual feeling, Flora's more overt sexuality is all the more tempting, while simultaneously exonerating Sir William from any suggestion of exploitation by providing the 'she asked for it' defence used by Glendinning's Bullingdon Huff. For Minny, Flora's angelic qualities are so rarely found in a woman of her class as to render her an object of curiosity, if not suspicion. The assumptions inscribed in this class discourse make Minny marvel at the uneducated Flora's powers, and at 'her unimpeachable moral status' (p. 49), indicated in her underwear being as clean as Minny's own. Flora's humble origins mean that her purity and spiritual vocation require further 'scientific' validation, and make it acceptable for her and her body to become an object of scrutiny in a way that would be unacceptable for a woman of Minny's class – *'their notions of modesty being so different to ours'* (p. 48). Sir William aims to show, through studying Flora, how the 'methods of science can clarify and explain spiritualistic occurrences' (pp. 20–2). Flora's spirituality is only validated even for Minny when her conduct has been subjected to the 'calm and objective scrutiny' (p. 34) of William himself. Science can apparently assist religion in differentiating the good woman from the bad.

The links established by Victorian psychology between the female body and the mind suggest, however, that most – if not all – women are inferior, invalidating their experience and views. For in women, 'mind' does not seem to equate with consciousness or intellect so much as the *un*conscious. This again in effect defines women in terms of the body, since the unconscious is the repository of the repressed and inadmissible drives and impulses which derive from the body. The body can, however, 'speak' what words cannot. Finding herself in front of Charcot's students, Flora decides, 'I must let my body shape words for me. [...] I must act my meaning through my body' (p. 127). But patriarchal gender discourse is only able to read the female body, and the unconscious, in terms of darkness. Flora feels at home in darkness, which lets her 'expand into something, someone, larger than a child or [her] ordinary daily self' (p. 31); it is the route to her spiritualist experiences. But for the medical profession, the darkness of the unconscious must, like the body, be exposed to the light of scientific scrutiny.

In the process, the powers of the medium, rather than being seen as evidence of female spirituality, are medicalised and declared invalid, as is clear from Sir William's changing response to Flora. Although readers are never given direct access to his point of view, according to Minny's letters, when he first studies Flora she produces materialisations of her spirit control, whose antiquity and nobility are evident in her behaviour. He observes:

> Where Flora is modest and shy, Hattie is outspoken and articulate; where Flora is simple and ignorant, Hattie discourses brilliantly upon a wide range of topics; where Flora rarely speaks of her deep Christian convictions, Hattie imparts mysterious hints of ancient gods and the mystical powers of certain arrangements of numbers in mathematics. (p. 96)

Modern readers may prefer to use the language of psychology to explain Hattie as the repressed side of Flora, or to speak of dissociation when Flora declares, 'Flora would never do what Hattie does. Flora is a good girl' (p. 123). But it is more important to observe that Sir William himself uses different discourses for his different purposes: the language of spiritualism to explain his need to be alone with Flora and to carry out 'medical examinations' of the spirit messenger, but the language of psychiatric medicine when he wishes to repudiate her. When Sir William requires photographic evidence of the existence of Flora's spirit-guide, Hat, he claims that Hat moves too fast, blurring the photographs, so that Flora must instead adopt the semi-pornographic poses which he claims are Hat's. But he goes to Salpêtrière 'to compare the physiology of persons endowed with mediumistic gifts with that of those afflicted with hysterical illnesses, having some intuition that the two conditions may [. . .] overlap' (p. 112), so that he can confirm the conclusions he has reached about the medium's unconscious. Sir William finally adopts the medical discourse of Dr Charcot, with all its moral overtones: 'all too many young female mediums partake of the moral degeneracy always found amongst hysterics' (p. 144). The familiar equation of female hysteria and immorality that characterises Victorian psychology is here explicit. As Susan Rowland puts it in her analysis of the novel's relationship to the evolution of Victorian psychology:

> By modelling William Preston on Crookes [William Crookes was a scientist interested in mediumship] and Jung, *In the Red Kitchen* posits a web of intersecting erotic, occult and medical narratives at the genesis of psychoanalysis and Jungian psychology, where gender is the silent term in these male-generated theories of the end of the nineteenth-century. (*Rereading Victorian Fiction*, p. 211)

In addition to invalidating Flora's claims to spiritual powers, her diagnosis as a hysteric also silences any suggestion of abuse she makes about Sir William. Even Flora's ability to imagine such abuse is proof of her wickedness: in a Catch-22 situation, she is either a genuine medium who never left her sofa to be touched by Sir William, or she is 'nothing but a hysteric who suffers from delusions' (p. 130). Rowland points out that these views echo Freud's changing view of female hysteria:

> Whereas Freud once believed that hysteria resulted from repressed memories of sexual abuse, he later decided that such abuse had no reality outside the mind of the patient, that it was in fact fantasy. Such a theoretical turn fuelled his concept of the Oedipus complex

with its female equivalent, the daughter's incestuous desire for the father. (*Rereading Victorian Fiction*, p. 208)

In the Red Kitchen can, then, be seen to demonstrate the evolution of psychiatric theories which can be used to silence women who threaten to speak out of their ordained roles, while affording protection to those who, in the name of science, use/abuse women's bodies and minds as their subject. In Paris, Charcot uses hypnosis to make his female patients act out their roles – he is 'ringmaster', 'magician', 'God', 'a great artist' (pp. 124–5). Flora consciously performs the role of a hysterical patient for an audience of doctors, her mimicry drawing attention to the nature of the hysteric as a construction, but she still serves the doctors' purposes.

It is not only scientific discourse, however, that colludes at the abuse of young women. Flora is the link between the two figures furthest apart in time, but linked by name – Flora's spirit-guide, the Egyptian princess Hat, and Hattie King – both of whom are subjected to abuse within religious contexts that deny its very existence. When the orphaned Hattie is left with the nuns, she attempts to tell Sister Julian that her uncle, acting *in loco parentis*, abuses her sexually, but the Sister accuses her of lying, because 'in that house of chaste women there was no room for a truth that included uncles' (p. 136). The reality of male power is once again suppressed by the silencing of the female voice. The house dedicated to the divine Father unknowingly colludes with the abuses of those who play the role of father on earth. Hat's case is more complex. In the first place, Hat appears to have all the power and control over her world that she needs. As she says, 'This little world is all mine. It encloses, expresses and reflects me' (p. 7). And in contrast to the women brought up in the Christian tradition, she is not made to feel that her sexuality is shameful. As Roberts herself says, 'within Christian cultures we've lost the idea of the body as sacred. Which they had in ancient Egypt; perhaps one reason why my medium in my present novel wishes she once lived in ancient Egypt.'[35] Hat therefore awaits her sexual initiation with anticipation rather than fear. Her union with her father is, moreover, celebrated as a sacred ceremony central to her culture. But since the taboo on incest is so powerful in modern Western culture, it is difficult not to see this relationship as yet another example of abuse sanctioned by religion, particularly since adopting a culturally relativist position would mean overlooking the parallels drawn between the three young women and the father figures who dominate their lives.

Whether or not she is the victim of abuse, Flora's sexuality still transgresses the limits set by Victorian gender ideology. And religious discourse stipulates that the only way in which women can redeem themselves from the sins of Eve is through obedience and motherhood. Minny is complicit with this discourse. In her depression she is completely obedient to her husband's directions that she should cease all mental and intellectual activity, expressing herself in language reminiscent of the narrator of *The Yellow Wallpaper*,[36] and on the surface Minny accepts childbirth as her natural, god-given role. But her attitude is deeply ambivalent. Her fear of childbirth is understandable given the rates for maternal death during the Victorian period.[37] But there are hints of more sinister feelings, suggested when, in her role of medium, speaking as baby Rosalie, Flora accuses Minny of 'smothering' her, using a word which contains the ideas of both death and the mother. This account evokes those atavistic fears of the female body which derive from a primordial association of birth with death, generating a sense of disgust. As Simone de Beauvoir puts it, 'the slimy embryo begins the cycle that is completed in the putrefaction of death [...]. Thus the Woman-Mother has a face of shadows: she is the chaos whence all have come and whither all must one day return.'[38] Flora herself lives in a house like a cemetery, 'full of Mother's dead babies'. Mothers in this novel consistently fail to nurture their daughters: Hattie's mother abandons her; Hattie feels she let her baby die in the womb; Flora's mother attempts to abort hers; Minny kills hers after birth. The body of the female medium epitomises the ambivalent nature of the maternal body: in the séance Flora reflects that 'in the medium's own body a death takes place. In the medium's body death squats and grins. [...] She has given birth to the pain, she has set it free' (p. 94).

Freudian interpretations add further complications to the figure of the mother. According to the Electra complex, the daughter wants to take the mother's place in the father's affections, but since the mother remains her first love-object, she wants also to be the child and retain the mother for herself. Flora knows that the daughter comes between mother and father, and feels guilty, knowing that 'if the daughter were out of the way, then the mother and father would be able to love each other truly, without restraint' (p. 127). But one night she dreams that 'she can go where he goes: into the warm sweet mother' (p. 128) because she belongs to him, is his 'sword'. This suggests both the child's desire to return to the womb, and her identification with the father, which causes her to violate and erase her mother. Hattie's recurrent nightmares of burglary and rape, experienced as a violent death inside her, are on one occasion textually juxtaposed with both Hat's sexual initiation and the death of her own baby, but in her dream she blames only her absent mother for abandoning her. Interpellated as guilty, because female, she displaces that sense of guilt onto her mother, rather than blaming the system which makes male abuse possible.

It is hardly surprising, therefore, that Flora does not wish to become, or even identify with, the mother, and a reproductive function which is a source of fear and loathing. She prefers to identify with the father who is the source of power. For whatever 'powers' Flora may possess as a medium, her only access to real power is through men, who control the language that defines, categorises and controls women. Her father is a printer, who shows her how to make little books out of scraps of paper, an activity which her mother cuts short insisting that Flora looks after the children. Sir William too can be seen as taking on the role of the father, with Flora dancing for him as she danced for her father. Even Hattie's absent father remains a powerful influence, complicated – as it is for Hat – by his embodying the power of the divine Father: the nuns tell her that her 'real Father' is in Heaven and that true joy will only come when she joins him there after death. Hat's initiation – in the mortuary temple and in darkness – is similarly associated with the rituals of death, but it is also her 'second birth', a rebirth which confirms her identification with the father and patriarchal culture. When her father comes for her, disguised as the god, she must yield herself utterly to the god's power. Her reward will be to feel herself part of the very mythology of that culture: 'I am at the beginning of the world [...] the start of creation.' The price of female power in this as in other mythologies is submission to the sexual needs of the male, to the Law of the Father.[39]

Hat's identification with her father is indeed so great that it obliterates any possibility of a maternal relationship or any identification with the female:

> during my infancy it is my father who carries me close to his heart, who bears me on his lap, who nurses me on the milk of his wisdom, who nourishes me with his great learning, the power of his words.[...]
>
> I do not need a mother [...]. I am my father's daughter. [...] I am better than other women, for I am both beautiful and wise, both clever and courageous, both understanding and powerful. [...] My destiny is to follow my father and one day to become as powerful as he. (pp. 53–4)

Here the abstract, symbolic functions of the father, providing 'wisdom' and 'learning', are substituted for the physical attributes associated with the maternal body – 'milk', 'nourishment'. The mother's role is most dramatically undermined in the mythology surrounding Hat's birth. In her father's account, she was conceived when the great god Amun made himself visible to her mother and father 'to the wonder and terror of all', while her soul was 'fashioned on a potter's wheel by other gods'. Hat herself is complicit in seeing the act of creation as all-male. She claims, 'It was my Father in his divine form who begot and birthed me; his earthly queen being merely the vessel for his power. It is my father through whom I live now and through whom I shall have eternal life' (p. 54). In this account, as in Christian stories of the annunciation and virgin birth, the mother is simply a vessel for a child created by a male god. There can be no identification with the female, no sisterhood, within such a culture. Just as Flora has to compete with her sister Rosina for a husband, so Hat has to murder her father's favourite concubine to secure her own position.

The story of King Hat, therefore, which seems to celebrate the existence of great female power before the Judeo-Christian tradition made it increasingly rare, turns out to be more problematic than it first appears. For the price of Hat's power is ultimately the denial of her femininity. On her father's death, she takes his last breath into her, saying, 'I have him now. He lives on in me.' But rather than taking over her father's role, it could be argued that it takes over her, so that once again a woman's body becomes the vessel for the reproduction of male power. She takes on his power only by ceasing to be a woman, as she declares: 'I am no longer Queen Hat [...]. The man in me has come forth and must be recognized. [...] I am man, I am Pharaoh, and I shall rule' (p. 100). This is not, moreover, simply a personal transformation, but an obliteration of the female from history, represented in Hat's final words in the novel, a sequence which begins 'KING HAT' and ends with 'O' (p. 145). Although Hat reassures herself that, like her father, she will experience rebirth in the spirit world, in the dreams which articulate her repressed fears she returns to a world in which she has been 'unwritten. Written out. Written off.' 'King Hat' no longer exists. She laments: 'I am lacking. I am a lack. I am nothing but a poor dead body that lacks the sign of life: I am female [...] I have lost the great male force that was once in me' (p. 133).

In Hattie's story, however, a more positive identification with the female becomes possible. Through cooking, she learns from the nuns, she acquires a sense of identity which combines the female associations of bodily nurture with the verbal power of the male symbolic: working with food gives her a sense of power, and in writing down recipes she 'unmade and remade the world, and, after a childhood in which [she] could not trust others' words, learned to discriminate, to speak' (p. 87). As an adult, grieving over her miscarriage, her interest in both food and life is revived by an old woman in a supermarket, reconnecting her with the world of female domesticity which is a source of comfort and motivation. Taking that woman's advice, Hattie restores a table probably used by Flora for her séances, and in Flora's kitchen, becomes aware of the spirit of Flora herself. As the novel's title suggests, this kitchen has a special significance as the place where Hattie connects her own past with both Flora's and a female history which is essential to her identity. In a French convent, a vision of Flora's 'cavernous underground kitchen, lit by the red glare of flames' (p. 11) is briefly imprinted on the confessional, a female world superimposing itself on the authority of patriarchal religion. The kitchen represents a uniquely female space in which women can create, and have control, and even certain kinds of power. As a child, sitting in her mother's lap, Flora feels she has 'power over those hands, that lap, that kissing mouth' (p. 18). She feels powerful, too, in darkness, which in this novel is reclaimed from its negative connotations and associated positively with the unconscious as the place where all that is repressed by patriarchy and hence designated as female can be found. So the red kitchen can be identified with the unholy passions conjured up in such formulations as the scarlet woman, and by Hattie's dreams of dismembering her uncle. But it is also an essential source of warmth, both physical and emotional: the kitchen 'keeps us alive, warm, fed' (p. 44), as Flora puts it. Hattie becomes part of that nurturing, life-giving world when she releases the howling four-year-old Flora from the cupboard in the corner where the adult Flora concealed herself during séances. When she holds Flora, the child's pain releases the child inside herself, together with all her memories of pain and abandonment, so that she can move on to a fully adult role. She conceives again, embarking on a pregnancy which appears to offer a more hopeful outcome.

Spiritualistic experiences in this novel can, then, either be taken at face value or as an expression of the unconscious of history, of those experiences and thoughts which have to be passed on by secret means, since history only obliterates or distorts them. The connections they forge create a female genealogy. Flora's role as a medium makes her just such a conduit, 'a hollow stick the spirits blow messages down. [. . .] The speaking tube in this house in Bayswater, a corridor for others' voices' (p. 93). This female consciousness moreover unites areas of experience usually kept separate by dualistic gender ideologies. For Hattie the sensual physicality of cooking blends with spiritual experiences, represented by the Word of God, as she says the Office with Sister Bridget, 'the words of that poetry working themselves into the foodstuffs between [their] fingers' (p. 12). As a woman of the twentieth century, Hattie has more opportunity to break out of the binaries that imprisoned earlier generations of women, but to achieve this breakthrough she needs to tap into the experiences of earlier female lives, as she does by cleaning the red kitchen, which leaves her feeling she has transcended the limits of her own ego. She records, '"I" no longer existed; "I" was just a linguistic convenience, not any kind of truth.' She sees the ten-year-old Flora in the kitchen, playing with metal type, using her father's language, the words of the symbolic order, to conjure up those women's lives which form a continuity with hers, even in their self-denial and sense of guilt: 'HAT. HATE. [. . .] HATTIE. HATE. I' (p. 105).

But the three voices of Hat, Hattie and Flora are not the only ones speaking through the novel. There are other minor but significant voices – those of Rosina and Minny – which contradict or undermine Flora's account and yet are allowed to stand, for in this novel there is to be no authoritarian privileging of one voice over another. As we begin the novel, it is difficult to establish whose voice we hear, or to whom they are speaking/writing, so that the effort to solve this mystery forces the reader to be involved actively in establishing the relationship of one voice to another, and the connections between women's consciousness at different periods. Each woman has a different reason for writing/ speaking, and these motives affect the reader's interpretation of events, and are themselves part of the story that this complex narrative structure articulates. Minny's account, which completely exonerates Sir William from blame and interprets his interest in Flora as entirely professional, could easily be dismissed as an attempt to prevent her mother from seeing the reality of her life, or even to hide herself from that reality. But it may be the truth. Rosina's damning account of her sister's behaviour lends support to Minny's view, but is addressed to Flora's former admirer, so may be the product of jealousy, and a desire for revenge, since Rosina lost her former lover to Flora. Flora claims to be writing her story simply to please herself, and to make her husband and son live again, but this alone cannot guarantee the truthfulness of her account, or the accuracy of her memory. Nevertheless, while Rosina has the last word in the novel, the power of Flora's narrative is such that its credibility survives this final attack. While none of these voices may provide the 'true' story of the novel, each carries a significant part of a bigger story that has been largely unwritten. Although *In the Red Kitchen* does not claim to be history, it adds a female perspective which is not represented in the official written record.

For history can only be written by those with access to the Word, as Hat understands:

> To write is to enter the mysterious, powerful world of words, to partake of words' power, to make it work for me. To write is to deny the power of death [...]. To inscribe a person's name on the wall of his tomb, to describe his attributes thereupon, is to ensure that he will live forever. [...]
>
> Writing, I live; [...] my existence continues throughout eternity. (p. 24)

But this proves to be only part of the story, because 'history' is also the result of reading and interpreting what has been written, and therefore always a contested terrain. Hat's own name and life are obliterated by historians who cannot fit the idea of a female pharaoh into their patriarchal version of history. When future generations find her female body, they will not believe she was a pharaoh because 'King Hat' has been hacked off the walls and columns of her tomb.[40] Her fear of oblivion fuels her desire to speak to future generations, linking her story to that of Flora, who is in effect the scribe Hat seeks to 'write down [her] name and let [her] live again' (p. 133). At the more personal level, Hattie articulates what is left implicit in the other stories, the sense that the female body is written on, interpreted by patriarchal language. In her case 'a *cancelled* notice' (p. 86) is imprinted on her forehead when she is abandoned as a child, but she can erase this by telling her own story of the union of body and spirit, and the union of male and female. She and her lover are able to deconstruct and bring together the binary oppositions embodied in male and female in productive and spiritual forms, since they are deep down 'made of the same substance' (p. 114); in their sexual union she feels totally connected to everything else, like an infant experiencing pre-Oedipal wholeness, while simultaneously aware of difference, and distinctness, with the creative artist's eye. *In the Red Kitchen* suggests that, by listening to the silenced voices, women can, like Hattie, reshape the meaning of gender difference.

* * * * * * *

All three of the novelists discussed, therefore, use spiritualism to explore Victorian ideas of femininity, and also show an awareness of how problematic the role of medium was for women. While it gave a sense of power rare for women of the period, a power that derives from a surrender of consciousness may simply reinscribe women in the role of hysteric. Under the pretext of merely being a vehicle for the spirit messenger, the medium may have been enable to transgress conventional ideas of femininity in speech and deportment, but may in the process become not so much 'human' and genderless, as subhuman and animal-like. What recurs in these stories is the sense that real power for women depends on using the conscious mind to write, to tell their own stories and resist the gender discourses that threaten to imprison them.

5
Degeneration and Sexual Anarchy

> A new fear my bosom vexes;
> Tomorrow there may be no sexes!
>
> – *Punch* (1895)[1]

This fear, voiced in *Punch* in 1895, sums up a growing anxiety felt by many Victorians towards the end of the century that the boundaries between the sexes were no longer as clear as they had been, and should be. Typical *fin-de-siècle* anxieties about social breakdown tended to focus on that 'sexual anarchy' which Elaine Showalter conveys so vividly in her book of that name. Specifically, they focus on woman, in spite of a dawning awareness that even masculinity might be problematic. To the Darwinian mathematician Karl Pearson, for instance, women constituted one of the 'two great problems of modern social life' (the other being labour).[2] Modern women, he argued, threatened the institutions of marriage and the family by rejecting the domestic sphere and invading the male public sphere. Many such women, moreover, challenged what had been 'scientifically' established as woman's nature by denying the need for either a mate or maternity, while others breached the norm of 'passionlessness' by laying claim to their sexuality. The response of the 'experts' is summed up by Flavia Alaya: 'the social and personal happiness of the future now seemed to rest on the accentuation, rather than the obliteration, of sex differences' (p. 279).

Where the mid-Victorians had hoped for continual progress through the processes of evolution, the late Victorians were instead haunted by the spectre of degeneration. Rebecca Stott identifies E. Ray Lankester's *Degeneration* (1880) as one of the earliest works to warn of the real possibility of degeneration among the European races: first delivered as a lecture, *Degeneration* 'articulates (scientifically) the widespread fear of "cultural drift", a drift *backwards* down the evolutionary scale'.[3] Those characteristics defined as degenerate could spread and threaten the moral purity and cultural health of entire nations. As Stott points out, this discourse was 'easily assimilated into biological, psychological and social theory', so that just as evolution had provided a scientific basis for women's role in society, the theory of degeneration provided 'scientific' evidence to show what happened when women ignored the evolutionary imperative. Such 'evidence' was provided, for example, by Cesare Lombroso, the Italian criminologist, and Havelock Ellis, whose work he influenced. The first six chapters of Lombroso's *The Female Offender* (1895) are devoted to detailed analysis of the physical characteristics, including skull measurements, 'cranial anomalies' and hairy moles, of female criminals.[4] In a typically authoritative – and revealing – assertion, Lombroso presents these as the features which he has '*pronounced to be* characteristics of degeneration' (my italics).[5] Such outward signs 'mark degeneration in the female subject' (p. 83). Lombroso also asserts that such women show, both physically and mentally, enough 'masculine qualities' to prevent them 'from being more than half a woman' (p. 153), a point also made by Havelock Ellis in *The Criminal* (1890). Ellis points out, however, that through evolution, sexual selection has reduced the threat these women pose to civilisation: 'Masculine, unsexed, ugly, abnormal women – the women, that is, most strongly marked with the signs of degeneration, and therefore the tendency to criminality – would be to a large extent passed by in the choice of a mate, and would tend to be eliminated' (*Embodied Selves*, p. 333). Lombroso clinches the argument: 'Man not only refused to *marry* a deformed female, but ate her' (p. 109). The suggestion that criminal women are masculine in look and temperament all too easily gives rise to the corollary that women who are 'masculine' are likely to have criminal tendencies. Greater policing of gender boundaries was thus scientifically justified by the risk of degeneration, whereas nineteenth-century feminists, as Penny Boumelha points out, 'could not predict with "scientific" certainty the effects of higher education or the vote upon the physiology of future generations' (quoted in Stott, p. 19).

Those women who did threaten gender boundaries were divided into different, if sometimes overlapping, categories. First there were the 'surplus' women mentioned in Chapter 3. Called 'Odd Women' in George Gissing's novel of 1891, their 'oddity' lay in their failure to become part of a heterosexual pair. The large numbers of 'odd men' were not, incidentally, seen as a problem, emphasising how differently men's role in society was perceived. In contrast to the surplus woman, the second category of 'New Woman' chose her single life in preference to marriage, and therefore constituted an even greater threat to society. She was also likely to contribute to degeneration by her 'unhealthy' tendency to feed her brain, with inevitable consequences for both her reproductive system and her nerves. Whether wilfully or not, all these women who deviated from the natural laws which dictated that maternity was woman's destiny constituted a danger to the health of society. Yet they could also resist attempts to categorise them along with other 'deviants' by rejecting sexuality altogether, advocating social purity and blaming degeneration on men rather than women, since, as New Woman and novelist Mona Caird puts it, 'Man in any age or country is liable to revert to a state of savagery' (quoted in Showalter, *Sexual Anarchy*, p. 45).

More consistently deviant were those women who challenged the sexual norms of Victorian gender ideology. Writing about the popularity of the *femme fatale* in the art and literature of the period, a phenomenon symptomatic of the growing anxiety about female sexuality, Rebecca Stott points out that the first recorded use of the word 'sexuality' in a recognisably modern sense, meaning 'possession of sexual powers or capability of sexual feelings' (*OED*), is dated 1889. The *Oxford English Dictionary* quotes from *Clinical Lectures on the Diseases of Women* by the physician James Matthews Duncan: 'in removing the ovaries you do not necessarily destroy sexuality in a woman'. Stott comments, 'The word appears, then, in medical discourse and involves a (problematic) female sexuality' (p. 25). Lombroso had looked for, and believed he had found, 'natural' organic causes for prostitution, believing it to be largely the result of a physically pathological nature resulting from evolutionary degeneracy (although he also took into account social and environmental factors). For him, sexuality in women was characteristic of a lower level of evolution: 'The primitive woman was rarely a murderess; but she was always a prostitute' (p. 111). But such rigid categories were increasingly difficult to sustain, since even 'respectable' women were beginning to demand recognition of their sexual needs. Both male and female members of the Men and Women's Club, founded in 1885, for instance, included sexuality as an essential element in their utopian vision of new kinds of male–female relationships.[6] Since such radical thinkers failed to put maternity at the top of their agenda, they too, however, could be dismissed as 'degenerate'. As Lombroso puts it, 'A strong proof of degeneration in many born criminals is the want of maternal affection' (p. 152).

But the most radical threat to the stability of Victorian gender roles came from those women described as 'inverts', who, according to the sexologists, rejected everything that defined woman's place in society. Their choice of female partners was associated by sexologists with feminism, and the demands of the New Woman for greater participation in public life. Describing female emancipation as a good thing on the whole, Havelock Ellis nevertheless holds it responsible for 'an increase in feminine criminality and in feminine insanity, which are being elevated towards the masculine standard,' and is not surprised to see lesbianism also increasing, since it 'has always been regarded as belonging to an allied, if not the same, group of phenomena' (quoted in Oram, p. 102). This blurring of categories was furthered by the tendency of New Women to adopt, like some lesbians, a more masculine style of dress as a sign of economic independence and feminist principles. What typifies debates about women in 'male' roles is the desire to classify perceived deviance in order to prevent these characteristics spreading through society, what Stott describes as the late Victorian 'instinct to define and measure culture by what it ought not to be' (p. 23).

Set in the 1890s, both Angela Carter's *Nights at the Circus* (1984) and Sarah Waters' *Tipping the Velvet* (1998) engage with and explode all such measurements and definitions. Their central female characters breach gender boundaries both sexually and professionally, taking on the so-called masculine traits in order to become 'New Women'. They court 'deviance' in order to further their own evolution, ignoring the social imperative of marriage and the evolutionary imperative of maternity. Their challenge is, moreover, a public and highly visible one, with a concomitant risk of public censure. As Barbara Brook suggests, 'The public spectacle of a woman's body enacts an antithesis to the identification of femininity with the private and domestic body.'[7] Carter and Waters explore how far women, by 'making a spectacle of themselves' and taking their 'deviance' into the public arena, can resist the effects of the normalising discipline of the male gaze, which measures women against the values inscribed in Victorian gender discourse. Can the performer draw attention to her body, and her defiance of gender norms, and yet evade or subvert that disciplining effect?

Nights at the Circus and *Tipping the Velvet* revisit Victorian ideas of sexual difference from a more overt late twentieth-century perspective than the novels discussed previously. Carter and Waters implicitly situate their challenge to Victorian ideas about the female body in relation to recent debates about the body in feminist theory. The nineteenth-century models of sexuality outlined above are evident in each text, but the novels' emphasis on the social functioning of the body exposes the ideological basis of those allegedly objective models. The novels make it clear that, as Stevi Jackson and Sue Scott put it, 'No bodily function can ever be outside the social.'[8] Referring to the theories of Judith Butler and Christine Delphy, they go on: 'Bodies have no meaning, no significance apart from cultural context, social situation and interaction with others. It is these cultural and social practices which render our bodies intelligible to ourselves and others, as indicative of our gendered and sexual being' (p. 21). The novels' emphasis on the performance of gender, whether in or out of the arena, challenges the idea of the 'naturalness' of sexual difference, according to which both social position and sexual identity are determined by the genitals.

The newly born woman: Angela Carter, *Nights at the Circus*

While every other British novel I discuss in this book was published in the 1990s, *Nights at the Circus* appeared in 1984,[9] Angela Carter typically anticipating a literary trend by a decade. The novel also stands apart from those novels in its use of fantasy. Often described as post-modern and 'carnivalesque',[10] it is nevertheless firmly grounded in the historical reality of the 1890s. Aidan Day describes it as a 'fantasy whose symbolic meaning can be recovered in rational historical terms'.[11] He also argues that the novel provides a critique of carnival's masculinist values.[12] Carter makes these 'masculinist' values evident both in the historical reality she constructs in the novel, and in the carnival world represented by the circus, but only to show them triumphantly subverted by a winged woman who embodies the worst fears of the degeneration theorists, combining in herself the sexualised *femme fatale* and the 'masculine' New Woman. *Nights at the Circus* is set at what Carter calls 'exactly the moment in European history when things began to change. It's set at that time quite deliberately, and [Fevvers] is the new woman.'[13]

Evidence of 'degeneration' is foregrounded in the representation of Fevvers' gross physicality, which is an affront to the ideal of femininity as delicate, ethereal and spiritual. In her dressing-room, even the air comes 'in lumps' (p. 8). When Walser, the young American journalist determined to discover the 'truth' about Fevvers, first sees her, his mind fills not with Romantic images but with images of powerful and predatory animals like basking sharks; even her amatory advances feel more like warlike assaults, 'a blue bombardment from her eyes' (p. 54). Nor is this just an assault on the eyes. Fevvers' body smells; it is sweaty and dirty. In her presence, no one can be unaware of all the processes in which the living body, even when female, engages: eating and excreting, farting and belching. Her manifest enjoyment of these bodily functions makes her an outstanding example of Mary Russo's 'female grotesque', her body typifying that 'grotesque realism' which is a central category of the carnivalesque text.[14]

Fevvers' overt sexuality is further evidence of degeneration. Hers is clearly what Jackson and Scott call the 'sexual body', as opposed to the 'gendered body'. They explain: 'For women a gendered body often means a sexualized body, a body disciplined into a sexually "attractive" appearance and demeanour. This performance of sexual desirability is often equated with "female sexuality", which is thus reduced to "the look".' No one could accuse Fevvers of 'disciplining' her body into the conventional image of desirability. Instead, as the 'sexual body', she is a 'sexual subject' rather than object: 'The sexualized body is often a passive body; the sexual body implies something more engaged, whether actively or passively, in sexual practices – a body capable of sensual pleasure.' Fevvers' insistence on her sensual pleasures, which clearly include the prospect, if not the experience, of sexual pleasure, prevents her from being the mere object of Walser's gaze. But nor can she be reduced to mere body, along traditional patriarchal lines. As Jackson and Scott insist, such a sexual body, in 'anticipating and experiencing desire and pleasure cannot be *just* a body abstracted from mind, self and social context' (p. 15). Fevvers' body is, moreover, neither the source of shame the female body represents to the moralists, nor the source of weakness it appears to the scientists. Challenging the view that the female body is dominated by a reproductive system which holds mind and spirit in thrall, the young Fevvers perceives hers as 'the abode of limitless freedom' (p. 41) and glories in its strength.

Paradoxically, however, Fevvers' wings make her the literal, if parodic, embodiment of the angel of Victorian ideology. She is sufficiently aware of virginity's mystique to maintain with Walser the fiction that she is 'the only fully-feathered intacta in the history of the world' (p. 294) until their love affair reveals otherwise. In Paris she appears as 'the English Angel' (p. 8), her legendary inaccessibility contributing to her virginal aura. Her sexual status is the final truth to be revealed, long after that of her wings, emphasising its centrality in the myth of woman. But Fevvers also attempts to demystify virginity, referring to it as merely 'a scrap of cartilege [sic]' (p. 80) rather than the essential attribute of female purity. When in Siberia she meets a group of men outlawed for taking revenge on those who dishonoured their women, she challenges them: 'Wherein does a woman's honour reside, old chap? In her vagina or in her spirit?' (p. 230). Fevvers claims the status of a virgin spirit, whatever her physiological status. Known in her youth as the 'Virgin Whore' (p. 55), she continues to be an anomaly, physiologically and otherwise, defying all the categorical certainties of the experts.

Marina Warner, moreover, explains that, according to Plato, a wing 'shares in the divine nature'.[15] In the London brothel to which Fevvers is taken as a foundling, she sits in the reception room dressed as Cupid, the – usually male – God of love. When her true wings arrive with the onset of puberty, Lizzie, Fevvers' mentor and mother-surrogate, sees this as an angelic transformation, with Fevvers standing in for the male Gabriel at the 'Annunciation' not of a nativity but of Lizzie's menopause. Warner also has relevant comments to make on the gendering of this figure. She suggests that the Christian angel derives from the figure of Nike, Greek Goddess of Victory, who was never associated with love or sex, and could therefore be 'appropriated to become a holy image of heaven, altered in sex, and as it were baptized, to emerge as an archangel' (p. 80). In implicitly seeing Fevvers as the archangel, Lizzie re-appropriates the divine for women, anticipating the moment when Fevvers graduates to the role of the Winged Victory herself, improving on the original by having arms to carry a ceremonial sword symbolising her challenge to phallic power.

Fevvers' account of her early life suggests, however, that any such challenge can be contained or negated by the power of the male gaze. The problematic nature of this phase of her existence is emphasised by the painting of Leda and the Swan, hanging over the mantelpiece in the brothel parlour. Since she claims she was herself 'hatched' from an egg, Fevvers sees the painting as representing something like the primal scene of her own conception. Anne Fernihough suggests that the popularity of the Leda myth with *fin de siècle* artists was because it expressed 'the new, degenerate woman's lasciviousness, as well as a desire to return woman to her "true" position of abject submission to male authority'.[16] But Fevvers identifies with the power of the male God disguised as a bird, rather than with the helpless human Leda, although this identification remains unrealised, as her abortive attempts to fly indicate: as a statue, she still exists 'only as an object in men's eyes' (p. 39), more woman than bird. Fevvers recognises that these early years were spent serving an 'apprenticeship in *being looked at*' (p. 23). Even her role as Victory is short-lived, since a 'large woman with a sword' has an inappropriate effect on the brothel's clientele. Even symbolic representations of female power must be obliterated if they threaten male dominance.

Fevvers' uniqueness can, moreover, be a source of as much danger as delight, since her deformity makes her 'always the cripple' (p. 19). In Madame Schreck's museum of women monsters, she is employed as a 'freak' to feed male sadomasochistic fantasies. Each of these 'monsters' is, like Fevvers, in scientific terms a 'physiological anomaly' (p. 15), such as would warrant a whole chapter in Lombroso's study. But they simultaneously embody in grotesque, parodic form the myths about women which pass for knowledge. The Sleeping Beauty, for instance, is an allegorical figure representing woman as sexual object, whose only function in life is to respond to the male desire implicit in the Prince's kiss. Her condition, which reduces her entirely to her bodily functions, so that she wakes only to eat and defecate, began with the onset of puberty, a grim alternative to the female destiny represented by Fevvers' wings. The Wiltshire Wonder, on the other hand, is a Thumbelina-like parody of the ideal dainty, diminutive woman, perceived as a child or toy, anticipating the fate which Fevvers herself barely escapes in St Petersburg. These characters function within the discourse of fairy tale, reflecting woman's role as the sexual 'other', both physically impaired and the embodiment of male fantasy, and evoking in Walser a mix of revulsion and enchantment. Intended as symbols of degeneration and degradation, these exhibits instead – in the view of Fevvers and Toussaint, the only male in the establishment[17] – reveal the degradation of the customers, which is evident in their eyes. But while challenging the authority of the white male gaze, neither Fevvers nor Toussaint is able to escape from its confining power.

The wings which, in the museum, make Fevvers the image of a petrified 'tombstone Angel' appear to promise freedom when she later turns her ability to fly into a professional stage act. But how can she escape further objectification and symbolisation when even Lizzie points out that the only way Fevvers can earn a living is 'to make a show of [herself]' (p. 185)? And for a woman to 'make a spectacle of herself' has been to risk censure well into the twentieth century, according to Barbara Brook:

> Theories of the disciplining functions of the 'male gaze' suggest that she enters public (masculine) space as a potentially disruptive, transgressive body and it is her position as spectacle (making a spectacle of herself) under the view of the masculine eye, that disciplines her back into line, returns her into a docile body. (p. 112)

Writing about the specific problems of nineteenth-century female aerial acrobats, Tracy Davis is equally sceptical about their ability to resist sexual objectification, arguing that 'the eroticized implications of male spectators viewing the scantily clad female aerialist at the turn of the century suggested an unequal balance of social power, especially since the female costume was often considered "morally objectionable"'.[18] Peta Tait, however, argues that their bodies, in active and continuous movement, provided circus audiences with a transgressive pleasure. Because the feminine body was culturally identified with restraint and passivity, it was the female performers who 'demarcated a site of Imaginary freedoms' (p. 29). The female aerialist also blurred the boundaries between femininity and masculinity, 'marking her body as feminine with her gestures, poses, and costume while performing athletic, courageous acts of strength and daring commonly aligned with masculinity' (p. 28). Fevvers' performance not only transcends gender stereotypes in this way, but further subverts the female stereotype with a body which by no means presents that image of insubstantial lightness characteristic of most female high fliers. And her flight is not a magical attribute acquired with her wings. She has to master the art of flight by study and practice, to the extent that she claims to have shared her expertise with scientists, rather than being simply a passive object of their curiosity. In other words, she achieves release from Victorian gender constraints and resists objectification when she is admired for what she does, rather than what she is, when her flight, rather than her wings, is the focus of attention.

Tait's description of the aerialist's freedom as 'imaginary' nevertheless suggests her transgressions are theoretical rather than real, that 'the domain of the aerial body was symbolically powerful, but this was not necessarily a contravention of social power' (p. 34). Only within the circus can the female body display such freedom. In Fevvers' case, however, this freedom is extended beyond the circus ring, surviving the destruction of the circus itself. She subverts the discipline imposed by the discursive frameworks of social control by herself exercising control over how she is seen, and indeed read. Her slogan, 'seeing is believing' (p. 15), implies that by controlling what others see, she can control how she is perceived. Her other slogan, 'Is she fact or is she fiction?' (p. 7) keeps both her audience and Walser in a state of uncertainty, depriving them of the power of 'knowing' her and imprisoning her in any discursive constructions. From their very first interview, Fevvers confounds Walser's attempts to establish the 'truth'. She keeps her private self hidden, keeping in her dressing room 'nothing to give her away' (p. 13). While demanding the audience's attention, she refuses to allow closer access: 'Look! Hands off! LOOK AT ME!'. Instead of constructing a character through his story, the experienced journalist becomes a 'prisoner of her voice' (p. 43). Consequently, where the image in the mirror represents for theorists like Lacan an ego ideal which gives birth to a sense of lack, for Fevvers the mirror is a source of constant satisfaction, for the image that she sees reflected back is the image that she has constructed for herself. Walser cannot initially believe that Fevvers has created herself, looking for some kind of Svengali figure to explain her phenomenal success. But in 'making a spectacle of herself', Fevvers puts the emphasis on making herself. Her self-representation breaks down the body/spirit binary underlying Victorian gender ideology, and insists on a 'singularity' that defies 'scientific' attempts at classification.[19]

That singularity nevertheless has a symbolic function which is central to the novel's meaning as well as to her own sense of self. Pondering the mystery of Fevvers' status, Walser concludes that, if she is 'fact', if her wings are real, she is no longer a brilliant artiste whose performance is to be admired, but only a freak to be gawped at: 'an exemplary being denied the human privilege of flesh and blood, always the object of the observer, never the subject of sympathy, an alien creature forever estranged' (p. 161). But the text proves him wrong, since Fevvers herself consciously foregrounds her 'exemplary' status while demanding recognition both as a 'real woman', and as a representative of the woman of the future who will no longer tolerate being 'the object of the observer'. In that future she will no longer be an alien, 'a singular being', but 'the female paradigm, no longer an imagined fiction but a plain fact' (p. 286). Her unique body has a symbolic power which she feels responsible for revealing to the public. Her wings not only embody her aspirations but represent womanhood as it might be. As the Winged Victory, she is, according to Ma Nelson, 'the perfection of, the original of, the very model for that statue which, in its broken and incomplete state, has teased the imagination of a brace of millennia with its promise of perfect, active beauty that has been, as it were, mutilated by history' (p. 37). Constantly battling to free herself from the symbolic use to which others attempt to put her, the mature Fevvers attempts to fulfil this 'promise', consciously constructing herself as the 'New Woman', in stark contrast to the 'symbolic woman' (p. 96) of the old order embodied in the baboushka of Petersburg, constantly moving between the roles of Mary, the spiritualised woman at prayer, and Martha, engaged in domestic chores. Fevvers as 'female grotesque' therefore constitutes as much of a political statement as Lizzie's more overt social commentary. That politics is articulated in her anticipation of a glorious future: 'All the women will have wings, the same as I. [...] The dolls' house doors will open, the brothels will spill forth their prisoners, the cages, gilded or otherwise, all over the world, in every land, will let forth their inmates singing together the dawn chorus of the new, the transformed – ' (p. 285).

Ma Nelson's awareness of what Fevvers represents further validates Fevvers' symbolic function. For Fevvers is not alone in her aspirations, as is evident from the female counter-cultures represented throughout the novel. The novel does, indeed, show prostitutes and prisoners escaping, as well as Fevvers' own escape from the miniature gilded cage with which the Russian Grand Duke threatens her. The brothel in which Fevvers' significant singularity is first realised contains, according to Victorian ideology, criminal degenerates with an insatiable sexual appetite. But contesting Baudelaire's view of prostitutes as '*damned souls* who did it solely to lure men to their dooms' (p. 38), Fevvers describes them simply as working girls inhabiting by choice a female world, a sisterhood ruled by 'a sweet and loving reason' (p. 39). Prostitution is represented here not as evidence of female insanity, but as a rational choice, taking place in a building belonging to the Age of Reason – 'in which rational desires might be rationally gratified' (p. 26). The brothel also implicitly deconstructs the feminine ideal of maternity. The scientific view that woman is 'in bondage to her reproductive system, [. . .] tied hand and foot to that Nature which [Fevvers'] physiology denies' (p. 283) is here firmly discredited. Acting as 'mothers' to the abandoned infant Fevvers, the prostitutes demonstrate that motherhood is a function distinct from biology, an idea reinforced by her dramatic claim that her 'natural mother' is London. Mothering is not to be despised, only chosen.[20] The association of the prostitutes with motherhood also challenges the separation of maternity and sexuality inscribed in the ideal of the Virgin Mother, the most revered Christian image of woman. The prostitutes cannot resist patriarchal law, as Ma Nelson's brother closes down the brothel after her death, but the novel continues to affirm that prostitution is a profession rather than a disease, providing an optimistic view of the possibilities opened up to women by the turn of the century. Carter comments: 'All the women who have been in the first brothel with her end up doing these "new women" jobs, like becoming hotel managers and running typing agencies and so on' (Katsavos, p. 13).

The second female counter-culture in the novel meets a similarly Utopian end, but with the emphasis on collective rather than individual liberation. The female prison introduced in Part Three of the novel has little bearing on the novel's plot, but reproduces Victorian gender ideology in the Siberian wastes, as if to reinforce the extent of patriarchy's empire.[21] Designed on 'the most scientific principles available' (p. 210), with the aid of a French criminologist with an interest in phrenology,[22] the prison is modelled on Jeremy Bentham's panopticon. Each prisoner sits 'in the trap of her visibility' (p. 211), never knowing when the Countess, in her swivel chair at the centre, might be watching her. Such a sense of perpetual surveillance is intended to make the prisoner internalise her guilt. In Foucault's words, 'The inmates should be caught up in a power situation of which they are themselves the bearers' (*Discipline and Punish*, p. 201). This 'scientific' system, designed to isolate both prisoners and warders, is nevertheless defeated by the power of female 'desire, that electricity transmitted by the charged touch of' two women (p. 216). Touch and look, the non-verbal language of the body, prove effective means of communication when speech is forbidden. The catalyst for revolution in the prison is the message which one of the prisoners writes to one of the guards, using her own menstrual blood, a product of the very reproductive process which – according to many of the sexual scientists of the time – both defines woman and defiles her. What so often provokes disgust here provokes an explosion of love: ceasing to see their charges as criminals, or objects of a scientific experiment, the guards are 'all subverted to the inmates' humanity through look, caress, word, image' (p. 217). The prolonged repression of these transgressive impulses gives rise to an equal amount of empowering psychic anger, enabling all the women to break out of the prison to 'inscribe whatever future they wished' on the white world outside (p. 223). But their plan to create 'a female Utopia in the taiga' (p. 240) is a problematic form of subversion, since it can only exist outside patriarchy, rather than transform it, and runs the danger of becoming its mirror-image. For while they can reject all fathers, abandoning use of the patronymic, the community's long-term survival depends on their use of frozen sperm donated by a male escapee. When Lizzie sourly wonders whether they will kill all the male babies, she conjures up visions of an infanticidal culture which bears all too close a correspondence to existing cultures which do not value female offspring.

Sandwiched, chronologically, between these two female counter-cultures is the mixed-sex world of the circus, the dominant image in the novel. Embodying the spirit of 'carnival', licensing behaviour which parodies or reverses the norms of the world outside, the circus appears to provide an arena in which dominant gender ideology can be challenged. A number of humorous reversals of this kind do occur, usually when Walser needs to be rescued from male rivals by women: Fevvers, for instance, uses the hosepipe on the Strong Man in what Walser feels is 'a disturbingly masculine fashion' (p. 166), shaking off the last few drips. But as Fernihough suggests, more often Carter's circus shows how these 'carnivalesque tropes' can 'serve very different ends from the radical, utopian ones emphasized by Bakhtin'. This circus serves, ultimately, 'to reinforce social hierarchies, not to subvert them' (p. 104), proving dangerous for women and other marginalised groups. The appropriately named Monsieur Lamarck, the Ape-Man, seduces the fragile, vulnerable Mignon 'solely to abuse her' (p. 140). But here too resistance comes through female desire, the love that develops between Mignon and the Princess of Abyssinia, the tiger tamer.

Each of these counter-cultures appears to suggest that in a patriarchal society, only same-sex relationships between women can subvert the heterosexual power structures that inflict so much damage on them. Part of Fevvers' 'singularity', however, is to envisage the possibility of heterosexual relationships which do not sacrifice female autonomy. Her relationship with Walser confounds conventional Victorian expectations, largely because it blurs the distinctions between the sexes just as the *Punch* author feared. Like Hélène Cixous' 'newly born woman',[23] the 'hatched' Fevvers transcends traditional gender boundaries, bearing such marks of 'masculinity' as the 'strong, firm, masculine grip' (p. 89), and 'Brobdingnagian' features which make Walser wonder whether she might even be a man. As the 'New Woman', she acts out roles thought by most Victorian commentators to be the prerogative of men. Walser is in turn 'hatched' by Fevvers as 'the New Man, [...] fitting mate for the New Woman' (p. 281) for the New Century about to start. His original persona as 'a man of action' (p. 10) breaks down under the clown's mask, and even more radically when he experiences amnesia and madness after the train crash. Woken, like Sleeping Beauty, with a kiss, his first word is 'Mama': he too is newly born, 'a perfect blank' (p. 222). He loses the 'wits' that he thought constituted his identity, becoming instead 'all sensibility', transposing the more familiar associations of masculinity with reason, and femininity with feeling. On finding him again, Fevvers' first thought is that he has become 'a wild, wild woman' (p. 250). He has indeed been 'feminized' by his experience of masquerade under the clown's make-up, and of vulnerability.[24]

In blurring sexual differences, the relationship between the New Man and the New Woman also disrupts the hierarchy built into theories of sexual difference. Walser has to abandon his attempt to construct Fevvers for public consumption through the normalising discourse of his writing while remaining secure in his own position as male observer. He is instead to be her 'amanuensis', to bear witness both to her uniqueness and to 'the histories of those women who would other-wise go down nameless and forgotten, erased from history as if they had never been' (p. 286). Walser's experience of the hallucinatory world of the Siberian shaman has left him unable to distinguish fact from fiction, unable even to draw any conclusions from his discovery that Fevvers has no navel, a 'fact' which he once thought would provide the final answer to her mystery. The 'reconstructed Walser' (p. 291) is ready to believe whatever Fevvers tells him, rather than trying to fit it into his own preconceptions about women. Just as the circus chimps, who appear to be studying Darwin's theory 'from the other end' (p. 110), lead Walser to question the accepted evolutionary hierarchy of man and beast, so Fevvers leads him to surrender the gender hierarchy that puts man in the position of privileged observer, and producer of knowledge. This subversion is vividly enacted in a reversal of the iconic image of Leda and the swan: when Fevvers couples with Walser, she takes the dominant position of the feathered god, smothering him in feathers and reducing him to helpless but willing passivity.

It can, nevertheless, be argued that Fevvers' desire for Walser is a betrayal of her role as the 'New Woman', who was commonly perceived to need only a career. Lizzie appears to endorse such a view with her numerous warnings that marriage is 'prostitution to one man instead of many' (p. 21). When, in Siberia, Fevvers longs 'to see herself reflected in all her remembered splendour in [Walser's] grey eyes' (p. 273), is she not guilty of needing the validation offered by the male gaze? Fevvers is aware of such dangers: when she finds him again, and does see herself in his eyes,

> instead of Fevvers, she saw two perfect miniatures of a dream. [...] She felt herself trapped forever in the reflection in Walser's eyes. For one moment, just one moment, Fevvers suffered the worst crisis of her life: 'Am I fact? Or am I fiction? Am I what I know I am? Or am I what he thinks I am?' (p. 290)

And she is not prepared to fulfil any man's 'dream' or fantasy. Unlike young Melanie, in Carter's *The Magic Toyshop*, who wants to see herself reflected in the eyes of her cousin Finn, because there is no mirror in the house, nothing else to tell her who she is, Fevvers seeks confirmation of the 'remembered splendour' she has seen for herself in her own dressing-room mirror.

That confirmation is primarily provided by her audience, 'the eyes that told her who she was' (p. 290). In Siberia, indeed, Lizzie warns her that she is 'fading' as if only the 'discipline of the audience' keeps her visible (p. 280). Walser's value to her is always partly that he represents that audience, so that, as Lizzie also observes, she acts 'more and more *like* [herself] [...] more and more like [her] own publicity' (pp. 197–8) when he is around. This observation emphasises Fevvers' success in constructing the identity that she hands out for public consumption, while acknowledging the part that her public plays in maintaining it. Walser's gaze is only one of the reflective surfaces that confirm her sense of self-worth. Fevvers' story is contrasted with that of the clowns to suggest that the self cannot be constructed in isolation, only through relationship. When Walser becomes a clown, he is excited by the idea that the clown mask gives him total freedom to be whatever he wants behind it, but Buffo the Great warns him that, once he has adopted the mask, and become his own construction, he will be reduced to it, so that when he takes it off, he will be nothing. To symbolise the nihilism inherent in this withdrawal from relationship, the clowns perform a 'dance of disintegration; and of regression; celebration of the primal slime' (p. 125). The dance offers an image of degeneration in contrast to Fevvers, who stands as an image of the evolution of woman, images which together confound Victorian concepts of degeneration and evolution.

In terms of its plot, *Nights at the Circus* appears to confirm the worst fears of the degeneration theorists about the catastrophes that will follow any breakdown of the hierarchies that have emerged through millennia of evolution. As Fevvers' lyrical evocation of the future when all women will have 'wings' predicts, prostitutes leave their brothels and infiltrate respectable society with impunity; murderers escape their prisons; outlaws blow up trains; even dumb animals take control of their own destinies. The celebratory conclusion of the novel, however, suggests great optimism not only about the empowered future for women of the twentieth century – with only a slight dampening effect from Lizzie – but also about the simultaneous survival of personal relationships. Love, whether between women, between men and women, or in the form of 'maternal' care, is shown throughout the novel to be a powerful and necessary force. And while Lizzie warns Fevvers of the dangers of giving herself to a man, Fevvers insists that because her being is 'unique and indivisible' (p. 280), it cannot be given or taken. She demonstrates this in her amusement over having fooled him for so long with her mythical virginity. Her consequent infectious laughter reverberates through the novel's final pages. But her laughter is, I suggest, not only about the success of her deceit, but an expression of her delight at the 'giant comedy' (p. 294) of life, in which we fool each other with our stories and fall in love with them. It is a delight in story and story-telling which is, of course, Carter's own, a delight in particular in women's ability to construct singular fictions of themselves to provide release from the straightjackets to which 'scientific' and other laws would confine them.

Performing gender: Sarah Waters, *Tipping the Velvet*

By the 1890s, when most of Sarah Waters' novel, *Tipping the Velvet*[25] is set, the difficulty of conceptualising lesbian identity had passed, and there was no shortage of literature attempting to classify different 'pathologies' within this group of women. In 1892, for instance, *Psychopathia Sexualis*, by the German psychiatrist Richard von Krafft-Ebing, was first published in English.[26] Including lesbianism in its list of 'perversions', it played a significant part in the development of a body of 'knowledge' about female homosexuality.[27] In 1892, lesbianism is similarly identified as a sexual perversion or '"inversion" of the sexual feelings', associated with 'temporary or permanent conditions of degenerative mental disturbance' in Tuke's *Dictionary of Psychological Medicine*, a standard work that indicates the mainstream contemporary approach.[28] Waters appears to refer to Krafft-Ebing when a well-educated upper-class lesbian claims that her own life story has been used by a doctor in a book with a Latin title in 'an attempt to explain our sort so that the ordinary world will understand us' (p. 311). Whether or not Krafft-Ebing had such an aim, his accounts of cultures in which women lived closely together, in harems or even simply in poverty, produced such sensational 'findings' about women developing huge clitorises that it simply endorsed the view of lesbianism as a pathological condition.

What is distinctively Victorian is the determination to find biological bases for this 'condition', which would make it easier to identify as a pathology. Havelock Ellis, for instance, cites evidence that lesbians have 'a very decided masculine type of larynx', and a 'comparative absence of soft connective tissue' (Oram, p. 34), making them 'unfeminine' to touch. It is ironic, then, that Nancy develops a distinctly 'masculine' musculature when engaged in 'women's work', housework, exposing the fictitious nature of such conventional gender paradigms. The sexologists of the period were generally agreed on defining lesbianism as a medical problem, whether physical or psychological. One American doctor, Allan McLane Hamilton, claimed in 1896 that a lesbian was 'usually of a masculine type, or if she presented none of the "characteristics" of the male, was a subject of pelvic disorder, with scanty menstruation, and was more or less hysterical or insane' (quoted in Faderman, p. 155).

A typical early work (1869), by the German psychiatrist Carl von Westphal, based its argument on a case study of a 'congenital invert', whose 'abnormality' was the result of hereditary degeneration and neurosis. Subsequently, medical journals were flooded with papers on this newly identified 'type' (Faderman, p. 239).

Nancy Astley, Waters' central character, would probably therefore have been included in the category of 'inverts', whom Havelock Ellis identifies as those who not only misdirect their sexual feelings towards their own sex, but also assume the characteristics and privileges of men. When she sees an advertisement in a shop window for a 'Fe-male Lodger' (p. 211), she sees herself in the hyphen, bridging female and male. Inversion involved an individual thinking, feeling and acting in ways typical of the opposite sex, which encroached on male prerogatives, unlike female homosexuality which referred purely to sexual desire for another woman. Such thinking rests on the assumption that sexual differences are rigid and clearly defined. The mere presence in a woman of any sexual or social assertiveness, therefore, any desire for independence and power, indicated that she was not really a woman. Like Fevvers, Nancy seeks a freedom, both in performance and in love, usually denied to women. But her desires are even more transgressive than Fevvers', since Victorian ideas about the 'naturalness' of sexual difference made heterosexuality the only 'normal' and therefore legitimate form of sexuality. Nancy's story therefore illustrates one of the central tenets of twentieth-century gender theory: that gender divisions sustain and are sustained by normative heterosexuality. To this extent contemporary perspectives ironically endorse the Victorian fear that lesbianism is as much about gender roles as it is about sexuality.

The opening chapters of *Tipping the Velvet* present a world recognisably like that of *Nights at the Circus*. Nancy's first meeting with the music-hall performer Kitty Butler in her dressing-room recalls Carter's opening chapter, in which another performer removes her greasepaint in the company of an admirer, but in Kitty's case the admirer is female rather than male. The dirty clothes, cigarette ends, filthy teacups are all there, creating the same sense of a solidly physical, if slightly sordid world, although the scene lacks the grotesque exaggeration characteristic of the earlier novel. Both novels offer picaresque accounts of a young woman's adventures in a wide variety of worlds, although Nancy sets out with an innocence of life never much in evidence in Fevvers. And both are in a sense about women with wings. Nancy notices that onstage as a male impersonator Kitty's step is lighter, 'as if the admiration of the audience lent her wings' (p. 17), and has a similar experience herself when 'performing' as a man in the real world. Cutting off her hair for the second time, she feels as if she had 'a pair of wings beneath [her] shoulderblades, that the flesh had grown over, and she was slicing free' (p. 405). But in the fantastic world of *Nights at the Circus*, Fevvers' wings are real, whereas Nancy's are metaphorical, representing the freedom that comes from dressing as a man.

Cross-dressing has a long history in the theatre, as anyone familiar with Shakespearean comedy will be aware. And even in the early nineteenth century, it was presented as a legitimate activity in such forms of popular culture as the broadsheet ballads. Later in the century, however, even the theatre came under suspicion as a location which congenital 'inverts' might exploit to turn susceptible young women into 'femmes'. Havelock Ellis, for instance, quotes a friend who worried that for girls to be cooped up together in dressing rooms 'in a state of inaction and excitement' encouraged the growth of lesbian feelings (quoted in Oram, p. 99). For women to dress as men onstage increased such dangers, since, as Oram explains, 'expressions of female desire for women can occur in the fantasy space of entertainment', which opens up 'complex sexual ambiguities and possibilities for women audiences' (p. 13). Nancy observes that the originality of Kitty's 'masher act', in which she masquerades as a fashionable young male womaniser, is that the transformation is complete, unlike earlier female impersonators who wore women's clothes with such male accessories as a man's hat and cane. Carol Wolkowitz explains the transgressive impact of such impersonation by suggesting that trousers paradoxically draw attention to sexual difference. While a woman's skirts confirm gender difference by conforming to gendered dress codes, they conceal the sexed body; trousers on women, in contrast, suggest the artificiality of gender difference while drawing attention to difference in the genital area.[29] Nancy also associates Kitty's appearance with other forms of transgression, observing, 'If I had ever seen women with hair as short as hers, it was because they had spent time in hospital or prison; because they were mad' (p. 12). Kitty's new manager, Walter Bliss, advises her to make her act even more convincing by scrutinising men in the street, so she can copy not just their external features, but their inner lives, 'their characters, their little habits, their mannerisms and gaits' (p. 83). So total is her adoption of the male role that she assumes with it the power of the male gaze: although dependent on the approval of the audience, Kitty can manipulate its response well enough to make the young women in the audience long for her gaze, to be the recipient of her parting look and the rose that she throws with it.

Kitty's act is, however, transgressive only within limits. The audience experiences a frisson of pleasure at seeing women wearing men's clothes and singing men's songs, while remaining distinctly female. When Nancy first sees Kitty on stage, she registers that her figure is 'boy-like and slender – yet rounded, vaguely but unmistakably, at the bosom, the stomach, and the hips, in a way no real boy's ever was' (p. 13). As Wolkowitz suggests, sexual difference is not eliminated by this kind of cross-dressing but enhanced, the masculinity of the clothing and hair bringing the femininity of the performer into sharper focus. In contrast, when Nancy first puts on male costume, she causes Kitty and Walter some anxiety because she looks too much like a boy, and her costume has to be altered to create the illusion of feminine curves which she does not possess. The theatre, like the circus and the carnival, licenses the temporary breaching of gender boundaries within its walls as long as it ultimately sustains the concept of sexual difference. Nancy notices, for instance, that when Kitty, as Prince Charming, kisses Cinderella in the pantomime, it is perfectly acceptable. The conventions of this traditional form of theatrical cross-dressing paradoxically reinforce the heterosexual norm.

A double act in which two women are dressed as men, however, threatens to destabilise that norm, exposing the limits of acceptable transgression. Although the act which Kitty and Nancy perform is initially popular for its originality, it is destroyed the moment that a drunk in the audience calls them 'Toms', a current and common slang term for lesbians, and sweeps aside the distinction Kitty tries to maintain between herself and Nancy and those 'Toms' who 'make a – a *career* – out of kissing girls' (p. 131). His intervention draws attention to the transgressive subtext underlying male impersonation – that it is not simply a matter of usurping male roles, but makes possible the more illicit pleasure of the female gaze. As Jackie Stacey puts it, the dominant convention of the male gaze identified by Mulvey is contradicted by texts which explore 'the fascination of one woman for another', and therefore cater for the pleasure of the female spectator who is 'invited to look or gaze with one female character at another, in an interchange of feminine fascinations'.[30] By identifying the performance of Nancy and Kitty as more than a mere act, as an extension of their private lives, the heckler's comments moreover cause Kitty to lose her hold over the audience for the first time, destroying the 'wings' of confidence and self-esteem which it gives her. The audience can turn Kitty into 'a woman in the grip of a drug, or in the first flush of an embrace' (p. 37) but it also enacts a powerful form of surveillance, because she internalises its judgement and is unable to withstand its impact. As she tells Nancy, 'so long as I am looked at, I cannot bear also to be – *laughed* at; or hated; or scorned' (p. 171).

While a successful male impersonator on stage therefore, offstage Kitty hides her desire for other women behind the mask of femininity which will prove her to be a 'real' woman. Her performance on stage is in fact, closer to 'reality', in the sense that it suggests her transgressive sexuality, than is her 'performance' in life. And that mask is given institutional force through her marriage to Walter, who appears to hold Havelock Ellis's view that 'normal' women could be distinguished from true inverts because relationships with men would bring their 'normal instincts... into permanent play' (quoted in Faderman, p. 241). Nancy's friend Tony Reeves unwittingly identifies Kitty 's strategy when he describes her as 'a bit of an oyster'. Nancy's father explains that, although all oysters look male because of their beards, the oyster is 'what you might call a real queer fish – now a he, now a she, as quite takes its fancy. A regular morphodite, in fact!' (p. 49). 'Morphodite' originally denoted a hermaphrodite, any creature with both male and female sex characteristics, and it is not evident whether Mr Astley understands its later use to denote a homosexual, especially 'one overtly manifesting features regarded as characteristic of the opposite sex' (*OED*, New Edition). Nancy, who was 'raised an oyster-girl' (p. 4), belongs to the second category, and Kitty immediately responds to what she senses in her, loving her the minute she smells the oyster-liquor on Nancy's fingers which pre-figures the smell of her own bodily fluids on Nancy's fingers when they make love. Nancy's biggest mistake is to assume that she and Kitty are as alike as two halves of an oyster.[31] On the night that she first kisses Kitty, when the River Thames starts to freeze, Nancy is awed by 'that extraordinary, ordinary transformation, that easy submission to the urgings of a natural law, that was yet so rare and so unsettling', a miracle that reflects the 'natural' but 'rare' thing that is happening to her and Kitty (p. 101). She too has 'journeyed against the current' (p. 86), and imagines walking across the river if it froze over, but Kitty is too afraid, just as she is too afraid to acknowledge her sexuality in public.

For Nancy, however, the intimacy and pleasure of their private acts feeds into their public act:

> A double act is always twice the act the audience thinks it: beyond our songs, our steps, our bits of business with coins and canes and flowers, there was a private language, – in which we held an endless,

delicate exchange of which the crowd knew nothing. This was a language not of the tongue but of the body, its vocabulary the pressure of a finger or a palm, the nudging of a hip, the holding or breaking of a gaze, that said, *You are too slow – you go too fast – not there, but here – that's good – that's better!* (p. 128)

And she is prepared to make their private relationship public. Like Fevvers, she is prepared to take her transgressive sexuality outside the theatre into the real world, seeing the streets as an extension of the theatre: 'Both are a curious mix of magic and necessity, glamour and sweat. Both have their types – their *ingénues* and *grandes dames*, their rising stars, their falling stars, their bill-toppers, their hacks...' (p. 203). Nancy initially adopts male dress in public to avoid being the object of the male gaze 'in a city where girls walked only to be gazed at' (p. 191). Now the glances slither past, and she can walk in freedom, 'as a handsome boy in a well-sewn suit, whom the people stared after only to envy, never to mock' (p. 195). But she also achieves her greatest success as a performer of masculinity here in the illicit, dangerous and sometimes degrading world of the 'renter'. By passing as a young male homosexual, she subverts the idea that gender and sexuality have a biological basis, suggesting instead a performative view of gender similar to that proposed by Judith Butler, who sees gender as a repeated 'reenactment and reexperiencing of a set of meanings already socially established'.[32] Clothes play a vital role in this 're-enactment', as Nancy knows, having already experienced the transforming effect of the dress Kitty bought her for Christmas: it is, paradoxically, 'practically a disguise', turning her into a 'grown-up woman' (pp. 94–5), and making Kitty in turn adopt a masculine pose, aggressively accusing Nancy of 'fancying' someone else. Male clothing appears to produce not only gender but sexuality. The further Nancy ventures into 'boyishness', the greater her desire for Kitty, as if taking on a male persona liberates her to be sexually assertive. As a site where walking and watching are the main activities, the street heightens this sense that all gender is performative. The 'feminine' qualities, constructed with 'lipstick and lavender', that signal Nancy's status as a rent boy are as false as her masculinity.

Nancy's story, however, largely reverses the trajectory followed by Fevvers. While Fevvers' spectacular success as a performer releases her from being the passive object of the male gaze, Nancy's early success as a performer is followed by a way of life that increasingly objectifies her. *Tipping the Velvet* therefore appears less optimistic than *Nights at the Circus* about the power of women's 'wings' to transcend the restrictions of Victorian gender norms. This is partly because, unlike the fantastic world that Fevvers inhabits, Nancy's world is presented as one in which verifiable social and historical forces operate. As narrator, Nancy draws the reader's attention to the realities of the lives of working-class people like herself: the misery of cold weather for the fish trade, and for the London poor, who bring their babies into the warmth of the music hall to prevent them dying of frostbite at home. Her experience of the London underworld suggests the vulnerability of those who have nothing but their bodies as a source of income, and even her time among the respectable poor suggests the particular vulnerability of women, such as Lilian, the young socialist whose belief in 'the free union' (p. 394) did not prevent her from being abandoned by her lover, thrown out of her lodgings, and dying shortly after childbirth without a midwife, because she was an unmarried mother. While similar threats are present throughout *Nights at the Circus*, Fevvers' wings always offer the potential for escape; Nancy's cross-dressing provides no such easy way out.

The moment Nancy becomes a renter, she once more subjects herself to the male gaze. She tries to avoid the feeling of objectification by rationalising that to be looked at and desired by men who think she too is homosexual is to be 'in some queer way, *revenged*' (p. 201). Through her impersonation she, as it were, subjects men to the male gaze, and makes them suffer for their desires as one man, Walter, made her suffer for hers. But her clients, like her, suffer what Oscar Wilde calls the 'love that dare not speak its name', unlike Walter, who is free to take his pleasure where he likes, so that her revenge misses its target. And as a 'male' prostitute, her body is just as much a commodity as that of those female prostitutes described by Victorian sexologists as deviant criminals. The very success of her impersonation, moreover, creates its own ironies. Not having an audience for 'such marvellous performances' (p. 206), she alone is conscious of her transgression of gender boundaries, so that its significance as a subversive act is nullified.

Nancy's experiences as a cross-dresser tend also to undermine the idea that homosexuality is in itself a transformative, subversive power, because they make it clear that all sexual experience is constructed and constrained by the social. Her decline from empowered performer to passive sexual object is dramatically evident in her relationship with the rich Diana Lethaby, even though Diana provides the admiring audience she has missed. Diana conforms to the type of lesbian described by Havelock Ellis as most commonly found in the upper ranks of society, 'for here we have much greater liberty of action', and as admirers of feminine beauty, unlike 'the normal woman whose sexual emotion is but faintly tinged by aesthetic feeling' (quoted in Oram, p. 101). What he unwittingly registers is the relationship between the gaze and the structures of power, for the controlling gaze is an effect of the power relations which have traditionally typified male–female relationships, but can be replicated even in consensual same-sex relationships, if one wields economic and/or social dominance over the other. Nancy initially believes herself to be part of 'a perfect kind of double act' (p. 282), enjoying once more 'the thrill of performing with a partner at [her] side, someone who knew the songs, the patter, the pose [...], playing whore and trick so well [they] might have been reciting a dialogue from some handbook of tartery!' (p. 235). But rather than being partnered by Diana, Nancy is owned by her. Diana's wealth enables her to 'buy' Nancy, as she might any other 'find' that she picks up 'for a song in some grim market' (p. 277). At Felicity Place, the house Diana has dedicated to Sapphic pleasure, Nancy is no longer in control of her own performance or her own identity. When Diana starts caressing her breasts, Nancy feels 'like a man being transformed into a woman at the hand of a sorceress' (pp. 239–40), and that Diana has 'created [her] anew' (p. 251). Diana becomes Nancy's only audience, so that she barely exists when Diana is not there: 'like a spectre – the ghost [...], of a handsome youth, who had died in that house and still walked its corridors and chambers, searching, searching, for reminders of the life that he had lost there' (p. 265). And she is eventually completely objectified, a 'living picture, a blonde lord or angel whom a jealous artist had captured and transfixed behind the glass' (p. 270), adopting poses for the entertainment and titillation of Diana and her friends, just as much a freak as Fevvers in the Museum of Monsters. Her primary function is to be displayed, although Diana fears that 'like a photograph [she] might fade, from too much handling' (p. 280), because she is also used, like Fevvers, for pornographic purposes. Dressed for Diana's birthday party as Antinous, favourite page of the Roman emperor Hadrian, she is told by a guest that she looks 'like a picture from a buggers' compendium' (p. 309). During this period, seeing Kitty in a double act with Walter, Nancy is horrified to see her 'saucy, swaggering Kitty [...] play the child, with her husband, in stockings to the knee' (p. 295), acting out a grotesque parody of marital relations. But she too has become little more than a theatrical prop, proof of Diana's daring, but demonstrating nothing of her own skills. Hearing Diana speak to her in the same tones she uses to her servants, Nancy has to recognise that bodies can be commodified in lesbian relationships as in heterosexual ones. She is still, in effect, a renter.

Felicity Place is, moreover, no more part of the real world than the theatre is: the subversive elements it embodies are as safely contained within its walls as those of carnival and the circus are contained by their structural limits. It feels 'timeless' to Nancy precisely because it fails to engage with historical and social reality and therefore to effect any change. Nor does her sexual liberation guarantee liberation in the wider sense. Her belief that she will be paradoxically freer with Diana, 'bound to lust, bound to pleasure' (p. 249), seems to accord with Foucault's view that, as the site of pleasure, the body holds a potential for resistance to power. Yet, as Jackson and Scott argue against Foucault, 'the body is inseparable from the totality of the self. If we forget this, foregrounding the body does not challenge body–mind dualism, but actually reinstates it' (p. 19).[33] Persuading herself that the submission or even degradation to which she subjects her body will have no impact on her emotional or intellectual life, Nancy's emphasis on her body and its sexual functions as 'performance' suggests just such a dualism, and denies the reality of those social forces which determine how her body is being used. Her 'performances', even in the intimacy of the sexual act, cannot escape the social.

For in spite of her apparent liberation from conventions of femininity, Nancy is totally lacking in social and political awareness until she meets Florence, whose radicalism pervades her understanding of both the political and the personal. The photograph of Eleanor Marx given to Florence by Lilian represents her social conscience and her political consciousness, as well as her love for Lilian. Constantly on view, this photograph is Florence's 'audience'. Joining Florence on her visits to the poor, to encourage them to join unions, Nancy realises with shame that the fine linen she wore at Diana's was created in conditions of dire poverty. And her naive suggestion that she could be a kind of wife, doing what most women do, while Florence and Ralph are at work, offers the 'worst argument' that she could use in the home of two socialist and feminist radicals. Her comment, 'It's natural, ain't it?' (p. 371) shows how limited is her understanding of the constructed nature of gender roles. Felicity Place, protected by the privilege of wealth, may be where she can enjoy wearing and being admired for her male clothing in complete liberty, but the East End is where she finds the freedom to take that masculinity into the streets, not as a 'renter', but as a worker. Poverty blurs the boundaries of the gendered dress code, trousers being more acceptable on women in Bethnal Green than in more respectable parts of London. And at the Frigate, a meeting-place for lesbian women, Nancy is surrounded by women dressed in men's clothing. *Tipping the Velvet*, like *Nights at the Circus*, suggests the potential for change in women's lives at the end of the century, but only after meeting Florence does Nancy find herself living and working with women who are actively involved in bringing about change, so that she can go beyond the 'subversive' masquerades of Felicity Place, which change nothing outside its walls. At the end of the Workers Rally in Hyde Park, Nancy concludes that 'it was Florence's passion, and hers alone, that had set the whole park fluttering' (p. 472), as well as her own heart. But, as Ralph tells his audience, 'you must do more than cheer. You must *act*' (p. 459).

Furthermore, Nancy has to learn to distinguish between acting as playing a part and acting as doing. She cannot engage effectively with the world around her until she takes control of her own life, rather than performing according to other people's 'scripts'. All too ready to surrender her own identity, she is happy to become 'Nan' or any other name, or to have 'gone nameless entirely' (p. 36), in order to become whatever her lovers want. In order to persuade Florence and Ralph to give her a home, she acts the part of an outcast, responding to Florence's prompts with a story similar to Lilian's: 'it was as if she was handing me the play text, for me to read it back to her' (p. 355). When she finds out about Florence's love for Lilian, she realises that she 'had believed [herself] playing in one kind of story, when all the time, the plot had been a different one – when all the time, [she] was only clumsily rehearsing what the fascinating Lilian had done so well and cleverly before' (p. 398). Even when Nancy puts her skills as a performer to political use, saving Ralph's speech at the rally from total disaster, Florence accuses her of bad faith because she speaks with such conviction without belief. Florence demands sincerity. Consequently, Nancy's final realisation of her love for Florence leaves her speechless. As she tells Florence, 'I feel like I've been repeating other people's speeches all my life. Now, when I want to make a speech of my own, I find I hardly know how' (p. 471). Her love finally dares to speak its name when she kisses Florence in public at the rally. Dressed in women's clothes, she no longer needs to masquerade as male to legitimise her love for women. The 'muffled cheer' and 'rising ripple of applause' (p. 472) coming from a nearby speakers' tent are not this time for her, but nevertheless are a symbolic acknowledgment that she can now act as herself in public, and use her own voice. Since she no longer needs to pretend, Nancy can exchange the admiration of an audience for the pleasures of the reciprocal gaze: Florence's words, 'that were so warm, had melted [their] gazes the one into the other' (p. 427).

Nancy learns therefore that sexual liberation, to be meaningful, has to be part of a wider social and political agenda. If men and women are social, rather than biological, categories, then the 'performance' of gender must have social implications. Although she and Florence joke about whether their transgressive sexuality contributes to the social revolution, anticipating some of the arguments of the second wave of the women's movement, they appear to take such a possibility seriously when they read to each other Edward Carpenter's poem, *Towards Democracy*.[34] Similarly, Nancy at first reads Florence's copy of Walt Whitman mockingly, but is ultimately moved by his utopian vision of equality: 'O my comrade! [...] O you and me at last – and us two only; O power, liberty, eternity at last! O to be relieved of distinctions! to make as much of vices as virtues! O to level occupations and the sexes! O to bring all to common ground!' (p. 393). The elimination of class and gender difference is here envisaged as a social and political act, not just a personal choice. And while Florence shares Fevvers' confidence in the coming of change in a future where she will not be the only woman with wings, Florence's vision includes a much more explicit sense of the processes through which that will be achieved:

> Things *are* changing. There are unions everywhere – and women's unions, as well as men's. Women do things today their mothers would have laughed to think of seeing their daughters doing, twenty years ago; soon they will even have the vote! If people like me don't work, it's because they look at the world, at all the injustice and the muck, and all they see is a nation falling in upon itself, and taking them with it. But the muck has new things growing out of it – wonderful things! – new habits of working, new kinds of people, new ways of being alive and in love... (p. 391)

Those nineteenth-century commentators who linked lesbianism with feminism as dangerous forces which subverted social stability were, therefore, astute in recognising their common ground and their potential combined power. As long as lesbianism remained hidden beneath the veneer of femininity, as it is in Kitty, it could be condoned or at least ignored. Only when it invaded public spaces and consciousness in the form of cross-dressing, or the kind of 'masculine' behaviour and demands associated with the New Woman, was it perceived as a real threat. As Faderman puts it:

> As long as [lesbians] appeared feminine, their sexual behavior would be viewed as an activity in which women indulged when men were unavailable or as an apprenticeship or appetite-whetter to heterosexual sex. But if one or both of the pair demanded masculine privileges, the illusion of lesbianism as *faute de mieux* behavior was destroyed. At the base it was not the sexual aspect of lesbianism as much as the attempted usurpation of male prerogative by women who behaved like men that many societies appeared to find most disturbing. (p. 17)

The sexologists therefore attempted to frighten women away from both lesbianism and feminism with theories which 'proved' that these were abnormal, but associated, conditions. The normative discourse of their allegedly 'scientific' work was intended to dissuade women from the public display of their 'deviance' by proving conclusively the biological bases of gender difference and sexuality. In *Nights at the Circus* and *Tipping the Velvet*, however, women 'perform' gender in defiance of prevailing norms, and yet ultimately evade the disciplining effect of Victorian gender discourse. Their success is of course the vision of writers privileged to have seen how triumphantly women have disproved the arguments of Victorian biological science.

6
Evolutionary Thought, Gender and Race

If degeneration was linked with the breakdown of gender boundaries, it was equally linked with the breakdown of the barriers between races. The science of evolution envisaged the nineteenth-century white male as its peak, looking down on women as a less evolved form of life, and looking back at the past as a lower stage of development. This European male observer similarly looked both down and back on what were perceived as more 'primitive' races. Although Darwin himself ultimately refuted concepts of racial purity, his model of development, differentiating between racial types, suggested different stages in human evolution, and contributed to the idea that 'lower' races belonged to a state of perpetual childhood similar to that occupied by women. 'Bushmen' and 'Hottentots', for instance, central to debates about racial groups in Africa, were thus seen to belong to the childhood of man. The similarities between this discourse of race and Victorian gender discourse indicate the common ideological function that they served.

The scientific study of racial difference can be said to have begun with the foundation of the Anthropological Society of London in 1863, and its potential social and political role was indicated by the Society's Treasurer, the Reverend Dunbar Heath, in an address in 1868: 'the best legislator or politician is he who best understands the elements he governs; or, in other words, the best practical anthropologist' (quoted in Stott, p. 16). By the 1870s, the central debate as regards race was between monogenist and polygenist views: between the traditional Christian view that all humankind had a common origin, and the view that different races were in effect different species.[1] Georges Cuvier (1769–1832), one of the most influential of the monogenists, had in the early years of the century argued that all humans came from a single creation, but had developed into three races: Caucasians, Ethiopians and Mongolians. These could interbreed, but had distinct physical differences, especially in the shape of the head, which indicated internal differences. According to Cuvier, 'It is not for nothing that the Caucasian race had gained dominion over the world and made the most rapid progress in the sciences while the Negroes are still sunken in slavery and the pleasures of the senses.'[2] Joseph-Arthur de Gobineau, the French ethnologist, in his notorious 'Essay on the Inequality of the Human Races' (1853–5), uses the same allegedly historical argument – that all human civilisations are the product of the white race – to warn against the adulteration of white blood by 'foreign' elements.[3] Cuvier's view of the correlation between brain size, which could be derived from measurements of the skull which housed the brain, and supposed difference in intelligence prevailed throughout the century, and was used, as I have indicated, to identify deviants of all kinds. Alfred Russel Wallace, closely involved like Darwin in the debate over evolution, wrote in 1870, 'all the most eminent modern writers see an intimate connection between the diminished size of the brain in the lower races of mankind, and their intellectual inferiority' (quoted in *Embodied Selves*, p. 370). Racial hierarchies are given 'scientific' validity by the same anatomical or medical discourse used to establish gender hierarchies.

If the white male represented the ideal or norm, then both women and other races represented deviations from it. As Sara Ahmed puts it, 'The scientific knowledges of the mid to late nineteenth century [...] were based around the normalization of the white male body and the pathologizing of difference.'[4] Barriers therefore needed to be established and maintained to prevent degeneration through the blurring of difference either through miscegenation or, as the previous chapter suggested, through the breakdown of traditional gender roles. Nancy Stepan suggests that racial biology was, by this time, 'a science of boundaries'. She explains:

> As slavery was abolished and the role of freed blacks became a political and social issue, as industrialization brought about new social mobility and class tensions, and new anxieties about the 'proper' place of different class, national, and ethnic groups in society, racial biology provided a model for the analysis of the distances that were 'natural' between human groups.[5]

Such separation was far more important to most people than any arguments about equality. In America, the land of democracy and equality, scientists maintained that through evolution women were necessarily reduced to the status of slaves as men's hunting and herding skills improved, reducing their dependence on women's help. Neither this nor other forms of slavery, they argued, should be undermined by fears of social inequality. As late as 1927, it was argued that 'inequality is the very precondition of organization and progressive adjustment'.[6] In Britain, even the biologist T.H. Huxley, committed to the development of women's higher education, draws analogies between the position of women and of slaves in America which suggest a belief in a 'natural' racial and sexual hierarchy.[7]

Both racial and sexual differences were, moreover, clearly written on the body. Ahmed suggests that we cannot understand the production of race without reference to embodiment, since 'racialization involves a process of *investing* skin colour with meaning, such that "black" and "white" come to function, not as descriptions of skin colour, but as racial identities' (p. 46). 'Racialisation' is not therefore simply a process of identifying racial differences, but of producing the 'racial body' through 'knowledge' of alleged differences. That is, nineteenth-century scientists did not simply use physical differences between races to extrapolate mental and emotional differences, as they did with sexual differences. To quote Ahmed again, 'Rather than *finding* evidence of racial difference, science was actually *constructing* or even inventing the very idea of race itself as bodily difference and bodily hierarchy' (p. 50). She sums up: 'The bodies of others hence became the means by which scientists attempted to mark out the difference and superiority of "the white race"' (p. 49). The invention of racial difference, tied to hierarchy, justified the expansion of nineteenth-century colonialism. Through such 'scientific' discourse, 'race' is assumed to be an intrinsic property of bodies, whereas it does not, according to Ahmed, precede 'ethnicity' – that is, 'the cultural inscription of group identity' (p. 46).[8] The characterisation of the ignorant and childlike Hottentot, for example, is the product of 'observations' of behaviour which play a greater part in their identification as a group than skin colour or brain size.

When the discourses of race and gender are brought together to define the black female, her place on the evolutionary ladder is made brutally clear. Cuvier described Sarah Bartmann, the 'Hottentot Venus', as an exemplar of 'a degenerate, barely human race'. As Fausto-Sterling puts it, 'he constructed her as the missing link between humans and apes' (p. 221). A black female shared the same reproductive system that served to differentiate the white female from the white male. But racial hierarchies required that she had also to be differentiated from the white female. This was achieved by making subtle distinctions between sexual characteristics central to women's reproductive function and those which indicate sexual proclivities. As far back as 1826, Willem Vrolik had argued that a wide pelvis was a sign of racial superiority, ensuring more successful childbearing, and had drawn attention to the relative narrowness of Sarah Bartmann's pelvis as yet another sign of the Hottentot's inferior racial status. Cuvier too had used pelvic width as part of his classification system to differentiate European from African women. In contrast, Hottentot women were thought by many to be identifiable by their steatopygia,[9] even though this feature was not originally observed as characteristic of any particular people. At the turn of the century, Havelock Ellis returns to this theory to argue that steatopygia is 'a simulation of the large pelvis of the higher races'.[10] Lacking the reproductive value of the genuine article, however, this simulation merely reinforces the role of the buttocks as secondary sexual characteristics which incite pleasure, so it becomes yet more evidence of excessive female sexuality in the Hottentot. Sander Gilman argues that the attention paid to the Hottentot woman during this period was because steatopygia provided a 'central icon' for the difference between black and European women, which built on existing stereotypes of 'primitive' women as highly sexualised.

Other alleged anatomical differences between black and white women were used to provide 'proof' that heightened sexuality was universal in black women, a defining feature, whereas it was a marker of degeneracy and deviance in white women. Fausto-Sterling argues that by the mid-nineteenth century, elongated labia and enlarged clitorises were described as genital abnormalities and associated with particular races, rather than as part of a wide range of 'normal' human variation. The availability of Sarah Bartmann for display and examination both before and after her death provided what seemed like conclusive evidence. Medical discourse could then 'explain' the sexual nature of black females as the result of their more developed sexual organs. And since the genitalia of the Hottentot could be likened to the diseased genitalia of prostitutes, ideas of racial inferiority could be used to reinforce the distinctions between the white woman as she should be, and what she could become if allowed to 'degenerate'. For although white women were also associated with the sexual body, they were able to rise above its dangers, if they subjected themselves to the protection and/or controls of their male betters. The displacement of sexuality onto the figure of the black woman, as onto that of the prostitute, allowed respectable white women's bodies to be represented as pure. The ideology of white supremacy therefore reveals the contradictions in patriarchal gender discourse, showing the concept of universal or true womanhood to be a false idealisation, since it excludes women of colour and lower class.

Such arguments, reducing the black female to body, simultaneously construct the white male as non-body. The white male becomes what Ahmed calls 'the place from which he thinks and knows *through*' the black female (p. 53). Toni Morrison, however, has argued that this process goes beyond gender: according to Margaret Homans, she is angry that in white American writing the 'Africanist presence', both female and male, has been required to signify the body 'so that mind can be white'.[11] The tendency to represent the black female as body is not confined to the discourse of nineteenth-century patriarchy, but has led to tensions between even feminist critics. While many European feminist critics have attempted to reinstate the female body as a source of value and empowerment from its despised position in Victorian discourse, any emphasis on 'writing the body' is problematic for those who feel they have always been written as body, represented as body and no more, and whose bodies have been literally written on by the branding iron. Black feminist critics have identified the dangers, summarised by Valerie Smith in her critique of the role of the black woman as historicising presence in recent feminist criticism:

> at precisely the moment when Anglo-American feminists and male Afro-Americanists begin to reconsider the material ground of their enterprise, they demonstrate their return to earth, as it were, by invoking the specific experiences of black women and the writings of black women. This association of black women with reembodiment resembles rather closely the association, in classic Western philosophy and in nineteenth-century cultural constructions of womanhood, of women of color with the body and therefore with animal passions and slave labor.[12]

Black women, it appears, can as easily function as the 'Other' for white women, as white women have done for white men. Homans goes further, arguing that even black feminist critics are guilty of using black women to represent 'experience, sensuality, emotion, matter, practice as opposed to theory, and survival' (p. 416).

Articulating this problem, however, usefully reinforces a thesis central to this study: the Victorian scientist's attempt to define woman in terms of her body was an essentialising project which evaded the fact that the body is not experienced in the same way by all women. Toni Morrison's *Beloved*, the last novel I shall discuss, provides a tentative conclusion to my analysis of the Victorian woman question by throwing the ideological function of these models of gender and racial difference into sharp focus. Introducing race into considerations of gender places the female body within a context which makes it impossible to ignore the social and political situation of the individual woman. If different meanings can be assigned to different female bodies, according to racial categories, it exposes all the cracks in the argument that all women, daughters of Eve, share a reproductive system which determines every aspect of their psychological and moral being.

'Ain't I a Woman?': Toni Morrison's *Beloved*

> That man over there says that women need to be helped into carriages, and lifted over ditches, and to have the best place everywhere. Nobody ever helps me into carriages, or over mud-puddles, or gives me any best place! And ain't I a woman? Look at me! Look at my arm! I have ploughed and planted, and gathered into barns, and no man could head me! And ain't I a woman? [...] I have borne thirteen children, and seen them most all sold off to slavery, and when I cried out with my mother's grief, none but Jesus heard me! And ain't I a woman?[13]

In her famous speech to a woman's convention in Akron, Ohio, in 1851, the visionary ex-slave Sojourner Truth demolished a clergyman's arguments against women's rights by using her own experience of slavery to expose the false idealisations and inherent racism on which his conception of womanhood rested. In doing so she made a powerful case for both gender and racial equality. Toni Morrison's novel, *Beloved*,[14] set in 1873, when the recent abolition of slavery left black men and women still scarred physically and psychologically, makes the same case. If the sexual woman, the violent woman and the black races were all considered as 'degenerate', then the novel's central character Sethe, who belongs to all these categories, is the ultimate degenerate. She nevertheless implicitly and explicitly challenges the very foundations of the ideologies that so define her.

Morrison historicises both gender and race by basing her novel on the true story of Margaret Garner, an escaped slave who killed one of her children rather than let it be returned to captivity. Unlike Sethe, Garner returned to slavery after her trial, though not before having killed another of her children, and her case was seen as a setback for the Abolitionist cause, since the court upheld the slave-owners' claim that they were entitled to the return of their property, under the 1850 Fugitive Slave

Law. Garner therefore avoided being tried for murder, because as mere property she did not possess the moral responsibilities accepted by whites.[15] But *Beloved* rejects the reductive association between the black female and the body which denies her spiritual and moral dimensions. In having Sethe face trial for the killing, Morrison refuses to relieve her of the moral responsibilities associated with equality, while paradoxically making that act her most powerful expression of Sojourner Truth's plea, 'Ain't I a Woman?'

Much of the novel's power lies in direct, physical forms of resistance to racism. *Beloved* is not simply about the sufferings endured by the female slave; it is a version of the slave-escape narrative in which women are the central agents. The driving force in the novel is the love between mother and child, but that love has none of the sentimentality of Victorian ideology, and operates as a force for destruction as well as devotion. Barbara Christian has argued that the sanctification of the slave mother in American culture occurred through the stereotype of the mammy, who was 'mythologized in America as the perfect worker/ mother, content in her caring, diligent in her protection of her master's house and children'. In reality, she points out, slave narratives, historical accounts and folklore reaffirm the critical role that mothers played 'through sacrifice, will, and wisdom, to ensure the survival of their children'.[16] And it is Sethe who gets her children to freedom, not Halle, their father. Her one source of pride, the only thing she ever does alone, is to save her 'best thing'. Her courage and passion for her children are what surely lead her lover Paul D to counter that she is in fact her 'best thing' (p. 273). *Beloved* is therefore the story of heroic women who challenge prevailing stereotypes of femininity as well as of race in historically specific ways which reveal that gender and racial identity are products of culture and history, and redefine the meaning of the word 'woman'.

Since the novel is set in the United States, rather than in the British Empire, it constructs a world where Victorian gender ideology is both confirmed, and yet rendered irrelevant by the experiences of its black male and female characters. The same gender discourse can be found in American scientific studies, conduct literature and periodicals as in Victorian publications, but America's history of slavery gives it a different inflection, compounded by equally 'scientific' discourses of race. The embodiment of these principles is the aptly named Schoolteacher, who is not content simply to exercise control over the slaves of Sweet Home, but wants to construct a systematic classification of them along 'scientific' principles. Sethe registers his use of the 'measuring string' (p. 191) to measure her head, nose and buttocks, his habit of counting her teeth and his numerous questions as sinister, even before she is fully aware of their purpose. Slaves were habitually recorded and evaluated as a function of their body parts; such objectification of the body characterises the discourse of those who claim knowledge of and therefore superiority over others. The moment Sethe overhears Schoolteacher telling his 'boys' to put 'her human characteristics on the left; her animal ones on the right' (p. 193) is the trigger for her to put her escape plan into action, since she instinctively recognises the link between such 'observations' and the brutal treatment of the slaves which they serve to justify, slaves being classified as little more than animals.[17]

Such theories of racial difference almost obliterate the sexual differences so forcefully asserted by nineteenth-century scientists, at least as far as they concerned the uses to which female bodies could be put. Both men and women were subjected to the same relentless labour and brutality. Not only Paul D but Sethe's mother is 'corrected' by a metal bit in her mouth. The most powerful image of how irrelevant Victorian gender ideology becomes, given the objectification of the slave body, is provided when Sethe is flogged for complaining to her owner Mrs Garner after the white boys steal from her pregnant and lactating body the milk intended for her baby daughter: Sethe tells Paul D, 'They dug a hole for my stomach so as not to hurt the baby' (p. 202). The hole protects the valuable property she carries in her womb, but there is no concession to the maternal body itself.

The reproductive functions that so rigidly differentiate women from men in nineteenth-century scientific discourse are, nevertheless, kept sharply to the fore throughout the novel, because of their importance to the slave economy. And the effect is to demonstrate how differently black and white women experience those functions. Schoolteacher measures Sethe's buttocks as markers of that racialised sexuality already discussed, a sexuality which legitimates sexual abuse by her white masters. As a slave, Sethe experiences sexuality as rape; even as a free woman she experiences it as part of a system of exchange, since it is all she has to pay for the inscription of the precious seven letters that constitute her daughter's name, 'Beloved', on a headstone. Virginity is no longer the central female virtue, since it is the slave's duty to satisfy her master's sexual desires: her virginity is simply another commodity which may increase her value. Sethe nevertheless exposes the falsity of racial stereotypes, as she attempts to create for herself the emotional and familial bonds which are believed to be antipathetic to the sexualised black female. In spite of their intense sexual frustration when she arrives on the farm, the Sweet Home men recognise the 'iron-eyed' (p. 10) Sethe's right to choose her own sexual partner, in the process refuting that other racial stereotype of the black male as little better than a rapist. And although sex before marriage and illegitimate births were not condemned among slaves, Sethe insists on a ceremony to celebrate her 'marriage' to Halle, the slave of her choice. Paula Eckard points out that slave marriages were very fragile, since they were not binding or recognised as legal: even when preachers were present, the marriage vows were changed to 'Until death or distance do you part' (p. 20). And once parted, slave women were expected to find new 'husbands' so that they could continue breeding. Sethe, however, demands the respect accorded to white unions, determined that hers shall form the basis of a true and permanent family.

Even wider, however, than the gulf which racial ideology established between black female sexuality and the idealised asexual white woman is that established between black and white experiences of motherhood, perceived by nineteenth-century scientists to be the defining purpose of the female body. The fecundity of southern white women in the 1850s, which meant that they were likely to be pregnant or nursing a baby every year of their married lives until their mid-forties, prompted one physician of the time to conclude that 'all women should be considered pregnant until proved otherwise'.[18] It confirmed that motherhood was woman's natural state. The black slave could similarly expect to begin childrearing at the age of twenty, and to have children every 2.5 years until the age of 35.[19] But her reproductive functioning was a measure of her productivity for her owner, who also expected productivity in the fields or house. Even the nurturing powers of the mother could be diverted, through wet-nursing, to another child. Where the middle-class European mother was increasingly encouraged to depart from aristocratic practice and breastfeed her own child,[20] the slave mother's milk is simply another product of her body, like the milk of a cow, which can be used for any purpose that the owner determines.

The ideology and system of slavery therefore ruptured the meaning of motherhood. It detached the 'scientific' view of reproduction as woman's defining function from the maternal ideal central to Victorian gender ideology, indicating how contingent that 'universal' ideal was upon economic and social circumstances. Once she becomes free, Sethe herself recognises its contingency, speculating, 'maybe I couldn't love em proper in Kentucky because they wasn't mine to love' (p. 162). Reproduction is in effect severed from motherhood because female slaves were forced to undergo the experience of pregnancy, childbirth and lactation, without necessarily being allowed to look after or even keep their own children.

Under this system, the child's relationship with its mother is simultaneously everything and nothing. It is everything, since a slave's child inherits its mother's status, even if it has a free man for a father, an ironically bitter form of matrilineal succession. And yet it is nothing, since the child of a slave does not belong to her; it belongs to its master. Giving birth sometimes helped to preserve the integrity of the slave 'family', since it proved the value of the slave in terms of her fecundity, and therefore postponed her sale. Sometimes mother and child were even sold together (see Eckard, p. 18). But such practices were governed by economic arguments, rather than the ideological argument that the mother provided the foundation for family and moral values which dominated white gender discourse. In *Beloved*, this breaking of the link between the maternal body and the maternal role is pitifully evident in Sethe's memories of lactation, both as mother and as child. After briefly being suckled by her natural mother, Sethe was fed by a black nurse, 'whose job it was' (p. 60), getting what little milk was left when the white babies had finished, and only knowing her mother as a distant figure in a field, pointed out to her by the nurse. When her mother was hanged, Sethe could identify her only by the brand under her breast, the sign written on her body by her owner. Sethe's greatest sense of violation is arguably occasioned not by her rape, but by having her milk taken from her body by white men, simply to assert that her body and everything that issues from it is always only a white man's property. Becoming a mother is here reduced to a purely biological function.

Sethe again, however, challenges racial ideology by laying claim to the same maternal rights and feelings as a white woman. She claims the right to be not simply a breeder, but a mother, with all the attributes inscribed with such authority in Victorian gender discourse. She echoes Sojourner Truth's 'ain't I a woman?' with an implied 'ain't I a mother?'. Such a claim entails huge emotional risks: 'For a used-to-be-slave woman to love anything that much was dangerous, especially if it was her children she had settled on to love' (p. 45). Maternal love, instinctive according to Victorian ideology, is in reality the privilege of the free and the prosperous: 'a place where you could love anything you chose – not to need permission for desire – well now, *that* was freedom' (p. 162). After her escape from Sweet Home, Sethe has twenty-eight days – 'the travel of one whole moon', a menstrual cycle – of such freedom, before Schoolteacher arrives to retrieve his possessions, including her newborn child. That time represents her first experience of womanhood as articulated in Victorian gender discourse, her first experience of being a mother who is part of a family and part of society: 'she had claimed herself'

(p. 95). The fact that she has to learn how to be a mother, because she has never had anyone to learn from, only emphasises the constructed nature of that concept. Hence her constant surprise at her 'crawling-already' daughter, whose development is hastened beyond the norms for a slave child by proper nutrition.

How radical Sethe's demands are can be better understood in the context of historical evidence. Faced with the realities surrounding reproduction, many female slaves totally repudiated the attributes allegedly natural to maternity. Barbara Bush argues that:

> tensions inherent in slave women's 'dual burden' of production and reproduction, combined with attempts by slave masters to manipulate these women's cultural practices and fertility, strongly influenced the responses of slave women to childbirth and infant rearing at both conscious and unconscious levels.[21]

Women's control over their own bodies became a major area of struggle, causing many women to reject or even kill their own babies, rather than acknowledge the intimacy of a relationship forced on them. Nan tells Sethe how her mother threw away the babies born to her as a result of rape by white men, only keeping Sethe because she was the child of a black man for whom she had feelings enough to embrace. Even those who do not reject their children are circumspect about their emotions: Baby Suggs, Halle's mother, barely glanced at Halle, her last-born, at birth, 'because it wasn't worth the trouble to try to learn features you would never see change into adulthood anyway' (p. 139). And in turning away from a child she cannot afford to love, the slave reinforces the view of her white masters that the black races are incapable of the emotional and moral sensibilities shared by 'civilised' people.

That view is apparently confirmed by the brutal infanticide which is the terrible secret at the heart of the novel, and which Morrison differentiates from the kind of responses described above by altering the facts of the original story. Garner's murdered child, recorded as having a light skin, was probably the child of her owner, the result of rape or forced breeding. And Barbara Christian suggests that women who killed such children 'might be seen as striking out at the master/rapist and resisting the role of perpetuating the system of slavery through breeding'.[22] Morrison, however, makes Sethe kill the child of the man she loves, so that such a rationale is not possible. Sethe's action is, instead, the most dramatic statement of her newly freed maternal love. It ironically affirms the nineteenth-century view that motherhood is more than a biological function, since it plants aspirations in women that go beyond biological destiny. It leads them to assert that they and their offspring are more than bodies, that life is about more than mere animal survival, that there is a fate worse than death. This is what Sethe is desperate to make Beloved, the incarnation of her murdered infant, understand:

> That anybody white could take your whole self for anything that came to mind. Not just work, kill, or maim you, but dirty you. Dirty you so bad you couldn't like yourself anymore. [...] The best thing she was, was her children. Whites might dirty *her* all right, but not her best thing. (p. 251)

This is why she gathers together 'every bit of life she had made, all the parts of her that were precious and fine and beautiful, and carried, pushed, dragged them through the veil, out, away, over there where no one could hurt them' (p. 163).

What Schoolteacher sees as the typical act of 'people who needed every care and guidance in the world to keep them from the cannibal life they preferred' (p. 151), and what causes even Paul D, Sethe's lover, to remind her that she has two legs, not four, is therefore not the act of an animal, but its opposite – the act of someone determined to prove she is not an animal. Sethe refuses to have her children's characteristics listed 'on the animal side of the paper'. And Schoolteacher confirms the nature of the forces she is resisting. In another departure from Garner's story, he abandons any claim on either Sethe, considering her as useless as an overchastised horse, driven wild, or her children, since a dead slave has even less value than an animal, whose skin can be sold.

While *Beloved* is therefore a novel about the power of reductive physical classifications to imprison both women and the black races, doubly subjugating the black woman, it also demonstrates the possibility of non-physical challenges to such systems of 'knowledge'. But the spirituality from which that possibility derives does not exist in opposition to the physical, for in *Beloved* the spiritual is rooted in, and manifest in the material world. And the belief that the spiritual can be reached through the body provides a further challenge to nineteenth-century ideologies of race and gender, since it implies a respect for the body which is absent from the dualistic traditions of patriarchal religious thought which underlie them. Jago Morrison suggests that where racial ideology sought to justify slavery by its emphasis on the 'soul-less' slave body, *Beloved* provides 'a rejection of this ideology – a *consecration* of black flesh. Rather than a refusal of embodiment, it is a liberatory reclamation of the body, *through* a redemptive affirmation of soul' (p. 128). This belief is articulated most eloquently by Baby Suggs 'holy', who for much of her free life is an 'unchurched preacher [...]. Uncalled, unrobed, unanointed' (p. 87). She tells her congregation in the Clearing where they meet that they must love their own bodies precisely because they are not loved by 'them':

> 'Here', she said, 'in this here place, we flesh; flesh that weeps, laughs; flesh that dances on bare feet in grass. Love it. Love it hard. Yonder they do not love your flesh. They despise it. They don't love your eyes; they'd just as soon pick em out. No more do they love the skin on your back. Yonder they flay it. And O my people they do not love your hands. Those they only use, tie, bind, chop off and leave empty. Love your hands! Love them. Raise them up and kiss them. Touch others with them, pat them together, stroke them on your face 'cause they don't love that either. *You* got to love it, *you!* And no, they ain't in love with your mouth. Yonder, out there, they will see it broken and break it again. What you say out of it they will not heed. What you scream from it they do not hear. What you put into it to nourish your body they will snatch away and give you leavins instead. No, they don't love your mouth. *You* got to love it. This is flesh I'm talking about here. Flesh that needs to be loved . . .' (p. 88)

This affirmation of the value of the material body contradicts the dualistic basis of dominant nineteenth-century theological positions which encouraged distrust of the body. The sermon is concluded by Baby Suggs dancing 'the rest of what her heart had to say', confirmation of her message that flesh and spirit are indissoluble, and her congregation answer with long musical notes that create a harmony, not just in music, but 'perfect enough for their deeply loved flesh' (p. 89).

As her name implies, Baby Suggs and her preaching mark the birth of a form of resistance to the values of the white race which is an intermittent but monstrous presence throughout the novel. But this response is rooted in the African tradition from which the American slave was torn, but often attempted to keep alive. Her preaching is reminiscent of the work of 'praying bands', which Gerda Lerner describes as typical of the struggle for women's religious agency amongst African Americans in the nineteenth century. She points out that, although evangelists like Sojourner Truth based their authority to teach and preach on mystical experiences and citations from the Bible, their 'churches' had their own language, symbolism, structures and traditions.[23] For their traditions derived from a system of beliefs originally based on a mother goddess, which celebrated the maternal body. Where birth, common as it was, remained the central mystery of life, the mother who gave birth was an obvious focus of veneration and awe, worshipped in the form of the Great Goddess, who gave her people life, provided them with material and spiritual nurturance, and in death took them back into the earth, her womb.[24] And the quest for the mother, whether it is Beloved's almost murderous quest for Sethe, or the quest for the nurturing power of the mother goddess which brings people to the Clearing and Baby Suggs, binds the individual's history to that of the race.[25] In contrast to the idealised maternal presence of Victorian ideology, the discourse of mother goddess mythology locates spirituality in the female body, rather than in opposition to it.

Sethe's murderous attack on her family, however, prompts Baby Suggs to give up her preaching, in the belief that such tragedies prove the irrelevance of everything she has previously said. And that view appears to be confirmed by physical manifestations of the spirit, brought into her house by Sethe's action, which are a force for evil, rather than good. Number 124, their home, is haunted by the ghost of Sethe's baby, operating as a malevolent poltergeist whose presence is so strongly felt that it drives away her two sons. At a personal level, this is a manifestation of guilt and memory. The baby's presence is on the one hand experienced as an act of revenge: 'Who would have thought that a little old baby could harbor so much rage?' (p. 5). But when re-embodied as Beloved, a young woman introduced in terms reminiscent of a newborn, with 'new skin', even on her feet, emerging out of water, she represents the child's demand for the love she feels has been denied to her. As Amy, the young white girl who acts as midwife to Sethe during her escape, says when she massages Sethe's swollen feet, 'Anything dead coming back to life hurts' (p. 35). Beloved's appearance is testimony to the power of the mother–child bond, even when broken under the most terrible of circumstances. Moreover, when Sethe attempts to persuade Beloved that she intended them all to die, to be together on the other side, Beloved responds unforgivingly with a lament that is effectively the whole history of slavery, of all the children denied their mother. In Rebecca Ferguson's words, in *Beloved* 'what is commonly called the supernatural is also the manifestation of history'.[26] Beloved is no ethereal presence, but one that leaves bruises on Sethe's neck, alongside the caresses that heal her anguish. And her dependence on Sethe ultimately becomes not that of a child on its mother, but that of a succubus or vampire on its victim, thriving as her mother becomes increasingly weak.

The presences summoned up in spiritualist séances in the novels discussed in Chapter 4 are pale, harmless wraiths in comparison. Even the voice of another infant killed by its mother, in *In the Red Kitchen*, is never as palpably real or demanding, but remains firmly in the spirit world whose boundaries are more clearly fixed in these representations of Victorian spiritualism.

Sethe is nevertheless the inheritor of the traditions of her mother-in-law, Baby Suggs. Even after Baby's death, she goes to the Clearing for her help in dealing with the appalling new images of Halle that Paul D has put into her mind, wanting to feel Baby's fingers again: even Baby's 'long-distance love was equal to any skin-close love she had known. The desire, let alone the gesture, to meet her needs was good enough to lift her spirits to the place where she could take the next step: ask for some clarifying word; some advice about how to keep on with a brain greedy for news nobody could live with in a world happy to provide it' (p. 95). Like Baby, Sethe also recognises the close ties between body and spirit. And her act against her child – however violent – is not only a radical statement about motherhood, but continues Baby's resistance to white systems of belief and power. The one word that she has carved on her daughter's tombstone, 'Beloved', is the only word from the Christian burial service that has meaning for her: it asserts the right to love which the black races are denied, even though love is the central tenet of the Christian faith. And although the female community who form a large part of Baby's congregation never condone Sethe's act of infanticide, they appear to recognise something of this, ministering to both her body and her spirit in actions which readmit her to the community and its traditions. Individual women who have learned about Sethe's plight from Denver, her surviving daughter, leave offerings of food. Subsequently, thirty women go to 124 to exorcise Beloved's presence, hollering together in a primeval wordless noise which explicitly challenges the very foundations of the Judeo-Christian tradition: 'In the beginning there were no words. In the beginning was the sound, and they all knew what that sound sounded like' (p. 259). Sethe feels as if the Clearing has come to her; she feels newly baptised, newborn in her own new beginning. Their actions relieve her of the burden of guilt which, in the form of Beloved, is destroying her. They turn away from Beloved herself, even though she is now pregnant, as if to reject the idea that the maternal tradition can be continued in this spirit of eternal and deadly vengeance.

The voices of these women act, therefore, as a form of magic, a transformative process which speaks for the maternal body, which is the true beginning of all human life. Their 'hollering' illustrates Kristeva's concept of the semiotic, a form of pre-verbal communication articulating the infant's basic drives and rhythms – the intake and release of breath, ingestion and expulsion, dark and light, and the liquid rhythms of the womb which remain as a memory – and evoking its ties with its mother.[27] Because they are pre-verbal, memories of the semiotic state cannot find expression in the symbolic order of language, but the semiotic disposition nevertheless remains latent in language, becoming most manifest in language that departs radically from the strict structures and fixed meanings to which the symbolic tends, such as the language of poetry or madness. Ferguson finds traces of this disposition in Beloved's interior monologues, which she describes as 'an open, seeking, concentrated language of elision, approaching most nearly Julia Kristeva's concept of the pre-Oedipal "semiotic"' (pp. 116–17). In the first of these monologues Beloved explicitly asserts the lack of boundary between child and mother: 'I AM BELOVED and she is mine. [...] I am not separate from her   there is no place where I stop   her face is my own and I want to be there in the place where her face is and to be looking at it too   a hot thing' (p. 210). But the stylistic characteristics of the semiotic – sound effects like rhythm, rhyme and repetition, and indeterminate syntax and semantics, reflecting the indeterminacy of identity when there is no separation between mother and child – are increasingly evident throughout this section. They culminate in the following passage, which is laid out more in the style of free verse than conventional prose:

You are my face; I am you. Why did you leave me who am you?
I will never leave you again
Don't ever leave me again
You will never leave me again
You went in the water
I drank your blood
I brought your milk
You forgot to smile
I loved you
You hurt me
You came back to me
You left me

I waited for you
You are mine
You are mine
You are mine (pp. 216–17)

In *Beloved*, however, such language articulates not only the child's dependence on the maternal body, but the individual's relationship to the cultural tradition which celebrates that body, both repressed by patriarchy. *Beloved's* 'memories' are racial memories, conflating stories of the 'middle passage' by which African slaves came to the Americas with their own experiences of suffering and loss. She is what Eckard describes as 'a living womb, a repository of stories from the horrifying annals of slavery' (p. 70). When Beloved describes how she crouched in the dark with other dead and dying bodies, while Sethe went into the sea and left her, she is drawing on a collective memory. Baby Suggs herself admits to throwing one of her babies overboard, so that Sethe too, belonging to the same generation as Baby's children, could easily have 'gone overboard', perpetuating the endless line of childless mothers and motherless children. Language here does not so much construct an individual identity as a collective history. The women on the slave ship are, moreover, able to use a language incomprehensible to white men, a language which Sethe can remember her mother sharing with Nan, Sethe's surrogate mother. Although Sethe has forgotten what the words mean, she recognises its 'message' as her inheritance from her mother, a reminder that she belongs to a world beyond the understanding of slave-owning societies.

Beloved nevertheless also articulates the dangers presented by the semiotic. The semiotic stage is a world of eternal 'play' and fluidity before the logical structures of the symbolic order intervene to differentiate, define and categorise. But the break with the semiotic and the mother's body must be made so that the subject can establish the borders between itself and its mother, achieving the separation necessary for the creation of the individual ego, and find its identity within the symbolic order. The desire to return to the pre-Oedipal state is therefore a form of regression, a desire for the loss of identity, for the dissolution of the self in the mother – in other words, a desire for madness or death.[28] Beloved is in such a state of regression, and in the process also threatens to destroy her mother. As an adolescent incarnation of the murdered child, she has never left the semiotic and therefore can have no sense of self, only the desperate sense of loss experienced by the child who has been torn from her mother: in saying, 'Me, me, me', and demanding that her mother's life should be absorbed by hers, to answer her greed for love, this child is also obliterating her own identity. Kristeva makes it clear that women cannot afford to risk such self-annihilation, which is also a self-silencing.

Eckard writes persuasively about the role of milk as a powerful symbol in the novel, 'a "privileged" sign of the maternal' and a 'metaphor for nonspeech in Kristeva's theorization' (p. 71), serving as a precursor to language in the novel. But it is not enough for the maternal body to 'speak' only in these terms, which the novel shows can be stolen, or even through the 'hollering' in the Clearing. For the female body needs a voice, if it is to be a source of power. It must be mediated through language, so that women do not remain mute presences in discourse. Baby Suggs retires to her bed and gives up her preaching when she becomes convinced that the bloodshed in her own backyard mocks her calling: 'The heart that pumped out love, the mouth that spoke the Word, didn't count. They came in her yard anyway' (p. 180). But her old friend Stamp Paid tells her she cannot 'quit the Word. It's given to [her] to speak' (p. 177). While allowing expression in their language to the semiotic, and all it signifies, women must nevertheless employ the symbolic as a shared linguistic base for understanding. For without the ordering control of the symbolic, language becomes mere psychotic utterance, sense and shared meaning overwhelmed by the unconscious drives articulated through the semiotic. The rhetoric of Baby Suggs' sermons, with its repetitions and rhythms and song-like qualities, incorporates the characteristics of the semiotic already noted in Beloved's monologues. But the sermons retain a basis in the ordering structures of conventional syntax and use of pronouns which is missing from the monologues, but which make shared meaning much easier.

The different insights acquired so painfully by Baby Suggs and Sethe are inherited by a third generation, Sethe's daughter, Denver, who is able to use them to rise to the challenge of Sojourner Truth's rhetorical question and fight against the constraints of both race and gender. Both Baby Suggs and Sethe are represented as celebrating the female body while simultaneously striving to prove that they are more than simply bodies, as racial ideology would have it, and Sethe passes on that belief in the sanctity of the body to Denver, telling her to listen to her body, to love it, and take pleasure in it. Denver, however, is painfully aware of the dangers of being reduced to the maternal body, as Sethe is by Beloved, who obliterates every other dimension of Sethe's life, including her love for Paul D. And watching her sister's monstrous and parasitic desire for her mother slide into madness, she is equally aware of the dangers of the semiotic. She understands that she must distance herself from this symbiotic and destructive dyad and connect again with the wider community. As Ferguson puts it, 'nothing the past can offer will make up for the loss of a future' (p. 123). Taking on the responsibility for feeding her family, the child takes on the responsibilities of the adult, continuing the maternal tradition inherited from mother and grandmother not by literally becoming a mother, but by taking on a maternal role towards Sethe, who – in thrall to Beloved – has in effect become a child. The narrator notes that when Denver goes to ask for work, it is ironically Lady Jones' response, '"Oh, baby," [...] said softly and with such kindness, that inaugurated her life in the world as a woman' (p. 248). Denver embodies a reconfiguring of the maternal in terms of function, rather than biology, exemplifying Sethe's own perception that 'motherhood' is more than simply a biological condition.

Denver also has reason to be aware of the dangers of self-silencing implicit in any retreat into the semiotic. Her first response to hearing that her mother murdered her own child is to retreat into deafness and total silence for two years, since communication has only brought her pain. Maturing, however, she appears to understand that women must use the symbolic if they are to engage with the historical and political realities that oppress them. Her desire to communicate again with the outside world coincides with the renewal of her formal education, through Lady Jones and the white Bodwins, activities that reflect the first concerted attempts to teach literacy to blacks that took place in the Reconstruction years (see Ferguson, p. 122). Here the novel's concerns connect with those of white Victorian women who demanded the right to education. Only through education could either the women or the black races cease to be prisoners of their anatomical differences from the white male. Only through education could there be 'evolution' for either group. And in seeking education, a young black woman like Denver challenges both gender and racial hierarchies.

In the process of reconstructing the image of the black female slave, *Beloved* reverses the hierarchy assumed in the European model of evolution. The novel represents the white man as the animal beyond comprehension: Stamp Paid, finding a red ribbon in the river, still attached to a scalp, asks in disbelief, 'What *are* these people? You tell me, Jesus. What *are* they?' (p. 180). Slavery, not black female sexuality, is the pathology. Morrison herself writes that whites have 'had to reconstruct everything in order to make that system appear true' (quoted in Ferguson, p. 110), but in this novel she deconstructs the system, showing – again in the words of Stamp Paid – that while 'whitepeople [*sic*] believed that whatever the manners, under every dark skin was a jungle', they created that jungle themselves, with the result that ultimately 'it invaded the whites who had made it. [...] The screaming baboon lived under their own white skin; the red gums were their own' (pp. 198–9). In this way Morrison challenges the certainties of nineteenth-century scientists regarding both gender and race in a narrative which reads at times more like a poem or prayer than a novel. While other novels discussed in this study also deal with the supernatural, or with fantasy, or subvert traditional chronology, the strong presence of the semiotic in *Beloved* marks its more radical departure from the traditions of realist fiction, so often associated with 'scientific' truth-telling. The novel responds to the question, 'What is a woman?', with another question – Sojourner Truth's question – articulated in language which undermines the truth claims of Victorian science at their very foundation, exposing their pretensions to objective knowledge as mere echoes of patriarchal ideology.

Afterword

The preceding chapters have argued that, amongst the various Victorian discourses explored in feminist fiction of the 1980s and 1990s, scientific discourse is one of the most significant – if only as a subtext. If this is so, it is perhaps because science is again playing a major role in our current 'knowledge' about gender and sexuality. Femininity is problematic: women are once more perceived to be victims of their bodies, although hormones, rather than individual organs, are now identified as the source of women's disposition. Whether the 'problem' is pre-menstrual tension or menopausal symptoms, medical intervention is advocated to 'normalise' a sex prone to irrational moods, sadness or anger. These 'syndromes' appear to be the latest manifestations of 'hysteria' resulting from female 'periodicity'. Interestingly, while the role of testosterone, particularly in male violence, has also been much debated, there has been no equivalent rush to provide hormone treatment to deal with this problem.

Medical management of female reproductive functions is also greater than ever, bringing with it demands for more control over women's choices. New forms of contraception and abortion have renewed the call to restrict women's access to such services. Since the 1980s, pregnancy and childbirth have been increasingly subject to medical intervention. As medical events, they can be monitored and controlled by the latest technology. Such monitoring may benefit the foetus but is also used to justify the imposition of moral and emotional pressures on women with regard to what they should eat, drink or otherwise ingest, and may determine the form of delivery offered to the mother. Women's reproductive health has thus become a matter of public health policy. The increase in new reproductive technologies has similarly led to demands for more social and legislative control over the maternal body.[1] The issues at stake include the question of which women should have the right to benefit from such technologies, and the nature of both paternal and foetal identity. These debates clearly also affect men, but their focus nevertheless remains the body of the pregnant woman. When describing these approaches to the reproductive body, gender theorists have used the same language that I have used to describe the disciplines to which the Victorian female body was subject. It has been suggested, for instance, that 'the new reproductive and genetic engineering technologies can be seen as disciplinary technologies governing the pregnant woman's body'.[2] Anne Balsamo argues that new developments in visualisation techniques produce 'a climate of visual, technological surveillance', which is matched by 'a climate of public, mass media surveillance of mothering'. And these surveillance techniques, she continues, are matched by 'technologies of confession', such as talk shows which encourage women to reveal their inadequate mothering practices and audiences to judge them (see Cranny-Francis et al., pp. 194, 195).

On a more theoretical level, the work of evolutionary psychologists has intensified the debate about the relationship between biological sex differences and the concept of gender. A Darwinian view of sexual differentiation has been evoked by such writers to explain and justify alleged behavioural differences, particularly in male and female sexual activity.[3] These are precisely the differences so forcefully challenged in Byatt's *Morpho Eugenia*. As Lynne Segal puts it, 'The eternal truths of Darwin's grand narrative have returned with a vengeance to reshape intellectual agendas this *fin de siècle*, just as strongly as they did the last.' Citing a report produced by the think tank Demos, which sets out 'the implications of evolutionary psychology for the shaping of social policy', she argues that the return to Darwinian fundamentalism is fuelled by a desire to 'legitimise predestined gender and sexual distinctions' in the face of feminist challenges and changes in gender practices. Once again an alleged crisis in masculinity and in society is presented as the result of women's greater freedom. The books and authors Segal holds most responsible for this view of the sexes offer 'genetic underpinning for male dominance and aggression, female passivity and domestication, in terms of "the optimising of reproductive fitness"'.[4] This argument, she points out, fails totally to take account of the complexity of women's lives today – just as the arguments of Victorian scientists failed totally to take account of the complexity of the lives of Victorian women.

Mary Jacobus has stressed the difficulties involved in developing a critical detachment from the discourses and ideologies that affect us

today, compared with the relative ease of developing a critical understanding of the past:

> The Victorian medical and social discussions of the female body [...]
> offer themselves readily to ideological dissection, revealing the
> economic and gender assumptions at stake. As we come closer to our
> own time, when science wields unprecedented cultural authority,
> and massive material investments guarantee its truths, demystification
> grows more difficult.[5]

By bringing a modern, feminist sensibility to the reconstruction of
Victorian women's lives, the novelists discussed in this book provide a
bridge between past and present, making it easier for the reader to
identify the ideological pressures at work on the experience of gender
identity today. If that were not enough, they offer the stylistic and
imaginative pleasures which are fiction's unique gifts.

Notes

Introduction

1. 'Wolfskins and Togas: Maude Meagher's *The Green Scamander* and the Lesbian Historical Novel', *Women: A Cultural Review*, 7 (1996), 176–88 (p. 176).
2. *On Histories and Stories: Selected Essays* (Chatto & Windus, 2000), p. 38.
3. Susan Rowland, 'Women, Spiritualism and Depth Psychology in Michèle Roberts's Victorian Novel', in *Rereading Victorian Fiction*, ed. Alice Jenkins and Juliet John (Basingstoke: Palgrave, 2002), pp. 201–13 (p. 207).
4. Quoted in Dana Shiller, 'The Redemptive Past in the Neo-Victorian Novel', *Studies in the Novel*, 29 (1997), 538–60 (p. 539).
5. *The Apparitional Lesbian: Female Homosexuality and Modern Culture* (New York: Columbia University Press, 1993).
6. 'Using the Victorians: The Victorian Age in Contemporary Fiction', *Rereading Victorian Fiction*, pp. 189–200 (p. 198).
7. 'The Re-Imagining of History in Contemporary Women's Fiction', *Plotting Change: Contemporary Women's Fiction* (Edward Arnold, 1990), pp. 129–41 (p. 134). For a different view, which values women's historical fiction for its return to the traditions and values of nineteenth-century social realism, see Lynn Pykett, 'The Century's Daughters: Recent Women's Fiction and History', *Critical Quarterly*, 29 (1987), 71–7.
8. See *Women and the Word: Contemporary Women Novelists and the Bible* (Basingstoke: Macmillan, 2000); and 'Women and the Word: Christa Wolf's *Cassandra*', *Journal of Gender Studies*, 3 (1994), 333–42.
9. *Genders* (Routledge, 2000), p. 18.

1 What is a woman? Victorian constructions of femininity

1. John Caspar Lavater, *Essays on Physiognomy*, trans. T. Holcroft (1789), quoted in *Embodied Selves: An Anthology of Psychological Texts 1830–1890*, ed. Jenny Bourne Taylor and Sally Shuttleworth (Oxford: Clarendon Press, 1998), pp. 8–18 (p. 15). This anthology, to which I am greatly indebted, provides an invaluable source of primary texts on Victorian psychology and related disciplines.
2. Alfred Lord Tennyson, 'Merlin and Vivien', *Idylls of the King*, lines 812–13, *The Poems of Tennyson*, ed. Christopher Ricks (Longmans, 1969), p. 1616. 'Merlin and Vivien' was written in 1856, and published as 'Vivien' in 1859.
3. See 'The Newly Born Woman', *The Hélène Cixous Reader*, ed. Susan Sellers (Routledge, 1994), pp. 37–45.
4. The full list is:

> Man is the most firm – woman the most flexible.
> Man is the straightest – woman the most bending.
> Man stands steadfast – woman gently trips.

> Man surveys and observes – woman glances and feels.
> Man is serious – woman is gay.
> Man is the taller and broadest – woman less and taper.
> Man is rough and hard – woman smooth and soft.
> Man is brown – woman is fair.
> Man is wrinkly – woman less so.
> The hair of man is more strong and short – of woman more long and pliant.
> The eyebrows of man are compressed – of woman less frowning.
> Man has most convex lines – woman most concave.
> Man has most straight lines – woman most curved.
> The countenance of man, taken in profile, is more seldom perpendicular than that of the woman.
> Man is most angular – woman most round. (pp. 17–18)

5. *The Victorian Period: The Intellectual and Cultural Context of English Literature, 1830–1890* (Longman, 1993), p. 7.
6. *Laws of Life, with Special Reference to the Physical Education of Girls.* See Margaret Forster, *Significant Sisters: The Grassroots of Active Feminism 1839–1939* (Penguin, 1986), p. 75.
7. See Kate Millett, 'The Debate over Women: Ruskin vs. Mill', in *Suffer and Be Still: Women in the Victorian Age*, ed. Martha Vicinus (Bloomington: Indiana University Press, 1972), pp. 121–39, for an analysis of the contrasted positions represented by the two writers.
8. S. Barbara Kanner provides a useful bibliography on the subject, particularly as it concerns the climate of opinion on women's social roles, in 'The Women of England in a Century of Social Change, 1815–1914', in *Suffer and Be Still*, pp. 173–206.
9. 'The Female Animal: Medical and Biological Views of Woman and Her Role in Nineteenth-Century America', *The Journal of American History*, 60 (1973), 332–56 (p. 333).
10. 'Passionlessness: An Interpretation of Victorian Sexual Ideology, 1790–1850', *Signs: Journal of Women in Culture and Society*, 4 (1978), 219–36 (p. 228). Cott also argues that the ideology of passionlessness offered women a way to assert control in sexual encounters, both outside and within marriage, reducing unwelcome sexual demands and unwanted pregnancies.
11. *Uneven Developments: The Ideological Work of Gender in Mid-Victorian England* (Virago, 1989), p. 10.
12. See the arguments presented by Davidoff and Hall to support their view that the spheres could never be truly separate in Leonore Davidoff and Catherine Hall, *Family Fortunes: Men and Women of the English Middle Class, 1780–1850* (Hutchinson, 1987).
13. 'Golden Age to Separate Spheres? A Review of the Categories and Chronology of English Women's History', *The Historical Journal*, 36 (1993), 383–414 (pp. 400, 411). This article provides an invaluable introduction to the debate, not only suggesting how the idea of the separate spheres has become 'one of the fundamental organizing categories, if not *the* organizing category of modern British women's history' (p. 389), but also providing an informed rebuttal of the view that women's lives were constrained by the 'woman's

sphere'. Robert B. Shoemaker, while essentially endorsing Vickery's view, adds that although the idea of the domestic sphere may not have halted the growth of women's participation in life outside the home, 'it may have contributed to the channelling of men's and women's activities into more definably masculine and feminine channels'. See *Gender in English Society 1650–1850: The Emergence of Separate Spheres?* (Longman, 1998), p. 317.

14. Eileen Janes Yeo, 'Some Paradoxes of Empowerment', in *Radical Femininity: Women's Self-Representation in the Public Sphere*, ed. Eileen Janes Yeo (Manchester: Manchester University Press, 1998), pp. 1–24 (p. 1).

15. 'The Order of Discourse'. See *The Postmodern Bible Reader*, ed. David Jobling, Tina Pippin and Ronald Schleifer (Oxford: Blackwell, 2001), pp. 8–12, for a helpful introduction to this essay.

16. ' "A Calculus of Suffering": Ada Lovelace and the Bodily Constraints on Women's Knowledge in Early Victorian England', in *Science Incarnate: Historical Embodiments of Natural Knowledge*, ed. Christopher Lawrence and Steven Shapin (Chicago: University of Chicago Press, 1998), pp. 202–39 (p. 206).

17. See, for example Rosenberg and Smith-Rosenberg; John S. Haller and Robin M. Haller, *The Physician and Sexuality in Victorian America* (Urbana: University of Illinois Press, 1974); *Victorian America*, ed. Daniel Howe (Philadelphia: University of Pennsylvania Press, 1976), and Thomas J. Schlereth, *Victorian America: Transformations in Everyday Life, 1876–1915* (New York: Harper, 1992).

18. 'Mind and Brain; or, The Correlations of Consciousness and Organisation: Systematically Investigated and Applied to Philosophy, Mental Science and Practice', in *Embodied Selves*, p. 176.

19. 'Mental Difference between Men and Women', *Nineteenth Century*, quoted in *Embodied Selves*, p. 384.

20. 'Science Corrupted: Victorian Biologists Consider "The Woman Question" ', *Journal of the History of Biology*, 11 (1978), 1–55 (p. 17).

21. Quoted in Cynthia Eagle Russett, *Sexual Science: The Victorian Construction of Womanhood* (Cambridge, MA: Harvard University Press, 1991), pp. 37–8.

22. *The Science of Woman: Gynaecology and Gender in England, 1800–1929* (Cambridge: Cambridge University Press, 1990), pp. 104–5. It is therefore all the more surprising to find a clergyman and Secretary to the Royal Institution, John Barlow, stating in a lecture to the Institution in 1843 that 'physiologists have demonstrated that the organs of thought are proportionally larger in woman than in man' (quoted in *Embodied Selves*, p. 245).

23. R. Barnes, 'An Address on Obstetric Medicine, and Its Position in Medical Education', *Obstetrical Journal of Great Britain and Ireland* (1875–6), quoted in Moscucci, p. 37.

24. See Elaine and English Showalter, 'Victorian Women and Menstruation', *Suffer and Be Still*, pp. 38–44 (p. 39).

25. See Thomas Laqueur, 'Orgasm, Generation, and the Politics of Reproductive Biology', in *The Making of the Modern Body: Sexuality and Society in the Nineteenth Century*, ed. Catherine Gallagher and Thomas Laqueur (Berkeley: University of California Press, 1987), pp. 1–41.

26. In J. Craig's *A New Universal Etymological, Technological, and Pronouncing Dictionary of the English Language: Embracing All the Terms Used in Art, Science and Literature*, quoted in Moscucci, p. 7.

27. William Pepper, 'The Change of Life in Women', quoted in Carroll Smith-Rosenberg, 'Puberty to Menopause: The Cycle of Femininity in Nineteenth-Century America', in *Clio's Consciousness Raised: New Perspectives on the History of Women*, ed. Mary S. Hartman and Lois Banner (New York: Harper & Row, 1974), pp. 23–37 (p. 24).

28. Quoted in Ann Douglas Wood, ' "The Fashionable Diseases": Women's Complaints and Their Treatment in Nineteenth-Century America', *Clio's Consciousness Raised*, pp. 1–22 (p. 3).

29. In John Forbes, Alexander Tweedie and John Conolly (eds), *The Cyclopaedia of Practical Medicine: Comprising the Nature and Treatment of Diseases, Materia Medica and Therapeutics, Medical Jurisprudence*, 4 Vols, quoted in *Embodied Selves*, p. 201.

30. Julia Kristeva has argued that the separation of maternity and sexuality has always been central to both Judaism and Christianity. See 'The War between the Sexes', and 'The Virgin of the Word', *About Chinese Women* (Marion Boyars, 1986), pp. 17–33.

31. *The Functions and Disorders of the Reproductive Organs in Childhood, Youth, Adult Age, and Advanced Life: Considered in Their Physiological, Social and Moral Relations* (1857), quoted in *Embodied Selves*, p. 180.

32. See Rosenberg and Smith-Rosenberg, p. 348.

33. William P. Dewees, *A Treatise on the Diseases of Females*, quoted in Wood, p. 3.

34. M.E. Dirix, *Woman's Complete Guide to Health* (New York, 1869), quoted in Smith-Rosenberg and Rosenberg, pp. 335–6.

35. Hermann von Helmholtz's principle of the conservation of energy in thermodynamics.

36. ' "Scenes of an Indelicate Character": The Medical "Treatment" of Victorian Women', *The Making of the Modern Body*, pp. 137–68 (pp. 145–6).

37. Quoted in Nancy Tuana, *The Less Noble Sex: Scientific, Religious and Philosophical Conceptions of Woman's Nature* (Bloomington: Indiana University Press, 1993), p. 75.

38. See Wood, p. 7. Wood's essay provides a helpful account of these conflicting arguments.

39. Maudsley, 'Sex in Mind and Education', and Anderson, 'Sex in Mind and Education: A Reply', *Fortnightly Review* (1874), quoted in *Embodied Selves*, pp. 379–84.

40. See Smith-Rosenberg and Rosenberg, p. 336.

41. Quoted in Mosedale, p. 1. *The Popular Science Monthly* was founded in May 1872, in part to provide a forum for the work of Herbert Spencer (p. 9).

42. 'Woman Physically and Ethically Considered', *Liverpool Medico-Chirurgical Journal*, quoted in Moscucci, pp. 15–16.

43. 'Insanity Produced by Seduction', quoted in Tuana, p. 98.

44. Quoted in Showalter and Showalter, p. 40.

45. St Bartholomew's Hospital Reports (1888), quoted in Moscucci, p. 107.

46. *The Female Malady: Women, Madness and English Culture, 1830–1980* (Virago, 1987), p. 29.

47. The word originally derives from the Greek *hystera* – womb. In Greek thought the womb was thought to wander up into the throat, impeding breathing, if a woman remained barren too long. Hysteria was therefore originally related to sexual deprivation.

48. See *Embodied Selves*, pp. 190–3.
49. See, for example, *Cyclopaedia of Practical Medicine* and Thomas John Graham, *On the Management and Disorders of Infancy and Childhood* (1853), quoted in *Embodied Selves*, pp. 184–8.
50. Breuer and Freud, *Studies in Hysteria*, quoted in Showalter, p. 158.
51. Dickens's child-brides are the most obvious examples. Darwin's view also parallels that of doctors like Michael Ryan, who saw puberty in the female as the point at which her development 'arrested', so that she preserved 'some of the infantile constitution' (quoted in Smith-Rosenberg, p. 26).
52. *The Origin of the Fittest*, quoted in Tuana, p. 43.
53. Board of Regents, University of Wisconsin, *Annual Report*, 1877, quoted in Smith-Rosenberg and Rosenberg, p. 342.
54. Russett argues that the concept of the unevolved woman also provided a hierarchy badly needed once the dominant status of the human race over the animal kingdom, guaranteed in the Bible, was threatened: 'Women and the lesser races served to buffer Victorian gentlemen from a too-threatening intimacy with the brutes' (p. 14).
55. *Darwin's Plots: Evolutionary Narrative in Darwin, George Eliot and Nineteenth-Century Fiction*, 2nd edition (Cambridge: Cambridge University Press, 2000), p. xxiv.
56. See Chapter 6 of this book, however, for a discussion of attempts to establish such racial differences while preserving the essentialist category 'woman'.
57. 'On the Real Differences in the Minds of Men and Women', *Anthropological Review*, quoted in Tuana, p. 40.
58. See *Myth, Religion and Mother Right: Selected Writings of J. J. Bachofen* (Routledge, 1967) and Robert Briffault, *The Mothers: A Study of the Origins of Sentiments and Institutions*, abr. Gordon Rattray Taylor (Allen & Unwin, 1959).
59. See Russett, pp. 130–33 and Elizabeth Fee, 'The Sexual Politics of Victorian Social Anthropology', *Clio's Consciousness Raised*, pp. 86–102.
60. *The Westminster Review*, 1857, quoted in Gilmour, p. 129.
61. 'Psychology of the Sexes' (1873), quoted in Tuana, p. 87. Even the American evolutionist Edward Drinker Cope, who took a great interest in feminism, shared Spencer's view that female sympathy would interfere with true justice. See Mosedale, pp. 24–32.
62. 'The Triumph of Complementarity', *The Mind has no Sex? Women in the Origins of Modern Science* (Cambridge, MA: Harvard University Press, 1991), pp. 214–31.
63. For fuller discussions of Victorian ideas of masculinity, see John Tosh, *A Man's Place: Masculinity and the Middle-Class Home in Victorian England* (New Haven: Yale University Press, 1999), Andrew Bradstock, *Masculinity and Spirituality in Victorian Culture* (Basingstoke: Macmillan, 2000) and Christopher Lane, *The Burdens of Intimacy: Psychoanalysis and Victorian Masculinity* (Chicago: University of Chicago Press, 1999).
64. See also William Acton on masturbation and spermatorrhea (*Embodied Selves*, pp. 211–14).
65. David Glover and Cora Kaplan, *Genders* (Routledge, 2000), p. 23.
66. 'The Probable Retrogression of Woman', quoted in Tuana, p. 39.
67. *The Language of Gender and Class: Transformation in the Victorian Novel* (Routledge, 1996), p. 22.

68. The most important of these are probably the Married Women's Property Acts (1870 and 1882), and the Guardianship of Infants Act (1886). For a fuller account of these changes in legislation see Philippa Levine, *Victorian Feminism 1850–1900* (Gainesville: University Press of Florida, 1994).

69. 'Sexual Inversion in Women', quoted in Charlotte Perkins Gilman, *The Yellow Wallpaper*, ed. Dale M. Bauer (Boston: Bedford Books, 1998), p. 245. A similar anxiety is expressed about the 'feminised' male homosexual, and manifested in the Labouchère Amendment to the Criminal Law Act (1885), which achieved the legal identification of homosexuality as deviant.

70. 'Why are Women Redundant?', *National Review*, quoted in Poovey, p. 1.

71. It is therefore refreshing, if amusing, to find the American zoologist W.K. Brooks following the argument that to be masculine is to be fully human to its logical conclusion: he argues that, for the human, 'possession of a beard must be regarded as a general characteristic of our race ... when a female, from disease or mutilation or old age, assumes a resemblance to the male, the change is an advance' (*The Law of Heredity*, 1883, quoted in Russett, p. 75).

72. 'The Traffic in Women: Notes on the "Political Economy" of Sex' (1975), quoted in Glover and Kaplan, p. xxiv.

73. For a detailed discussion of the contribution of Romanes and other Victorian scientists to the debate about inherited and acquired characteristics in relation to gender and education, see Mosedale.

74. 'Victorian Science and the Genius of Woman', *Journal of the History of Ideas*, 38 (1977), 261–80 (p. 265).

75. 'Lectures on the Comparative Physiology of Menstruation', quoted in Moscucci, p. 33.

76. See *Darwin's Plots* and *Open Fields: Science in Cultural Encounter* (Oxford: Oxford University Press, 1996).

2   The Darwinian moment: The woman that never evolved

1. Full title – *On the Origin of Species by Means of Natural Selection, or the Preservation of Favoured Races in the Struggle for Life.*

2. 'The Origin of Species and the Science of Female Inferiority', in *Charles Darwin's 'The Origin of Species': New Interdisciplinary Essays*, ed. David Amigoni and Jeff Wallace (Manchester: Manchester University Press, 1995), pp. 95–121 (p. 118).

3. *Journal of Researches into the Natural History and Geology of the Various Countries Visited during the Voyage of H.M.S. Beagle Round the World* (London, 1839).

4. Jenny Diski's novel, *Monkey's Uncle* (Weidenfeld & Nicolson, 1994) also engages in a very ambitious and adventurous way with Darwin's ideas – as well as those of Marx and Freud – but registers their impact on twentieth- rather than nineteenth-century consciousness.

5. It will be apparent throughout this chapter that I am heavily indebted to Professor Beer's work on the relations between science and literature, in particular to her work on the impact of Darwinism.

6. *Journal of Researches into the Natural History and Geology of the Various Countries Visited during the Voyage of H.M.S. Beagle Round the World*, 11th edition (Ward, Lock: Bowden, 1892), p. 39.

7. 'Science and Women's Bodies: Forms of Anthropological Knowledge', in *Body/Politics: Women and the Discourses of Science*, ed. Mary Jacobus, Evelyn Fox Keller and Sally Shuttleworth (Routledge, 1990), pp. 69–82 (p. 69).

8. Lilian Faderman records that the number of single women increased disproportionately with each census from the 1850s onwards, rising from 2,765,000 in 1851 to 3,228,700 in 1871. See *Surpassing the Love of Men: Romantic Friendship and Love between Women from the Renaissance to the Present* (Women's Press, 1985), p. 184.

9. First published by Norton, the novel was published in Britain by Flamingo in 1999. All page references will be to the British edition, and will follow the relevant quotation in the text.

10. Beer points out that all such journeys were also, however,

> an expression of the will to control, categorize, occupy, and bring home the prize of samples and of strategic information [...]. And natural history was usually a sub-genre in the programme of the enterprise, subordinate to the search for sea-passages or the mapping of feasible routes and harbours. (*Open Fields*, p. 59)

11. I have used the archaic term 'Esquimaux' throughout this chapter, rather than the term 'Innuit', used by the indigenous Arctic population themselves, to reflect Anglo-American/European usage at the time.

12. Boerhaave's view is largely based on that set out by Louis Agassiz and A.A. Gould in *Principles of Zoology* (1851), and quoted as the epigram to Chapter 8.

13. Elisha Kent Kane was one of the many explorers who led an expedition with the same aim as the fictional voyage of the *Narwhal*, to search for Sir John Franklin.

14. Max Jones, 'Science and Sacrifice: The Royal Geographical Society and British Exploration', paper delivered at *Locating the Victorians* conference, Imperial College, London, July 2001.

15. Lisa Bloom, *Gender on Ice: American Ideologies of Polar Expeditions* (Minneapolis: University of Minnesota Press, 1993), p. 6. Although Bloom deals primarily with twentieth-century polar exploration, her arguments about its relationship to models of masculinity and race are also relevant to the situation evoked in *The Voyage of the Narwhal*.

16. The novel also draws attention to the similar impact of colonial ideology on the English view of the Irish, two much more closely related peoples, when Ned, the *Narwhal*'s Irish cook, compares the meticulous individual burials of members of the *Narwhal* with the treatment of the famine dead, 'stacked like firewood or tossed loosely into giant pits' (p. 114).

17. In contrast, when Oonali's wife gives Erasmus part of the sole of a boot which may have been used for cannibalism, Erasmus tries to keep it secret, failing to include it in his list of finds, so that when it is lost, there is no written evidence to support its existence and he is discredited.

18. Saartje Baartman, a young Khosian woman from Southern Africa known as the Hottentot Venus, was put on display for six years in nineteenth-century Britain and France as a sexual freak because of her large posterior and genitalia. After her death in 1816, scientists interested in 'primitive sexuality' dissected

her body and used her genitalia as 'proof' of African women's sexual appetite. Her remains were displayed in Paris's *Musée de l'Homme* until 1974. Sander Gilman, 'Black Bodies, White Bodies: Toward an Iconography of Female Sexuality in Late Nineteenth-Century Art, Medicine, and Literature', in *Race, Writing and Difference*, ed. Henry Louis Gates (Chicago: University of North Carolina Press, 1985), pp. 223–61.

19. Kane's errors, which condemned his men to two years of isolation in the polar regions, and many of which are shared by Zeke, were identified in the narrative of Johan Peterson, a member of the crew. See Oscar Villarejo, *Dr Kane's Voyage to the Polar Lands* (Philadelphia: University of Pennsylvania, 1965).

20. *The George Eliot Letters*, ed. Gordon S. Haight, 9 Vols (New Haven: Yale University Press, 1955), V, p. 107.

21. See, for instance, W.R. Greg, 'Why Are Women Redundant', *National Review* 14 (1862), 434–60.

22. Margaret Penny is said to be the first European women to winter at Baffin Island, accompanying her husband on a whaler in 1857, and keeping a record of the journey. See W. Gillies Ross, *This Distant and Unsurveyed Land: A Woman's Winter at Baffin Island, 1857–1858* (Montreal: McGill-Queen's University Press, 1997). But it is estimated that as early as 1853 one in six American whaling captains were accompanied by their wives. Bloom argues, however, that even the achievements of women who were Arctic explorers in their own right were feminised in male accounts, the emphasis being placed on their supportive role and self-sacrifice, so as to reduce those achievements to the performance of a wife's traditional role under adverse circumstances (p. 7).

23. Tackritow was the most famous female Innuit traveller, taken to Britain – where she was popularly known as Anne – with her husband and son in 1853, and being exhibited widely before returning home in 1855. See Ross, pp. 52–7.

24. Margaret Penny notes that the Esquimaux believed that the soul could escape the body more easily when the flesh was removed (Ross, p. 165).

25. See Londa Schiebinger, 'Skeletons in the Closet: The First Illustrations of the Female Skeleton in Eighteenth-Century Anatomy', in *The Making of the Modern Body*, pp. 42–82, on nineteenth-century attempts to identify gender and race from skeletal remains. Schiebinger argues that, although there are differences between the male and female pelvis, they have often been exaggerated in response to changing social and political circumstances.

26. *On Histories and Stories*, p. 81. Chapter 4, 'True Stories and the Facts in Fiction' (pp. 91–122) provides an account of the writing and meaning of both *Morpho Eugenia* and *The Conjugial Angel* which should be the starting point for anyone interested in either novella.

27. The novella was published together with *The Conjugial Angel*, as *Angels and Insects* (Chatto & Windus, 1992). All further references to the novella will be to the Vintage edition (1995), and will follow the relevant quotation in the text.

28. Byatt states that she puts into Harald's mouth the arguments of the Harvard biologist Asa Gray, including his reference to those parts of Darwin's early work in which he still talks of a Creator (*Histories*, p. 118).

29. '*Morpho Eugenia*: Problems with the Male Gaze', *Critique*, 40 (1999), 399–411 (p. 399). This persuasive essay argues that the novella subverts that gaze by illustrating its reductive repercussions, and by demonstrating that William himself becomes one of the observed.
30. A.S. Byatt, *Writers and Their Work* (Northcote House, 1997), p. 36.
31. The Captain reappears in *The Conjugial Angel*, the second novella in the book. In 'The *Odyssey* Rewoven: A.S. Byatt's *Angels and Insects*', *Classical and Modern Literature*, 19 (1999), 217–31, Judith Fletcher describes Papagay as an Odyssean wanderer linking the two stories.
32. *Ecological Revolutions: Nature, Gender, and Science in New England* (Chapel Hill: University of North Carolina Press, 1989), p. 251.
33. *The Woman That Never Evolved* (Cambridge, MA: Harvard University Press, 1999), p. xiii.
34. *The Sexes throughout Nature*, quoted in Hrdy, p. 12.

3   'Criminals, idiots, women and minors': Deviant minds in deviant bodies

1. Quoted in Elaine Showalter, *Sexual Anarchy: Gender and Culture at the* Fin de Siècle (Bloomsbury, 1991), p. 129.
2. Roberta McGrath provides examples of such 'mapping' in her study of the relationship between the history of anatomical illustration and changes in the practice and theory of anatomy. See *Seeing Her Sex: Medical Archives and the Female Body* (Manchester: Manchester University Press, 2002).
3. *Regulating Motherhood: Historical Essays on Marriage, Motherhood and Sexuality* (Routledge, 1992), p. 7. Anyone interested in exploring the legal dimension further should consult this excellent study.
4. Smart lists: the Offences against the Person Act (1861), the Contagious Diseases Acts of 1866 and 1869, the Infant Life Preservation Act (1872) and the Criminal Law Amendment Act (1885) (p. 13).
5. 'Criminals, Idiots, Women, and Minors', *Fraser's Magazine*, in '*Criminals, Idiots, Women, and Minors': Victorian Writing by Women on Women*, ed. Susan Hamilton (Ontario: Broadview Press, 1995), pp. 108–31 (pp. 110, 111, 118).
6. For a fuller discussion of hysteria see Ilza Veith, *Hysteria: The History of a Disease* (Chicago: University of Chicago Press, 1965).
7. *On the Pathology and Treatment of Hysteria* (John Churchill), pp. 33, 50 and 153. Middle-class women were generally seen as more likely to suffer hysteria as a consequence of the repression of sexual feeling, and of their education and lifestyle. For this reason and because of the existence of masculine hysteria, Carter, for instance, rejects as untenable the theory that hysteria derived entirely from changes in the reproductive system, maintained by some doctors.
8. *Difference and Pathology: Stereotypes of Sexuality, Race, and Madness* (Ithaca: Cornell University Press, 1985), pp. 43, 55.
9. *Traité clinique et thérapeutique de l'hystérie*, 1859, quoted in Evelyne Ender, *Sexing the Mind: Nineteenth-Century Fictions of Hysteria* (Ithaca: Cornell University Press, 1995), p. 37. Ender describes this work of 700 pages, based on over 400 cases, as a 'monument of a positivist science' which nevertheless rests on untested assumptions about female 'nature'.

10. Isaac Baker Brown was the most famous obstetrician to carry out such operations, sometimes without the consent of the patient, until being expelled from the Obstetrical Society in 1867 and being denounced in the *Lancet*. See *Embodied Selves*, p. 302.

11. The story was first published in *New England Magazine*, 1892. See also 'Why I Wrote the Yellow Wallpaper?', in *The Yellow Wallpaper*, ed. Dale M. Bauer (Boston: Bedford Books, 1998), pp. 347–9.

12. 'The Eye of Power', *Power/Knowledge: Selected Interviews and Other Writings 1972–1977*, ed. and trans. C. Gordon (Hemel Hempstead: Harvester, 1980), p. 155.

13. *What a Man's Gotta Do: The Masculine Myth in Popular Culture* (Grafton Books, 1986), p. 43.

14. *Confession: Sexuality, Sin, the Subject* (Manchester: Manchester University Press, 1990), p. 135. I am indebted to this book for much of the argument underlying my analysis of *Alias Grace*.

15. *Critical Practice* (Methuen, 1980), p. 112.

16. All references to this novel, first published in 1996 (Toronto: McLelland & Stewart), will be to the Virago edition of 1997, and will follow the relevant quotation in the text.

17. In an interview with James Bone, Atwood makes it explicit that *Alias Grace* is an attempt to get beyond such a dualistic view of woman as either a *femme fatale* or 'some kind of put-upon, weak, angelic being who doesn't know any better'. See *The Times Magazine*, 14 September 1996, pp. 13–16 (p. 14).

18. *Life in the Clearings versus the Bush*, originally published in 1853 (Toronto: McClelland & Stewart, 1989), pp. 209, 21. Atwood's use of Moodie and other contemporary sources suggests that the varied representations of 'the celebrated murderess' are a central issue in the novel. See also Magali Cornier Michael, 'Rethinking History as Patchwork: The Case of Atwood's *Alias Grace*', *Modern Fiction Studies*, 47 (2001), 421–47.

19. Susan Rowland describes Jordan as 'a prototypical C. G. Jung both in using Jung's early technique of word association and particularly in describing Grace as an "anima"' ('Imaginal Bodies and Feminine Spirits: Performing Gender in Jungian Theory and Atwood's *Alias Grace*', in *Body Matters: Feminism, Textuality, Corporeality*, ed. Avril Horner and Angela Keane (Manchester: Manchester University Press, 2000), pp. 244–54 (p. 250)).

20. In the chapter 'Secret Drawer', Jordan discusses with Grace a quilt pattern called Pandora's Box, the same image being used twice.

21. Michel Foucault, *The History of Sexuality: An Introduction*, trans. Robert Hurley (Harmondsworth: Penguin, 1990), p. 104.

22. Grace's ethnicity plays an important role at her trial, linking the murder with the Irish question so that the murder of a Tory gentleman becomes equivalent to 'the insurrection of an entire race' (p. 91).

23. DuPont's demonstration follows the example of the real-life Dr Charcot, who used hypnotism in his clinic in Paris to treat hysteria. See Showalter, *The Female Malady*, pp. 147–51, for a relevant discussion of Charcot's practice.

24. See *Embodied Selves*, pp. 70–2, for a discussion of the place of this concept in nineteenth-century psychology.

25. It is worth noting that hysterical women were thought to be particularly good subjects for hypnosis. See, for instance, Cesare Lombroso, *The Female Offender* (T. Fisher Unwin, 1895), pp. 219–20.

26. In a very persuasive article, Stephanie Lovelady assesses the likelihood of Grace having a split personality, faking or even being possessed by Mary's ghost. Although my conclusion is slightly different, her arguments are worth consideration. See 'I am Telling This to No One But You: Private Voice, Passing, and the Private Sphere in Margaret Atwood's *Alias Grace*', *Studies in Canadian Literature*, 24 (1999), 35–63.

27. The novel was first published by Virago in 1999. All references to the novel will be to this edition and will follow the relevant quotation in the text.

28. The author has established through correspondence that Sarah Waters read *Alias Grace* towards the end of writing *Affinity*, and that she was 'a bit perturbed, rather than intrigued' by the similarities between them, as her own novel had not yet been published.

29. See Michel Foucault, 'Panopticism', *Discipline and Punish: The Birth of the Prison*, trans. Alan Sheridan (Harmondsworth: Penguin Books, 1991), pp. 195–228.

30. I am indebted to *Surpassing the Love of Men* for much of my understanding of the nature of female friendship in the second half of the nineteenth century. Similar arguments, deriving from the separation of spheres, can of course be applied to male friendships, as I shall argue in the following chapter.

31. In some respects, therefore, it reflects Terry Castle's argument that in Victorian fiction lesbians were associated with ghostly, spectral presences. Castle suggests that until around 1900, lesbianism manifested itself in the Western literary imagination primarily 'as an absence [...] a kind of love that, by definition, cannot exist' (pp. 30–1), a view which Margaret's diaries arguably reflect.

32. It is worth noting, however, as Faderman points out, that Thomas Hardy describes the passionate kisses which Miss Aldclyffe gives to her maid, Cytherea, in *Desperate Remedies*, as 'motherly', without any apparent sense of contradiction (p. 172).

33. Waters is arguably being a little anachronistic in putting such thoughts into Margaret's mind, since one might expect the gap between 'deviant' criminal women and the Victorian lady to have kept her in relative ignorance of sexual matters.

34. Selina names Margaret 'Aurora' after the eponymous heroine of Elizabeth Barrett Browning's novel-poem *Aurora Leigh*. When anticipating running away abroad with Selina, Margaret books a ticket for her in the name of Marian Earle, who figures in *Aurora Leigh* as a poor seamstress and unmarried mother, and reads to her mother the passages in which Aurora proposes that Marian should live with her in the home she plans in Tuscany.

35. See Chapter 4 of this book for an explanation of the Swedenborgian principles on which Selina's theories draw.

36. See 'Compulsory Heterosexuality and Lesbian Existence', *Adrienne Rich's Poetry and Prose*, ed. Barbara Charlesworth Gelpi and Albert Gelpi (New York: W.W. Norton, 1993), pp. 203–24.

4 Subversive spirits: Spiritualism and female desire

1. Quoted in Vieda Skultans, 'Mediums, Controls and Eminent Men', in *Women's Religious Experience: Cross-Cultural Perspectives*, ed. Pat Holden (Croom Helm, 1983), pp. 15–26 (p. 16).
2. *The Darkened Room: Women, Power and Spiritualism in Late Nineteenth Century England* (Virago, 1989), p. 233. This is an invaluable source for readers looking for a history of women in spiritualism.
3. A.N. Wilson, *The Victorians* (Hutchinson, 2002), p. 439.
4. See Owen, p. 237.
5. *Electricity* (first published by Hutchinson, 1995). All page references to this text will be taken from the Arrow Books edition (Random House, 1996), and will follow the relevant quotation in the text.
6. It is worth again pointing out that although contemporary fictions set in the Victorian period frequently suggest different discourses at work, Victorians working in a wide variety of disciplines – scientific, religious and cultural in the wider sense – would have felt they shared a discourse.
7. See J.D. Bernal, *Science in History*, Vol. 2, *The Scientific and Industrial Revolutions* (Harmondsworth: Penguin, 1969), pp. 564, 613.
8. The reference is to Hertha Ayrton (1854–1923), who became a highly successful electrical engineer and physicist, also active in women's causes. See Evelyn Sharp, *Hertha Ayrton, 1854–1923: A Memoir* (Edward Arnold, 1926).
9. The name Godwin in such a context inevitably recalls William Godwin, radical father of Mary Shelley, whose anti-hero Frankenstein is arguably destroyed for using electricity to usurp the uniquely female power to give birth to another human being.
10. Although the term 'attraction' had a scientific meaning long before it acquired its popular modern usage, the language used to explain electricity more often borrows from the vocabulary of human interaction, particularly in nineteenth-century science textbooks of the more popular kind. Henry Noad's *Lectures on Electricity, Comprising Galvanism, Magnetism, Electro-Magnetism, Magneto- and Thermo-Electricity, and Electro-Physiology* (George Knight & Sons, 1849), which aims to present a popular view of the current state of knowledge of the subject, shows clearly how central such terms as 'bodies', 'attraction', 'repulsion' and 'excitement' are to its discourse. See also John Cook's account of frictional electricity:

    > if an excited stick of sealing-wax be brought near, the pith instantly flies to its embrace, only, however, to be in a moment cast off [...]. Banished from the wax, it will now find favour with the glass for an instant again; and thus a continual exchange of sympathy for the one or the other electrified body may be kept up as long as the excitement continues. (*Magnetism and Electricity* (Chambers, 1875), p. 20)

11. See, for instance, A.J. Bloch's account of examining a two-year-old girl thought to be suffering the effects of excessive masturbation. He explores her genitalia to ascertain exactly which area produces the 'true phenomena' of sexual excitement in order to justify a clitoridectomy ('Sexual Perversion in the Female' (1894) quoted in Bauer, p. 232).

12. The use of electricity for such conditions is described in A. de Watteville's prescription for 'uterine neuralgia', seen as the probable cause of hysteria. A current is passed for eight to ten minutes between 'poles' placed on the cervix and the abdomen, over one of the ovaries. (*A Practical Introduction to Medical Electricity* (Lewis, 1878), pp. 115–16.)

13. *Madness and Civilisation: A History of Insanity in the Age of Reason* (Tavistock, 1967).

14. Entropy means that in a closed system, fast (hot) molecules and slow (cold) molecules would mix and become intermediate (tepid), resulting in an absence of surplus energy.

15. 'Seating the Séance', *Times Literary Supplement*, 7 April 1995, p. 24.

16. *Nights at the Circus* (Pan, 1985), p. 216.

17. The novella was published together with *Morpho Eugenia*, as *Angels and Insects* (Chatto & Windus, 1992). All further references to the novella will be to the Vintage edition (1995), and will follow the relevant quotation in the text.

18. *Brewer's Dictionary of Phrase and Fable*, revised by Ivor H. Evans (Cassell, 1970), p. 1115.

19. *Literature and Gender*, ed. Lizbeth Goodman (Routledge, 1996), p. 48.

20. Visitors to her home describe the historical Emily Tennyson as 'a shadow of her former self'. See *Tennyson: 'In Memoriam'*, ed. Susan Shatto and Marion Shaw (Oxford: Clarendon Press, 1982), p. 168.

21. Mitoko Hirabayashi, 'Aged Sleeping Beauty: "Prince's Progress" as "Women's Text"', paper presented at *Victorian Women Revisited* conference, University of Aberdeen, April 2001.

22. Although I use the term 'the fictional Emily', that figure has a very strong basis in biography, if the novella is compared to the documentary evidence cited in Ann Thwaite's monumental work, *Emily Tennyson: The Poet's Wife* (Faber, 1996).

23. See for example, 'My Arthur, whom I shall not see / Till all my widowed race be run' (IX.17) and 'tears of the widower' (XIII.1).

24. Examples in the poem include: 'hands so often clasped in mine' (X.19), and 'Reach out dead hands to comfort me' (LXXX.16).

25. 'On Some of the Characteristics of Modern Poetry', the *Englishman's Magazine*, 1831, quoted in *The Broadview Anthology of Victorian Poetry and Poetic Theory*, ed. Thomas J. Collins and Vivienne J. Rundle (Toronto: Broadview Press, 2000), pp. 541–55 (p. 545).

26. For Tennyson's hope that spiritualism might offer proof of such an afterlife, see Philip Elliott, 'Tennyson and Spiritualism', *Tennyson Research Bulletin*, 3 (1979), 89–100. Elliot argues that although the poet attended séances, showed an interest in the Society for Psychical Research and talked of spiritualism in very positive terms, he was never satisfied by the proofs of immortality that it offered.

27. See Elaine Pagels, *The Gnostic Gospels* (Weidenfeld & Nicolson, 1980), and Anne Baring and Jules Cashford, 'Sophia: Mother, Daughter and Bride', *The Myth of the Goddess: Evolution of an Image* (Harmondsworth: Penguin, 1993), pp. 609–58.

28. Byatt herself describes spiritualism as, like Swedenborgianism, 'the religion of a materialist age' *Passions of the Mind: Selected Writings* (Chatto & Windus, 1991), p. 62.

29. See Donne's 'Elegie: Going To Bed'; 'Licence my roaving hands, and let them go, / Behind, before, above, between, below.'
30. See 'Revolution in Poetic Language', *The Kristeva Reader*, ed. Toril Moi (Oxford: Blackwell, 1986), pp. 89–136.
31. Byatt quotes Swedenborg's 'scornful' attitude to women at some length in an article on Henry James's novel *The Bostonians* ('The End of Innocence', *The Guardian Saturday Review*, 6 September 2003, 34–5).
32. The novel was first published by Methuen in 1990. All page references to the novel will be taken from the Minerva edition (Mandarin, 1991), and will follow the relevant quotation in the text.
33. Roberts acknowledges this in her Author's note, citing as her source an essay by Alex Owen, reprinted in *The Darkened Room*.
34. The most dramatic expression of deceptive innocence occurs in Minny's dream, when Flora appears dressed in the bridal white of chastity with a bloody knife in her hand and the body of Minny's baby, which she proceeds to eat.
35. *Women Writers Talk: Interviews With Ten Women Writers*, ed. Olga Kenyon (Oxford: Lennard Publishing, 1989), pp. 149–72 (p. 169).
36. For instance, when Sir William tells her not to 'mope', Minny is concerned not to be a burden to her over-worked husband, sure he has her best interests at heart, and yearns to take up her 'duties as a wife and mother' (p. 6) again.
37. In 1874, deaths in childbirth reached the highest level ever recorded in England (70 per 10,000). See Irvine Loudon, 'Maternal Mortality in Britain from 1850 to the Mid-1930s', *Death in Childbirth: An International Study of Maternal Care and Maternal Mortality 1800–1950* (Oxford: Clarendon Press, 1992), pp. 234–53.
38. *The Second Sex*, trans. H.M. Parshley (Pan, 1988), pp. 178–9.
39. The paradigmatic example of this pattern is probably the Greek myth of Apollo and Cassandra, in which Apollo promises Cassandra the gift of prophecy if she will submit to him sexually.
40. I am indebted to Sarah Falcus for pointing out that Hat is probably based upon Hatshepsut (1473–1458 BC), one of only four women to reign as 'king' in ancient Egypt, who is depicted in male clothing on her monuments. Her eventual fate is uncertain, and her co-regent, Thutmose III, had her name removed from her monuments after her death. *Corpses in the Church and Mouths of Men: Mothers, Daughters and the Maternal in Selected Novels of Michèle Roberts*, unpublished PhD thesis, Aberdeen, 2001.

5 Degeneration and sexual anarchy

1. *Punch* (1895), quoted in *Sexual Anarchy*, p. 9.
2. 'Woman and Labour', *Fortnightly Review* (1894), quoted in *Sexual Anarchy*, p. 7.
3. *The Fabrication of the Late-Victorian Femme Fatale: The Kiss of Death* (Basingstoke: Macmillan, 1992), p. 18. The concept gained even greater currency after the publication in 1895 of the first English translation of *Degeneration* by the Austrian Max Nordau, a book which condemned much of late nineteenth-century European culture.
4. The same techniques were applied to other social groups, as Nancy Stepan points out: 'By the late nineteenth century, the urban poor, prostitutes,

criminals, and the insane were being construed as "degenerate" types whose deformed skulls, protruding jaws, and low brain weights marked them as "races apart", interacting with and creating degenerate spaces near at home.' See 'Biology and Degeneration: Races and Proper Places', in *Degeneration: The Dark Side of Progress*, ed. J. Edward Chamberlin and Sander L. Gilman (New York: Columbia University Press, 1985), pp. 97–120 (p. 98).

5. *The Female Offender* (T. Fisher Unwin, 1895), p. 101.

6. The Club, a group of socialist and feminist intellectuals, was founded by Karl Pearson, and met from 1885 to 1889. See *Sexual Anarchy*, p. 47.

7. *Feminist Perspectives on the Body* (New York: Pearson Education, 1999), p. 111.

8. 'Putting the Body's Feet on the Ground: Towards a Sociological Reconceptualization of Gendered and Sexual Embodiment', in *Constructing Gendered Bodies*, ed. Kathryn Backett-Milburn and Linda McKie (Basingstoke: Palgrave, 2001), pp. 9–24 (p. 12). The underlying premise of this important collection is that 'the sociology of the body provides an opportunity to study the body as integral to social action and social being' (p. xviii).

9. The novel was first published by Chatto & Windus. All page references will be to the Picador edition (1985) and will follow the relevant quotation in the text.

10. Susan Watkins provides a helpful introduction to this novel as a post-modern text, in the sense that it dismantles key nineteenth-century narratives of truth, subjectivity and representation. See *Twentieth-Century Women Novelists: Feminist Theory into Practice* (Palgrave, 2001). Discussions of the carnival element occur in virtually every discussion of the novel.

11. *Angela Carter: The Rational Glass* (Manchester: Manchester University Press, 1998), p. 175.

12. Carter is openly sceptical of the subversive powers sometimes claimed for carnival, noting that it is a licensed interlude which must always come to an end. See 'Angela Carter Interviewed by Lorna Sage', in New Writing, ed. Malcolm Bradbury and Judith Cooke (Minerva Press, 1992), pp. 185–93 (p. 188).

13. Anna Katsavos, 'An Interview with Angela Carter', *Review of Contemporary Fiction*, 14 (1994), pp. 11–17 (p. 13).

14. *The Female Grotesque: Risk, Excess, and Modernity* (New York: Routledge, 1995), p. 62. Susan Swan's novel, *The Biggest Modern Woman in the World* (Allen & Unwin, 1983), based on the true story of the Nova Scotia giantess, Anna Swan, provides an interesting historical companion to Fevvers' story. Swan joined Barnum's American Museum in New York around 1863, and went on to tour America and Britain.

15. *Monuments and Maidens: The Allegory of the Female Form* (Vintage, 1996), p. 132.

16. '"Is She Fact or is She Fiction?" Angela Carter and the Enigma of Woman', *Textual Practice*, 11 (1997), 89–107 (p. 97). This essay provides an excellent analysis of the relationship between body and identity in the novel.

17. Toussaint is a black man with no mouth, signifying his role as the silenced racial other. His later post-operative eloquence suggests Carter is here alluding to the Caribbean ex-slave, Toussaint L'Ouverture – 'he who makes an opening' – who led the St Dominguan revolution and became its ruler in 1800. See Cora Kaplan, 'Black Heroes/White Writers: Toussaint L'Ouverture and the Literary Imagination', *History Workshop Journal*, 46 (1998), pp. 32–62.

18. Quoted in Peta Tait, 'Feminine Free Fall: A Fantasy of Freedom', *Theatre Journal*, 8 (1996), 27–34 (p. 32).
19. Fernihough suggests that the prominent yet uncertain nature of Fevvers' body makes her 'an exaggerated version of "woman" as posited by late nineteenth-century doctors, sexologists and psychoanalysts. [...] Carter's dual perspective means that the concept of "the enigma of woman" is both foregrounded and systematically undermined in this novel' (p. 90).
20. When chosen, motherhood can be transforming, as it is for Fanny the 'freak', who becomes a successful adoptive mother in spite of not feeling biologically equipped for maternity, because she has eyes instead of breasts.
21. Havelock Ellis finds evidence for his view of the correlation between levels of female criminality and women's incursion into male territory in 'the Baltic provinces of Russia, where the women share the occupations of the men' (quoted in *Embodied Selves*, p. 334).
22. Carter is probably alluding to Alphonse Bertillon (1853–1914), who developed a new system of measurement specifically to identify criminals.
23. See 'The Newly Born Woman', *The Hélène Cixous Reader*, pp. 35–46.
24. To underline Walser's representative function, his transformation is ironically prefigured in his fellow performer, the Strong Man, the epitome of masculine power and violence. When the Strong Man's heart is broken by his unrequited love for Mignon, the narrator comments, 'Out of the fracture, sensibility might poke a moist, new-born head' (p. 167).
25. The novel was first published by Virago in 1998. All page references will be to this edition, and will follow the relevant quotation in the text.
26. *Psychopathia Sexualis: With Especial Reference to Antipathic Sexual Instinct: A Medico-Forensic Study*, trans. Charles Chaddock (F.A. Davis, 1892).
27. The book was recommended as a useful source in a House of Lords debate on an attempt to make lesbian as well as male homosexual acts illegal. See Alison Oram and Annmarie Turnbull, *The Lesbian History Sourcebook: Love and Sex between Women in Britain from 1780 to 1970* (Routledge, 2001), p. 167.
28. D. Hack Tuke (ed.), *A Dictionary of Psychological Medicine*, 2 Vols (J. & A. Churchill, 1892), II, pp. 1156–7.
29. 'The Working Body as Sign: Historical Snapshots', in Backett-Milburn, pp. 85–103 (p. 93).
30. Sarah Waters herself draws attention to Stacey's argument in 'Wolfskins and Togas: Maude Meagher's *The Green Scamander* and the Lesbian Historical Novel', *Women: A Cultural Review*, 7 (1996), 176–88 (p. 181).
31. Oysters recur as a symbol not just of sexuality but of nurturing when Nancy uses her mother's oyster recipes to stimulate the appetite of Florence, her final lover, who is unhealthily underweight. This more practical use of the oyster anticipates the more grounded and ultimately secure nature of this relationship.
32. *Gender Trouble: Feminism and the Subversion of Identity* (New York: Routledge, 1990), p. 140.
33. Angela Carter similarly resists presenting the body of a young Victorian woman as purely the site of transgressive pleasure, and she punctuates Fevvers' story with near-disastrous encounters with powerful men. As Fernihough puts it, 'by making her winged flesh into her means of survival,

Fevvers is always at risk, and always a commodity. [...] Two ideas of flesh, one positive, one negative, flesh as self-assertion and flesh as vulnerability and risk, are precariously played off against one another in the novel' (p. 101).

34. Carpenter was a widely read socialist and sex reformer, but his book *The Intermediate Sex* (privately published in 1895) was condemned by medical practitioners, perhaps because he refused to see this condition as a sign of disease or degeneration. Carpenter argues that the mix of male and female characteristics in each individual is what enables the sexes to understand each other. This 'normal' arrangement is merely more pronounced in the 'intermediate sex', which he bases on the Austrian writer K.H. Ulrich's concept of 'Urnings': those born with the biological characteristics of one sex, but with the mental and emotional characteristics of the other. To Carpenter it is perfectly logical that such individuals would love their own sex rather than the opposite sex, although that love may not always be sexual in nature (see Oram, p. 106).

6 Evolutionary thought, gender and race

1. For a full account of this debate, see Nancy Stepan, *The Idea of Race in Science: Great Britain 1800–1960* (Basingstoke: Macmillan, 1982).
2. Quoted in Anne Fausto-Sterling, 'Gender, Race and Nation: The Comparative Anatomy of "Hottentot" Women in Europe, 1815–1817', in *Feminism and the Body*, ed. Londa L. Schiebinger (Oxford: Oxford University Press, 2000), pp. 203–33 (p. 212).
3. See Jago Morrison, *Contemporary Fiction* (Routledge, 2003), p. 55.
4. 'Racialized Bodies', in *Real Bodies: A Sociological Introduction*, ed. Mary Evans and Ellie Lee (Basingstoke: Palgrave, 2002), pp. 46–63 (p. 54).
5. 'Biology and Degeneration: Races and Proper Places', in *Degeneration: The Dark Side of Progress*, ed. J. Edward Chamberlin and Sander L. Gilman (New York: Columbia University Press, 1985), pp. 97–120 (p. 98).
6. Graham Sumner and Albert Galloway Keller, *The Science of Society*, quoted in Russett, p. 142.
7. See 'Emancipation: Black and White' (1865), quoted in *Embodied Selves*, pp. 374–7.
8. Since the 1950s, the United Nations have refuted nineteenth-century racial theory by arguing that while the species *Homo sapiens* can be divided into groups and populations in various ways, 'race' is not one of these (see Ashley Montagu, *Statement on Race: An Annotated Elaboration and Exposition of the Four Statements on Race Issued by the United Nations Educational, Scientific, and Cultural Organization* (New York: Oxford University Press, 1972)).
9. A protuberance of the buttocks, due to an accumulation of fat in or behind the hips and thighs.
10. Quoted in Sander Gilman, *Difference and Pathology: Stereotypes of Sexuality, Race, and Madness* (New York: Cornell University Press, 1985), p. 90. Gilman's essay, 'The Hottentot and the Prostitute: Toward an Iconography of Female

Sexuality', pp. 76–108, provides a persuasive analysis of the links between these two images of sexual deviance.

11. '"Women of Colour" Writers and Feminist Theory', in *Feminisms: An Anthology of Literary Theory and Criticism* (revised edition), ed. Robyn Warhol and Diane Price Herndl (Basingstoke: Macmillan, 1997), pp. 406–24 (p. 407).

12. Valerie Smith, 'Black Feminist Theory and the Representation of the "Other"', in *Feminisms*, pp. 311–25 (p. 316).

13. *The Vintage Book of Historical Feminism*, ed. Miriam Schneir (Vintage, 1996), pp. 94–5.

14. The novel was first published by Chatto & Windus in 1987. All page references will be to the Picador edition (Basingstoke: Macmillan, 1988) and will follow the relevant quotation in the text.

15. Morrison's primary source is *Reminiscences* (Cincinnati: Routledge, 1876), the memoirs of Levi Coffin, an activist on the underground railroad moving escaped slaves north. See Jago Morrison, pp. 128–9.

16. Quoted in Paula Gallant Eckard, *Maternal Body and Voice in Toni Morrison, Bobbie Ann Mason, and Lee Smith* (Columbia: University of Missouri Press, 2002), pp. 21–2.

17. Schoolteacher's equally careful record-keeping of the variety of corrections which he develops 'to re-educate them' (p. 220) recalls the similarly meticulous records of Nazi concentration camps.

18. Quoted in Sally McMillen, *Motherhood in the Old South: Pregnancy, Childbirth and Infant Rearing* (Baton Rouge: Louisiana University State Press, 1990), p. 32.

19. See Eckard, p. 19.

20. Advice manuals for mothers not only extolled the virtues of breastfeeding but stressed the importance of doing it in the right frame of mind. See, for example, Pye Henry Chavasse, *Advice to a Mother on the Management of Her Children, and on the Treatment on the Moment of Some of Their More Pressing Illnesses and Accidents*, 12th edition (Churchill, 1875), p. 36, and Isabella Beeton, *Mrs Beeton's Book of Household Management*, enlarged edition (Chancellor Press, 1861), p. 1034.

21. 'Hard Labor: Women, Childbirth, and Resistance in British Caribbean Slave Societies', in Schiebinger, pp. 234–62 (p. 235).

22. Quoted in Jago Morrison, p. 130.

23. *The Creation of Feminist Consciousness: From the Middle Ages to Eighteen-Seventy* (Oxford: Oxford University Press, 1994), p. 107.

24. Many historians and anthropologists believe goddess-centred religions preceded patriarchal systems of belief. See, for instance, Baring and Cashford, *The Myth of the Goddess*.

25. Alice Walker explores similar ideas in *The Temple of My Familiar* (New York: Harcourt Brace Jovanovich, 1989). Her Mother Goddess is African and black, and the geographical source of spiritual truth is Africa, not the Mediterranean.

26. 'History, Memory and Language in Toni Morrison's *Beloved*', in *Feminist Criticism: Theory and Practice*, ed. Susan Sellers (Harvester Wheatsheaf, 1991), pp. 109–27 (p. 113).

27. See 'Revolution in Poetic Language', p. 95.

28. See Kristeva, 'I Who Want Not To Be', *About Chinese Women*, trans. Anita Barrows (New York: Marion Boyars, 1986), pp. 39–41.

Afterword

1. See Margrit Shildrick, 'Leaks and Flows: NRTs and the Postmodern Body', *Leaky Bodies and Boundaries: Feminism, Postmodernism and (Bio)ethics* (Routledge, 1997), pp. 180–210. It is interesting to compare current demands for more social and medical control of the maternal function with Victorian debates over the same issues. See Sally Shuttleworth, 'Demonic Mothers: Ideologies of Bourgeois Motherhood in the Mid-Victorian Era', in *Re-Writing the Victorians: Theory, History and the Politics of Gender*, ed. Linda M. Shires (Routledge, 1992), pp. 31–51.
2. Anne Cranny-Francis and Wendy Waring, Pam Stavropoulos and Joan Kirkby, *Gender Studies: Terms and Debates* (Basingstoke: Palgrave, 2003), p. 193.
3. See, for example, David Buss, *Evolution of Desire: Strategies for Human Mating* (New York: Basic Books, 1994); and Randy Thornhill and Craig T. Palmer, *A Natural History of Rape: Biological Bases of Sexual Coercion* (MIT Press, 2000).
4. *Why Feminism?: Gender, Psychology, Politics* (Oxford: Blackwell, 1999), pp. 79, 80.
5. *Body/Politics*, p. 4.

Bibliography

(The place of publication is London, except where stated otherwise.)

Ahmed, Sara, 'Racialized Bodies', in *Real Bodies: A Sociological Introduction*, ed. Mary Evans and Ellie Lee (Basingstoke: Palgrave, 2002), pp. 46–63.

Alaya, Flavia, 'Victorian Science and the Genius of Woman', *Journal of the History of Ideas*, 38 (1977), 261–80.

Anderson, Linda, 'The Re-Imagining of History in Contemporary Women's Fiction', *Plotting Change: Contemporary Women's Fiction* (Edward Arnold, 1990), pp. 129–41.

Atwood, Margaret, interviewed by James Bone, *The Times Magazine*, 14 September 1996, pp. 13–16.

——, *Alias Grace* (Virago, 1997).

Bachofen, J.J., *Myth, Religion and Mother Right: Selected Writings of J. J. Bachofen* (Routledge, 1967).

Bainbridge, Beryl, *Master Georgie* (Gerald Duckworth, 1998).

Baring, Anne and Jules Cashford, *The Myth of the Goddess: Evolution of an Image* (Harmondsworth: Penguin, 1993).

Beauvoir, Simone de, *The Second Sex*, trans. H.M. Parshley (Pan, 1988).

Beer, Gillian, *Open Fields: Science in Cultural Encounter* (Oxford: Oxford University Press, 1996).

——, *Darwin's Plots: Evolutionary Narrative in Darwin, George Eliot and Nineteenth-Century Fiction*, 2nd edition (Cambridge: Cambridge University Press, 2000).

Beeton, Isabella, *Mrs Beeton's Book of Household Management*, Enlarged edition (Chancellor Press, 1861).

Belsey, Catherine, *Critical Practice* (Methuen, 1980).

Bernal, J.D., *Science in History*, Vol. 2, *The Scientific and Industrial Revolutions* (Harmondsworth: Penguin, 1969).

Bradstock, Andrew, *Masculinity and Spirituality in Victorian Culture* (Basingstoke: Macmillan, 2000).

Breuer, Joset and Sigmund Freud, *Studies on Hysteria*, trans. James and Alix Strachey (Hogarth Press, 1895).

Briffault, Robert, *The Mothers: A Study of the Origins of Sentiments and Institutions*, abr. Gordon Rattray Taylor (Allen & Unwin, 1959).

Brook, Barbara, *Feminist Perspectives on the Body* (New York: Pearson Education, 1999).

Brown, Isaac Baker, *On the Curability of Certain Forms of Insanity, Epilepsy, Catalepsy and Hysteria in Females* (Robert Hardwicke, 1866).

Buss, David, *The Evolution of Desire: Strategies for Human Mating* (New York: Basic Books, 1994).

Butler, Judith, *Gender Trouble: Feminism and the Subversion of Identity* (New York: Routledge, 1990).

Byatt, A.S., *Passions of the Mind: Selected Writings* (Chatto & Windus, 1991).

——, *Angels and Insects* (Vintage, 1995).

——, *On Histories and Stories: Selected Essays* (Chatto & Windus, 2000).

——, 'The End of Innocence', *The Guardian Saturday Review*, 6 September 2003, pp. 34–5.

Carter, Angela, *Nights at the Circus* (Pan, 1985).

Carter, Robert Brudenell, *On the Pathology and Treatment of Hysteria* (John Churchill, 1853).

Castle, Terry, *The Apparitional Lesbian: Female Homosexuality and Modern Culture* (New York: Columbia University Press, 1993).

Chavasse, Pye Henry, *Advice to a Mother on the Management of Her Children, and on the Treatment on the Moment of Some of Their More Pressing Illnesses and Accidents*, 12th edition (Churchill, 1875).

Cixous, Hélène, 'The Newly Born Woman', in *The Hélène Cixous Reader*, ed. Susan Sellers (Routledge, 1994), pp. 35–46.

Clarke, Edward H., *Sex in Education, or, A Fair Chance for Girls* (Boston: James R. Osgood, 1873).

Cobbe, Frances Power, 'Criminals, Idiots, Women, and Minors', *Fraser's Magazine*, in *'Criminals, Idiots, Women, and Minors': Victorian Writing by Women on Women*, ed. Susan Hamilton (Ontario: Broadview Press, 1995), pp. 108–31.

Cook, John, *Magnetism and Electricity* (Chambers, 1875).

Cott, Nancy, 'Passionlessness: An Interpretation of Victorian Sexual Ideology, 1790–1850', *Signs: Journal of Women in Culture and Society*, 4 (1978), 219–36.

Cranny-Francis, Anne, Wendy Waring, Pam Stavropoulos and Joan Kirkby, *Gender Studies: Terms and Debates* (Basingstoke: Palgrave, 2003).

Darwin, Charles, *The Origin of Species by Means of Natural Selection, or the Preservation of Favoured Races in the Struggle for Life* (John Murray, 1859).

——, *The Descent of Man and Selection in Relation to Sex* (John Murray, 1871).

Davidoff, Leonore and Catherine Hall, *Family Fortunes: Men and Women of the English Middle Class, 1780–1850* (Hutchinson, 1987).

Day, Aidan, *Angela Carter: The Rational Glass* (Manchester: Manchester University Press, 1998).

Duncker, Patricia, *James Miranda Barry* (Serpent's Tail, 1999).

Easthope, Antony, *What a Man's Gotta Do: The Masculine Myth in Popular Culture* (Grafton Books, 1986).

Eckard, Paula Gallant, *Maternal Body and Voice in Toni Morrison, Bobbie Ann Mason, and Lee Smith* (Columbia: University of Missouri Press, 2002).

Elliott, Philip, 'Tennyson and Spiritualism', *Tennyson Research Bulletin*, 3 (1979), 89–100.

Ellis, Henry Havelock, *Man and Woman: A Study of Human Secondary Sexual Characteristics* (W. Scott, 1894).

Ender, Evelyne, *Sexing the Mind: Nineteenth-Century Fictions of Hysteria* (Ithaca: Cornell University Press, 1995).

Evans, Ivor H., *Brewer's Dictionary of Phrase and Fable* (Cassell, 1970).

Faderman, Lillian, *Surpassing the Love of Men: Romantic Friendship and Love Between Women from the Renaissance to the Present* (Women's Press, 1985).

Falcus, Sarah, *Corpses in the Church and Mouths of Men: Mothers, Daughters and the Maternal in Selected Novels of Michèle Roberts*, unpublished PhD thesis (Aberdeen, 2001).

Fausto-Sterling, Anne, 'Gender, Race and Nation: The Comparative Anatomy of "Hottentot" Women in Europe, 1815–1817', in *Feminism and the Body*, ed. Londa L. Schiebinger (Oxford: Oxford University Press, 2000), pp. 203–33.

Fee, Elizabeth, 'The Sexual Politics of Victorian Social Anthropology', in *Clio's Consciousness Raised*, ed. M. Hartmann and L. Banner (New York: Harper & Row, 1974), pp. 86–102.

Ferguson, Rebecca, 'History, Memory and Language in Toni Morrison's *Beloved'*, in *Feminist Criticism: Theory and Practice*, ed. Susan Sellers (Harvester Wheatsheaf, 1991), pp. 109–27.

Fernihough, Anne, ' "Is She Fact or is She Fiction?" Angela Carter and the Enigma of Woman', *Textual Practice*, 11 (1997), 89–107.

Forster, Margaret, *Significant Sisters: The Grassroots of Active Feminism 1839–1939* (Penguin, 1986).

Foucault, Michel, *Madness and Civilisation: A History of Insanity in the Age of Reason* (Tavistock, 1967).

——, 'The Eye of Power', *Power/Knowledge: Selected Interviews and Other Writings 1972–1977*, ed. and trans. C. Gordon (Hemel Hempstead: Harvester, 1980), pp. 146–65.

——, *The History of Sexuality: An Introduction*, trans. Robert Hurley (Harmondsworth: Penguin, 1990).

——, 'Panopticism', *Discipline and Punish: The Birth of the Prison*, trans. Alan Sheridan (Harmondsworth: Penguin, 1991), pp. 195–228.

——, 'The Order of Discourse', in *The Postmodern Bible Reader*, ed. David Jobling, Tina Pippin and Ronald Schleifer (Oxford: Blackwell, 2001), pp. 8–12.

Gallagher, Catherine and Thomas Laqueur (eds), *The Making of the Modern Body: Sexuality and Society in the Nineteenth Century* (Berkeley: University of California Press, 1987).

Gilman, Charlotte Perkins, *The Yellow Wallpaper*, ed. Dale M. Bauer (Boston: Bedford Books, 1998).

Gilman, Sander, *Difference and Pathology: Stereotypes of Sexuality, Race, and Madness* (Ithaca: Cornell University Press, 1985).

Gilmour, Robin, *The Victorian Period: The Intellectual and Cultural Context of English Literature, 1830–1890* (Longman, 1993).

——, 'Using the Victorians: The Victorian Age in Contemporary Fiction', in *Rereading Victorian Fiction*, ed. Alice Jenkins and Juliet John (Basingstoke: Palgrave, 2002), pp. 189–200.

Glendinning, Victoria, *Electricity* (Random House, 1996).

Glover, David and Cora Kaplan, *Genders* (Routledge, 2000).

Goodman, Lizbeth (ed.), *Literature and Gender* (Routledge, 1996).

Hallam, Arthur, 'On Some of the Characteristics of Modern Poetry', *The Englishman's Magazine*, 1831, quoted in *The Broadview Anthology of Victorian Poetry and Poetic Theory*, ed. Thomas J. Collins and Vivienne J. Rundle (Toronto: Broadview Press, 2000), pp. 541–55.

Hirabayashi, Mitoko, 'Aged Sleeping Beauty: "Prince's Progress" as "Women's Text" ', paper presented at *Victorian Women Revisited* conference (University of Aberdeen, April 2001).

Homans, Margaret, ' "Women of Colour" Writers and Feminist Theory', in *Feminisms: An Anthology of Literary Theory and Criticism* (Revised edition), ed. Robyn Warhol and Diane Price Herndl (Basingstoke: Macmillan, 1997), pp. 406–24.

Howe, Daniel (ed.), *Victorian America* (Philadelphia: University of Pennsylvania Press, 1976).

Humble, Nicola, 'Seating the Séance', *Times Literary Supplement*, 7 April 1995, p. 24.

Ingham, Patricia, *The Language of Gender and Class: Transformation in the Victorian Novel* (Routledge, 1996).

Jackson, Stevi and Sue Scott, 'Putting the Body's Feet on the Ground: Towards a Sociological Reconceptualization of Gendered and Sexual Embodiment', in *Constructing Gendered Bodies*, ed. Kathryn Backett-Milburn and Linda McKie (Basingstoke: Palgrave, 2001), pp. 9–24.

Jacobus, Mary, Evelyn Fox and Sally Shuttleworth (eds), *Body/Politics: Women and the Discourses of Science* (Routledge, 1990).

Jordanova, Ludmilla, *Sexual Visions: Images of Gender in Science and Medicine Between the Eighteenth and Twentieth Centuries* (New York: Harvester Wheatsheaf, 1989).

Kanner, S. Barbara, 'The Women of England in a Century of Social Change, 1815–1914', *Suffer and be Still: Women in the Victorian Age* (Bloomington: Indiana University Press, 1972), pp. 173–206.

Kaplan, Cora, 'Black Heroes/White Writers: Toussaint L'Ouverture and the Literary Imagination', *History Workshop Journal*, 46 (1998), 32–62.

Katsavos, Anna, 'An Interview with Angela Carter', *Review of Contemporary Fiction*, 14 (1994), 11–17.

Kenyon, Olga (ed.), Interview with Michèle Roberts, *Women Writers Talk: Interviews With Ten Women Writers* (Oxford: Lennard Publishing, 1989), pp. 149–72.

King, Jeannette, 'Women and the Word: Christa Wolf's *Cassandra*', *Journal of Gender Studies*, 3 (1994), 333–42.

——, *Women and the Word: Contemporary Women Novelists and the Bible* (Basingstoke: Macmillan, 2000).

Krafft-Ebing, Richard von, *Psychopathia Sexualis: With Especial Reference to Antipathic Sexual Instinct: A Medico-Forensic Study*, trans. Charles Chaddock (F.A. Davis, 1892).

Kristeva, Julia, *About Chinese Women* (Marion Boyars, 1986).

——, 'Revolution in Poetic Language', *The Kristeva Reader*, ed. Toril Moi (Oxford: Blackwell, 1986), pp. 89–136.

Lane, Christopher, *The Burdens of Intimacy: Psychoanalysis and Victorian Masculinity* (Chicago: University of Chicago Press, 1999).

Lerner, Gerda, *The Creation of Feminist Consciousness: From the Middle Ages to Eighteen-Seventy* (Oxford: Oxford University Press, 1994).

Levine, Philippa, *Victorian Feminism 1850–1900* (Gainesville: University Press of Florida, 1994).

Lombroso, Cesare, *The Female Offender* (T. Fisher Unwin, 1895).

Loudon, Irvine, 'Maternal Mortality in Britain from 1850 to the Mid-1930s', *Death in Childbirth: An International Study of Maternal Care and Maternal Mortality 1800–1950* (Oxford: Clarendon Press, 1992), pp. 234–53.

Lovelady, Stephanie, 'I am Telling This to No One But You: Private Voice, Passing, and the Private Sphere in Margaret Atwood's *Alias Grace*', *Studies in Canadian Literature*, 24 (1999), 35–63.

Martin, Valery, *Mary Reilly* (New York: Random House, 1990).

McGrath, Roberta, *Seeing Her Sex: Medical Archives and the Female Body* (Manchester: Manchester University Press, 2002).

McGrail, Anna, *Mrs Einstein* (New York: Doubleday, 1998).

McMillen, Sally, *Motherhood in the Old South: Pregnancy, Childbirth and Infant Rearing* (Baton Rouge: Louisiana University State Press, 1990).

Meagher, Maude, *The Green Scamander* (New York: Houghton Mifflin, 1933).

Merchant, Carolyn, *Ecological Revolutions: Nature, Gender, and Science in New England* (Chapel Hill: University of North Carolina Press, 1989).

Michael, Magali Cornier, 'Rethinking History as Patchwork: The Case of Atwood's *Alias Grace*', *Modern Fiction Studies*, 47 (2001), 421–47.

Mill, John Stuart, *The Subjection of Women* (Longmans, Green, Reader and Dyer, 1869).

Millett, Kate, 'The Debate over Women: Ruskin vs. Mill', in *Suffer and Be Still: Women in the Victorian Age*, ed. Martha Vicinus (Bloomington: Indiana University Press, 1972), pp. 121–39.

Montagu, Ashley, *Statement on Race: An Annotated Elaboration and Exposition of the Four Statements on Race Issued by the United Nations Educational, Scientific, and Cultural Organization* (New York: Oxford University Press, 1972).

Moodie, Susanna, *Life in the Clearings versus the Bush* (Toronto: McClelland & Stewart, 1989).

Morrison, Jago, *Contemporary Fiction* (Routledge, 2003).

Morrison, Toni, *Beloved* (Basingstoke: Macmillan, 1988).

Moscucci, *The Science of Woman: Gynaecology and Gender in England, 1800–1929* (Cambridge: Cambridge University Press, 1990).

Mosedale, Susan Sleeth, 'Science Corrupted: Victorian Biologists Consider "The Woman Question" ', *Journal of the History of Biology*, 11 (1978), 1–55.

Naslund, Sena Jeter, *Ahab's Wife: Or The Star-Gazer* (New York: William Morrow, 1999).

Noad, Henry, *Lectures on Electricity, Comprising Galvanism, Magnetism, Electro-Magnetism, Magneto- and Thermo-Electricity, and Electro-Physiology* (Knight, 1849).

Oram, Alison and Annmarie Turnbull, *The Lesbian History Sourcebook: Love and Sex between Women in Britain from 1780 to 1970* (Routledge, 2001).

Owen, Alex, *The Darkened Room: Women, Power and Spiritualism in Late Nineteenth Century England* (Virago, 1989).

Pagels, Elaine, *The Gnostic Gospels* (Weidenfeld & Nicolson, 1980).

Poovey, Mary, '"Scenes of an Indelicate Character": The Medical "Treatment" of Victorian Women', in *The Making of the Modern Body: Sexuality and Society in the Nineteenth Century*, ed. Catherine Gallagher and Thomas Laqueur (Berkeley: University of California Press, 1987), pp. 137–68.

——, *Uneven Developments: The Ideological Work of Gender in Mid-Victorian England* (Virago, 1989).

Pykett, Lynn, 'The Century's Daughters: Recent Women's Fiction and History', *Critical Quarterly*, 29 (1987), 71–7.

Rich, Adrienne, 'Compulsory Heterosexuality and Lesbian Existence', in *Adrienne Rich's Poetry and Prose*, ed. Barbara Charlesworth Gelpi and Albert Gelpi (New York: W.W. Norton), pp. 203–24.

Roberts, Michèle, *In the Red Kitchen* (Mandarin, 1991).

——, *Fair Exchange* (Little, Brown, 1999).

Romanes, George, 'Mental Differences between Men and Women', *The Nineteenth Century*, 21 (1887), 654–72.

Rosenberg, Charles, Carroll Smith-Rosenberg, John S. Haller and Robin M. Haller, *The Physician and Sexuality in Victorian America* (Urbana: University of Illinois Press, 1974).

Rowland, Susan, 'Imaginal Bodies and Feminine Spirits: Performing Gender in Jungian Theory and Atwood's *Alias Grace*', in *Body Matters: Feminism, Textuality, Corporeality*, ed. Avril Horner and Angela Keane (Manchester: Manchester University Press, 2000), pp. 244–54.

——, 'Women, Spiritualism and Depth Psychology in Michèle Roberts's Victorian Novel', in *Rereading Victorian Fiction*, ed. Alice Jenkins and Juliet John (Basingstoke: Palgrave, 2002), pp. 201–13.

Ruskin, John, 'Of Queen's Gardens', *Sesame and Lilies: Two Lectures Delivered at Manchester in 1864* (Smith, Elder, 1865).

Russett, Cynthia Eagle, *Sexual Science: The Victorian Construction of Womanhood* (Cambridge, MA: Harvard University Press, 1991).

Russo, Mary, *The Female Grotesque: Risk, Excess, and Modernity* (New York: Routledge, 1995).

Sage, Lorna, interview with Angela Carter, in *New Writing*, ed. Malcolm Bradbury and Judith Cooke (Minerva Press, 1992), pp. 185–93.

Schiebinger, Londa, 'The Triumph of Complementarity', *The Mind Has No Sex? Women in the Origins of Modern Science* (Cambridge, MA: Harvard University Press, 1991), pp. 214–31.

Schlereth, Thomas J., *Victorian America: Transformations in Everyday Life, 1876–1915* (New York: Harper, 1992).

Schneir, Miriam (ed.), *The Vintage Book of Historical Feminism* (Vintage, 1996).

Segal, Lynne, *Why Feminism?: Gender, Psychology, Politics* (Oxford: Blackwell, 1999).

Sharp, Evelyn, *Hertha Ayrton, 1854–1923: A Memoir* (Edward Arnold, 1926).

Shiller, Dana, 'The Redemptive Past in the Neo-Victorian Novel', *Studies in the Novel*, 29 (1997), 538–60.

Shoemaker, Robert B., *Gender in English Society 1650–1850: The Emergence of Separate Spheres?* (Longman, 1998).

Showalter, Elaine, *The Female Malady: Women, Madness and English Culture, 1830–1980* (Virago, 1987).

——, *Sexual Anarchy: Gender and Culture at the Fin de Siècle* (Bloomsbury, 1991).

Shuttleworth, Sally, 'Demonic Mothers: Ideologies of Bourgeois Motherhood in the Mid-Victorian Era', in *Re-Writing the Victorians: Theory, History and the Politics of Gender*, ed. Linda M. Shires (Routledge, 1992), pp. 31–51.

Skultans, Vieda, 'Mediums, Controls and Eminent Men', in *Women's Religious Experience: Cross-Cultural Perspectives*, ed. Pat Holden (Croom Helm, 1983), pp. 15–26.

Smart, Carol, *Regulating Motherhood: Historical Essays on Marriage, Motherhood and Sexuality* (Routledge, 1992).

Smith, Valerie, 'Black Feminist Theory and the Representation of the "Other"', in *Feminisms: An Anthology of Literary Theory and Criticism* (Revised edition), ed. Robyn Warhol and Diane Price Herndl (Basingstoke: Macmillan, 1997), pp. 311–25.

Smith-Rosenberg, Carroll, 'The Female Animal: Medical and Biological Views of Woman and Her Role in Nineteenth-Century America', *The Journal of American History*, 60 (1973), 332–56.

——, 'Puberty to Menopause: The Cycle of Femininity in Nineteenth-Century America', in *Clio's Consciousness Raised: New Perspectives on the History of Women*, ed. Mary S. Hartman and Lois Banner (New York: Harper & Row, 1974), pp. 23–37.

Sontag, Susan, *The Volcano Lover: A Romance* (New York: Jonathan Cape, 1992).

Stepan, Nancy, *The Idea of Race in Science: Great Britain 1800–1960* (Basingstoke: Macmillan, 1982).

——, 'Biology and Degeneration: Races and Proper Places', in *Degeneration: The Dark Side of Progress*, ed. J. Edward Chamberlin and Sander L. Gilman (New York: Columbia University Press, 1985), pp. 97–120.

Stott, Rebecca, *The Fabrication of the Late-Victorian Femme Fatale: The Kiss of Death* (Basingstoke: Macmillan, 1992).

Swan, Susan, *The Biggest Modern Woman in the World* (Allen & Unwin, 1983).

Tait, Peta, 'Feminine Free Fall: A Fantasy of Freedom', *Theatre Journal*, 8 (1996), 27–34.

Tan, Amy, *The Kitchen God's Wife* (New York: Ivy Books, 1991).

Tambling, Jeremy, *Confession: Sexuality, Sin, the Subject* (Manchester: Manchester University Press, 1990).

Taylor, Jenny Bourne and Sally Shuttleworth (eds), *Embodied Selves: An Anthology of Psychological Texts 1830–1890* (Oxford: Clarendon Press, 1998).

Tennant, Emma, *Tess* (Harper Collins, 1993).

——, *Two Women of London* (Faber & Faber, 1989).

Tennyson, Lord Alfred, *The Poems of Tennyson*, ed. Christopher Ricks (Longman, 1969).

——, *Tennyson: 'In Memoriam'*, ed. Susan Shatto and Marion Shaw (Oxford: Clarendon Press, 1982).

Thornhill, Randy and Craig T. Palmer, *A Natural History of Rape: Biological Bases of Sexual Coercion* (MIT Press, 2000).

Thwaite, Ann, *Emily Tennyson: The Poet's Wife* (Faber, 1996).

Tosh, John, *A Man's Place: Masculinity and the Middle-Class Home in Victorian England* (New Haven: Yale University Press, 1999).

Tremain, Rose, *Restoration* (Hamilton, 1989).

Tuana, Nancy, *The Less Noble Sex: Scientific, Religious and Philosophical Conceptions of Woman's Nature* (Bloomington: Indiana University Press, 1993).

Tuke, D. Hack (ed.), *A Dictionary of Psychological Medicine*, 2 Vols (J. & A. Churchill, 1892).

Veith, Ilza, *Hysteria: The History of a Disease* (Chicago: University of Chicago Press, 1965).

Vicinus, Martha (ed.), *Suffer and Be Still: Women in the Victorian Age* (Bloomington: Indiana University Press, 1972).

Vickery, Amanda, 'Golden Age to Separate Spheres? A Review of the Categories and Chronology of English Women's History', *The Historical Journal*, 36 (1993), 383–414.

Walker, Alice, *The Temple of My Familiar* (New York: Harcourt Brace Jovanovich, 1989).

Warner, Marina, *Monuments and Maidens: The Allegory of the Female Form* (Vintage, 1996).

Waters, Sarah, 'Wolfskins and Togas: Maude Meagher's *The Green Scamander* and the Lesbian Historical Novel', *Women: A Cultural Review*, 7 (1996), 176–88.

——, *Tipping the Velvet* (Virago, 1998).

——, *Affinity* (Virago, 1999).

Watkins, Susan, *Twentieth-Century Women Novelists: Feminist Theory into Practice* (Basingstoke: Palgrave, 2001).

Watteville, A. de, *A Practical Introduction to Medical Electricity* (Lewis, 1878).

Wilson, A.N., *The Victorians* (Hutchinson, 2002).

Winter, Alison, '"A Calculus of Suffering": Ada Lovelace and the Bodily Constraints on Women's Knowledge in Early Victorian England', in *Science Incarnate: Historical Embodiments of Natural Knowledge*, ed. Christopher Lawrence and Steven Shapin (Chicago: University of Chicago Press, 1998), pp. 202–39.

Winterson, Jeanette, *The Passion* (Vintage, 1987).

——, *Sexing the Cherry* (Bloomsbury, 1989).

Wolkowitz, Carol, 'The Working Body as Sign: Historical Snapshots', in *Constructing Gendered Bodies*, ed. Kathryn Backett-Milburn and Linda McKie (Basingstoke: Palgrave, 2001), pp. 85–103.

Wood, Ann Douglas, '"The Fashionable Diseases": Women's Complaints and their Treatment in Nineteenth-Century America', in *Clio's Consciousness Raised*, ed. M. Hartmann and L. Banner (New York: Harper & Row, 1974), pp. 1–22.

Yeo, Eileen Janes, 'Some Paradoxes of Empowerment', in *Radical Femininity: Women's Self-Representation in the Public Sphere*, ed. Eileen Janes Yeo (Manchester: Manchester University Press, 1998), pp. 1–24.

Index